Heartland

VOLUME TWO

by Lauren Brooke

SCHOLASTIC INC.
New York Toronto London Auckland Sydney
Mexico City New Delhi Hong Kong Buenos Aires

Taking Chances, ISBN 0-439-13025-5, copyright © 2001 by Working Partners Ltd., London.

Come What May, ISBN 0-439-13026-3, copyright © 2001 by Working Partners Ltd., London.

One Day You'll Know, ISBN 0-439-13035-2, copyright © 2001 by Working Partners Ltd., London.

Heartland series created by Working Partners Ltd., London.

12 11 10 9 8 7 6 5 4 3 2 1   5 6 7 8 9 10/0

Printed in the U.S.A.   23

This edition created exclusively for Barnes & Noble, Inc.

2005 Barnes & Noble Books

ISBN 0-7607-9585-1

First compilation printing, August 2005

Contents

With special thanks to Linda Chapman

Heartland

❧

Taking Chances

To my parents,
for buying me my first pony
and making my dreams come true

Chapter One

Amy finished filling up a water bucket and glanced at her watch. It was twelve-thirty. Soraya would be arriving any minute. She placed the bucket in Solo's stall and headed to the top of the drive to wait for her friend.

On either side of the driveway, horses and ponies grazed contentedly in the turnout paddocks, the October breeze ruffling their coats and sending the occasional red or gold leaf skittering across the short grass.

Only one paddock was empty. In the middle stood a single oak sapling, the soil still fresh around its base.

Amy walked over to the wooden gate and leaned against it. "Pegasus," she whispered, a wave of sadness flooding over her as she looked at the young tree. She could hardly believe it was only three weeks since her favorite horse had been buried there.

1

Amy pictured the great gray horse. In his younger days, he had been one of the most famous show jumpers in the world. But Amy remembered him better as the horse that had let her play around his legs when she was little and had nuzzled her when she was upset. To her, he was the horse that had helped her through the nightmare of her mom being killed in a road accident four months ago and the horse that had been her dearest friend.

Amy swallowed as she looked at the sapling. *Everything's changed so much in the last few months,* she thought to herself. *Mom's gone. Pegasus is gone. Lou's come back.*

The return of Lou to Heartland was one of the few good things that had happened. Until recently, Amy's older sister had worked in Manhattan, but when their mother died she decided to leave her banking job and live permanently at Heartland, the equine sanctuary their mom, Marion, had set up on their grandpa's farm.

The sound of a car coming up the drive roused Amy from her thoughts. She looked around.

Soraya Martin, her best friend, was waving from the front passenger seat as her mom's car neared. Amy took a deep breath, swallowing hard and pushing down the ache of painful memories. She waved back, forcing herself to smile, burying her inner sadness.

"Hi!" Soraya called, winding down the window. "Sorry I'm late. Mom had to pick up some groceries on the way over." The car drew to a halt, and Soraya jumped out, black curls bouncing on her shoulders. "See you later, Mom," she said. "Thanks for the ride."

"Sure," Mrs. Martin said, smiling at Amy. "Now, you girls have fun."

Amy and Soraya grinned at each other. "We will," they both said at once.

✲

Half an hour later, Amy tightened her fingers on Sundance's reins and looked toward the fallen tree that lay across one side of the trail. "Come on, boy," she whispered. "Let's jump it!"

"Be careful, Amy," Soraya called. "It's a big one."

"Not for Sundance," Amy replied, turning her buckskin pony toward the tree trunk.

Seeing the jump, Sundance threw his head up in excitement and plunged forward, but Amy was ready for him. Her body moved effortlessly in the saddle. "Easy now," she murmured, her fingers caressing his warm neck.

The pony's golden ears flickered as he listened to her voice — and then he relaxed, his neck lowering and his mouth softening on the bit.

Amy squeezed with her legs. In five strides they reached the tree trunk. It loomed up in front of them — massive, solid. Amy felt Sundance's muscles gather as he took off perfectly and gracefully rose into the air. Amy caught a glimpse of thick, gnarled bark flashing by beneath them, felt a moment of suspension as if she and Sundance were flying, and then heard the sweet thud of his hooves as he landed cleanly on the other side. They were over!

"Good boy!" Amy cried in delight.

"He looks so good!" Soraya said, letting Jasmine trot forward to meet them. "He's jumping better than ever, Amy."

"I know!" Amy grinned, patting Sundance's neck. "He's incredible!"

As the two ponies reached each other, Jasmine stretched out her neck to say hello. With an angry squeal, Sundance threw his head in the air, his ears back. "Stop it, Sundance!" Amy exclaimed, turning him away. "Jasmine's your friend."

The buckskin nuzzled her leg affectionately. Even though he was stubborn and difficult with most horses and people, he adored Amy. She had first seen him at a horse sale. Thin and unhappy, he lashed out at anyone who tried to come through the gate of his pen. But Amy had a special feeling about him and persuaded her mom to buy him. They took him back to Heartland, where Amy gradually gained his trust and affection.

"Are you planning to go to any shows with him?" Soraya asked as they started along the trail again.

Amy shook her head. "There's no time. All the stalls have been full since the day of the open house, and there's a waiting list of people who want to bring their horses here."

Just two weeks ago, Lou had organized an open house at Heartland. People had been invited to come find out about Heartland's methods for curing physically and emotionally damaged horses. Amy and Ty, Heartland's seventeen-year-old stable hand, had given demonstrations, and the day had been a great success. Ever since then, they had been inundated with inquiries from owners of problem horses.

"It's good, though, that you've got lots of horses boarding," Soraya said. "I mean, it must be such a relief to know that you can carry on your mom's work and not stress too much about money."

Amy nodded, remembering the difficulties Heartland had faced before the open house. After her mom died, Heartland had come close to shutting down because of the lack of customers. They had been extremely close to running out of money and losing everything. But now, thankfully, it was different. Business was booming.

"Yeah, I'm glad we're busy," she said. "Even if it does mean that I don't have much time to go to shows." She patted Sundance's neck. "Still, things might get easier now that Ben will be working for us."

Ben was eighteen and the nephew of Lisa Stillman,

the wealthy and successful owner of Fairfield Arabian Stud. After Amy had cured one of Fairfield's prestigious show horses, Lisa had been so impressed that she arranged for Ben to come to work at Heartland so he could learn their methods. He was expected to arrive that afternoon.

Soraya glanced at Amy. "Do you think he has a girl-friend?"

"Why?" Amy grinned. "Are you interested?" She and Soraya had both met Ben briefly when he had dropped off the problem horse that Amy treated. Tall and good-looking, he had seemed OK, but he wasn't really Amy's type.

"You have to admit he *is* cute," Soraya said. She raised her eyebrows. "Poor guy. I guess he's not going to know anyone around here. I'll just *have* to offer to give him a tour."

Amy feigned innocence. "Don't go out of your way, Soraya. I'm sure Ty can do it — he's looking forward to having another guy around the place."

"Oh, *no*," Soraya said quickly. "I'm sure I'd make a *much* better guide than Ty."

"Well, I'm looking forward to seeing Ben's horse," Amy said. "He's a show jumper. Ben said he'd only work at Heartland if he could bring his horse, too."

"So what time's he coming?" Soraya asked.

"Two o'clock."

Soraya glanced at her watch. "We should get a move on, then. It's almost one-thirty."

Amy gathered up her reins. "What are you waiting for? Let's go!"

✌

Amy and Soraya rode down the trail that led to the back of Heartland. Coming out of the trees, they could see Heartland's barns and sheds spread out before them — the turnout paddocks with their dark wooden fencing, the two training rings, the twelve-stall back barn, and the front stable block that made an L-shape toward the white, weather-boarded farmhouse.

As Amy halted Sundance, she heard the sound of hooves thudding angrily against the wall of the barn.

"Steady now!" Amy could hear Ty's raised voice from inside the barn. "Easy, girl!"

"It sounds like Ty could use some help," she said.

"You go," Soraya said. "I'll take care of Sundance."

"Thanks." Amy threw Sundance's reins at her friend and headed into the barn. A wide aisle separated the six stalls on each side. From a stall near the back came the crash of hooves striking the wall. Amy realized it was Dancer's stall.

Dancer was a paint mare who had been neglected.

She was half starved and left on a tiny patch of land where an animal charity had found her. The charity volunteers called Heartland, and Amy and Ty had immediately agreed to help. Dancer had arrived only two days ago, and her recovery was progressing slowly.

"You OK, Ty?" Amy called.

Ty looked over Dancer's door. His dark hair was disheveled. "Yeah," he replied, wiping his bare forearm across his face.

"What's up?" Amy asked, looking into the stall. Dancer was standing by the back wall, her body trembling.

"All I did was pick up her hoof, and she went crazy," Ty said, shaking his head. "She broke her lead rope and started kicking in every direction. She had me cornered for a bit, but I managed to get out. Now she's all worked up."

Amy looked at the frightened mare. "Maybe we should try some chestnut powder to calm her down," she suggested, remembering it had been one of her mom's favorite remedies for traumatized horses.

Ty nodded. "Good idea. You wait with her, I'll get it." He hurried off.

The mare shifted uneasily at the back of the stall. Her muscles were tense and her ribs protruded painfully through her shaggy coat. Around her face were scars where her old halter had been digging into her skin, and her fetlocks were covered with rope burns from hobbles that had been tightly tied around her legs to stop her from wandering away.

"It's OK, girl," Amy said softly. "You're safe now. No one's going to hurt you anymore."

Amy watched as the mare's ears flickered uncertainly. She knew her recovery would take time.

Ty returned with a small tin. He handed it to Amy. "Here," he said. "It might be better if you try. I don't want to upset her again."

Amy unscrewed the lid of the tin. Inside there was a gritty gray powder. Taking a little, she rubbed it onto the palms of her hands. Then she stepped forward, her shoulders turned sideways to the mare, her eyes lowered.

Dancer shifted nervously. Amy stopped, offered her palm for the mare to sniff, and waited.

After a few moments, the mare turned and snorted. Stretching her muzzle out toward Amy's upturned hand, she breathed in, her nostrils dilating. Amy waited a few moments, and then, talking softly, she gently reached out and touched Dancer's neck with her other hand. As her fingers stroked and caressed, she felt the mare gradually begin to relax. Amy's fingers massaged the mare's neck until she came to her head. When Dancer seemed to trust her, Amy took hold of the lead rope.

"Nice job," Ty said in a low voice. Rubbing a little of

the powder onto his own palms, he approached the mare. She looked at him cautiously but then stretched out her head and let him stroke her, too. "Poor girl," he said, rubbing her neck. "Your life hasn't been too great up to now, has it?"

"Well, it's going to be a lot better from here on," Amy said.

For a moment they stood in silence, both stroking the mare.

She looked at the deep scars on Dancer's brown-and-white legs. "Maybe when you touched her feet she thought that you were going to put hobbles on her," she suggested.

Ty nodded. "I guess we'll just have to take things slowly."

"As always," Amy said, smiling at him.

She didn't know what she'd do without Ty. He was so good with the horses. After her mom had died, he had taken over the running of the yard while the family came to terms with their loss. She knew they were lucky to have him. He never seemed to treat working at Heartland as just a regular job — he seemed as devoted to Heartland as Amy.

Ty looked at the tin in his hand. "Your mom's magic powder did it again."

Amy nodded. Her mom had been told about the powder by an old horseman in Tennessee. It contained herbs ground up with chestnut trimmings — the masses that grow on the insides of horses' legs. Marion had written down the recipe, and they had used it at Heartland ever since.

"Your mom was amazing," Ty said, turning the tin over in his hands. "She had great instincts and knew so much about horses. Sometimes I wonder if I'll ever be half as good as she was."

"You're pretty good already, Ty," Amy said, surprised.

"But not good enough," Ty said. He shook his head. "I was learning so much from her, Amy. Since she's been gone, I'm just struggling to keep up. I feel like there's a lot left to learn, but I don't know how. And I hate it."

"You can't think like that, Ty," Amy said quickly.

"Why not?" Ty replied. "I keep thinking if I only knew more, I'd have a better shot at really helping these horses."

Amy stepped closer to Ty, wanting to let him know that she understood. "You know, I felt the same when Pegasus was really sick, and I couldn't help him. But then I realized I just had to accept that there are things I don't know, and all I can do is try my best." She paused, her eyes searching his. "You have to trust yourself. You know Mom would have said the same thing."

Ty nodded slowly. "Yeah, I guess."

They stood for a moment, neither of them speaking. The silence was interrupted by the sound of footsteps running down the aisle. "Hey, you guys! There's a trailer coming up the drive!" Soraya reached Dancer's door and looked over. "It's looks really nice. Come check it out."

"It must be Ben," Amy said, looking at Ty.

He nodded. Leaving Dancer, they hurried down the yard. A gleaming white trailer, with green and purple stripes and a black crest with the words FAIRFIELD ARABIANS emblazoned on the side, was pulling up in front of the house. The truck stopped, and Ben Stillman jumped out.

"Hey," he said, straightening his tall frame.

Amy stepped forward. "Hi, I'm Amy. We met when you brought Promise over for your aunt. This is my friend Soraya Martin," she said, pushing Soraya forward.

"Hi," Soraya grinned.

"Yeah, I remember," Ben smiled. "Hi."

"And you've met Ty," Amy said.

"Welcome back to Heartland." Ty offered his hand.

As they shook hands, the farmhouse door opened and Lou came out. She had also met Ben when he dropped Promise off at Heartland. "Hello again," she said, smiling at Ben.

"Good to meet you properly this time," Ben said.

"I'll see you later — I'm just going into town," Lou said, walking toward her car with her keys in hand.

Just then, from inside the trailer, came the sound of a horse stamping impatiently.

"Sounds like Red wants to get out," Ben said. "He's fine when we're on the road but can't stand being in the trailer after we've stopped."

"Here, I'll give you a hand," Ty volunteered.

Ben disappeared inside the trailer while Ty unbolted the ramp. Amy watched eagerly, wondering what Ben's horse would be like.

Ty lowered the ramp to the ground. There was a clatter of hooves, and, suddenly, a bright chestnut horse shot nervously down the ramp, with Ben holding tightly on to the end of the lead rope. Once out, the horse stopped and looked around, his head held high.

"Wow!" Amy exclaimed. "He's gorgeous!"

"He's called Red, but his show name is *What Luck*," Ben said, looking pleased. "He's a Thoroughbred–Hanoverian cross."

Amy walked closer, admiring Red's handsome head, broad back, and strong, clean legs. Standing, she guessed, at around sixteen-two hands, he looked every inch a show jumper. "How old is he?" she asked, letting Red sniff her hand and then patting his muscular neck.

"Six," Ben said. "My aunt bought him for me when he was three." He glanced at the trailer. "I guess there are *some* advantages to having a rich aunt who's into horses."

Hearing a strange note in his voice, Amy glanced at

him. For a moment she saw what she thought was a look of bitterness cross his face.

"*Some* advantages?" Ty said. He was putting the ramp up and obviously hadn't seen Ben's expression. "That's the understatement of the year!"

"Yeah." Ben coughed, his face suddenly clearing and his voice becoming light again. "I guess you're right. So which stall should I put him in?" he asked Amy.

"The one at the end," Amy replied, pointing toward the stable block. "It's all bedded down and ready for him."

"Come on, boy." Ben clicked his tongue and Red moved forward.

Leaving Soraya and Ty to clear out the trailer, Amy went on ahead of Ben and opened the stall door. "Do you compete much on Red?" she asked.

Ben nodded as he started taking off the pillow wraps that had protected the gelding's legs on the journey over. "He's got real talent. I've been taking him in Prelim Jumper classes, but with the way he's been winning I figure he's going to upgrade real quick." He stood up with the wraps in his arms. "We're going to make it to the top," he said confidently. "I'm sure of it."

Amy looked at him in surprise; he didn't sound like he had any doubts.

"So," Ben said, walking out of the stall, "what's it like living around here?"

"It's OK," Amy replied.

"You'll have to show me around," Ben said.

Amy remembered what Soraya had said and saw the perfect opportunity. "Well, I'm always pretty busy with the horses," she said as they walked across the yard toward where Soraya and Ty were standing by the trailer. "But Soraya has tons of spare time."

"Did I hear my name?" Soraya asked, turning to face them.

"Yeah, I was just telling Ben that you'd be happy to give him a tour," Amy answered, giving her a meaningful look.

"Yeah, of course!" Soraya said, stepping forward eagerly. "Anytime."

"Thanks." Ben smiled at her. "I might just take you up on that."

"Do you want to check out the other stable?" Amy offered. "You've got all the horses to meet, and then we can start telling you about our work here at Heartland."

"Actually, you know, I might leave all that till tomorrow," Ben said, yawning. "I want to go to my new place and start unpacking. Then I think I'll just crash for a while."

"Oh . . . right," Amy said, a bit taken aback. She knew that if she was about to start work at a new stable, the first thing she would want to do was look at the horses. "Well, sure. Go ahead."

"Great," Ben said. "Well, I'll just unload Red's tack, then I'll be off."

Amy, Ty, and Soraya helped him carry the mountain of blankets, tack, and grooming equipment up to the tack room. When they were done, Ben unhitched the trailer and got into his truck. "I'll be back to feed Red later," he said, starting the engine.

❦

Not long after he had driven off, Lou got back. "I think I passed Ben on the road. Did he leave already?" she asked, getting out of her car.

Amy nodded.

"But I was going to ask him if he wanted to stay for supper tonight," Lou said, frowning. "Oh, well, I guess I can call him. I've got his phone number." She looked at Soraya and Ty. "You're both welcome to stay, too."

"That would be great," Ty said. "Thanks."

"Oh, I can't," Soraya said ruefully. "I'm going out tonight for my mom's birthday. But thanks anyway, Lou."

Lou looked down the drive. "It's a bit odd that Ben didn't stick around longer. I thought he'd be here for a couple of hours, anyway. Grandpa will be sorry to have missed him." Shaking her head, she went back into the house.

"So what do you think?" Amy asked Ty and Soraya as they walked back across the yard.

"Of Ben?" Soraya inquired. "Definitely cute!"

"And after all, what else matters?" Ty teased.

Soraya pretended to punch him.

Amy grinned. "Come on, what do you think, Ty?"

"He seems fine," Ty said, shrugging.

"And?" Amy pushed for more.

"And nothing," Ty said. He looked at Amy and Soraya's expectant faces. "Well, what else do you expect me to say?" he demanded. "I only met the guy for about five minutes."

"Well, I only met him for five minutes, too, and I think he seems really nice," Amy said. She turned to Soraya. "He was telling me about Red. He's been competing in Prelim Jumpers. Ben thinks they'll move up pretty quick."

"I wonder when we'll get to see him ride," Soraya said. Her eyes looked dreamy. "I bet he looks great on Red!"

"Oh, please!" Ty grimaced. "You think he looks great, period." Shaking his head, he went into the tack room.

Exchanging grins, Amy and Soraya followed him. In the middle of the tack room floor was a mound of Ben's stuff.

"Three saddles," Ty commented, starting to make space on the already crowded saddle racks.

"And all top quality," Amy added, picking up a forward-cut jumping saddle and admiring the well-oiled leather.

"I wish I had a rich aunt who would buy me a horse like Red and all this stuff," Soraya said.

Ty nodded as he hung up a bridle. "Ben sure is a lucky guy."

Amy thought about the look she had seen pass across Ben's face just after he'd unloaded Red. At that moment he hadn't seemed exactly thrilled with his good fortune. Still, it must have been wonderful to have grown up on a huge horse farm with lots of money. Maybe he was having a hard time leaving Fairfield and wasn't sure about the arrangement his aunt had made with Heartland. "Imagine living at a place like Fairfield," she said out loud.

"Yeah," Ty said nodding. "I wish."

Amy looked at him. Ty's family had very little money. He had first started working as a part-time stable hand at Heartland when he was only fifteen, to help out his parents. But money was still tight, so he approached Marion a year later about hiring him full-time.

"Do you know why Ben grew up with his aunt instead of his parents?" Soraya asked.

"I think it was something to do with his parents getting divorced when he was younger," Amy said, remembering a conversation between Lou and Lisa Stillman when they'd first discussed the possibility of Ben coming to Heartland. "But I don't really know that much about it. We might find out more tonight."

"I wish I could stay," Soraya said longingly. "Promise you'll find out all the gossip about him — like whether he's got a girlfriend or not."

"Oh, you mean the real *important* stuff." Amy grinned at her. "Don't worry. Of course I will."

Chapter Two

❧

Ben arrived back at Heartland just as Amy and Ty were mixing the evening feeds. "Are you unpacked?" Ty asked when Ben joined them in the feed room.

Ben nodded. "Yeah, thanks." He looked around at the huge metal bins, stone-flagged floor, and thick strands of dusty cobwebs hanging from the wooden ceiling beams. "So this is where you keep the grain, right?"

"Yeah," Amy said. "Just help yourself to whatever you want for Red. There's cod liver oil and other supplements in the cabinets over there." She pointed to a corner of the feed room. "And you can use any of those buckets in that pile — they're all spare."

"Here," Ty said, getting a bucket for him.

"Thanks," Ben said. "But I've brought Red's buckets for him. They're in the trailer."

He returned a few minutes later with a couple of steel buckets, each embossed with the Fairfield crest and with Red's name in neat black lettering on the side. Ben scooped some oats and alfalfa cubes into one of the buckets and then looked in the cupboard.

"Wow!" he exclaimed, staring at the packed shelves, crammed with dried herbs and country remedies — honey, bicarbonate of soda, vinegar, chalk. "You sure use a lot of supplements here."

"Well, we don't just use herbs as feed supplements," Amy said. "We use them to help deal with behavioral and physical problems. If you want, when we're done feeding, Ty and I can start giving you an idea of what some of the herbs do."

"Sure," Ty said enthusiastically. "The healing properties are pretty amazing."

"Yeah, maybe some other time," Ben said casually. "I think I'll go see Red now." Quickly adding a little more grain to the bucket, he carried it out of the feed room.

Amy frowned at Ty. "That's strange. I thought he'd be really interested. After all, he is here to learn about what we do." Past the feed room door, she could hear the horses in the front stable block banging their doors impatiently. They would have seen Ben walk past with Red's bucket. "And he could have offered to help us feed the other horses," she said, feeling slightly irritated. "Now the others are going to be wild until they get fed."

"I know what you mean," Ty shrugged. "But he just got here and probably wants to make sure Red's settling in."

"I guess," Amy said. She picked up a pile of buckets. "Well, we'd better get feeding before they kick all the stalls down."

Ɂ

At seven o'clock, Lou came out from the house. "Dinner's almost ready!" she called.

Amy and Ty came out of the tack room just as Ben appeared from Red's stall.

"How is he?" Ty asked.

"He's doing just fine," Ben replied, walking down the yard with them.

The delicious smell of baked ham filled the kitchen. Jack Bartlett, Amy and Lou's grandfather, was draining a pan of black-eyed peas at the sink. "Hi," he said to Ben, turning and offering his hand. "Jack Bartlett."

"Pleased to meet you, sir," Ben said, shaking hands.

As Ty and Amy began to set the table and Lou fixed drinks, Ben spent a few moments looking at the photographs that covered the kitchen walls.

"Is this your mom in these pictures?" he asked Amy.

She nodded and joined him by the pine cabinet. "Yeah. She was competing in England. We lived there when I was little."

"So why did you move back here?" Ben said.

"Because of Daddy's accident," Amy said.

"Oh, my aunt told me about that," Ben said. "He was riding in a jump-off, wasn't he?"

Amy nodded. Her father had been riding Pegasus in the World Championships. Pegasus had caught his legs on the top rail of a fence and fallen. Both he and her father had been badly injured. Having been only three at the time, Amy had no real memory of the event. But as Ben spoke, she saw Lou look around and frown. Lou had been eleven, and Amy knew she remembered it all much more clearly.

"So what happened to your dad after the accident?" Ben asked Amy.

"Well, he really injured his spine and was in a wheelchair for a bit," Amy explained. "He did get better, but the doctors said that it would be too dangerous for him to ever ride again." Her voice hardened. "It was really hard on him, and he couldn't cope with the situation, and so he ran off, abandoning us and the horses. He didn't want anything to do with us or his old life anymore, so Mom decided to move back here to live with Grandpa."

"Come on, Amy. That's not true!"

Amy turned. Lou was staring angrily at her. "Dad did try to get back together with Mom. And you know it. Did you forget about that letter? It's proof that he just needed time."

There was no way Amy could have forgotten the

letter. It had been a real shock when she and Lou had found the note from their dad, begging their mom for a reconciliation. They had found it while clearing out Marion's room.

Lou's blue eyes flashed. "If Mom had stayed in England instead of running off to the States, then maybe there's a chance that they *would* have gotten back together!"

"You don't know that," Amy said hotly. "And what was Mom supposed to do? Wait around patiently until Dad decided he was ready to come back?"

"Yes! That's precisely what she should have done!" Lou exclaimed.

"Amy! Lou!" Jack Bartlett said, stepping forward. "That's enough!" His voice softened. "I know both of you have strong feelings, but a lot of stuff went on at the time that neither of you know about. Don't judge your parents now."

Lou turned abruptly and went back to the sink. Amy knew that her sister didn't feel the same about their father as she did. Devastated by his disappearance, Lou had refused to accept that he wasn't coming back. When Marion had told them of her plans to move back to Virginia, she had refused to go, begging to be allowed to stay at her English boarding school instead. When their mom had been alive, Lou had made it abundantly clear that she saw the move to Virginia as a betrayal of their father.

Ben cleared his throat. "So your mom came here to live?" he said, breaking the silence.

Amy spoke more quietly. "Yeah, my mom and I came here with Pegasus. He was emotionally traumatized, and conventional medicine was only helping his physical wounds, so my mom began to explore alternative therapies. When Pegasus recovered, Mom started Heartland to put the methods she had learned into practice — with the aim of helping other horses."

"And your mom never competed again?" Ben asked.

"No, she was far more interested in her work here."

"What about you, Amy?" Ben asked, sitting down. "Do you show?"

"Occasionally," Amy replied. "When I get the time, I take Sundance, my pony, in the Large Pony Hunter division."

"How about you, Ty?" Ben asked.

"No," Ty said. "I'm not interested."

"Not at all?" Ben said, looking surprised.

Ty shook his head. "I've had a few people ask me to take their horses in classes, but competing doesn't really do it for me. I think working with damaged horses is more satisfying."

Amy smiled at Ty, knowing just how he felt.

Ben didn't look as if he understood them at all. "I just couldn't be like that," he said, shaking his head. "I mean, how do you prove that you're really good at what you do? I love the thrill of competing and putting in a really good ride. It's great to get the ribbon and know that everyone has seen you do your best."

Ty shrugged. "I guess I just don't care that much about what other people think."

For a moment, Ty and Ben's eyes met, and Amy felt a certain tension creep into the air.

"OK, guys," Jack Bartlett announced. "Dinner's ready."

With the sudden bustle of movement, the tension dissolved. Chair legs scraped as they all sat down, and Lou began to hand out platefuls of baked ham, a basket of cornbread, and a bowl heaped with black-eyed peas.

"This looks incredible," Ben said, helping himself.

"I'd like to propose a toast to the latest addition to Heartland," Jack said, lifting his glass when everyone's plate was piled high. "Welcome, Ben," he said. "And I hope you have a very happy time here."

They all raised their glasses. "To Ben!" they echoed.

Ben raised his glass back with an easy smile. "To Heartland," he said.

❧

When Amy's alarm clock rang as usual at six o'clock the next morning, she hit the off button with a groan.

She hadn't gone to bed until after midnight, and the last thing she felt like doing right now was leaping up to face the day. However, the horses, as always, were waiting.

Yawning, she climbed out of bed, and with eyes half closed pulled on her jeans. Not bothering to brush her long hair, she went downstairs and slipped on her boots.

Going out into the yard, she thought about Ben. He had been a fun guest to have over for dinner. He had talked to Lou about her old job in Manhattan and to Grandpa about his farming days. Amy had even managed to find out that he wasn't dating anyone — a piece of information that she knew would please Soraya tremendously.

She refilled the water buckets and had just started to mix the feeds when Ty arrived. "Morning," he said, coming into the feed room. "Any sign of Ben yet?"

Amy shook her head as she added scoopfuls of soaked beet pulp to the grain in the buckets. "No." Ben was supposed to start work at seven o'clock, the same as Ty, but he hadn't arrived. "He'll probably be here any minute," she said.

However, Ben's truck didn't appear until more than an hour later. Hearing the engine, Amy looked out of Sundance's stall.

"Hi, there!" Ben said, jumping out of the truck. "Great morning, isn't it?" he said enthusiastically.

Amy had expected him to be full of apologies for being so late. "Yeah, I guess so," she replied.

Ben seemed to sense her reserve. "Hey, sorry I'm a little late," he said. "You don't mind, do you? I overslept. I guess I'm just tired from yesterday's move."

"It's OK," Amy said, pushing down the little voice in her head that was suggesting that maybe an hour and a half was more than a *little* late.

"OK, then," Ben said. "What do you want me to do?"

"I guess I should show you where things are first," Amy said. "And then you can help Ty and me. We've already finished the feeding and are mucking out the stalls. Then we sweep the barns and groom and exercise until lunchtime. Come on, I'll introduce you to the horses."

"Hang on a sec," Ben said. "I just want to say hi to Red."

Amy waited patiently as Ben went up to the tall chestnut and patted him and spoke to him in a quiet voice. Amy watched the horse nuzzle Ben's shoulder. He obviously adored his owner.

Ben joined her after a few minutes, and she began to take him around the stalls. "This is Jake," she said, stroking the bay Clydesdale in the stall next to Red's. "He's twenty-one." Jake pushed hopefully against her hand, and taking the hint, she fished out a packet of mints from her pocket. "Mom rescued him at a horse sale," Amy explained. "He has really bad arthritis and can't be rehomed."

"How many horses do you have here?" Ben asked.

"There are seven boarders and ten rescue horses," Amy said. "Eight of the rescues will hopefully recover enough so we can find them new homes. Two of them are here permanently — Jake and my pony, Sundance." She kissed Jake's nose. "I hate saying good-bye to horses when they leave. You get so attached to them." She glanced at Ben to see if he understood, but he was moving on to the next stall.

"That's Gypsy Queen," she said, going after him. "She's here to be cured of her bucking habit." She was about to explain more about Gypsy's history and her owner, but Ben was already walking to the next stall.

He showed a similar lack of interest when Amy started to tell him about the different therapies they used at Heartland. She showed him the medicine cabinet filled with her mom's books, herbal treatments, aromatherapy oils, and Bach Flower Remedies.

"What's the point of all this?" Ben said at last. "I mean, why not just trust the vet?"

"We do," Amy said. "It's just that Mom believed that you can use natural remedies to complement traditional medicine. Our vet, Scott, pretty much agrees." She saw the skeptical look on Ben's face. "Our methods *do* work, you know. Don't forget, we cured your aunt's horse, Promise, when nobody else managed to."

"I suppose," Ben said, but he still looked less than convinced. He stepped toward the door. "You said the stalls need finishing off. Should I get started? Ty looked like he could use some help."

Amy nodded and Ben strode off.

Amy stared after him, feeling confused. Lisa was paying for Ben to be at Heartland, but he didn't seem at all interested in their work — in fact, he acted like he didn't even think their methods could help.

❧

When they stopped for lunch, Ben got out his grooming kit and tack. "Aren't you going to eat?" Amy asked. "We still have ham for sandwiches."

"I'm going to ride first," Ben replied, heading in the direction of Red's stall.

"So what do you think of him now?" Amy asked Ty as they went into the kitchen.

"What — apart from him being an hour and a half late, taking two hours to muck out four stalls, and not showing any interest in the work we do here?" Ty replied dryly.

Amy smiled. "Yeah, despite that. What do you think?"

Ty shrugged. "I don't know. It'll probably take him time to adjust. Ask me in a week or so."

As Amy made herself a sandwich, she looked out the window and saw Ben walking Red up the path to the schooling ring. "Want to sit outside and watch him ride?" she said.

Ty nodded and, taking their lunch with them, they headed toward the training ring.

Ben was cantering Red in a figure eight. With light and fluid movements, the chestnut executed a perfect flying change in the center of the ring. Amy saw Ben stroke Red's neck, his lips moving in praise as they cantered on, his body still in the saddle, his back straight, and his hands maintaining light, steady contact with the horse's mouth.

"They look good," she said in a low voice to Ty.

Seemingly oblivious to their presence, Ben turned Red down the center of the ring, steering to where there was a four-foot jump. With barely a change in his stride pattern, Red approached and cleared it as easily as if it had been a fence half the height. To Amy, watching at the gate, the bond between horse and rider was unmistakable, but at the same time, she had to question whether Red was warmed up properly before Ben started jumping him.

As Ben cantered past, he seemed to notice them for

the first time. In one easy transition, he brought Red from a canter to a walk. "Hey," he said, circling Red back toward them.

"Hi," Ty replied.

"You jumped that well," Amy said.

Ben smiled. "Thanks." He patted Red. "I thought I might take him out on a trail ride for a bit. Do either of you feel like coming? It would help to have someone show me the trails around here."

"Sure, I'll come out on Sundance," Amy said. She glanced at Ty. "How about it, Ty? Are you going to come?"

"I'd better not," Ty said. "Solo, Charlie, and Moochie need working in the ring, and there is a lot of grooming to do."

"You're right." Amy felt guilty. "Maybe I should stay."

"No, it's OK. You go," Ty said. "Ben needs someone who knows the trails, and Sundance could use the exercise."

"Great, it's settled, then," Ben said, looking at Amy. "I'll walk Red around and cool him off while you get ready."

"Are you sure you don't mind?" Amy asked Ty as Ben walked Red away.

"It's fine," Ty replied. "You just go ahead and enjoy yourself," he teased. "Don't worry about me. I'll stay and do all the work — as usual."

"That's right," Amy said with a grin. "I never do anything around here."

"You said it." Ty said, dodging quickly as she swung a playful punch at him.

As Amy walked to the ponies' turnout field to catch Sundance, she felt another flicker of guilt. Now that they had so many horses boarding, Ty was working harder than ever — he was working until late in the evening and never taking his days off. *Oh, well,* she thought as she reached the paddock gate and called to Sundance, *hopefully now that Ben's here to help, things should start getting easier for him — for both of us.*

It only took Amy five minutes to run a brush over Sundance's coat and tack up. She mounted and went up to the ring. "I'm ready."

"Great," Ben said. "Let's go."

They rode out of the yard to Teak's Hill, the wooded mountain that rose up behind Heartland. Just before the trail left the fields and entered the trees, Amy stopped Sundance. "I love this view," she said, looking at Heartland stretched out below them, the barns and paddocks bathed in the glow of the October sun.

"It's beautiful up here," Ben said, looking around.

"Your aunt's barn is great, too," Amy said. "It must have been amazing to grow up there."

"Yeah," Ben said, with the hint of a dry, unamused laugh. "I guess it was."

Amy glanced at him.

Ben gathered up his reins. "So what are we waiting for?" he said, trotting Red on. "I thought you were supposed to be showing me around."

Amy trotted after him. Patches of sunlight filtered through the treetops and dappled the shady track. "That leads up to Clairdale Ridge," Amy said, pointing out the trail as they rode past it. "And the trail we're going to take up here on the left leads down to the creek."

They approached the fallen tree that Sundance had jumped the day before. Seeing it, the buckskin's ears pricked forward.

"Can we jump that?" Ben asked. "Is it safe?"

"Yeah, it's fine," Amy said, holding Sundance back. She let Ben go first and watched as he cantered Red toward the tree trunk. As he neared it, the young horse spooked at the unfamiliar jump and stopped.

Amy gasped as Ben immediately brought his crop down on Red's neck. With a snort, the chestnut shot backward, head in the air. Clamping his legs on the horse's sides, Ben turned again toward the tree trunk. Amy saw the horse's ears prick forward in alarm and his stride shorten as his muscles tensed in defiance.

"Go on!" Ben said angrily, pounding his legs against Red's sides.

"Ben! He's scared!" Amy exclaimed as the chestnut began to back away from the trunk.

"He has to learn," Ben shouted back.

Amy cantered over. "Don't upset him. I can give you a lead on Sundance if you want," she appealed in a calm voice.

Ben ignored her. Using his heels and his seat, he urged Red forward. The horse took two short strides and plunged toward the trunk. Ben brought his crop down on the horse's shoulder, and Red took off in a massive leap. As they landed on the other side, Ben patted Red's shoulder and praised him. "Good boy!" He turned triumphantly to Amy. "See? He had to learn there was nothing to be afraid of."

But did he have to learn that way? Amy thought, looking at the sweat that had broken out on the chestnut's neck. She wanted to tell Ben that scolding a horse to overcome fear is not a good way to build trust. However, she bit back the words. Seeing Ben pat Red now, she knew that he hadn't meant to be cruel. He obviously just used different methods from those she used — the kind of forceful methods that most of the horse world used. But Amy couldn't figure out why anyone would train with force when you could accomplish just as much — even more — through cooperation and understanding.

"There are other ways to get a horse to do what you

want," she said to Ben. Clicking her tongue, she cantered Sundance in a circle.

"You're not really going to jump it, are you?" Ben called in surprise. "Isn't it a bit big for him?"

Ignoring him, Amy turned Sundance toward the tree. His ears pricked up, his stride lengthened confidently, and in one smooth leap they were over.

"Way to go!" Ben exclaimed, looking very impressed. "For a pony, he sure can jump!"

Amy nodded as she trotted over. "He's won Large Pony Hunter Champion three times now. But I don't get many chances to show him. I'd like to try a few junior jumper classes, though."

"You should," Ben said. "With form like that, he'd have a great chance."

Amy patted Sundance, pleased at Ben's approval. "We rescued him from a sale. He probably would have been sold for glue if not for my mom and me," she said. "He was so bad tempered no one could cope with him. Now we get tons of offers for him. But I'll never let him go."

"I know how you feel," Ben said. He stroked Red's shoulder. "I'd never sell Red, either. No matter what anyone offered me."

Seeing Red turn and nuzzle Ben's hand, Amy began to forgive Ben for how he had behaved earlier.

She smiled back at Ben, and they continued along the track.

Ben patted Red. "I'm entered in a show next month with him. I thought I'd do a couple of classes to keep him going over the winter and then take the circuit seriously next summer." He looked at Amy. "We could do some shows together. My trailer takes up to three horses. You could really go for it with Sundance, too."

Amy was flattered, but she shook her head. "Thanks, but I couldn't be away from Heartland for that long."

"You know it's a waste," Ben said. "You could be really good."

Amy shrugged. "Heartland's more important to me than competing."

"Nothing's more important to me than competing," Ben said, his voice suddenly sounding determined. Shortening his reins, he leaned forward in his saddle. "Come on, I'll race you to the bend in the track!"

Chapter Three

When Amy and Ben got back to Heartland, Ty was riding Moochie. "We'd better get back to the grooming," Amy said.

"Sure," Ben replied. "I'll be with you as soon as I've put Red away."

Amy thought that Ben meant that he would just give Red a quick rubdown before returning him to his stall. However, it was almost an hour before he eventually reappeared. "OK, who do you want me to start on?" he asked.

Amy was just finishing Jasmine. There were only three horses left to groom. "Can you do Jake and Sugarfoot?" she said, feeling slightly irritated that he'd been gone so long.

Ben nodded cheerfully and fetched a grooming kit.

When he came back, Amy was just going into Dancer's stall. "This is Dancer, right?" Ben said.

Amy nodded.

Ben stepped into the stall and reached to pat Dancer's neck, but he moved too quickly, and the mare reacted like lightning. Throwing her head up with a squeal, she snapped at Ben's arm.

"Hey!" Ben shouted, smacking her in the jaw.

"Ben! No!" Amy cried in horror, grabbing his arm.

It was too late. Dancer's eyes flashed with white, and she started kicking in fear.

"Get out!" Amy cried, brushing past Ben and yanking on his arm.

She dragged him out of the stall and shut the door just as Dancer's hooves smashed into the side wall. Almost beside herself with anger, she turned to Ben. "How could you do that!" she cried. "Dancer's scared enough of people as it is!"

Ben stared at her. "But she tried to bite me!"

"So? We don't *hit* horses here."

"You mean you just let them bite?" Ben exclaimed. "That's crazy! How will they ever learn to respect you if you let them get away with things like that?"

Amy's gray eyes flashed. "You don't need to hit a horse to get it to respect you. Especially a horse like Dancer, who has been abused."

"So what *do* you do?" Ben said. "She's not going to stop biting on her own."

"If you treat them with the respect they deserve, show them understanding, and let them realize that there is nothing to be afraid of, you'll be surprised how some horses will change. Have you seen the scars on Dancer's head?" Amy demanded. "They're from a halter being on so tight that her skin was rubbed raw. That halter was left on for more than a year. Of course she tried to bite you when you put your hand up to her head like that. You'd have done the same. You can't blame her."

Ben looked slightly ashamed. "I didn't realize." He looked at the mare, now standing trembling at the back of her stall. "Hey, I'm sorry if I scared her."

Amy took a deep breath to try to control her anger. "Look, just make sure you remember that we never hit any of the horses here. Every single one of them is damaged in some way. What we need to do is gain their trust, not frighten them even more."

Ben swallowed hard. "OK, I get it." He looked at Dancer again. "Is there anything you can do to calm her down?"

"I'll see," Amy said. Leaving the halter on the floor, she walked quietly into the stall. Dancer stared at her warily.

"It's OK, girl," Amy told her softly, feeling in her pocket for the packet of mints and offering her one. "I won't hurt you."

Dancer watched Amy for a moment and then stepped forward cautiously, her neck outstretched, her brown-and-white nostrils blowing in and out. Amy let the mare snuffle the mint up from her hand and then moved quietly to stand beside her shoulder. Dancer shifted uneasily in the straw. Very gently, still speaking soothingly to the frightened horse, Amy put her hand lightly on Dancer's shoulder and began to move her fingers in a series of small circles, each circle moving on to a new patch of skin.

Forgetting about Ben watching from the doorway, she concentrated totally on the mare. As the minutes passed, she felt the horse's muscles begin to relax slightly, and Amy slowed the circles down, moving them gradually up Dancer's neck toward her head. Every time the mare tensed, she lightened her touch, but gradually Dancer started to relax more and more until she was allowing Amy to work tiny circles over her muzzle, nostrils, and lips.

As Amy worked, the mare yawned and slowly lowered her head, her eyes half closing. At last, Amy stopped, and moving quietly to the door, she picked up the halter and slipped it over Dancer's nose.

Dancer didn't even flinch. Buckling it up, Amy led the now calm mare toward the front of the stall.

"That's amazing," Ben said in surprise. "She's OK now just because of a massage?"

"It's not really massage," Amy explained. "It's a form of therapy called T-touch." She tied Dancer up. "See? Force isn't the best way to get a horse to do what you want."

Ben frowned. "I get your point with horses like Dancer," he said. "But a regular horse responds to discipline. Look at Red. I'm firm with him, but you would never say that he's scared of me, and we work great together."

"But why use force when you can get a horse to work just as well without it?" Amy asked.

Ben shrugged. "It's just what I've always done. Red and I have a lot of training to do. He has a lot to learn about being a jumper, and we've got a system that works for us." Ben saw Amy's face. "Look, don't worry, I'll respect your rules with Heartland's horses. Just don't expect me to change what I do with Red." He picked up the grooming kit again. "Now, I'd better get started grooming that Shetland — Sugarfoot, right?"

Amy nodded and started to brush Dancer. She didn't know what to make of Ben. He seemed so skeptical. He was not at all prepared to accept Heartland's methods and ideas, and yet he was obviously a good rider and completely devoted to Red. Amy didn't think he needed to resort to crops and harsh treatment to train his horse. She thought that over time she and Ty would be able to persuade him to change his ideas. She patted Dancer. She hoped she was right.

❧

At five o'clock, Amy and Ty started to fill the evening hay nets. They were running late as usual. "At least all the horses have been exercised," Amy said to Ty as they stuffed sweet-smelling meadow hay into the nets.

"Yeah, and with three of us we should be able to stack the rest of the hay delivery in the feed room in no time," Ty said. "That's if we all put our backs into it."

Just then, there was the sound of footsteps. Ben looked over the door. "I'm finished grooming, so I'll be heading out."

Amy stared at him. "Going? But we haven't fed the horses yet."

"I'm off at five," Ben said in surprise.

Amy was at a loss for words. He was right of course. But working with horses wasn't like a regular job; you didn't just leave when your hours were up.

"I usually stay 'til things are done," Ty said pointedly.

"Great," Ben said cheerfully. "If you're staying, then I'm OK to go, right?"

"Well, actually, Ben, if you could stick around until the feeds are done, it would help a lot," Amy said quickly, seeing that he hadn't taken the hint.

Ben looked taken aback. "I guess I could."

"Good," Amy said, feeling awkward that she had to ask. "You could start mixing the feeds, and we'll finish these nets off."

Ben did as Amy suggested. As they heard the rattle of the buckets being put out on the floor, Amy and Ty exchanged glances. They continued filling the hay nets in silence.

At last the horses were fed. "See you tomorrow," Ben said.

Amy nodded, not able to bring herself to mention that the hay delivery still needed to be dealt with.

She watched Ben drive off. "Well," she said to Ty. "I don't know what to think of that."

"I guess he's used to his aunt's barn. They probably have enough staff to get everything done during normal working hours," Ty said.

Amy thought about Lisa Stillman's immaculate breeding stable with its army of stable hands and thought Ty must be right. "It's gotta be a big change for him. Ben's probably not even used to cleaning stalls and doing things like that."

Ty looked at her. "Well, you think he'll get used to it here?"

Amy remembered what had happened earlier that afternoon. "I'm sure he will," she said, trying to be positive. "It'll just take time."

For a moment, Ty didn't say anything, but then he nodded. "Well, we'll just wait and see."

🙢

Ben didn't arrive the next morning until Amy was going into the house to get changed for school. She didn't have time to ask why he was late. She hardly had a chance to think about it. School mornings were always hectic, and as usual, none of her school stuff was organized. She showered in two minutes flat, pulled on some clean clothes, and raced downstairs.

"What about breakfast, Amy?" her grandpa said despairingly, as she grabbed her sneakers and started to pull them on.

"I don't have time!" Amy said. "I'll miss the bus!"

"But Amy, you can't go without breakfast," Jack Bartlett said.

"Why do we have to go through this every morning?" Lou said from the kitchen table. "Why don't you get your stuff together the night before and come in from the barn at a decent time?"

"Here, take this," her grandpa said, shoving a muffin into Amy's hand.

"Thanks, Grandpa!" Amy said, giving him a kiss as she slung her backpack over her shoulder. "See you later. Bye, Lou!"

With that, she ran out of the house.

Ty was standing by the tap filling up a water bucket. "Have a good day," he called.

"Like that's going to happen," Amy said, pausing briefly. "I've got two periods of math first thing."

Ty grinned. "Better you than me."

"See you later!" said Amy, jogging off down the drive.

She made it to the stop just as the bus arrived. Soraya had saved a seat beside her. "So, come on — tell me all the gossip about Ben," she said as Amy sat down.

"Well, he's not very good at being on time," Amy said as she caught her breath. "He's been late both mornings since he got here."

"And you're *never* late," Soraya grinned, looking at Amy's flushed face and disheveled hair.

Amy grinned back. "OK, OK."

"Did you find out if he has a girlfriend?" Soraya asked.

"Yes," Amy said. "And he doesn't."

"Now *that* really is interesting," Soraya said slowly. "So how's he fitting in at Heartland?"

As Amy started to tell her all about Ben she noticed that the girl sitting in a seat across the aisle kept looking at her. "Who's that?" Amy whispered to Soraya when the girl looked away.

"I don't know," Soraya replied. "Maybe she's new."

The girl glanced at them again. She had short brown hair and a heart-shaped face.

"Hi," Soraya said, smiling in her usual friendly way. The girl turned red. "Oh . . . hi," she said nervously.

"Did you just start at Jefferson High?" Soraya asked, leaning forward.

The girl nodded. "Yes. My name's Claire Whitely."

"We thought you might be new," Soraya said. "Where are you from?"

"Philadelphia," the girl said. "We moved here because of my mom's job."

"Well, I'm Soraya Martin, and this is Amy Fleming," Soraya told her. "If you want to know anything about school, just ask us."

Amy nodded.

"Thanks," Claire said. Her cheeks became a bit pinker. "Actually, I couldn't help overhearing your conversation," she said, looking at Amy. "Do you — do you live at Heartland?"

"Yeah," Amy replied, feeling surprised.

Claire's blue eyes widened. "I read about Heartland in an issue of *Horse Life*. It sounds amazing. I knew it was somewhere in Virginia, but I had no idea it was *here*."

"Do you ride?" Amy asked her.

"Yeah," Claire said shyly. "My dad just bought me my own horse. My parents are divorced, and he just left to go work in Europe for a few months. So he gave me Flint before he left — that's my horse. He's a Thoroughbred."

"That's a pretty nice gift!" Soraya said.

Clare nodded. "I've wanted a horse forever. I think my dad feels bad that I don't get to see him much. But Flint's just brilliant. He was really expensive, but he's won a lot of awards, so he must be worth it."

Looking at the glow in Claire's eyes as she talked about Flint, Amy forgave her for bragging a bit. She just seemed so excited to have her own horse.

Claire looked at her and swallowed. "Would you — would you like to come and see him?" she asked hesitantly. "You, too, Soraya. You could come after school today. I'm going to the stable anyway. But you don't have to unless you want to," she added hurriedly.

"No, I'd like to see him," Amy said.

"Me, too," Soraya said.

"You would?" Claire looked as if she could hardly believe it.

Amy nodded. "Where is your stable?"

"Green Briar," Claire replied eagerly. "Do you know it?"

Amy and Soraya's eyes met. They knew it all too well. Green Briar was a large hunter/jumper barn that specialized in producing push-button horses and ponies that always racked in the ribbons. The stable was run by Val Grant. Her daughter, Ashley, was in the same class as Amy and Soraya at school, and whenever Amy took

Sundance to local shows, Ashley was one of Amy's fiercest rivals.

"Yeah, we know it," Soraya replied dryly.

"Great," Claire said, oblivious to the look that had passed between them. "Do you want to come by this afternoon?"

"I have to go home first and make sure everything's OK," Amy said. "But we could meet you there." She didn't particularly want to go to Green Briar, but she thought it would be nice to be friendly with Claire, and it would be interesting to see Flint.

"OK," Claire said, her eyes shining. "That would be great."

❧

School seemed to drag by that day. All Amy could think about was whether Ben and Ty were getting along at Heartland and how things would go when she and Soraya went to see Claire's horse. Soraya phoned her mom at lunchtime, and Mrs. Martin agreed to give them a ride to Green Briar.

"See you later," Amy said to Soraya and Claire as she got off the bus.

"Yeah, bye," they called.

Amy hurried up Heartland's winding drive. When she reached the top, she saw Ty coming out of the tack room. "Hi," she said, going over to him. "How's it been today?"

"Busy," Ty said. "But almost everyone has been worked. There's just Ivy and Solo left."

"I'll do them," Amy offered. "But do you mind if I go over to Green Briar first?"

"Green Briar?" Ty echoed. "What do you want to go there for?"

Amy told Ty about Flint. "I'd like to see him, and Soraya's mom said she'd drive us. It shouldn't take long."

"That's fine," Ty said. "I'll get Ben to help sweep — when he's finished riding Red."

"He's riding Red?" Amy said, surprised that Ben was riding his own horse when there was still work to be done.

Ty nodded. "Yeah. And he rode him for an hour this morning." He looked concerned. "Don't you think two workouts is a lot for a young horse?"

"Well, Ben did say that he's got a show next month," Amy said. "And lots of competition horses get ridden twice a day."

"Yeah, but they don't normally jump three-foot courses each time," Ty said. "I could understand him riding once in the ring and once on the trails, but he did heavy work, and he rode more than an hour both times."

Amy frowned. Ty was right. Two hour-long training

sessions was a lot of work for any horse, let alone a young horse like Red.

"And it's not like there wasn't anything else to do," Ty added.

Amy nodded. "Maybe we should talk with him later."

She went to get changed. As she came out of the house, Ben was walking Red down the path from the training ring. "Hi!" he called, catching sight of her and stopping Red. "He's been great today."

Amy didn't know what to say. She wanted to yell at him for jumping Red twice that day and not helping Ty more, but she didn't know how to start. And she didn't think it would be right. It was a tricky situation when his aunt was paying for him to be there. Under any other circumstance she wouldn't have hesitated to speak out and let her thoughts be known, but this was different.

"Good," she said. "I, er, think Ty could use a hand in the barn."

"Sure," Ben said. "I'll just cool Red down first."

"OK, but don't take too long," Amy said sharply.

Ben looked surprised.

Just then, the Martins' car came up the drive, and Amy realized that the conversation with Ben would have to wait.

"Hi, Ben," Soraya said, getting out of the car.

Ben smiled at her. "Hi. How are you doing?"

"Great," Soraya said with a smile.

Seeing that Soraya looked as if she was about to start a conversation, Amy grabbed her arm. They didn't want to be late for Claire. "Hello, Mrs. Martin," she said as she pulled Soraya into the back of the car.

"Hi, Amy," Mrs. Martin replied, turning the car around.

"Did you see the way Ben smiled at me?" Soraya said with a giggle. "He is *so* cute!"

"Soraya Martin!" her mom said, overhearing. "I thought you liked going to Heartland because of the horses."

"I do!" Soraya protested. "Besides, Ben just started working there."

But then, shooting Amy a sideways look that her mom couldn't see, she grinned.

Amy smiled back at her friend, but inwardly she was worried by the situation with Ben.

❦

Claire was waiting for them in the paved parking lot at Green Briar. "Flint's stall is in that barn over there," she said, leading them across the immaculate yard toward a spacious modern barn. They passed a large, all-weather training ring where three beautiful horses were being schooled over a line of fences. In the middle of the ring stood Val Grant. With a cell phone clipped onto the back of her tight maroon breeches and a lunge whip in her hand, she called out instructions to the riders. Amy hurried past, not wanting to be seen. If she could see Flint and get away from Green Briar without having to talk to Val Grant or Ashley, she would be amazingly relieved. She cringed as there was a rattle of poles, and she heard Val Grant's voice yell out in strident tones, "What do you think your crop's for, Yvonne? Use it!"

Amy exchanged looks with Soraya as they hurried into the barn.

"That's him," Claire said. "Five stalls down on the left. The dark gray."

Amy looked down the row of stalls to where a beautiful iron-gray Thoroughbred was looking over his half door. His elegant ears were pricked, his brown eyes were large and thoughtful.

"He's very handsome," Amy said, going over. "Hi, boy."

Flint looked at her with an odd expression on his face.

Amy peered over the stall door. He was a fantastic-looking horse, very athletic with strong, clean legs and a noble head.

Soraya and Claire joined her. "He *is* handsome, isn't he?" Claire said, waiting for their approval.

"He sure is," Soraya said.

Amy nodded in agreement. "Are you going to ride him?" she asked.

Claire seemed suddenly hesitant. "Ummm, well, I don't know."

"Oh, you've got to!" Soraya said.

"OK," Claire agreed slowly. "I'll get my tack."

A few minutes later, Claire returned with her saddle and bridle. Her fingers fumbled with the bolt as she let herself into the stall. As she moved toward Flint, he tossed his head into the air.

"Steady, boy," Claire said, her voice sounding nervous.

Flint sidestepped away from her and moved to the back of his stall so his hindquarters were pointing in Claire's direction. Putting his ears back, Flint lifted one back hoof and stamped it on the ground. Claire jumped back quickly.

"Is he always like this?" Soraya asked.

"Not always, but most of the time," Claire said, grateful for the excuse to step back to the door. "He was OK at first, but he's been getting worse. Sometimes it can take me almost an hour to brush him and tack up."

Amy stared at her in astonishment. "An hour!"

"He just keeps lifting his back foot at me like that," Claire said, her face turning red. "I'm not sure what to do."

Amy frowned. She had seen the way Flint had been watching Claire as he stood in the corner, his ears pricked, his eyes bright. He didn't look mean. In fact, she had a strong feeling that he was just taking advantage of Claire's lack of experience. "Here, do you want me to try?" she said.

Claire gratefully handed her the bridle.

Ignoring the way Flint lifted his back hoof from the floor, Amy marched around to his head, grabbed his mane so that he couldn't swing away, and deftly tossed the reins over his head. "Got you!" she said. Taking hold of his nose, she slipped the bit in his mouth and pulled the headpiece over his ears. Flint looked at her determined face and didn't object.

"I think you're going to have to be a bit firmer with him," she said to Claire. "He's just being difficult."

She finished tacking Flint up and then led him outside and handed the reins to Claire.

Claire glanced at the main training ring. Val Grant was still working with the three riders. "We'll take him to the back ring," she said quickly.

Amy and Soraya followed her around to a smaller training ring behind the barns. Claire led Flint in through the gate and then mounted.

As soon as she was in the saddle, Flint started to sidestep. "Steady," Claire said, her hands grabbing at the reins. Looking at Amy and Soraya, she tried to smile. "I'll just walk and trot him for a bit," she said.

As she rode off, Soraya turned to Amy. "She doesn't seem very confident," she said.

"I know," Amy said in a low voice as Flint jogged around the ring. Although Claire's position in the saddle was basically good, she was stiff and tense. "And he's quite a handful."

As they watched, Flint began to settle down, and Claire seemed to relax. But she didn't canter him.

After a bit, she rode Flint over to the gate. "He's great, isn't he?" she said proudly.

"Yeah," Amy agreed.

"But he does look like he could be high strung," Soraya said.

"That horse just needs someone in the saddle who can actually ride," a voice said behind them.

Amy swung round. Ashley Grant was standing there, arms crossed, platinum blond hair falling onto her shoulders.

"I told you, Flint's too much horse for a beginner like *you*," Ashley said to Claire. She shrugged. "But if you want, I guess I could spare the time to ride him and teach him a few things."

"Thanks, but I think I'll bring him in now," Claire said quickly. She hurriedly started to dismount. "He's done enough today."

Ashley laughed and turned to Amy. "So how's business at . . . Heartland?" she said, her eyebrows raising in an irritatingly mocking way as she said Heartland's name.

"Extremely busy, actually," Amy said coldly, moving to open the gate for Claire. "All our stalls are full, and we've got a new stable hand."

Ashley looked surprised. "What happened to Ty?"

"The new hand is in addition to Ty," Amy said as Claire led Flint out of the ring

Ashley crossed her arms. "You're never going to keep Ty, you know. He's good — even Mom says so. He could go places."

"He could, but he doesn't want to," Amy said.

"I wouldn't be so sure if I were you." Ashley said. "Does he know that we've just started looking for a new head groom? He might want to apply."

Amy laughed incredulously. "Get real, Ashley. Ty would never want to work somewhere like *here*."

Ashley looked round at the immaculate surroundings. "Oh, really? So Ty wouldn't want to work at a stable with three training rings, a cross-country course, three state-of-the-art barns, efficient staff, and top-quality horses? Think about it, Amy," she said sarcastically. "Working here is every stable hand's dream. Particularly when you think of what Ty puts up with instead — one run-down stable with two dinky barns, two small rings, and a bunch of horses that no one wants."

Amy longed to say something clever back, but the truth in Ashley's words hit home. "Ty wouldn't come here!" she said, desperately wanting to reassure herself, but she was feeling less convinced.

"Mom would pay a lot to get someone like him," Ashley said. "Maybe I'll tell her to give him a call," she added casually.

"Do whatever you want!" Amy exclaimed, feeling her temper start to rise. "But Ty won't leave Heartland!"

Ashley's lips curved into an mischievous smile. "Oh, really?" she said. Her green eyes challenged Amy. "Well, I guess we'll just have to see about that."

Chapter Four

Amy was still furious with Ashley when Mrs. Martin dropped her off at Heartland half an hour later. She was sure that Ty wouldn't leave Heartland. Soraya had tried to reassure her, but Ashley had lodged a nagging doubt in her mind. Amy couldn't imagine how much Val Grant would offer Ty to steal him away. Whatever it was, Amy knew that Lou would never be able to match it. Extra money was something they didn't have at Heartland. And what about the opportunities he'd have at Green Briar? It was four times as big as Heartland.

Amy pushed away the questions. She was being ridiculous. Ty loved Heartland. She told herself that she knew him well enough to realize he would never consider leaving.

As she walked across the yard she saw Ben coming out of Red's stall. "Hi," he said.

Amy remembered that she had been planning to talk to him some more. She went over, wondering how to begin. "He's in great condition," she said, patting Red's muscular neck.

Ben nodded. "Yeah. I ride him twice a day."

"Isn't that a bit much for a young horse?" Amy said, trying to get the conversation around to what she wanted to talk about.

Ben shook his head. "If I want to make it to the top he needs to be fit."

"Yeah, but you don't need to school him twice a day," Amy said. "Ty said you jumped him both times you rode today. He was a little concerned."

"What does he know?" Ben said, looking angry. "He doesn't even ride competitively."

"He knows a lot!" Amy said, jumping to Ty's defense. "And he only mentioned it because he was worried about Red."

"Well, I don't need him to look out for my horse!" Ben said defiantly. "I know what's best for Red." He looked at her and changed his expression. "You should appreciate the demands of training a top competition horse, Amy. You saw your mom and dad do it."

Amy didn't want to get into a huge fight with Ben on only his second day. "I guess," she said, reluctantly backing down. She guessed that he had done the same at Fairfield, and Lisa Stillman had felt it was reasonable training for a show horse.

Just then the phone rang. "I'll get it!" Amy heard Ty yell as he came out of the tack room.

Five minutes later, he walked back toward the barn. Amy was filling Jake's water bucket. "Who was it?" she called.

Ty walked toward her, his dark eyes amused. "You will *never* guess."

"I have no idea," Amy said, shaking her head.

"It was Val Grant," Ty said. "And she just offered me a job at Green Briar." He had a huge grin on his face.

Amy was stunned. "Val Grant!"

Ty took in her expression and burst out laughing. "I'm not sure why she asked me. She hadn't said more than two words to me before," he said, shaking his head.

"What did you say?" Amy asked with concern.

"What do you mean?" Ty said, looking at Amy. "It's not really my thing. I mean, the money would be better, and it would be cool to be head groom, but I don't think it's a good move. She just doesn't see things the same way that I do."

"What?" Amy said sarcastically. "Val Grant, who would have a crop surgically attached to her arm if possible, doesn't see things like you?"

"Exactly," Ty said with a laugh and a smile, and then turned back toward the tack room.

Amy felt better knowing Ty wasn't really considering it, but some of her concern still lingered. She and Ty could joke all they wanted, but Amy knew it was a serious matter. If Ty left, it would change everything.

❧

That night, as the family sat down to dinner, Lou asked how Ben was settling in.

Amy didn't know what to say.

"There isn't a problem, is there, Amy?" Grandpa said, seeing her hesitate.

"No . . . no, he's OK," Amy said, reaching out for the water pitcher.

Jack Bartlett frowned. "Just OK?" Amy could tell that he thought she was trying to hide something. "Amy, what's on your mind?"

"Nothing." Amy saw her grandpa's eyebrows rise. "It's just that he's got some different ideas than we have," she tried to explain. "But I don't think it'll be a major problem."

Just then the phone rang.

"I'll get it!" Amy said, glad for the distraction. She jumped up and grabbed the receiver. "Heartland, Amy Fleming speaking."

"Hi, Amy. It's Scott."

Hearing the familiar voice of their local vet, Amy smiled. "Hey, Scott."

Scott cleared his throat. "Is Lou there?" he asked.

"Yeah," Amy said, nodding. "Let me get her." She held the cordless phone out to her sister. "It's Scott," she said, grinning.

Lou's cheeks turned pink. "For me?"

"Yes," Amy replied, her eyes glinting teasingly at her sister. "For you."

Lou took the phone. "Hello, Scott?" she said, walking away from the table and turning her back to Amy. "Yes, I'm fine. How are you?"

Amy grinned at their grandpa as she sat back down, forgetting the conversation about Ben. "I bet Scott's going to ask Lou out on a date!" she said.

Jack Bartlett shook his head, but Amy saw him smile as he looked away. Although Grandpa would never say anything, she knew that he would be just as pleased as she would if Scott and Lou were to start dating. For the last couple of months — ever since Lou had broken up with her past boyfriend — she had become increasingly friendly with Scott. So far nothing had happened, but this was the first time that Scott had called just to talk to Lou.

Amy turned hopefully in her chair. She could just hear what Lou was saying. "I'd love to, Scott! That sounds great. OK, I'll see you then."

"Well?" Amy demanded as Lou put the phone down. "Did he ask you out?"

"Yes," Lou said, turning round and looking stunned. "He did. We're going out on Saturday."

"Oh, Lou! That's wonderful!" Amy cried, jumping to her feet and hugging her sister. "You and Scott are totally perfect for each other."

"It's only one date, Amy," Lou laughed, but despite her practical words her blue eyes sparkled.

❧

The next day on the school bus, Amy told Soraya the news. "Isn't it awesome?" she said.

"I wonder if Matt knows," Soraya said.

Matt was one of their best friends and Scott's younger brother. As soon as he got on the bus they told him.

"Cool," he said. He looked hopefully at Amy. "You know, we could always see if they want to make it a double date."

"Like they'll want us tagging along," Amy said.

"We could go somewhere else," Matt said.

"Oh, Matt. You know I'm just too busy with Heartland," Amy said. "Maybe another time."

Matt sighed theatrically. "Rejected again."

Amy grinned at him. "You'll get over it." Matt had been trying to persuade her to go out with him for almost a year now, but somehow she just couldn't see him as a boyfriend. She caught Soraya looking at her. She knew Soraya thought she was crazy to keep turning Matt down. He was cute, intelligent, popular, and great fun to be around.

"So who's the new girl you were talking to yesterday?" Matt said, glancing toward the front of the bus to where Claire was sitting.

"Claire Whitely," Amy replied.

"She just moved here from Philadelphia," Soraya said. "We went to see her horse yesterday. She's keeping it at Green Briar."

"How's she getting along with the Grants?" Matt said.

"She seemed a bit in awe of Ashley," Amy said, remembering the way Claire had stammered and turned red when Ashley had spoken to her.

"I don't blame her," Matt joked. "Ashley can be pretty intimidating."

Amy smiled. "Well, I think Claire's going to have to learn to stand up to her — if she plans to keep Flint at Green Briar, anyway."

"I feel bad for her," Soraya said genuinely. "It's bad enough seeing Ashley at school every day. Imagine having to see her after school as well." She nodded toward the front of the bus. "You know, she looks like something's wrong — I've been watching her."

Amy looked to the front of the bus. Claire was hugging her bag and looking out the window, obviously lost in thought.

When they arrived at school, Amy pushed forward to catch up with Claire as she got off the bus. "Hi. How are you?" she asked.

"Fine," Claire said quickly. Just then, Matt and a group of his friends jumped off the bus and pushed past them. One of their bags knocked against Claire's arm. "Ow!" she gasped, clutching her arm.

"What's the matter?" Amy demanded.

Claire bit her lip. She looked like she was struggling not to cry.

"Are you OK?" Soraya said, joining them and glancing at Claire, clutching her arm. "What's wrong?"

"It's my arm," Claire said. She moved to one side to let the rest of the students get by and then shrugged off her jacket. She was wearing a long-sleeved T-shirt underneath. When she rolled up the sleeve both Amy and Soraya gasped. On her upper arm there was a massive bruise. Black and deep purple, it radiated out from a pale imprint of teeth marks in the center.

"What happened?" Soraya asked.

Claire swallowed and pulled her jacket back on. "It was Flint," she said. "He bit me last night after you left."

"What did your mom say?" Amy asked.

"I haven't told her," Claire said. "And the worst thing

is, she's coming to watch me ride tonight. If he bites me when she's there, she'll want to get rid of him." Her eyes filled with tears. "She didn't want Daddy to buy him in the first place. She says I'm not ready to own a horse of my own."

Soraya glanced at Amy. "Maybe Amy could help. She's knows what to do with aggressive horses."

"Could you?" Claire said, hope lighting up her eyes as she looked at Amy.

Amy didn't know what to say. "Well, there's not much I can do while he's at Green Briar. Val Grant wouldn't be happy if she knew I was helping you at her stable." She saw Claire's face start to crumple and didn't know what to do. "Well, I could give you some advice on how to deal with him. And maybe I could come and help you tack him up tonight so that your mom doesn't see him being difficult. It's not going to solve the problem, but at least it will give you more time."

Claire nodded. "Oh, would you, please? If I can just stop Mom finding out, I'll work with him — I'll do whatever you say. I'm sure he'll get better."

"OK then. I'll come over right after school." Amy spoke lightly, but deep down she was worried. It was one thing for her to tell Claire what to do about Flint but quite another for Claire to carry out her instructions. From what Amy had seen of the Thoroughbred, it was clear that he needed an advanced rider, and nothing she could *say* was going to give Claire the experience she needed.

ℒ

When she got back to Heartland after school, Amy persuaded Grandpa to drive her over to Green Briar. "I'll be back in an hour," he said as he dropped her off outside the stately white gates.

"OK. See you later," Amy replied. As she walked through the gates, she saw Claire hurrying toward her.

"I'm so glad you're here. Mom will be here in about twenty minutes." She panted as she reached Amy. "And we've got to get him groomed and tacked up before then. But I warn you, he's acting pretty nasty."

Claire had already carried her grooming kit to Flint's stall. As she opened the door, he threw his head up and pinned his ears back. Claire hesitated. "That's a good boy," she said nervously. Flint stamped the ground and swished his tail. "That's what he was doing yesterday," Claire told Amy. She took a cautious step toward the horse. "Here, boy."

Flint swung his teeth at her, and Claire jumped back with a gasp.

Amy decided to take charge. She pushed past Claire. "That's enough!" she said sharply to Flint. He looked at her, his head held high, his eyes seeming to measure her up.

Amy took the halter from Claire and moved in swiftly beside Flint's head. In one quick movement, she pulled the halter over his nose and flicked the headpiece over his ears. As she went to buckle it up, he tossed his head up. "No!" she said. Flint looked at her and gave in.

Amy patted his neck and looked thoughtfully at his head. Her mom had always said you could tell a horse's personality by looking at its face. Flint had a slight moose nose, large eyes, and large, open nostrils. All of these attributes suggested that he was a highly intelligent horse. Amy looked at his ears. They were long and narrow — the sort of ears that were often found on horses that were difficult and temperamental. *Highly intelligent but difficult and temperamental,* Amy thought as she stroked Flint's straight nose. *Totally the wrong horse for a timid, unskilled rider.*

Amy's mom had taught her that most horses that were aggressive acted that way because they were scared. However, Amy was inclined to believe that Flint was one of the exceptions to this rule. She had a strong feeling that he was being aggressive with Claire simply because he thought he could get away with it. *And he's right,* she thought.

"What should I do with him, Amy?" Claire asked.

"You're just going to have to be firm," Amy said. She saw Claire's face. "I don't mean hit him, just firmly reprimand him when he misbehaves, and try not to be nervous." She began to tie Flint up. "We should get moving. Your mom will be here soon."

At first when Claire tried to help with the grooming, Flint swished his tail, but a firm word from Amy soon stopped his display of bad manners. "You've just got to let him know that you're in charge," she said.

At last, Flint was ready. They saddled him up and led him to the small training ring. As Claire put her foot in the stirrup, Flint danced on the spot. Claire tightened the reins nervously. "Stand." She tried to sound firm, but it didn't work. Her voice was too high and too faint. Flint sidestepped. Giving up trying to get him to stand still, Claire mounted and Flint started to walk before she was settled in the saddle.

Claire walked him around the ring. After one circuit, she let him trot. He pulled impatiently at the bit, with his head held high and his hindquarters sidling inward.

Suddenly, Flint caught sight of a cat running from under a pile of jumps at the end of the ring and spooked violently. He threw his head, and the sudden movement took Claire by surprise. She lost a stirrup and lost grip of the reins. Feeling the tension on his reins loosen, Flint thrust his head down and bucked three times.

"Hang on, Claire!" Amy cried from the gate.

Claire stayed on for the first buck, but as Flint's head went down between his knees for the second time, she lost her other stirrup and landed on his neck. The third buck sent her flying over his shoulder, and she crashed to the ground.

"Claire!" Amy exclaimed, her heart pounding as she scrambled over the gate.

But her voice was drowned out by a scream from behind her. "Claire! Oh, my goodness!"

Amy swung round. A woman with shoulder-length brown hair was rushing toward the gate.

"Mom!"

Amy looked back at Claire. She was sitting up, looking at the woman with horror in her eyes.

Chapter Five

❧

Amy hesitated and then ran to the center of the ring. "Are you OK?" she demanded, reaching Claire.

To her relief, Claire nodded. "Yeah, I think so." Her voice trembled as she watched her mom opening the gate. "That's it, Amy. There's no way she'll let me keep him now."

"I'll get Flint," Amy said, not knowing what else to do.

"Claire!" Mrs. Whitely cried, her voice high.

"I'm OK, Mom," Claire said, getting up and walking slowly toward her.

Amy went to catch Flint. He was grazing nonchalantly on a patch of grass at the side of the ring. As Amy approached, he looked up at her, his muscles visibly tensing beneath his coat.

Amy pulled out a packet of mints from her pocket and held one out to him. "Here, boy," she said calmly.

She stood still and waited. Flint gazed at her for a moment longer, and then the lure of the mint became too strong for him. Stretching out his muzzle, he walked over to her.

"Good boy," Amy said, quietly taking hold of his reins.

As Flint crunched on the mint, he regarded her with his intelligent dark eyes.

Amy shook her head. "Now, Flint, that wasn't a nice thing to do." She patted his iron-gray shoulder. Flint might have a nasty streak, but she liked him. He was young and full of spirit.

She glanced over to the gate. Claire and her mom seemed to be arguing. "Looks like it's time to face the music," Amy said to Flint, her heart sinking. Clicking her tongue, she led him on.

"He has to go, Claire!" she heard Mrs. Whitely saying as she got near. "He's dangerous. Anyone can see that. Your father was a fool getting you a horse like that. I don't trust him."

"He's not dangerous, Mom!" Claire exclaimed. "He's just energetic."

"Energetic? He's going to break your neck!"

"No, he's not, Mom. He wouldn't do that!" Claire protested, turning to Amy for support. "Please tell her, Amy."

"He's just high-spirited," Amy said quickly. She saw the shock and concern on Mrs. Whitely's face and stepped forward, holding out her hand. "Hi, I'm Amy. I go to school with Claire."

"I told you about Amy, Mom," Claire put in. "She's the one who works at Heartland — the rescue center for horses."

Mrs. Whitely nodded distractedly. "Yes. Yes, I remember. Pleased to meet you, Amy." She looked back at Claire. "Oh, sweetheart," she said, shaking her head, "I just don't know what to do. I can't let you keep riding him if he's going to buck like that. What would you do if he threw you like that when no one was here?"

"But, Mom!" Claire protested.

"Maybe Claire could get some help with him," Amy broke in. "Have some lessons. He's really not dangerous, Mrs. Whitely. He's just taking advantage of her. Claire needs to learn to be firmer."

"I don't know," Mrs. Whitely sighed. She looked at Flint. "I guess I could ask Val Grant to work you into her schedule."

"No!" Claire interrupted. "I don't want to work with Val Grant. She'll make me hit him. I want Amy to help."

"I told you, I can't — not while he's here," Amy said. "Val Grant wouldn't allow it."

"Then we'll move him to Heartland," Claire said. "Won't we, Mom?"

Amy stared in surprise.

"Claire!" Mrs. Whitely exclaimed quickly. "You can't just make a decision like that."

"Why not?" Claire said. "I don't like it here. Val Grant is really hard on her horses. It's not at all like what I read about Heartland. Besides, Flint's really good with Amy. She can teach me what to do." She turned to Amy. "You will help, won't you?"

"Well, all our stalls are full at the moment," Amy said. She saw Claire's face fall. She desperately wanted to help, but there wasn't really room, and they were already so busy. "Well, it's still pretty warm," she said, thinking fast. "So I guess my pony, Sundance, could be turned out full-time. But only for a few weeks. Flint could have his stall."

Mrs. Whitely looked as if she didn't know what to say. "Well, that's very kind of you," she began, "but we've already paid this month's board."

"But, Mom," Claire begged her. "I'll do anything — just please say yes. Please let Flint go to Heartland."

Mrs. Whitely shrugged helplessly. "OK, then," she said at last. "If Amy thinks she can help, then I'll give him a second chance. But just for a month. If he hasn't improved, then he has to go, Claire."

"He'll get better," Claire said. "I just know he will!"

When Amy got back to Heartland, she found Lou and her grandpa paying the bills in the kitchen. She told them about Flint. "He can have Sundance's stall," she explained. "Sundance can live out in the field for a while."

Grandpa nodded. "He'll love that, and it sounds like this friend of yours could use some help."

"When's the horse arriving?" Lou asked, opening the stable calendar so that she could schedule Flint's arrival.

"Mrs. Whitely said she'd try to rent a trailer for Saturday," Amy said.

"I could take ours over to get him," Grandpa said. "I don't have anything else planned."

"Great!" Amy said. "I'll call Claire's mom and let her know."

"Have you told Ty?" Lou asked.

"No. Do you know where he is?" Amy asked.

"In the feed room, I think," Lou said. "He'd been working on something for Dancer."

Amy hurried to the feed room. Ty was looking through one of Marion's books. She told him about Flint. "Her mom said she'll give him a month. If he's not improving in that time, she's going to sell him."

"Sounds like it's a case of the wrong horse with the wrong rider," Ty said. "They're just not a good fit."

Amy nodded. "Yeah, but Claire's desperate to keep him. And he's a fantastic horse. We've got to try to help.

If Claire can just learn to be firmer with him, then he'll start to respect her and stop taking advantage."

"It might take more than a month," Ty said, marking his place in the book before closing it.

"No, it won't," Amy said optimistically. "He's fine with me."

"But you've been around horses all your life," Ty said. "You just can't teach someone that kind of experience. It only comes with time."

Amy shrugged off his concerns. "It'll work out, you'll see." She changed the subject. "So where's Ben?"

"Guess," Ty said dryly.

"With Red?" Amy said, her heart sinking.

Ty nodded. "He's riding him up in the ring — for the second time. You know, he's probably only done about two hours' yard work today. If I ask him to do something, he does it. But if I don't, he just hangs around in the tack room or Red's stall. Half the time it's easier to do the job myself than to waste time tracking him down. I tried saying something, but it made no difference. "

"Do you want me to talk to him again?" Amy offered.

Ty shrugged. "We could get Lou to. He might listen to her."

"Let me try first," Amy said. Somehow involving Lou made it seem like an official complaint, and she was still hoping that Ben was just taking time to settle in.

"OK," Ty said in a reluctant tone. "Good luck."

As Amy walked up to the schooling ring, she wondered what she was going to say.

Ben was cantering Red around the ring. Along one side he had set up a line of fences. As Amy reached the gate, he turned Red toward them.

Amy frowned. Red's neck and shoulder were drenched with sweat. Seeing the jumps, Red threw his head high and plunged sideways to the left. Ben yanked on the reins and pulled Red into a tight circle, trying to get him to bend to the right.

Amy stopped and watched. Red was fighting Ben. He looked totally wound up.

Again, Ben made a small practice loop and turned Red toward the fences, and again Red plunged excitedly forward.

"No!" Ben shouted, pulling on Red's mouth and forcing him to back up several steps.

Amy flinched when she saw Red throw his head up as he fumbled backward.

Ben turned Red into a tight circle again, harsh thumps of his legs driving the horse forward. Amy knew that he was trying to stop Red from rushing too fast to the fences — but the firmer he got, the more excited Red became.

Amy forgot that she had come to talk to Ben about work. She ran to the gate. "Give him a break, Ben! Can't you see you're confusing him even more? He doesn't know what you want."

Ben pulled Red into a halt and swung around in the saddle. "What?" he demanded.

His eyes looked angry, but Amy refused to back down. "You're just frustrating him more by making him canter in small circles like that!" she exclaimed.

"He has to learn!" Ben said. "The show's in three weeks."

"He's not going to learn anything in that state," Amy protested. "Look, just take him out on the trails and let him cool off a bit. You can try again tomorrow."

Ben shook his head stubbornly. "I'm not giving in to him. He's going to learn *now*, or else this was all for nothing."

Red snorted and sidestepped. Shortening his reins again, Ben pushed him into a canter.

"Ben!" Amy exclaimed, feeling her temper rise.

But Ben took no notice. He cantered Red in a circle, ignoring Amy's protest. Other than throwing herself in front of the horse, there was nothing Amy could do except watch.

To her relief, however, she realized that the moment's halt at the gate had calmed Red down slightly. Instead of fighting Ben, he was now cantering smoothly, lowering his head, and softening his jaw.

Ben turned him into the line of jumps. Amy held her breath.

"Steady, boy!" she whispered as Red approached the fences with his ears pricked but in a much calmer state of mind. Ben let him go, his stride lengthened before the first fence, and they flew over all three with perfect pacing.

At the far end of the ring, Ben pulled him up. "Good boy!" he exclaimed, patting him hard.

He rode Red down the ring toward Amy. The stubborn angry look had vanished from his eyes.

"See!" he said triumphantly as he got close. "That was much better! *Now* I'll take him out for a trail ride. You should never give in to a horse, Amy," he said as she opened the gate for him. "They have to learn to do what you want, when you want. If they don't learn that, then you'll never have complete control."

With that, he rode Red out of the gate and headed toward the woods. "See you later."

Amy watched him go, not knowing how to argue her point and make Ben understand. Although he had succeeded with Red using his methods, there was no way she could agree with him. What was the point in having complete control if the horse didn't want to work for you? She truly believed a horse and rider were far more successful when they formed a partnership. And if that meant sometimes giving in to the horse or accepting that the horse was a living, breathing creature that was going to have off days just like humans, then so be it. As far as she was concerned, it was a small price to pay to have a horse that loved you and that would try, heart and soul, to please you.

She walked slowly down to the barn. Like a lot of competitive horse people, Ben clearly didn't share her beliefs. But then she didn't have to put up with seeing those other people riding their horses every day. It really bothered her watching a horse being trained in this manner at Heartland.

"Did you talk to him?" Ty asked, appearing from the tack room. "Is he going to cut down on his time with Red and put more into barn work?"

Amy suddenly remembered that she had gone to the training ring to talk to Ben about his contribution to Heartland. "I — I didn't get around to it," she admitted. "He's taken Red on the trails to cool him down."

"What?" Ty exclaimed. "That's all he's done all day! If he isn't riding Red, he's grooming him or cleaning his tack. There's still sweeping to do and the feeding, not to mention that he was supposed to exercise Jasmine today."

Amy saw the frustration in his eyes. "Look, don't worry, I'll talk to him when he gets back — I promise."

❧

Amy was sweeping up the loose straw around the muck heap when Ben rode back into the yard on Red.

He saw her and dismounted. "Working hard?" he said, patting Red.

Amy straightened up, feeling hot and annoyed. She pushed back the hair that stuck to her damp forehead. "Well, someone has to," she said shortly.

Ben looked at her in surprise. "What's up with you?"

"Ben!" burst out Amy, beginning to lose her temper with him. "You're supposed to be working as a stable hand here. You can't just ride Red all the time and leave all the work to me and Ty!"

"I don't!" Ben protested. "I helped Ty today. I mucked out six stalls and filled all the water buckets."

"Big deal!" Amy raised her voice. "What about the other twelve stalls and the grooming. What about working the horses!"

"Are you saying I'm not pulling my weight?" Ben said.

"Yes!"

"OK," he said shortly. "Then I won't ride Red at all in the day. I'll ride him after work."

"Good!" Amy exclaimed. "Maybe then we can get things done around here."

"Fine." Ben turned and marched across the yard with Red.

Ty came out of the back barn. "What was all that?" he said to her.

"Ben," Amy said. She saw Ty open his mouth to speak. "Don't even ask." She sighed. "I think I might have been too harsh. I better go say something to Lou, so she knows. I don't want her to find out another way."

She headed toward they house, telling herself to keep calm. Losing her temper wouldn't do any good. She had to keep reminding herself how Ben had come to be at Heartland in the first place, how they should be grateful to have the extra help — and the extra money.

Seeing Ben come out of Red's stall, she went over. "Look, Ben, I didn't mean to go off on you like that. It's just that we need you to help out more."

"Yeah. Fine," Ben said shortly.

Amy bit back the angry words that flew into her head. "Come on, Ben. I'm really sorry. I didn't mean to start a fight." But Ben didn't change his expression. Amy wondered if Ben was still upset with Red's behavior in the ring. Maybe that was what was on his mind. "You know, there are lots of supplements you could use to help calm Red down. Honey's good, and valerian. They're great for helping a horse's concentration. We could add some to his grain."

"Red doesn't need calming down," Ben said, shutting

the stall door with a bang. "He just needs to learn discipline."

"Discipline!" Amy exclaimed. "He was so dizzy he couldn't even see the fence!"

"He's my horse, and I'll decide how to train him," Ben said angrily.

"Even if you stress him out?" Amy shot back. "It's normal for young Thoroughbreds to be high-strung. I don't see why you don't want to try a supplement."

"No way — I'm not giving him any of that herbal crap," Ben said.

"Crap!" Amy gasped.

"Everyone knows that stuff doesn't work," Ben said. "Give what you want to the other horses here, but Red's sticking to his regular feed." He picked up his tack and turned to go and then hesitated. "Listen, Amy, what you do at Heartland is your business, but keep in mind that I never *asked* to come here and learn about it." With that, Ben marched off before Amy could respond.

OK, Amy thought, *that's it. I can't take any more of this.*

She stormed up to the back barn to find Ty. She had *tried* being patient with Ben. She had tried giving him time. But she was not going to stand around and listen to him trash her mom's remedies and berate their work at Heartland.

"So how'd it go?" Ty asked casually. Then he looked at her expression. "OK — not good."

"You will *not believe* what Ben just said!" Amy exclaimed. The words tumbled out of her as she told Ty about her conversation with Ben.

"He said that?" Ty said.

"Yes!" Amy cried. "This is just so crazy! Why's he here? He doesn't believe in alternative remedies, I hate the way he treats his horse, and he hardly does any work!" Her eyes flashed. "Well, I've had enough! He's made it clear he has no real interest in being here. I'm going to talk to Lou."

"Well, what are you going to say?" Ty said.

"That we should get rid of him!" Amy said, with exasperation. "Right away!"

Chapter Six

Amy threw open the back door. Lou was busy updating the billing on her laptop. She looked around in surprise as Amy burst in.

"I need to talk to you," Amy said.

"What's up?" Lou asked, concerned. Just then the phone rang. "Hang on a sec," she said.

Amy sat down impatiently at the table. She wanted to get this sorted out right away. She knew the arrangement with Lisa was really convenient. Heartland needed the money and the help, but there was no escaping the fact that Ben just wasn't right for Heartland.

"Oh, hi, Lisa," Lou said into the phone. "Yes, this is Lou."

Amy turned around in surprise. "Lisa Stillman?" she mouthed at Lou.

Lou nodded at her.

Amy groaned inwardly. *What bad timing!*

"Yes, yes, Ben's settling in just fine," Lou said. Amy started to shake her head frantically but Lou had turned away and didn't see. "Yes, I'm sure," Amy heard her say. "No, there haven't been any problems. Why, did you get a different impression?"

There was a pause. Amy could just imagine what Lisa was saying. Amy wondered if Ben had told her anything. When Lou spoke her voice was serious.

"I understand," she said. "Yes . . . yes, I guess it is best that we know."

Amy felt surprised. What was going on?

There was another silence.

"I see," Lou said at last. "Oh, I'm sorry to hear that. Ben's been through a great deal."

Amy stared. What *was* Lisa saying?

"Well, like I said," Lou continued, "he seems to be doing just fine. But I'll let you know if there are any problems. Yes, of course, I won't say anything. You have my word. Thanks for calling, Lisa. Bye."

"What was that about?" Amy demanded as Lou hung up the phone.

Lou turned, a small frown creasing her forehead. "It's Ben."

"Yeah, I figured," Amy said impatiently.

Lou sat down slowly at the table. "Look — I'll tell you what she said, if you promise not to repeat it."

"OK," Amy replied, intrigued. "I promise."

"Lisa was checking in to see how Ben is doing," Lou explained. "She was worried he might have been a bit reluctant to take on some of the chores and really devote himself to working here. She said he's had a troubled background and he's had some problems adjusting in the past."

"Like what?" Amy asked, prepared to hear Lou out.

Lou sighed. "Well, his parents divorced when he was ten, and after that he started skipping school and basically got into a lot of trouble. Lisa said that because his mom wasn't coping very well with the divorce, she decided it was better if Ben didn't live with her. So she sent him to live with Lisa, thinking a new school and a fresh outlook might do him good. Lisa said it was a rough transition for Ben when he came to Fairfield. She thinks that, at first, Ben felt his mom was abandoning him, just as his dad had done. Then, after about a year or so, he got into riding. She said he was a natural, and once he started spending his time in the stables, he really loved being at Fairfield. The stable became his life."

Amy was stunned. "I had no idea about any of that."

"Lisa said she's a little worried that Ben now thinks that she's abandoning him — since she kind of volunteered him to come and work with us. That's why she was calling — to see how he was doing and make sure he's all right." Lou frowned. "But he's been fine, hasn't he?"

"Well . . ." Amy wondered what to say. "Actually," she admitted, "there have been some problems."

"But the other night you said everything was OK," Lou said quickly.

"No, I didn't," Amy said. "But I didn't get a chance to explain because Scott called. At first I thought it was just because Ben was new and he was getting used to Heartland. But things have gotten worse." She told Lou about her argument with Ben and how she had been coming to ask Lou to fire him.

"Oh, gosh," Lou said, when she'd finished, "that's not good." She looked at Amy quizzically. "And do you still feel the same?"

Amy hesitated. "I don't know," she said slowly. "I mean, I feel bad about all he's been through, but he pretty much said that he doesn't want to be here. Maybe he just wants to go back to Fairfield."

"Think of what Ben's been through, Amy," Lou said. "Lisa really thinks this is a good opportunity for him. That he'll feel more important at Fairfield after he's had a chance to learn and share all of Heartland's remedies. She thinks it's a good chance for Ben to feel like he belongs. After all that's happened to him, I don't want to take that chance away. I think he'll come around. We just need to be patient and give him some more time."

Amy thought about everything that Ben had said. "I'm not so sure he'll ever accept Heartland's ideas."

"Amy, we need to give him time to think about it," Lou persuaded.

"But why should we?" Amy demanded. "Worse things have happened to us, and we haven't gone around expecting people to give us special treatment. At least Ben's still got his mom — we don't!"

"No, we don't," Lou said quietly. "But what we do have is the knowledge that Mom loved us every minute of her life. Despite everything that happened, we've never had any reason to doubt that." She took Amy's hand. "Amy, you grew up here — at Heartland — with both Mom and Grandpa to love and care for you. Ben hasn't had that kind of stability." Lou shook her head. "Think about it. How would you have felt if Mom hadn't been as strong as she was and had sent you away after she and Dad separated?"

Amy was silent as Lou's words sank in. It was a thought too horrible to even contemplate.

Lou's voice softened. "Come on, Amy. Let's not turn our backs on Ben. This must be a difficult time for him, and, somehow, I can't help thinking that Heartland might be the best place for him right now." She squeezed Amy's hand. "Can't we at least try to help?"

Slowly, Amy nodded. "OK," she said. "If you really

think he's better off here, he can stay. I'll try to be more understanding."

Lou looked relieved. "Thanks, Amy, I really appreciate it. And you know, I think it might be best if we don't let him know that we know about his past," she added. "He might be upset with Lisa for telling us."

"I won't say a word to him," Amy agreed. "And I won't tell anyone — except Ty."

"No, Amy. You can't even tell Ty," Lou said hurriedly. "I promised Lisa that I wouldn't tell anyone. I'll explain the situation to Grandpa, but we have to keep it in the family."

"But I can't keep it from Ty!" Amy argued. "What will he think when I tell him that we're not going to fire Ben? This affects him, too. If Ben doesn't pull his weight more, and we don't put some kind of pressure on him, Ty is going to get suspicious."

"Just tell him I insisted that Ben was given a bit more time," Lou said. "Say that we owe that much to Lisa since she is paying us to train him in the first place. I don't mind if you blame it on me and the finances. But promise you won't tell him, Amy."

Amy looked at her reluctantly and sighed. "OK, I promise."

"Listen, Amy," Lou said gently, "things will work out — I'm sure of it. Ben just needs some time." She smiled at her. "We help horses with problems all the time at Heartland. Can't we help Ben as well?"

❧

Amy walked back to the yard, deep in thought. Ty was filling a water bucket at the faucet. "How did it go?" he said. "What did she say?"

"She wants to give Ben a second chance," Amy replied.

"You told her what he said about Heartland and not even wanting to be here?" Ty said in surprise.

Amy nodded. "She still felt we should give him more time."

Ty frowned. "Why aren't you mad at her?"

For once, Amy wished that Ty didn't know her so well. "Well, maybe she's right. Ben might just need more time to settle in."

She saw Ty look at her in astonishment.

"Anyway, we owe it to Lisa to try to make it work," she said quickly. "And as much as I'm not sure he'll ever fit in, I guess we've got to respect that. And a little extra help is better than none, right?"

Ty shrugged but didn't say anything.

"I'll go and talk to him again," Amy said. "Where is he?"

"Bringing Jake and Solo in from the field," Ty said.

Amy smiled weakly and then turned to go up to the turnout paddocks. She felt awful not telling Ty the entire truth.

She found Ben walking through the gate with the two horses. "Do you want a hand?" Amy said quietly, stepping forward to take Solo's lead rope.

"Thanks," Ben said.

Amy fidgeted with Solo's lead, not able to look Ben in the eye. *This is* so *awkward*, she thought. "Look . . ." she started.

"Amy . . ." Ben began at the same time.

They both stopped. "Go on," Ben said.

"I was just going to say that I'm sorry we argued before," Amy said.

"No, it's me who should be sorry," Ben said apologetically. "I overreacted. You guys have been good to have me here, and I just haven't been pulling my weight." He patted Jake. "I'll do a lot more from now on. Sometimes I just get so focused on Red that I lose track of everything else."

"OK," Amy said, surprised but pleased by his apology. "That would be good."

"I was frustrated with how things went with our ride today," Ben went on. "But I shouldn't have taken it out on you like that." The corners of his mouth flickered into a smile. "If one of the stable hands at my aunt's place had said those things, she'd have fired him."

Amy suddenly felt horribly guilty. Ben seemed genuinely sorry about what he'd said earlier. "Oh, we're not going to do that," she said lightly. "Come on."

They began to lead the horses toward the barn. "My mom called me today," Ben said. "She wants to come and watch me and Red at the show." He sounded casual, but Amy saw a tightness around his mouth. "I don't see her very often, you know."

"Oh, right. Why — why not?" Amy said uncomfortably.

Ben shrugged. "My parents got divorced when I was ten. Mom didn't deal with it very well and I was shipped out to live with Aunt Lisa when I was twelve. I guess Mom thought a break would do me good. It's been pretty permanent, though."

"Has she come to watch you at shows before?" Amy asked, trying to be positive.

"No," Ben said, and his voice was suddenly quiet. "If she makes it, this will be her first time."

"So you want to do your best then," Amy said, trying to sound sympathetic.

"I'd want that whether she was coming or not." Ben put his shoulders back. "I don't care what she thinks. Riding is about me and Red."

Amy glanced at him — for a moment he had shown her a much more vulnerable, likable side — but the barriers were back up again, and he had his old determined look back on his face.

As Amy put Solo away, she thought about what Ben had said. She didn't believe that he didn't care what his mother thought. She could tell that he cared deeply — maybe more than he wanted to. She wondered if that was why he had been so hard on Red in the ring earlier.

She was glad Lou had convinced her to let Ben stay. Things were pretty complicated for him. It seemed like the scars from his past were a long way from being healed.

❧

For the next few days, when Amy was home from school, she noticed that Ben was making more of an effort to help around the yard, and he seemed more willing to stay late if necessary. However, it was clear that he was still not interested in learning about Heartland's real work. Although he pulled his weight, he didn't get involved in the healing side of things, and he didn't volunteer to work any of the problem horses.

On Saturday, Grandpa picked up Flint from Green Briar. When Amy saw the trailer coming back along the drive, she left the stall she was mucking out and came to meet him.

"How is he?" she asked, as Grandpa got out of the truck.

Jack Bartlett raised his eyebrows. "A bit of a handful. He just wouldn't let Claire lead him into the trailer. I had to do it in the end."

"Thanks, Grandpa," Amy said, feeling relieved that he had been there.

"Are you certain you're going to be able to help Claire with him, Amy?" Jack asked, looking concerned. "She's obviously very inexperienced with such a bold horse."

"I know, but I think I can help," Amy said, her gray eyes determined. "I really do."

Her grandpa looked at her for a moment and then smiled — a smile tinged with sadness. "Sometimes you remind me so much of your mom," he said quietly.

Amy met his eyes. So much of her time was taken up with just carrying on, but the loss and grief were always there, and it only took a time like this to bring her feelings flooding to the surface. For a moment the emotion threatened to overwhelm her, but just then Mrs. Whitely's car drew up and stopped beside the trailer.

Amy smiled at her grandfather and blinked hastily as Claire opened the door and jumped out.

"Wow!" Claire said, looking around at Heartland's barns and paddocks. "It looks just like in the magazine."

"I guess it does," Amy said, pushing her feelings back down and forcing her voice to sound light. She smiled at Claire. "I'm glad you like it."

There was a kicking sound from inside the trailer.

"We'd better let this horse out," Jack Bartlett said, beginning to unfasten the bolts on the ramp and the side door.

Glad to have something to do, Amy stepped into the

trailer. Claire followed her. Seeing Claire, Flint flattened his ears and snaked his head forward.

"Here, I'll take him," Amy said as Claire shrank back. She moved swiftly in beside Flint's neck and untied the lead rope. Flint shook his head, but she held on. "Easy now," she said, stroking him until he calmed down.

"OK!" she called to her grandpa outside.

Jack Bartlett lowered the ramp, and Amy backed Flint out.

Ty and Ben had come to see what was going on. "Nice horse," Ben said appreciatively as Flint snorted and looked around.

"Very," Ty agreed. "He looks like he's got a fair amount of spirit."

Claire stepped forward. With a squeal, Flint struck out with his front hoof.

"Be careful, Claire!" her mom gasped.

"He's just feeling unsettled," Amy said, uncomfortably aware of Mrs. Whitely's presence. "He's a little nervous. It's all new to him, that's all." She started to lead Flint around to try to calm him down.

"Can I get you some coffee?" Jack offered.

Amy was relieved to see Mrs. Whitely nod. If Flint was feeling wild, then the last thing she wanted was to have Mrs. Whitely watching. After all, they were trying to persuade her he was safe.

"So what do you think?" Amy said to Ty.

"He doesn't look naturally aggressive," Ty said.

"You must be joking!" Ben exclaimed. "You saw what he just did."

Ty looked at him impatiently. "You can tell by looking at his head he's not naturally aggressive. He looks intelligent, strong willed, and difficult, but not mean."

Amy smiled at him. She was glad to know that he saw the same traits in Flint's face that she did.

However, Ben looked less than impressed. "Yeah, and next you'll be telling me that you're checking his astrology sign as well!"

Amy tried to explain, hoping to gain his interest. "Ty's right," she said to him. "You *can* tell a horse's personality from its head. The shape of a horse's eyes, ears, muzzle, and lips all give you clues to what its personality's like."

Claire looked fascinated. "Really? So what does Flint's head say about him?"

Amy looked at the Thoroughbred. "Well, his large eyes and nostrils and slight moose nose suggest that he's intelligent and bold, but his long, flat chin, long mouth, and the way his ears are set close together also suggest that he might be strong willed and difficult. He looks like the sort of horse that needs to respect his rider."

"You can tell all that just from his face?" Claire said in astonishment.

Amy nodded.

"So what do I have to do to get him to stop him biting me?" Claire asked.

Amy hesitated. "You have to gain his respect. But it might not be easy."

"I don't care," Claire said. "I'm prepared to put in the hours and do whatever it takes to make it work. I just don't want to have to sell him."

"Well, we'll help you all we can," Amy said. "Won't we, Ty?"

"Sure," Ty said. He smiled at Claire. "If you're really determined to keep him, then there's no reason why things shouldn't work out."

"Well, I am," Claire said.

Just then, Mrs. Whitely came out of the house. "Are you coming home with me now, Claire?" she asked.

Claire looked uncertainly at Amy.

"I think it might be best just to let him get used to his new surroundings today," Amy said. "We'll start work tomorrow."

"OK," Claire said. "I'll see you tomorrow then." She glanced at her horse. "Bye, Flint."

The gelding stared into the distance and ignored her.

Claire looked at him for a moment longer and then hurried away.

"So," Amy said, beginning to walk Flint across the yard to the back barn, "do you think Claire will learn to handle him?"

"It's not going to be easy," Ty said seriously.

"That's for sure!" Ben said, joining in the conversation. "I'd say it'll be next to impossible! It's obvious a girl like that's never going to be able to handle a high-spirited Thoroughbred like Flint. I don't know why you're even bothering."

Ty swung around. He was obviously fed up with Ben's negative attitude. "No, Ben," he said. "I guess you wouldn't."

"What's that supposed to mean?" Ben demanded as Amy led Flint into the stall.

"How could you possibly understand why we want to help Claire? You're not remotely interested in how we work around here!" Ty snapped.

Amy came to Flint's door. "Ty . . ." she said, seeing the expression drop on Ben's face.

Ty ignored her. He seemed to have something he wanted to say. "Do you know what it's like to really want something, Ben?" he asked. "To want something so bad that you're prepared to fight for it? I'm guessing that you've had it easy all your life. So Claire's not as confident as you, but if she wants to fight to keep Flint, then we'll help her. Heartland's not just about helping horses, it's about helping people, too." He shook his head. "Not that you'd ever understand that." Glaring at Ben, he turned and walked away.

"What's up with him?" Ben exclaimed. "What did I do to deserve that?"

Amy let herself out of the stall, not knowing what to say. Ty hardly ever lost his temper. However, she was sure that Ben's comments about Claire had pushed Ty over the edge. The strain of putting in so many hours, now that they had a full yard, was obviously getting to Ty. And she understood how frustrating it had to be for him to have to deal with Ben, whose heart just obviously wasn't in it.

"He'll be OK," she said awkwardly. "He's just been working really hard lately and he's tired." She smiled at Ben. Trying to avoid further discussion, she changed the subject. "Look, how about we finish with the stalls and go out for a ride?"

❧

After she had finished her share of the stalls she went to find Ty. She hadn't seen him since his outburst because she wanted to give him some time to cool off.

She found him lunging Moochie in the training ring. When he saw Amy standing at the gate, he brought the big bay hunter to a halt.

"Whoa, there," he said, gathering up the lunge line and leading the horse over to her.

"Hey," she said.

"Sorry about earlier," he said, glancing at the ground. "I really lost it back there. Who does Ben think he is? Telling us that we shouldn't bother with a horse and rider. That's what Heartland's all about." He shook his head. "He's really getting to me."

"I noticed," Amy said with a smile. She cleared her throat, wondering how Ty was going to take the news that she was just about to go on a trail ride with Ben. "I'm going out on the trails with him," she said. "We're going to take Solo and Gypsy." Ty just stared at her. "They could do with the exercise. Umm, you could come, too," she offered quickly.

"No thanks." Ty shook his head. "I don't get it, Amy. A few days ago you wanted to see him out of here as much as I did, so why are you now going out of your way to spend time with him?"

Amy avoided his gaze. "I just think he needs more time to get used to this place. I'm doing it for Lou. She thinks if we try he'll decide to get more involved." She looked up. "Come on, why don't you come? You could bring Moochie. It'll be fun."

"Wild horses couldn't drag me," Ty said with a faint smile, and turning Moochie away from the gate, he walked off.

Amy felt awful. She felt as if she had betrayed him. Sure, he'd made light of the situation, but she knew that, deep down, he must be feeling very confused and frustrated with her as well.

"See you later then," she said.

Ty nodded briefly in reply.

❧

Twenty minutes later, Amy and Ben were out on the trails and cantering along a wide grassy track. Amy glanced across at Ben. He was a very good rider, and he controlled headstrong Gypsy very well. A sixteen-hand, Dutch-bred mare, Gypsy had been sent to Heartland so they could cure her of her bucking habit. She was now almost ready to go home. Although she was still a spirited ride, she had stopped her frequent bucking rampages.

"Do you want to trot?" Amy called.

Ben nodded and eased the powerful black mare down into a trot. He patted her neck as she eased her pace.

Amy slowed Solo and brought him to a trot beside Gypsy. "She goes well for you," she said.

"She's a nice horse," Ben said. "What do her owners do with her in the show ring?"

"Mainly dressage," Amy said. "But I think they hope to do some eventing as well, now that she's stopped bucking. She's only five years old."

"What did you do to stop her bucking?" Ben asked curiously.

"We strapped a dummy on her back and let her buck as much as she wanted until she realized the dummy wouldn't come off no matter how hard she bucked. Once she realized that, she pretty much stopped. We changed her diet and used herbs and lavender oil to calm her down, and then we got on her ourselves. She was still pretty feisty at first, but she's doing well."

Ben smiled teasingly. "And I guess you analyzed her personality, too. That must have helped."

"It did, actually," Amy replied. "If you look at her head you can see that her forehead slopes back from above her eyes to her ears, and she's got a sloping muzzle and narrow nostrils. Those things suggest that she might be stubborn and willful. We've been working to encourage her to cooperate with people rather than resist them. We'll just need to have the owner come for some training sessions to learn how best to work with her personality."

Ben laughed. "You really believe all that stuff, don't you?"

"Yes," Amy said simply.

"OK," Ben challenged her. "So what's Red like?" He grinned. "Go on — analyze his personality."

Amy envisioned the big chestnut horse. "Well, he's got a wide forehead, a long mouth, and a flat, narrow chin, which suggest that he is very intelligent and probably a fast learner," she said thoughtfully. "His almond-shaped eyes and fluted nostrils also say that he's likely to be trusting and cooperative."

"Go on," Ben said.

Amy looked at Ben with a half smile and continued. "However, the slight dish in his face suggests that he is quite sensitive and needs to be handled carefully. He needs understanding. If you push him too hard he will lose confidence." Amy glanced at Ben. His forehead was furrowed in a slight frown. "Well? What do you think?" she asked. "You know him best. How'd I do?"

"It's actually not that far off," Ben admitted.

"See!" Amy said, triumphantly.

"Yeah, but you know him pretty well now," Ben said quickly. "How do I know that you can tell all that from his head and not just from seeing him in action?"

"You don't. You just have to trust me," Amy said. "It's like a lot of our work. It might not make exact sense, but we get the results." She looked at him. "And that's what matters."

"Maybe," Ben said. Then he patted Gypsy. "But I think I'll stick to science."

Despite his words, Amy thought that she sensed a slight change in his attitude.

They rode round a bend, and the trail widened out again. "Come on," she said, deciding not to persuade him anymore for now. "Let's canter!"

Chapter Seven

After lunch, Amy went to check on Flint to see how he was settling in. "I think I'll take him out in the training ring for twenty minutes or so," she said to Ty.

He nodded. "Do you have any idea how to help Claire?"

"Well, first I thought I'd get her to do some T-touch on him," Amy said. "Then she can start working him from the ground, lunging him to start, and then moving on to work him without the lunge line."

"That's a good idea," Ty said. "That should build the relationship between them."

Amy looked at Flint standing at the back of his stall. "He's not exactly what you'd call a friendly horse, is he?"

"Maybe there's something else behind his behavioral

106

problem," Ty said thoughtfully. "Do you know anything about his history?"

Amy shook her head. Normally she would have asked about the horse's history, but she hadn't taken on Flint in the usual way. "I'll ask Claire first thing tomorrow though," she said. She went into the stall. "Come on, Flint. Let's do some work."

Just as she had explained to Ty, she was planning to have Claire start working Flint from the ground, controlling him with a lunge line attached to his halter, and getting him to work through the gaits, change direction, back up, and come to the center when she told him to. The eventual aim was for Claire to be able to work Flint without a lunge line, just using voice commands. Amy was sure that this sort of work, called liberty work, would help Claire and Flint to develop a bond based on mutual trust and respect.

However, before Claire started, Amy wanted to find out whether Flint had ever been lunged before. She snapped the line onto his bridle, picked up the whip, and led Flint out of his stall.

Although at Heartland they never used whips to hit a horse, in liberty work the lunge whip was used as a guide for the horse — you could place it in front of him to slow him down, point it at his shoulder to keep him out at the side of the ring, or snap the whip on the sand to encourage the horse forward. Marion had always told Amy to think of a lunge whip not as a whip but as an extension of her arm.

Once in the circular training ring, Amy sent Flint out to the end of the lunge line. It quickly became obvious that he had been through this routine before. On command, he walked, trotted, and cantered circles around her.

After ten minutes, Amy decided to start teaching him some new commands, but she needed someone to help her out. She was about to go and ask Ty when she saw Ben with his pitchfork, standing by the muck heap. She thought that he was watching her. In fact he looked as if he might have been there for a while.

"Hey," she called over to him.

Ben raised his hand in greeting.

Amy made a snap decision. "Do you want to come help? I could use a hand."

Ben hesitated and then he nodded. "Sure," he called back.

When he reached her, Amy explained what she was going to do. "I need to teach him to change direction on command," she said. "Can you lead him on the outside and then encourage him around when I say 'turn'?"

"Sure," Ben replied with a shrug of his shoulders.

Amy clicked her tongue and told Flint to walk on. After a full circle, she said, "Turn."

Ben guided Flint around.

They repeated the exercise a few times. "So why are we doing this?" Ben asked.

"It's the first step toward liberty work," Amy said. "You teach the horse the commands on the lunge line, and when he's learned the commands you remove the lunge line to see if he will still obey you when he's free."

"But why?" Ben said.

"Because it helps develop the relationship between horse and rider," Amy explained.

Ben gradually started to move away from Flint's head until the horse was turning with no guidance apart from Amy's voice.

"That'll be enough for today," Amy said. She was pleased, both with the speed of Flint's learning and with how helpful Ben had been. He might say he didn't believe in alternative techniques, but when he dropped his skeptical act he seemed far more open-minded. He had seemed to sense exactly when Flint had needed his guidance and when to back away.

"Thanks," Amy said to him. "You were great."

Ben shrugged. "No problem."

As Amy led Flint back to his stall, Ty looked out from Dancer's stall. "How was he?" he asked.

"Great," Amy replied. "I got Ben to help, and we started teaching him to turn on command."

"You got *Ben* to help?" Ty echoed. "How'd you manage that?"

"Ty," Amy said in a pleading tone, leading Flint into his stall and undoing the bridle. "Will you please give Ben a chance? He was actually very good with Flint."

She came out of the stall. Ty was standing in the aisle, his arms crossed, a frown on his face. "I have given him a chance. I keep giving him chances, and he never changes around me," he said. "I'm starting to think he's not worth my time. But you — you are always giving him the benefit of the doubt, and that's not like you."

"Thanks a lot!" Amy said, trying to laugh it off.

But Ty continued to frown. "No, I mean it. Something's going on. You're spending all this time with him — taking his side. Why?"

"Lou asked me to, you know that," Amy said quickly.

Ty raised his eyebrows. "Yeah, and you always do what Lou says," he said sarcastically. "Come on, Amy. It's more than that. This is me you're talking to."

Amy so wanted to tell him the truth. How would Lou even know if she told him? But she knew she couldn't — not because of Lou, but because of Ben. "Well, you know I'm trying to get along better with Lou. And besides, I happen to think that she's right," she said. "She really wants it to work out with Ben. So I want to try. We have too much at stake in our relationship with Lisa Stillman. And he just showed that he is capable of learning — he just needs to be approached in the right way." She saw the skepticism in Ty's eyes, and her voice rose

defensively. "Look, you say it's not like me to be so patient, Ty. Well, it's not like *you* to be so judgmental. Why
can't you just give Ben a break?"

She saw the hurt flash across Ty's face. "Amy, those
are all the same reasons you gave before. I'm not being
judgmental — I'm being honest." Without saying another word he turned and started to walk off.

Amy couldn't handle lying to Ty. She had to offer
some sort of explanation. "OK, OK," she said desperately. "You're right. There *is* something."

Ty swung round.

Amy caught herself. "But — but I can't tell you what
it is."

Ty stared. "What do you mean, you can't tell me?"

Amy saw the disbelief in his eyes. She shook her head.
"Lou made me promise," she whispered.

A shutter seemed to fall across Ty's face. "OK," he
said coldly.

"I really want to tell you," Amy burst out. "You have
to believe me. I just can't break my promise to Lou. It's
really not that big a deal — I just can't say anything."
She looked at him pleadingly. "Please try to understand."

Ty's eyes were filled with disappointment as he looked
at her. "You know, Amy, I can't understand what's going
on. I feel like I don't even understand you anymore." He
held her in his gaze. "I've gotta get back to work."

Amy felt horrible. From the very beginning, when Ty had started working full-time at Heartland, her mom had always made a point of telling him everything about the business, and after she had died, he had been like one of the family — sharing their grief and fighting with them to keep Heartland going. But now that Amy was keeping something from him, she felt like she was deliberately cutting him out of the family he had become a part of.

She didn't want it to be that way. But she had given Lou her word, and Lou was firm that only the Flemings should know. Amy could see that if things could work out for Ben without too many people knowing about his personal life, it would be for the best in the long run. She felt sure that if Ty understood the situation, he'd feel the same way.

But there's no way he'll understand about Ben, she thought, *unless I tell him.*

❧

That night, when Amy went into the house, she went up to her sister's bedroom. Lou was getting ready for her date with Scott.

"What's up?" she said, seeing Amy hovering at her bedroom door.

"Ty," Amy said, sighing. "Lou, I feel I've just *got* to tell him about Ben. He can't figure out why I'm siding with him, and he's really upset about it."

"I understand, Amy — I really do," Lou said gently. "But please, let's give Ben a bit more time. Ty'll come around once Ben adjusts to being with us." She stepped forward, her eyes sympathetic. "I'm really sorry to put you in this situation, but I want to honor my word to Lisa. She's trying to protect Ben. Grandpa agrees with me — it's the right thing to do."

Amy didn't say anything. She could see Lou's point of view. She knew that if she were in the same situation, she wouldn't want everyone to know about her past and talk about her problems behind her back.

"I'm sorry," Lou went on, "but I'd really appreciate it if you'd trust me on this one."

"It's . . . fine," Amy sighed, wishing it could be different.

Lou smiled. "Thanks, Amy. You know, I'm here for you if you need to talk more about it. You know that, don't you?"

Amy bit her lip as she nodded. "What time's Scott coming?" she asked.

"Any minute now," Lou said, glancing at her watch. "I'd better get a move on or I'll be late."

Suddenly, there was the sound of a car arriving outside. Amy looked out the window. "That's him!" she said, smiling at her sister.

Lou followed Amy down the stairs as she raced to open the door.

"Hi, Amy," Scott said, as he came into the kitchen. He caught sight of Lou. "Hey," he said, "you look great!"

"Thanks," Lou said, blushing. "So do you." She started looking around quickly. "I'll — I'll just get my coat."

"It's in the hall," Amy said, secretly enjoying the way her usually very composed sister seemed to be falling to pieces now that Scott was here. It was good to see Lou's more vulnerable side sometimes.

Lou reappeared from the hall with her coat, and Scott opened the door.

"Have a great time, kids," Amy teased.

"Don't worry, we will," Scott said, smiling at Lou.

🙖

Amy woke up in the early hours of Sunday morning to the sound of the front door shutting and a car driving off. Glancing at the luminous hands on her bedside clock, she saw that it was two o'clock. She smiled. Things must have gone well with Lou and Scott!

There was no sign of her sister when Amy got up. It was Ty's and Ben's day off, but as usual Ty came by to help. He was quiet as they measured out the feeds.

"I'll start with the stalls in the back barn," he said to her once the horses had been fed and watered. Hardly even waiting for her answer, he strode off.

Amy sighed. She hated keeping a secret from him, and now that he knew she was hiding something, things were worse. But she didn't know what to say to make things better between them.

After a while, Amy saw Lou come out of the house. She hurried over. "So how did it go?" she asked eagerly.

Despite still looking half asleep, Lou smiled. "It was really fun! We had so much to talk about. And he was so funny."

"So are you going out again?" Amy prompted.

"Maybe," Lou said coyly.

"When?"

Lou smiled. "Tonight."

"Oh, Lou! That's great!" Amy said, hugging her in delight. "Wait till I tell Matt and Soraya!"

"Really, Amy, stop being such a matchmaker," Lou said. "It's only our second date."

🌿

Claire arrived later in the morning. Amy decided to take it one step at a time. "OK, come into the stall," Amy said, holding Flint by the halter. Claire walked in nervously. Flint put his ears back. "No!" Amy told him sharply. "It's OK, Claire. Just come up to him and pat him," she said kindly.

She made Flint stand still as Claire patted him.

"First, you're going to learn how to do the T-touch,"

Amy said. She showed Claire how to use the pads of her fingers to push Flint's skin lightly over his muscles in small circles and explained how the therapy worked.

"After you've finished one complete circle, slide your fingers to a new part of his neck and do another," Amy said. "And go slowly. The slower you go, the more he will relax."

Amy watched Flint's eyes carefully. He didn't look like he was particularly enjoying the treatment, but he wasn't objecting to Claire's touching him, either. After a minute or two, he seemed to relax slightly.

"Go all along his neck and down the top of his back to his hindquarters," Amy said.

After about ten minutes, she let go of Flint's halter. He stood quietly while Claire worked.

"I like doing this," Claire said, looking up.

"We use it on all the horses here," Amy said. "It's particularly good for the ones that are tense or oversensitive, and it really improves your relationship with a horse."

After a bit, they took Flint up to the ring. Amy lunged him first. He was excited at the beginning, but after he had cantered several circles and thrown in a couple of high-spirited bucks, he began to calm down and to listen to Amy's commands.

"OK, you can take over now, Claire," Amy said, bringing him to a halt.

"He still looks a bit wild," Claire said uneasily.

"He'll be fine," Amy replied. "Trust me."

Claire reluctantly came into the ring. Amy smiled at her reassuringly and handed her the lunge rope before moving to the gate.

"Walk on," Claire said hesitantly.

Flint didn't move.

"Walk on." Claire's voice shook, as she moved the whip toward him.

Flint stamped his hoof into the sand and put his ears back threateningly. Claire quickly withdrew the whip. "He's not moving," she said, looking helplessly at Amy.

"Sound like you mean it," Amy said, feeling slightly exasperated.

Claire tried again, but this time Flint moved toward her, his ears flat. Claire gasped and jabbed at him with the whip. Then the end of the whip wrapped loosely around her ankle. As she bent down to unravel it, she lost her balance and stumbled to the ground. "Amy," she cried.

Flint reared up in surprise.

"No!" Claire cried, covering her face with her hands.

Amy was already scrambling over the gate. She reached Flint just as he came to the ground. "Easy now!" she said, grabbing hold of his bridle.

Snorting loudly, the Thoroughbred stared warily at Claire.

"Are you OK?" Amy demanded.

Claire nodded. "I thought he was going to attack me!" she said, getting to her feet.

"It's OK. You just startled him," Amy said. "He wasn't trying to attack you, he was just reacting to your fall. It's OK." She looked at Flint's tense eyes. This was getting them nowhere. "How about you watch for a bit more, and I'll talk you through what I do?" she said to Claire, who nodded gratefully.

She worked Flint for twenty minutes and then looked toward the gate. She knew Claire needed to work with Flint, but she didn't want to lose ground with him — he was being really good for her. She didn't want to finish the training session on a bad note.

She asked the gray gelding to halt, and he stopped on a dime. "I think I'll bring him in now," she called to Claire.

"OK," Claire said, looking relieved that she wasn't going to have to work him again. But Amy still felt a little guilty.

Amy led Flint over to the gate. "So do you know anything about Flint's past?" she asked. "How he was with previous owners — stuff like that."

"Um, a bit," Claire replied. "I know he was bred by a woman who kept him until he was five. She trained and showed him. He's six now, and I think he's had two other owners besides me in the last year."

"So it sounds like he's been through a lot of changes recently," Amy said. "Maybe that explains some of his behavioral problems. With three different owners in a year, no wonder he's feeling unsettled."

"I hadn't thought about it like that," Claire said. "But I guess you're right. It was probably pretty hard on him." She smiled rather sadly. "I kind of know how he feels."

Amy looked at her curiously. "What do you mean?"

"Well, since Mom and Dad separated, Mom's always getting new jobs and we keep moving," Claire explained. "I'm always starting at new schools and have to make friends over again. Since the divorce, we haven't stayed anywhere more than a year."

"That can't be easy for you," Amy said sympathetically.

Claire shrugged. "It's OK." Her voice lifted. "Mom seems to really like it here, though — maybe she won't want to move again. And we're closer to where my dad lives so I can see him more often. I can't wait for him to get back and see Flint again."

"Well, now that we know what's going on with Flint, we can use some essential oils and flower remedies to help calm him down," Amy said. "As he gets calmer, he'll hopefully be more willing to form a new relationship with you. The T-touch will also help. And we have to get you working him from the ground."

"I hope it works," Claire said hopefully.

Amy smiled reassuringly at her. "I'm sure it will."

🙠

Ben arrived at lunchtime. "I'll give you a hand with the rest of the chores when I'm done with Red," he said when Amy went over to say hi.

"But it's your day off," Amy said in surprise.

He shrugged. "I haven't got anything else to do."

"Well, thanks then," Amy said, smiling at him. She was happy that he was making more of an effort.

"Mom called again last night," Ben told her as they walked to the tack room together. "I thought she might be calling to cancel, like she's done before, but she said she's definitely going to come." He picked up his grooming kit. "So I'd better get moving. Red and I have some work to do."

Amy started gathering a bunch of brushes that needed to be cleaned. After a bit, Ben led Red up to the training ring. She was just filling a bucket with bleach and water when Ty came marching up to the faucet.

"That's it!" he exclaimed, his eyes dark and angry. "I've had enough. I just can't believe that guy anymore!"

Amy didn't think she had ever seen Ty look so furious. "What is it?" she said, alarmed.

"Just come and see what he's doing to Red!" Ty exclaimed.

He stormed off toward the training ring.

Amy ran after him. "Ty! Wait!" But Ty didn't stop.

She hurried up to the ring to find Ben cantering an exhausted-looking Red in small circles, right in front of a jump.

"What does he think he's doing?" Ty demanded as Red fought for his head, his mouth foaming with saliva and his sides stained with sweat. "Could he be any harder on that horse? I can't stand by and watch this."

Amy took a deep breath and tried to rationalize the situation. She *hated* her new role as diplomat! "He's just trying to stop Red from rushing his fences," she said quickly. "Listen — this show he's going to in a few weeks is really important to him." Like Ty, she hated seeing Ben ride Red into the ground and she wished he would stop, but she was trying hard to understand him — to accept that he wasn't going to change his riding style overnight.

Ty turned on her. "So you actually approve of what he's doing?" he said incredulously.

"Of course I don't," Amy said. "But what can we do? Red is Ben's horse."

"But he's riding him on Heartland property," Ty said. His mouth hardened. "Well, if you won't say anything, Amy — I will."

"Wait, Ty!" Amy pleaded as she grabbed his arm to hold him back.

But it was too late. Ty shook her arm loose and headed straight to the fence. "What do you think you're doing, Ben?" he exclaimed.

Ben pulled Red to a halt. "What?" he said in surprise.

"Riding Red like that — look at him!" Ty pointed to the sweat foaming on Red's neck. "What are you going to accomplish by spinning the horse in circles?"

Ben's eyes grew colder. "Can't you see he's rushing at the jumps?"

"Oh, right, and you think what you're doing is going to stop him?" Ty demanded.

"Like you know anything about it!" Ben snapped.

"I know that if you get a horse upset like that it can't even think, let alone learn," Ty snapped back. "It's the stupidest thing I've ever seen."

"Well, thanks for your opinion," Ben said, digging his heels into Red's sides so that the horse broke into a canter again. "But I don't need your help."

Amy didn't want the situation to get out of hand. She rushed into the ring. "Ty, look — just let it go," she said.

He swung around. "Let it go?" he questioned. For a moment, Amy thought he was going to grab her shoulders and shake her, but then he seemed to stop himself. "You've never let something like this go in your life. You're always the first to speak out when a horse is mistreated. When did you let it all go?"

"But Ben's not mistreating Red — at least he's not being outright cruel," Amy argued desperately.

Ty looked to the top of the ring where Red was still making tight circles, his head bent, his neck foaming with sweat. "So you think *that's* not mistreating a horse?" he said, turning so that his eyes bored into hers. "It's one step from abuse."

Amy didn't say anything. She couldn't. She knew he was right.

Ty's eyes held hers for a moment, and then, shaking his head in angry disbelief, he pushed past her and walked away.

Chapter Eight

For the rest of the day, Amy felt that Ty was avoiding her. Instead of hanging around to talk like he usually did, he left right after the horses had been fed.

"He was in a weird mood all day," Ben commented, joining her as she watched Ty's car bump away down the drive.

Amy shrugged. There was no way she was getting into this conversation with him. "Oh, I guess. He's probably just in a bad mood."

"If you ask me, he's always in a bad mood," Ben said. "Doesn't he *ever* lighten up?"

"You don't know him," Amy said defensively. "He's OK. He's more than OK."

"Yeah, if you're an astrologically challenged horse," Ben said.

Amy glared at him and walked away.

"Hey, Amy! I'm sorry," Ben said, going after her.

She stopped.

"Look, don't get me wrong," Ben sighed. "I know you and Ty get along really well and that he's great with the horses you have here, but I wish he'd stop trying to tell me what to do with my horse."

"He only said those things because he cares about Red," Amy said.

"Are you saying I don't?" Ben demanded

"Well . . . not in the same way . . ." Amy began.

"Amy, Red is *the* most important thing in my life," Ben interrupted her. "I would never do anything to hurt him in any way."

"What about this afternoon? What about when things don't go your way?"

"Look — you and Ty might not agree with my methods," Ben went on. "But they're *my* methods, and I'm using them with *my* horse, and if either of you don't like that, then that's your problem, not mine. I'm not the only person who uses these kinds of techniques, you know."

Amy took a deep breath. Part of her wanted to yell at him to stop being so stubborn, to listen to Ty — to listen to her. But she knew it wouldn't do any good. She couldn't force him to change how he trained. That would only turn him against her, as well as against Ty. All she could do was be patient, give him time, and try to win him over.

❧

The atmosphere in the yard did not improve over the next few days. Ty avoided Ben as much as possible and was painfully reserved with Amy whenever she was around. To take her mind off Ty, Amy threw herself into working Flint.

Claire came to Heartland every night after school. She was getting increasingly confident using the T-touch circles and massaging him with diluted oil, a remedy that Amy hoped would help settle him down. In the stall, at least, Flint seemed to be accepting Claire more and more. But as soon as he was out in the training ring, everything changed.

Claire seemed to lose all confidence once Flint was in an open space. She always ended up giving the lunge line to Amy and going to watch from the gate.

Amy told herself that it didn't matter. They were just taking things slowly, and it was better that Flint was at least learning the voice exercises with someone. She also had to admit that she loved working Flint. His intelligence meant that although he was a challenge, he was also a very quick learner. Amy was pleased to sense a bond growing between them.

On Friday afternoon as she walked up to his stall after

school, she noticed how relaxed he was. He was looking out over his stall door. He whinnied softly when he saw her.

Amy was delighted. It was one of the first signs of affection that Flint had shown. She hurried forward, digging a packet of mints out of her pocket. "Hi, boy."

He pushed his dark gray muzzle softly against her arm as she took a mint from the packet.

Just then, Ty came out of Dancer's stall.

"He's getting friendlier," he said, looking at Flint nuzzling Amy.

She nodded. "Did you hear him whinny?"

"Yeah."

Amy glanced up. Ty was watching her. "What?" she said, seeing concern in his eyes.

"He's supposed to be forming a bond with Claire, Amy, not with you."

"I know," Amy said quickly.

"So why are you the one who's working him?" Ty said.

"Well, Claire doesn't want to," she said defensively. "And anyway I'm not doing the hands-on work in the stall, Claire's doing it all now." She saw that Ty's eyes were still looking concerned. "Claire just needs more time to become confident!"

"She'll never gain confidence while you do everything for her," Ty said.

"But if she starts doing the ground exercises now, Flint could get worse," Amy protested. "I just want him to keep improving!"

"You're supposed to be thinking about Claire, too," Ty said. "She needs to improve, too. Or have you forgotten that? She'll never be comfortable with him if she feels like she's competing with you."

Amy felt the rush of color flood her cheeks. Deep down, she knew he was right, but she didn't want him to be. "I'm the one who's supposed to be treating him!" she said, her embarrassment giving her a defensive tone. "And I'll make the decisions!"

Ty stared at her. "*You'll* make the decisions?" He stared at her. "Since when do you make all the decisions? We used to treat the horses *together*. Or does my opinion not matter around here anymore?"

Amy swallowed, the color in her cheeks deepening as she realized what she had said. "I — I didn't mean it that way." She felt horribly uncomfortable. She had never spoken to Ty in such a way before. Since her mom had died, they had really relied on each other and decided on the treatment of the horses together.

Just then, Claire appeared at the top of the aisle. "Hi!" she called out, oblivious to the tension in the air. She hurried toward them. "How are you, Ty?"

"Fine," he replied, stepping back from Amy. He

smiled briefly at Claire. Amy had noticed that he always seemed to make a special effort to be friendly toward her.

"I've got a favor to ask," Claire said, looking at them both.

"Ask away," Ty said.

"Well, when we brought Flint here, I was in such a rush to get away that I left three of his blankets at Green Briar." Claire looked a little awkward. "I don't want to go there on my own in case I run into Val or Ashley. I was hoping that —"

"That one of us would come with you?" Ty finished for her.

Claire nodded. "Would you?" she said hopefully.

"Sure," Ty said with a shrug. "We can go in my car."

"Yeah, I'll come, too," Amy said. She smiled at Claire, trying to forget the argument with Ty. "We'll protect you from Ashley."

They got into Ty's car. Still oblivious to the tension crackling between him and Amy, Claire chatted away. Now that she had gotten over being shy, she was a lot of fun to be with.

When they reached Green Briar, there was no sign of the Grants. "I'll go with Claire to get the blankets," Amy said to Ty. "We'll be right back."

Ty nodded. "I'll wait here."

Amy and Claire found Flint's rugs.

"At least we haven't seen anyone," Claire said as they hurried back down the main stable aisle.

"I'm afraid you spoke too soon," Amy whispered. As they turned the corner toward the car, she had seen Ashley leaning against it, talking to Ty.

Claire stopped dead. "Oh, no."

"Come on," Amy urged. "Just stand up to her."

Ashley's back was turned to them. As they got nearer, they saw her flip her hair back and laugh and then lean closer to Ty.

Amy felt a surge of anger. She gritted her teeth and marched toward them.

"We could really use someone with your skills at Green Briar, Ty," she heard Ashley say. On the word *skills*, Ashley's voice dropped huskily. "You know, my mom would do anything to get you to work here."

"Ty's already got a job, Ashley!" Amy said.

Ashley turned. "Hi there, Amy," she said coolly. "Ty and I were just —" she glanced back at Ty with raised eyebrows — "chatting."

"Yeah, I heard!" Amy said angrily. "Well, Ty's not leaving Heartland. Are you, Ty?"

Ty gave a small shake of his head but glared at Amy. When she saw his face, she flinched. She couldn't believe she answered for Ty like that. She had just said exactly what she wanted to believe — that Ty would never leave Heartland. Things had been so difficult lately, she couldn't help thinking that Ty might actually be tempted by the Green Briar offer. And if he was, she hadn't done much to convince him to stay.

"That's too bad," Ashley went on, looking at Ty through her long eyelashes. "We could have a lot of fun. Still," she said, "it's not too late to change your mind. The position's still open. In fact, I bet you could name your price."

Amy threw the rugs on the backseat of the car. "Come on! Let's go!" She felt so mad at Ashley that she almost could have hit her. How dare Ashley try to talk Ty into going to Green Briar right in front of her! Seeing Ashley smile at Ty again, she almost exploded. "Come on, let's go!" she repeated, flinging herself into the front seat. She realized she was being rude and bossy, but the situation was almost making her ill.

"See you," Ty said to Ashley.

Amy slammed the door.

Claire hastily got into the backseat on Amy's side. "Too scared to come without reinforcements?" Ashley said to her under her breath, a sneer in her voice. "Get a backbone, Claire."

Claire looked away.

"Bye, Ty," Ashley called as Ty started the engine. "And don't forget about us."

❧

Amy was so frustrated that she didn't say a word all the way back to Heartland. Her stomach was in knots she was so upset. Once they arrived, she went straight to the feed room and tried to release her anger by making up the evening hay nets.

Claire came to find her. "Flint's ready," she said.

"OK," Amy said. She was hot from shaking up the hay and stuffing it furiously into the nets, but she felt slightly calmer.

"Ashley really got to you, didn't she?" Claire said tentatively as they walked down to the tack room together to get Flint's bridle and the lunging equipment. "Was it the way she was coming on to Ty?"

"Don't even mention Ashley to me," Amy muttered angrily. "She's not worth it."

"Oh — OK," Claire said. There was a pause. "So what are you going to do with Flint tonight?"

"Well, I'll work him on voltés — they're small circles," Amy said. "And then I think you should have a go and put him through the paces."

Claire looked panic-stricken. "Are you sure he's ready for me? I mean, he's being so good for you."

"Yeah, but he needs to be good for you," Amy said, remembering what Ty had said. "He's been a lot better with you in the stall. If you're firm with him, I think you'll find he'll be good outside as well."

Claire didn't look convinced.

Amy worked Flint for five minutes and then decided that it was time to hand him over to Claire. She halted Flint and called Claire into the middle.

"Are you sure?" Claire said nervously.

Amy nodded. "You'll be fine."

Claire walked cautiously into the center of the ring.

"Just stand beside me as I lunge him," Amy said. She sent Flint forward at a trot again and after three circles gave Claire the lunge rein. "OK, now you take over."

"No," Claire said quickly, trying to hand the line back.

"Go on," Amy said, refusing to take it. "It's OK. You need to do this, Claire."

But sensing Amy's lack of concentration, Flint slowed down and looked toward the middle of the ring. "Tell him to trot on," Amy said quickly to Claire.

"Trot on!" Claire said nervously.

Flint slowed to a walk.

"Go on — make him do it," Amy said more firmly.

But Claire shook her head and gave the lunge line back to Amy. "You do it. He'll do it for you."

With a sigh, Amy took the line back.

"Amy!" She looked out toward the gate and saw Ty. She wondered how long he had been watching.

"What?" she called.

"I need to talk to you a minute."

Amy brought Flint to a halt. "Can't it wait?"

"No," Ty said. "Not really."

Amy called Flint to her. The gray horse walked over obediently. Amy turned him to bring him in, wondering what it was that Ty needed to talk about so urgently.

"Claire can hold him for you, right, Claire?" Ty said.

Claire looked startled. "Well — er —"

"We won't be long," Ty said, smiling at her. "Just walk him around. Do some T-touch with him."

"OK," Claire agreed.

Amy walked over to the gate. "Yeah?"

"Let's not talk here," Ty said. "Come down toward the barn."

Amy followed him away from the gate. "So what's going on? Is everything OK?" she demanded.

"It will be," Ty said. "But only if you give Claire a real chance to bond with Flint. You have to let her work him on her own."

Amy stared at him. "What do you think I was trying to do? I forced her to take the lunge rope from me, but she made me take it back."

"You shouldn't have taken it." Ty shook his head. "I know you're only tying to help, Amy. But can't you see? While you're there, Claire doesn't stand a chance. Flint will turn to you for direction, and Claire will back down every time."

"So what do you expect me to do?" Amy said.

"Have some faith in her," Ty said. "Give her another chance."

Amy shook her head. "I have to think of Flint. His progress is too important. The horse has to come first. The horse always comes first."

Ty looked at her. "What about with Ben and Red?"

Amy looked defiantly at Ty. "That's not fair! You know it's not."

"Why not?" Ty said.

"I don't like the way Ben treats Red any more than you do," she cried angrily, "but there's nothing we can do about it. Not now, anyway. Look, if you're so willing to stand up for Claire, why aren't you more understanding about Ben?"

Ty laughed scornfully. "What's there to understand? He's a rich kid who cares more about winning than he does about his horse."

"That is *not* true!" Amy said. "Ben does care about Red — he cares a lot."

"Well, he's got a strange way of showing it!" Ty snapped. He shook his head. "I can't stand the way he treats Red. I know it takes a lot to train a jumper, but I think he pushes the limits. And it's hard to deal with something like that happening at Heartland. Look, I came here to work with your mom and follow her ideals, and I just don't think she'd be happy with what's going on." Just then, the phone started to ring in the house. "I'll get it," he said, and he walked swiftly away.

Feeling overwhelmed, Amy hurried back to the ring. Right now, she felt like she was being pressured from all sides, and it was all beginning to get to her. Everyone wanted something different from her, and she couldn't cope with it anymore. Then, as she turned the corner, she stopped dead. Claire was standing in the middle of the ring, and Flint was facing her.

"Go on, Flint. Away!" Amy heard her say. Flint hesitated, and Claire flicked the ground with the whip. "Go on!"

Amy held her breath, watching Flint's reaction.

Slowly, Flint walked to the outside of the ring.

Amy took a step back. She didn't want Claire to see her and be distracted. Amy wondered if she was actually going to try to lunge him.

Then she saw Claire tap the lunge whip on the ground. "And trot!"

Flint looked at her. "Trot on!" Claire said, using the whip on the ground again.

To Amy's surprise, Flint began to trot. She saw a flash of joy cross Claire's face. "And walk!" she told him, pointing the whip toward the front of his shoulder as Amy normally did. Flint slowed to a walk.

"Good boy!" Claire praised. "And turn!"

Claire almost tripped over the lunge line as Flint did

as she said. "And trot on!" she called. An amazed smile lit up her face as Flint broke into a trot again.

Amy felt a surge of delight, but she stopped herself from running up to the gate to yell congratulations. She didn't want to disturb Claire when she was doing so well.

After a few more minutes, Claire brought Flint to a halt again and then called him to the middle. He walked toward her.

"Good boy!" she cried, stepping forward to pat him.

Flint rambunctiously threw his head in the air, and Amy's heart stopped for a moment as she anticipated Claire shrinking back and letting Flint get away with it. But Claire had newfound confidence, and she stood her ground.

"No!" Amy heard her say firmly. Taking up the slack on the rope, Claire stepped closer and patted the gray's neck again.

This time Flint accepted her affection. He let out a snort, and then, bringing his head around, he looked at her.

Claire rubbed his forehead and smiled.

A wave of relief and delight overwhelmed Amy. She knew it was just the first step for Claire and Flint, but they were on their way to building a new relationship. And really, they owed it all to Ty. He had known that they were ready. Amy suddenly wanted to find Ty and tell him. Suddenly, all the arguments of the past ten days faded. She knew that their disagreements didn't really matter because they shared the same vision of what was most important.

She could hardly wait to share the good news with him. She looked in the feed and tack rooms and then remembered the phone ringing and wondered if he was still on the phone. The kitchen door was open. She ran toward the house. As she got near, she heard his voice carrying on a one-sided conversation. She slowed down, not wanting to disturb him.

"Yeah, the salary is extremely generous," she heard him saying. "And two days off a week sounds great."

Salary? Amy stopped. *Days off?*

There was a pause.

"Yeah, of course, I'll let you know, Mrs. Grant," she heard Ty say.

Mrs. Grant! Amy froze. Ty was talking to Val Grant about salaries and days off. And he was saying he'd let her know. Was he really considering taking the job at Green Briar?

She backed away from the house, then turned and ran across the yard and into the feed room. She sat down on a bale of hay, her stomach churning. Ty couldn't leave. How could she run Heartland without him? She buried her head in her hands and tried to fight back the tears.

A few minutes later, she heard footsteps coming up to the barn. Wiping the arm of her sweatshirt across her face, she jumped to her feet.

Ty entered. He stopped when he saw her. "What are you doing in here?" He frowned. "What's up?"

"Nothing," she said quickly.

"Are you OK?" he said, stepping closer.

"Yeah." Amy looked down as she felt the tears rise in her throat again.

"Amy?" Ty took hold of her arm. "What's wrong?"

"Nothing's wrong!" Amy cried, hurt and betrayal flooding through her as she looked at his concerned face. How could he look at her like that when he was planning on leaving? She knew things hadn't been easy for him since Ben had arrived, but she didn't think things were that bad. Even though she hadn't been completely open with him, she at least would have expected him to tell her if he really wanted to leave. She felt that it was all her fault. If she had been honest with him, things would never have gone so far. But there wasn't anything she could do, and it was probably too late to change his mind.

"Is there anything I can do?" Ty asked.

Suddenly, something snapped inside her. She wrenched her arm away. "No," she said. "This is something I have to deal with on my own. You can't do anything."

Ty's face paled, as if he took her words to mean much more than she intended. "Well, OK," he said, and walked out of the barn.

Amy collapsed onto the hay bale again and this time completely gave way to her tears. She couldn't face the thought of Ty leaving. She couldn't even talk to him about it.

Chapter Nine

Ten minutes went by before Amy had enough control of herself to go up to the training ring. She splashed some water on her face from Flint's water bucket and then went to see how Claire was coping. She had a responsibility. Mrs. Whitely trusted her with Claire and Flint's well-being. Amy took several deep breaths and hoped everything would be OK.

She found Claire lunging Flint again. He was cantering around her. Seeing Amy, she brought him to a halt. "Look!" she said in delight. "He's letting me lunge him!"

"That's great," Amy said, going into the ring.

Claire frowned. "Are you OK? You look — odd."

Amy managed a faint smile. "I'm OK, thanks."

"Ty was looking for you."

"Yeah, he found me. He just wanted to talk about one

of the horses," Amy lied. She patted Flint. "It really is great that you got him to lunge on your own."

"I know!" Claire said, caught up in her own delight. "I walked him around for a while and then did some T-touch. He was being good so I thought I'd just try lunging him, and he was fine. He was great!" She grinned. "I can't wait to tell Mom."

❧

When Claire told Ty about her success with Flint back in the barn, he congratulated her warmly. "I knew you could do it!" he said.

"Thanks," Claire said, smiling at him. "I know I'm going to have to keep at it to build a really good relationship with him, but at least it's a start."

"That's great," Ty said.

After Claire had gone, Ty hardly said a single word to Amy until he left that evening. "I'm taking my day off tomorrow," he said curtly as he got his coat from the tack room. "So I'll see you Sunday."

Amy nodded. "Bye."

She watched Ty walk away, thoughts tumbling through her mind in a confused mess. Part of her wanted to run after him, to beg him not to leave Heartland, to tell him that she couldn't run the place without him. But there was another part of her that felt desperately hurt and utterly resentful that he would consider betraying her by going to Green Briar.

She swallowed. What was she going to do?

🙠

The next morning, Claire arrived at nine o'clock. Amy had never seen her at Heartland so early before. "I can't wait to try lunging him again," she said. "Mom's not picking me up me till this afternoon. I thought maybe I could lunge him twice."

"Sure, as long as you keep both sessions short," Amy said. "So he stays focused."

"I could do some T-touch on him in between," Claire said. "And maybe let him graze a little."

Claire's first lunging session with Flint went well, and the second went even better. Amy watched from the gate. "You're doing great! He's really listening," she said encouragingly.

Just then, Ben joined her. "She has gotten better, hasn't she?" he said.

Amy nodded. "It's all about confidence," she said as Claire made Flint turn and canter in the opposite direction. "Now that she knows she can make Flint do what she wants, her confidence is really growing. Hey, Claire!" she called. "How about trying him without the lunge line?"

Claire brought Flint to a halt. "What? Really?"

"Yeah," Amy said. "Just use the whip as you've been doing," Amy said. "It's the same signals, just without the line. Let's see what he does."

Claire led Flint over to the gate, unsnapped the lunge line, and handed it to Amy. "Here goes."

She led Flint back to the center and then let go of his bridle. "Away," she told him. Flint obediently walked away, and then suddenly he seemed to realize that the lunge line was missing. He stopped.

"Use the whip!" Amy said quickly.

Claire tapped the whip on the floor. "Walk on."

Flint hesitated. Amy held her breath, but then to her relief the gray horse moved on.

"And trot!" Claire said quickly, tapping the whip on the floor again.

With no line attaching him to her, Flint broke into a trot. He trotted easily around the circle.

"And turn!" Claire called.

Spinning quickly on his haunches, Flint changed direction.

"That's amazing!" Ben said to Amy.

"Good job!" Amy shouted.

After a few more circuits, Claire brought Flint to a halt and called him to her. "That's a good boy!" she said, patting him in delight. "I'll do some more tomorrow. But I'd like to stop for the day. Wasn't he fabulous?"

"You both were!" Amy said, opening the gate as Claire led Flint over.

"I didn't think I could do it," Claire said, looking totally astonished. Her eyes shone. "Did you see the way he changed direction? He was so quick!"

Amy nodded. She had, and more important than that, she had seen the respect and trust in Flint's eyes as he had reacted to Claire's commands.

"He's like a different horse," Ben said to her as they followed Claire and Flint down the yard. "I mean, a week ago he wouldn't let her near him."

"And now he's willingly responding to her direction," Amy agreed. "Not because he's forced to, but because he wants to. And the stronger the bond between them gets, the harder he will try for her." She looked at him. "When they start to show, they'll have a real partnership. And he'll really try his hardest for her. What more could a rider want?"

Hoping her words would sink in, she walked away. The last thing Amy wanted was to sound preachy, but the only way things were going to work out at Heartland was if she could get Ben to start seeing things more like she and Ty did. She didn't want to have to ask Ben to go, but most of all she hoped that he would eventually want to stay.

✥

Before Claire left that afternoon, she asked Amy whether she could ask her mom to come see Flint work the next day.

"Sure," Amy said.

"I think she'll be really impressed," Claire said happily. "OK, see you tomorrow then!"

"Yeah, see you," Amy replied.

She thought about what the next day would bring. How would she react to Ty? Would he tell her that he was leaving? In a way, she felt like she should tell him that she had heard him talking to Val Grant. But how would she bring it up? She couldn't tell him that she had listened to his private conversation, and if she did and he said that he was leaving, what was the point?

Amy was mucking out a stall when Claire and her mom arrived on Sunday morning.

"Hello, Amy," Mrs. Whitely said. "Claire said it was OK if I came to watch today."

Amy nodded. "Sure."

"I'll go and groom Flint. Then can I take him to the ring?" Claire asked eagerly.

"Yes, but you might want to do some T-touch on him first," Amy said.

"OK," Claire said. She turned to her mom. "Come on,

Mom. I'll show you what T-touch is." Her eyes lit up. "You could even do some!"

Amy looked at Claire in surprise. She had never seen her look so happy and enthusiastic. The success of the day before really seemed to have changed her. *I just hope that Flint's as good with her today,* Amy thought. *It would be awful if he acts up with Mrs. Whitely here.*

Five minutes later, Ben arrived, even though it was his day off. He came to find her. "I'm going to take Red out for a ride," he said. "Do you want to come?"

"Thanks, but I'd better not. Mrs. Whitely is here to see Claire work Flint." Amy said. She put her pitchfork down. "I hope he's good."

Ben nodded. "I'm sure he will be. See you later then."

Amy finished the stall and decided to go see how Claire was doing. As she walked up the yard, she saw Ben heading off toward the trails on Red.

"Have a good ride," she called.

Claire was working T-touch circles on Red's forehead. Flint's neck was low and relaxed and his eyes half closed. Amy felt relieved.

Mrs. Whitely smiled when she saw Amy. "Claire's been explaining this T-touch to me. It's fascinating."

Claire looked around. "Do you think he's ready for the ring now?"

Amy nodded. "Start off on the lunge rope, and then when he's settled you can let him off."

Claire set off to the tack room.

Mrs. Whitely watched her go. "I can't believe the change in Claire," she said to Amy. "She's been so happy these last few days. She's hardly stopped talking for a moment!"

Amy nodded. "I think it's really helped her confidence to be able to get Flint to do what she wants."

"So she really is OK to handle him on her own?" Mrs. Whitely asked. "When she said I could come and watch her today, I have to admit I had my doubts. This improvement seems to have happened so fast."

"We've been treating him with some violet leaf oil to help calm him down, and the T-touch Claire's been doing has helped develop a bond between them," Amy explained. "But the real breakthrough came when Claire worked him on her own yesterday." She saw that Mrs. Whitely was intent to hear more. "I think she suddenly realized that if she was firm, he would do what she wanted. So she stopped feeling so scared of him," Amy went on. "Flint has started to respect her, and now, hopefully, their relationship can develop into a real partnership."

"You know an impressive amount for a fifteen-year-old," Mrs. Whitely said.

"My mom taught me," Amy said. "Now that she's not here, Ty and I work together with the horses. It's been great experience."

As the words left her mouth, she realized what she was saying. Her breath caught in her throat. It was so natural to talk about working the horses together with Ty and for her to take their relationship for granted. And now it could be very close to coming to an end. Ty had hardly spoken a word to her since that morning, and whenever she had caught sight of him around the yard, his face had been serious and his eyes hard.

Just then, Claire came back. "OK," she said, snapping the lunge line on Flint. "Here goes."

She led Flint up to the training ring. "Remember, he can be a bit excitable at first," Amy warned, seeing the Thoroughbred's ears prick and his tail lift as he jogged up the path.

Claire nodded.

Amy opened the gate, and Flint pranced into the ring. "Be careful, honey," Mrs. Whitely said.

Claire walked to the center of the ring. "Away!" she said to Flint.

With a joyful bolt, Flint plunged to the outside of the ring and bucked twice. Amy's heart stopped in her chest. *Stay confident, Claire,* she thought.

"And trot!" Claire said firmly, bringing the whip down on the sand behind him. "Trot on!"

Amy looked at her face. Claire's eyes were fixed on her horse. Her shoulders square to his, she urged him on. For a moment Flint hesitated and looked as if he was about to plunge again, but Claire brought the whip down on the ground again. "Flint — trot!"

With a toss of his head, the gray obeyed. Amy's hopes lifted as she watched.

"And canter!" Claire told the gelding firmly. Flint broke into a canter. Claire played out the lunge line and let him canter in large circles, and at last he started to relax and lower his head.

Amy felt like she could breathe normally again.

"Hey, she's doing really well," Mrs. Whitely said.

Claire slowed Flint and turned him before sending him off at a canter on the other rein. Her eyes were focused on the horse, and her face shone with a new confidence. After a bit, she halted him. "I'll take him off the lunge line now," she said.

"Are you sure that's a good idea?" Mrs. Whitely said.

Claire nodded. "He'll be fine, Mom."

Unsnapping the lunge line, she sent Flint to the outside of the ring. "And canter!" she said. Flint was just as responsive as the day before.

Watching Flint so willingly obey the commands and seeing the pride and delight on Claire's face, Amy felt a lump suddenly rise to her throat. She was so happy to see a horse and a human working together as equals, trusting and respecting each other. It was what Heartland was all about.

Hearing a noise behind her, she turned. Ty was standing a little way off. Suddenly, he saw Amy looking at him, and he walked away.

In the ring, Claire stopped Flint. "What do you think, Mom?" she said, leading him over, her eyes shining.

"It's amazing," Mrs. Whitely said in astonishment. "He did just exactly what you told him to."

"I know. He's so wonderful." Claire stopped Flint. "I *can* keep him, can't I, Mom?"

Mrs. Whitely smiled. "Yes, you can."

"Oh, thank you!" Claire cried. She threw her arms round Flint's neck. "Did you hear that, Flint? I can keep you!"

Flint nickered and nuzzled her arm as she hugged him.

Claire looked around in astonishment. "He's never done that before! He must be starting to like me."

"Well, now that we've decided you're keeping him, I guess we're going to have to start looking for a house with some land," Mrs. Whitely said to Claire.

Claire looked at her in surprise. "But we're already renting a house."

Mrs. Whitely smiled. "I was talking about a house to *buy*. I was thinking we could plan to stick around here for a while. My work's going well, and it seems like you're happy here." She paused. "And it would be nice for you to be close to your father. What do you think?"

"Oh, Mom, that would be fantastic!" Claire exclaimed. She turned to Amy. "Oh, Amy, isn't this great?"

Amy grinned. "You'll have to see Ashley every day!"

"Who cares?" Claire said. She kissed Flint's soft gray nose. "I've got Flint. Nothing else matters."

❧

Amy had just said good-bye to Mrs. Whitely and Claire when the phone started to ring. She ran to answer it.

"Hello, Heartland," she said. "Amy Fleming speaking."

"Hi," a woman's voice said. "Is it possible to speak to Ben Stillman, please?"

"You could, but he's out on a ride," Amy said. Suddenly, she caught sight of Red coming down the path. "Actually, he just got back. Who should I say is calling?"

"It's his mom."

Amy put the phone down and went to the door. "Ben! It's your mom!"

Ben dismounted and handed Red's reins to Amy. "Can you hold him for me?"

"Sure," Amy said.

She took hold of Red's reins, and Ben ran to the kitchen. Red was still breathing heavily from his ride. It looked like Ben had been riding him hard. Deciding she should start to cool him down, Amy started to walk him around.

Five minutes later, Ben came out of the house.

"What did your mom want?" Amy asked. Suddenly, she saw that his face was dark and angry. "Was it bad news?"

"She's not coming!" Ben said.

"Not coming?" Amy echoed.

"To the show."

"Oh, Ben, I'm sorry," Amy said.

Ben grabbed Red's reins. "I was stupid to believe that she really would. She always cancels at the last minute — always." His face hardened. "Well, from now on I'm just not going to care. She can do what she wants. It's just me and Red — that's all that matters." He put his foot in the stirrup and mounted.

"What are you doing?" Amy said in surprise.

"I'm going to practice for this show," Ben said. "Mom might not be there, but that doesn't matter. We'll show everyone just how good we are."

He clicked his tongue and Red walked forward.

"But, Ben, you just got back from a ride," Amy protested, walking beside him. "Red's still hot."

"That was just a trail ride," Ben said as he trotted Red toward the ring.

Hearing the clatter of hooves, Ty came out of the feed room. "What's Ben doing?" he demanded, coming across the yard. "I thought he jumped him hard yesterday."

"He did," Amy said. "And he took him out on the trails this morning. But he got a phone call from his mom, and then he went kind of crazy. He said he's going to take Red over some courses, but Red seemed awfully hot to me. He was really blowing."

"Well he shouldn't overdo it." Ty said grimly. "I think we should check it out."

He hurried across the yard. Amy followed him.

When they reached the training ring, Ben was cantering Red toward a jump. It was a three-and-a-half-foot spread that looked really high. All the fences in the ring were set higher than three feet.

"Ben! Stop!" Amy called, running up to the gate.

But Ben ignored her. He brought his whip down on Red's neck, and the chestnut just cleared the fence. Pulling him to a halt, Ben dismounted and raised the pole another foot.

"What are you doing, Ben?" Ty said, striding into the ring.

"Jumping my horse!" Ben said through gritted teeth. He swung himself onto Red's back. "Get out of my way!"

Ty didn't move. Pulling on Red's reins, Ben cantered the horse past him.

"Ben! No!" Amy said, her heart leaping into her mouth as she saw Ben turn Red into the jump. For one horrible moment she had a vision of her father jumping

Pegasus and the pole catching between Pegasus's legs, bringing the horse and rider crashing to the ground. Things had gone far enough! She couldn't handle Ben's being so careless — even if it was his own horse. She ran across the sand toward the jump. "Will you *stop*! Red's tired! It's too much for him! Let him have a rest."

But Ben wouldn't back down. He brought his stick down twice on the chestnut's neck. For one moment as Red approached the towering jump, it looked like he was going to take off, but then his courage failed him and he stopped abruptly, his hooves skidding in the sand.

"Come on!" Ben shouted, reaching back and hitting Red's quarters with the crop.

The horse panicked and bolted away from the jump, straight toward where Amy was standing. For a moment, all Amy saw was Red's frightened eyes and foaming mouth, and then she felt Ty grabbing her by her shoulders and pulling her out of the way.

"You idiot!" Ty howled at Ben, still gently holding Amy's shoulders.

Amy's heart felt like it would burst through her chest, it was hammering so hard. She caught the look of shock on Ben's face, and then his eyes darkened again. Turning Red toward the fence, he brought the whip down on Red's quarters.

"Stop it, Ben!" Amy screamed.

Seeing the jump, Red panicked and rose into the air. Taken by surprise, Ben threw himself forward onto Red's neck to stay on. Ty let go of Amy and ran across the sand, prepared to grab Red's reins as the chestnut landed.

Red shot backward in alarm but Ty hung on. "Steady, boy, steady!"

"What are you doing?" Ben shouted at Ty, recovering his seat and trying to yank the reins away from him. "Let go of my horse."

Ty held tight to the reins and gently patted Red's sweaty neck. The chestnut's chest was still heaving with deep breaths.

"I won't let go until you get off and let him cool down," Ty said. "Red's exhausted. You're working him too hard, too often, and he needs a break."

"Don't tell me how to deal with my horse," Ben said.

"It's your choice, but not while you're at Heartland."

Ben glared at Ty.

"Just get off," Ty unexpectedly yelled. "Now!"

Ben let out a huff and pulled his leg over the saddle. He stared at Ty for a moment and then, turning swiftly, grabbed Red's reins and led him out of the ring.

Amy didn't know what to do. She looked at Ty's furious face and then at Ben disappearing across the yard. She stepped forward.

"Don't go after him, Amy," Ty said intensely.

Amy stopped and looked at him. "I have to. I just *have* to."

Ty's eyes bored into hers. "If you go, I'm leaving," he said. "I've had enough, Amy — I've *compromised* more in the last two weeks than in the rest of my life. I'm not prepared to stand by when I see cruelty like that, not even for you."

"What do you mean?" Amy whispered.

Just then there was the sound of shouting. Ben came running up to the gate. "Amy!" he yelled. "Amy! It's Red! Come quick!"

Chapter Ten

For a second, Amy glanced beseechingly at Ty and then ran to the gate.

"Red's collapsed in his stall!" Ben gasped.

Amy raced down the yard. When she got to Red's stall, she saw that the chestnut was violently trying to roll. "Colic!" she said, grabbing the halter from his door. "Quick! Get him up!"

Ben had taken Red's saddle and bridle off. Grabbing Red by his mane, he urged him to his feet. The chestnut scrambled up, but almost at once his legs began to buckle again. "Walk him around," she said, fastening the halter quickly. "You can't let him roll like that, or he could twist his intestines. I'll get Ty."

"Don't waste your time," Ben said. "Just call the vet!"

"I'll get Ty first," Amy said. She saw Ben's face drop.

"Ben — Ty is good at this stuff. He'll do whatever he can to help. This is more important."

She raced back across the yard. Ty was walking down from the training ring, his face set.

"Ty!" Amy gasped. "Red's got colic. It looks bad. Ben's walking him around." She grabbed his hand. "Please, Ty! You've got to come look at him. Please?"

Ty stared at her pleading expression. "You honestly think that I'd refuse to help because it's Ben's horse?"

"No, Ty — that's not it," Amy began to stammer.

Ty just shook his head and then strode across the yard toward Red's stall.

Ben was walking Red along the paddock. The horse's sides were damp with sweat and each step he took looked like a huge effort. When Ben saw Ty, his face tightened. But Ty ignored his expression. "Do you have any idea what could have caused it?" he demanded.

For a moment, Ben looked like he wasn't going to acknowledge Ty, but then his concern for his horse overcame him. "None. He was fine out on the trails," he said, stopping Red.

"Did he eat anything while he was out?" Ty asked.

"No. Well, nothing out of the ordinary. I stopped for a bit and let him graze on some grass at the side of a field."

"Mowed grass?" Ty said quickly.

"Of course not!" Ben said angrily. "And I didn't let him drink a troughful of water after it, either. I'm not stupid. I didn't purposely try to give him colic, you know."

"It's OK, Ben!" Amy said. "Ty's just trying to help."

Ben ran a hand through his hair. "Yeah, OK. I'm sorry. No, it wasn't cut grass." Just then Red's legs started to fold again. "Up, boy!" Ben cried, making him move forward.

"Amy, will you call Scott?" Ty said.

"Yeah."

Amy ran inside. But the receptionist at Scott's veterinary office told her that Scott was out on a call. "I'll get the message to him as soon as possible," she told Amy.

"Please hurry," Amy begged, looking out the window and seeing Red kick at the ground and try to reach around and bite at his flanks.

As she put the phone down, Lou came into the kitchen. "What's going on?" she asked, seeing Amy's worried face.

Amy quickly explained.

"That sounds bad," Lou said. "Is there anything I can do?"

Amy shook her head. "Not really, although you could call Scott's office back in ten minutes and see if they've gotten through and if they know how long he's going to be."

"Sure," Lou said. "And I'll get Grandpa."

Amy hurried outside and told Ben and Ty what was

happening. "They're trying to get in touch with Scott, but he's out on a call."

Grandpa and Lou came hurrying out of the house. Jack's eyes swept over the distressed horse. "It's colic, right?" he said to Ty.

Ty nodded. "But we don't know what caused it."

Suddenly, Red seemed to stagger. "He's getting worse!" Ben said.

"Keep him walking," Jack Bartlett instructed.

Ben moved Red on. "I can't believe it hit so quickly," he said. "Colic doesn't normally get bad so fast, does it?"

"Maybe it's not just colic," Ty said thoughtfully.

Ben turned on him. "Of course, it's colic! You can see the way he keeps trying to roll. What else could it be?"

"Do you have any ideas, Ty?" Jack said quickly.

"It could be some kind of poisoning," Ty said. "Colic might be just one of the symptoms."

"Poisoning!" Amy echoed, her heart dropping.

Ty was already hurrying over to Red. "Hold him still," he said to Ben. He opened the horse's mouth. "It could be poisoning, all right. Look at his gums — they're inflamed!" He turned to Ben. "What's he been eating?"

"Nothing, only grass!" Ben said desperately. "And I checked it out. There weren't any weeds or anything. It was just plain grass at the side of a field."

Amy's heart pounded. She knew that when treating

cases of poisoning you had to act quickly, but it was also vital to know exactly what type of poisoning it was so that the right remedy could be used, or there could be other side effects. How could they find out before it was too late what had poisoned Red?

"Where did you say the field was?" Ty demanded.

"I don't know," Ben said. "It was out to the south. It looked like it had just been seeded."

"Just been seeded?" Ty repeated.

"Do you think you know what the poison is, Ty?" Grandpa said.

Ty didn't answer. Instead he raised a hand quickly in front of Red's face. The chestnut shied back clumsily. Ty nodded. "That's it," he said grimly.

"What?" Amy demanded.

"Mercury poisoning," Ty said.

Ben stared at Ty. "But Red hasn't been anywhere near any mercury!"

"Organic mercury compounds are sometimes used as seed dressings," Ty said. "It's my bet that the field had been treated and some of the seeds drifted into the grass at the side."

Ben's face paled. "But mercury's really toxic."

Grandpa spoke quickly. "Is there anything we can do, Ty? Can we drench him? Give him something?"

"If it *is* mercury poisoning, then we have to get the mercury out of his system as fast as we can," Ty replied.

"If we don't, his kidneys will fail. We can try drenching him with a saturated sodium bicarbonate solution. That should help clear the mercury out."

"But what if it isn't mercury poisoning?" Amy whispered, looking at Red and then back at Ty. "What if the sodium bicarbonate doesn't help — or even makes things worse?"

"It's a risk," Ty admitted. "But there's no way to know exactly what it is right now. If we wait for Scott to get here, it might be too late." He looked at Ben. "It's your choice, Ben."

Ben hesitated. Red groaned and his knees buckled. "Treat him!" he said suddenly, as Red collapsed on the ground. "Do whatever you can!"

"Amy, Jack, can you help Ben get Red into his stall?" Ty said, starting to run across the yard. "It'll be better to work in a confined space. I'll make up the solution. Lou, can you call Scott's again and tell them that it's more than colic?"

Everyone did as Ty asked. Amy, Grandpa, and Ben forced Red to his feet. His legs were unsteady, but they managed to get him into his stall. Ben's face was pale as he turned Red in circles to stop him from lying down. "I don't know what I'll do if anything happens to you," he said, rubbing Red's face.

Ty appeared with three old plastic bottles filled with a saturated solution of sodium bicarbonate.

"It's OK. You can let him lie down," he said. "Just don't let him roll."

Ben let Red sink down onto the straw. Ty knelt down beside the horse's head and opened the first bottle. "Come on, boy," he said, tilting the horse's head back. "I know you're not going to like this, but I'm afraid we've got no choice."

Red struggled to get his head away as Ty began to tip the liquid down his throat. Ty slid his thumb in the side of Red's mouth to make sure the solution went down, but Red kept trying to pull away.

"Here, I'll hold him," Ben said, moving swiftly to Ty's side and steadying Red's head. With Ben there, Red calmed down.

"Don't hold his head too high, or he might choke," Ty said. "Angle it lower."

"Come on, boy," Amy whispered, kneeling beside him and stroking his hot neck. "You gotta do this to get better!" She glanced at Lou and Grandpa who were standing by the stall door watching tensely.

Ty finished one bottle and started on the other. "Are you sure this is right?" Ben said, looking at the stream of liquid being poured steadily down Red's throat.

"It's the fastest way to wash the poison out," Ty said. He finished the second bottle. "OK, let him rest a minute."

Ben let go of Red's head and, making a wisp from some straw, began to dry Red's sweating sides.

Amy saw the horse look uneasily around at his stomach.

"It's OK, boy," she said, moving up to his head and starting to work T-touch circles on his ears and face. "It's going to be just fine."

Amy's fingers worked skillfully. Horses that were ill often responded well to ear work. In a short while, Red stopped looking at his stomach and let his head hang low.

"He seems to like that," Ben said, coming and joining her. "Will you show me what to do?"

Amy explained how to do the circles, and Ben took her place at the Red's head.

Amy felt the chestnut's sides. His skin was still hot and damp, his flanks trembling slightly.

"His breathing's really shallow," she said in a low voice to Ty.

"Let's drench him again," Ty said, looking worried.

"I'll make some more solution," Grandpa said.

They kept up the routine for another half hour, alternately drenching and using T-touch circles.

"Come on, boy," Ben pleaded after they finished the third drenching. "You can make it!" He turned to Ty. "Isn't there anything else you can give him?"

Ty shook his head.

Ben buried his head in his hands. "He's got to get better."

"Keep working," Ty said grimly.

Just then, there was the sound of the phone ringing. "I'll get it!" Lou said, rushing toward the house.

A few minutes later, she came running back. "That was the vet's — Scott's on his way. They think he should be about twenty minutes." She looked at Ty in concern. "Will that be soon enough?"

"I hope so," Ty said.

Ben squared his shoulders. "It will be!" He started to work on Red's ears again. "It has to be."

Grandpa reappeared in the stall doorway and looked at the sodden, soiled bed. "He could do with some clean straw. Come on, Lou, give me a hand."

As Lou and Grandpa brought some clean straw and began to spread a thick layer over the bed, Amy felt Red's sides again. With relief, she realized that the skin under her fingers was not as steamy and no new patches of sweat were breaking out. "Hey!" she said. "I think he's calming down. In fact, I'm sure of it."

The others looked at Red. His head was still resting on the straw, but his eyes had lost the panic-stricken look of earlier, and his nostrils were no longer flaring with every breath.

"You're right!" Ben said. "Come on, boy!" he said dramatically. "You're going to make it."

Amy went to work with renewed vigor. *Oh, please,* she prayed, *please let this mean that Red is going to pull through.*

❧

Twenty minutes later there was the sound of car tires screeching to a halt outside the house.

"Scott!" Amy cried in relief as the vet appeared in the stall doorway.

"I came as fast as I could," Scott said, kneeling down next to Red.

"We think it's mercury poisoning," Ty said quickly. He explained about the grass that Red had eaten. "He was showing signs of nervousness and muscle weakness and had severe colic. We didn't know when you'd get here, so we took a chance and treated him. We've been drenching him with sodium bicarbonate solution."

Scott looked in Red's mouth and then stroked Red's neck. "You did the right thing. In fact, acting when you did probably saved his life." He looked at Ben. "He's your horse, right?"

Ben nodded. "Is he going to be OK?" he asked anxiously.

"I hope so. I'll inject him with some calcium disodium versenate," Scott said, checking Red's mouth again as he spoke. "It will offset any remaining mercury so it will pass through his system harmlessly. I'll take a sample of his stomach contents for analysis. But I think Ty made the right diagnosis. It looks like mercury poisoning to me." He stood up. "I'll get my things from the car."

"So he'll make a full recovery?" Jack Bartlett asked.

Scott nodded. "He'll need several more injections over the next couple of days, but I think he'll be back on his feet again soon."

As Scott hurried out of the stall, Amy sat back in the straw, feeling half dazed with relief. She pulled her legs to her chest and rested her head on her knees. Suddenly, all the tension that had been building up inside her over the course of the afternoon overwhelmed her. She gave a sob.

Ty and Ben looked around in surprise.

"Hey," Ty said, sitting down beside her and putting his arm around her shoulders. "You heard Scott. Red's going to be OK."

Amy nodded and sniffed. She felt so mixed-up and confused. She was delighted that Scott thought Red was going to be fine, but that didn't wipe away the events of the afternoon.

⁂

When Scott had finished treating Red, he started to put his things back in his bag. "Looks like he's been through a war," he said, pointing to the whip marks still visible from earlier. "How did he get those?"

Amy glanced at Ben. His face was bright red. "Um — I —"

"Oh, that happened when he was turned out in the field," Ty said quickly. "He was just playing around with the other horses."

Amy saw Ben look at Ty in astonishment.

"Oh, right," Scott said, straightening up.

Grandpa had gone back to the house, but Lou still stood by the stall door. "Do you want to come in for a drink?" she asked Scott.

Scott smiled at her. "Sure," he said, picking up his bag. "That sounds good."

Lou opened the door for him, and they walked toward the house together.

Ben turned to Ty. "Thanks," he said quietly.

Ty shrugged.

"I mean it, Ty," Ben went on. "And not just for telling Scott that Red got those welts in the pasture. Thanks for everything — for realizing what was wrong with Red and for doing what you did. If it hadn't been for you, who knows what would have happened?" He crouched down in the straw and stroked the chestnut horse. "Red means more to me than anything," he said quietly. "He's all I have."

Ty looked questioningly at Ben.

Ben laughed bitterly at Ty's reaction. "Oh, I know you think I'm real lucky, that I've got it all, but it isn't as simple as that. My dad ran off when I was ten, and after that things fell apart. I started getting into trouble in school. My mom couldn't deal with me, so she sent me to live with my aunt." He looked Ty straight in the eye. "My aunt's been great, but she's always made it clear that she's got her own life to lead. I owe her a lot since she got me interested in horses and she gave me Red, but I never really knew if I belonged there. I felt like I was in the way. Then she told me that she wanted me to come and work here, and I resented it. All my life I've been shuffled around." He turned back to Red. "Anyway, I know I haven't handled things here well at all and that I'm not the only one who has stuff to deal with. It's just that I didn't want to be here in the beginning." He looked up at Amy and Ty. "I didn't want to have to start over again. I should have said something. I'm sorry to drop all this on you now."

"Actually, I — I knew about your parents getting divorced," Amy admitted. "Lisa told Lou." She felt Ty look at her.

"Did you all know?" Ben said, obviously embarrassed.

Amy shook her head. "Ty didn't."

Ben looked at Ty. "Well, now you do," he said. "And not that it's an excuse, but at least now you know. I'm not so good at dealing with people. Most of the time I feel like the only one who understands me or cares about me is Red."

"Ben," Amy reassured him, "that's just not true. Life isn't all black and white like that. There were reasons why your mom sent you to live with your aunt — I'm sure some were good and some were bad. Just like when Lisa sent you here. She probably did it because she hoped you'd get something out of it. She definitely cares about you. You have to know that."

"Maybe," Ben said. He smiled. "She got me Red, anyway." He gently touched the horse's face. "Training him was the first thing I was ever good at. My aunt bought him for me when he was three. No one else could ride him, but I did. And then when we started showing and we were winning, it was like something was finally going right."

Suddenly, Amy began to understand why Ben seemed so driven to win. He didn't just like it — he *needed* it.

Ben sighed. "I know we've had ups and downs since I got here, but I have enjoyed it — and I'll be sorry to go."

"Go?" Amy said in surprise.

"Yeah." He looked at her. "There's no way you're going to want me to stay after how I've been acting. And what I did to Red was wrong." He shook his head. "It was more than wrong. I was upset, and I took it out on him. There's no excuse for that."

"No, there isn't," Amy said honestly. "But if you're

really sorry, then we can try and work it out. But it's not just up to me. It's also up to Ty." She looked at Ty, who was staring intently at Ben.

Ben averted his gaze. "But I thought you'd hate me for what I did," he said to Amy. "I went against what Heartland stands for."

"I hate *what* you did," Amy said. "But I don't hate you." She looked at Red. "I know you care about Red, and you didn't mean to hurt him."

Ben nodded. "I'd never *mean* to hurt him, but I did. Now I have to try to regain his trust." He stroked Red's mane. "The worst part is, if he hadn't gotten sick from that grass, I wouldn't have thought twice about over-working him and forcing him to jump those fences. But seeing him so sick, I suddenly realized how much he meant to me and how right you were. I don't want Red to listen to me because he's scared, I want him to really want to work with me so we're a team." He met Ty's steady gaze. "If I can't stay, I'll understand. A lot has happened between us. But I want you to know I've learned a valuable lesson that I'll remember no matter where I am."

Amy looked at Ty, hoping he felt the same way she did.

He nodded. "It's OK, Ben," he said quietly. "You can stay."

Amy felt a rush of relief as she saw Ben's eyes light up.

"I'll work hard," he said quickly. "And I'll learn fast. I want to be a real part of Heartland."

Suddenly, Red nickered softly, half lifting his head from the straw.

"Hey, boy," Ben said softly, reaching out to stroke him. "You feeling better?"

Amy tried to swallow her tears as she saw Red lift his nose to Ben's hand and gently nuzzle his palm. Amy knew they had a strong bond, but she was sure that this would make the horse and rider even closer.

✦

Leaving Ben and Red in the stall, Amy and Ty went outside. "So how long have you known?" Ty said when they were out of earshot of the stall.

Amy knew what Ty was talking about. "For about two weeks," Amy admitted. "I couldn't tell you. Lou made me promise not to. She said it would be hard for Ben if he found out that we all knew. But it's been *so* hard keeping it from you. I know it wasn't fair. And I knew you'd be more understanding with Ben if I could tell you. It was so frustrating. I'm really sorry, Ty."

"Lou was probably right," Ty said. He ran a hand through his hair. "But it was really hard knowing that there was something you weren't telling me." He shook his head. "That's just not the way we are with each other.

At least now I know *why* you were sticking up for Ben — even if I still don't agree with it."

Looking at his tangled hair and the weariness in his eyes that reflected the stress of the afternoon, Amy realized there was something else she was keeping from Ty. "Oh, Ty," she said desperately. "Please don't leave. I need you here — we all do. Heartland wouldn't be the same. It would be nothing without you!"

"What are you talking about?" Ty asked, confused.

"I know you're thinking about going to Green Briar," Amy rushed on. "I'm sorry, but I heard you on the phone with Val Grant. I heard you say you'd think about it and let her know. But please, please don't go!"

There was a silence. "Amy," Ty said, his eyes searching hers. "Tell me honestly. Did you think, even for a second, that I wouldn't help Red because of what happened with Ben and me?"

Amy didn't hesitate. "No," she said desperately.

"Just like you know that I would never consider leaving Heartland to go to work at Green Briar," Ty said.

"But I heard —"

"You heard me say I'd let Val Grant know if I wanted to consider her offer." Ty said. "I told her I wasn't leaving Heartland, and she said to call her if I changed my mind. That's it," Ty said emphatically.

"But today," Amy replied, "today you said you'd leave if I went after Ben."

"Amy, if you had followed him, I would have been pretty mad and would have taken off. But I never would have left for good." Ty looked at Amy as his words started to sink in.

"So you're not going?" Amy said hesitantly.

"No," Ty said, shaking his head. "I'm not. I never even considered it."

"Oh, Ty!" Amy said, her eyes starting to shine with relief and delight. "I'm so glad! I feel bad that I thought you might go to Green Briar. I couldn't handle the idea of being at Heartland without you."

"Well, you don't have to." Ty took her hand and looked into her eyes. "My future's here at Heartland, Amy — with you." Ty said.

Amy smiled gratefully, relieved that things between her and Ty were back to the way they had been, knowing that they shared the same dream — the same future at Heartland.

Heartland

❧

Come What May

To the five gray horses that have touched my life —
enriching it beyond measure

Chapter One

A cold November wind blew across the training ring, tossing Amy Fleming's light-brown hair in all directions. She hardly noticed. All her attention was focused on the black mare cantering around her. Seeing Gypsy begin to slow, Amy pitched the coiled line in the direction of the mare's hindquarters.

"Go on!" she urged.

Gypsy snorted and plunged forward again, her hooves thudding into the damp sand, the muscles rippling under her shining coat. Amy watched intently, moving in the center, so that her shoulders stayed square to the horse's.

After two more circles around the ring, Gypsy's inside ear flopped slightly, the point of it seeming to fix on Amy, and then her head and neck came down toward the ground, her mouth opening and closing.

179

Amy recognized the signal. In her own language — the language of gesture and body positioning — the mare was saying that she wanted to cooperate. Dropping the rope to her side, Amy broke eye contact and turned her shoulders sideways to the horse. It was time to show that she was no threat — to invite the mare to be a team with her.

Gypsy's hooves slowed down and stopped. Amy waited. There was a long pause, and then she heard the plod of the mare's hooves as she began to move toward her. Amy held her breath. Suddenly the mare appeared at her side. Her soft muzzle reached out and touched Amy's shoulder.

It was join-up! Delight surged through Amy as she slowly turned and rubbed Gypsy's lowered forehead.

Join-up was a technique that Amy had learned from her mom, Marion. By communicating with horses in their own language, a bond based on trust and understanding could be developed between horse and human. At Heartland, the equine sanctuary that Marion had set up to cure physically and emotionally damaged horses, join-up was the first stage of treatment. Before her death five months ago, Amy's mom had used join-up on all the horses that came to Heartland.

Amy turned away from Gypsy and walked across the ring. The mare followed. Wherever Amy went, so did the horse. Stopping at last, Amy turned toward the gate where Ty, Heartland's seventeen-year-old stable hand, was watching.

"Well, what do you think?" she called to him, clipping the longline onto Gypsy's halter.

"She's doing really well," Ty replied. He swung himself over the gate and came across the ring to meet her, the wind ruffling his dark hair. "She's a different horse from when she arrived," he said, patting the black mare.

Amy nodded. Five-year-old Gypsy belonged to a dressage rider named Pamela Murray. The horse had arrived at Heartland two months ago, nervous and uncooperative and with a bad habit of launching into a series of corkscrew bucks when she got excited. Working together, Amy and Ty had treated her nervousness by using aromatherapy oils and Bach Flower Remedies and had then encouraged her to cooperate through join-up. Gradually Gypsy had relaxed and become less stubborn. She hadn't bucked now for more than three weeks, and each time Amy joined-up with her, the process seemed to occur more quickly and smoothly.

Amy looked at Gypsy nuzzling the collar of Ty's coat. "Do you think she's ready to go back to Pamela's yet?"

A frown crossed Ty's deep green eyes. "I'm not sure. I know she's been behaving, but I'm still not convinced that she won't try bucking again. And if she does and manages to throw her rider, then we'll be back to square one, because she'll have learned that bucking works."

"You're right," Amy agreed, "I feel that way, too." She smiled at him, glad that their instincts were the same. Since the road accident that had killed her mom, Amy had shared all the decisions about the horses with Ty. Apart from one awful moment when she had thought he was going to leave Heartland, they had always gotten along well together, and Amy knew that she owed him a lot. Without Ty, she doubted whether Heartland could have kept going. While he helped her treat the horses, Amy's grandpa, who owned Heartland farm, looked after the house and the land, and Lou, Amy's older sister, took care of the business side of things.

"I'll call Pamela today," Ty said, "and explain that we need to keep Gypsy a while longer." He opened the gate and they led the mare down to her stall.

As they passed the back barn, tall, blond Ben Stillman, Heartland's new stable hand, appeared, pushing a laden wheelbarrow. Seeing them, he stopped. "How did Gypsy do today?"

"Good, thanks," Amy replied.

"All six stalls in the stable block have been mucked out," Ben said efficiently. "And I've done four of the ones up here," he said, nodding toward the twelve-stall barn.

"I'll come and give you a hand with the rest," Ty said.

"Me, too," Amy said, feeling slightly guilty that Ben had been working. "I'll just sort Gypsy out."

Just then, the back door of the farmhouse opened, and Lou came out. "Breakfast's ready!" she shouted.

Amy thought about the muffins, eggs, and ham that would be waiting inside the house for them. "We can finish the stalls after breakfast," she said quickly to Ty and Ben, her stomach starting to rumble. Her grandpa always cooked a big breakfast for everyone at Heartland on Saturday mornings in the winter. "Come on," she said, leading Gypsy forward. "Let's go in."

Ty fell into step beside her, but Ben stayed by the wheelbarrow. Amy glanced over her shoulder. "Aren't you coming, Ben?"

"I think I'll pass," Ben said.

Amy stopped in surprise. "What? You're going to skip one of Grandpa's famous breakfasts?"

Ben shrugged. "There's too much to do. I'll finish up the stalls." He must have seen Amy's astonished expression. "It's no big deal. I'm really not hungry." Taking hold of the handles of the wheelbarrow, he headed up the yard toward the muck heap. "See you later," he called.

Amy looked at Ty. It wasn't the first time that week that Ben had refused to take a break.

Ty raised his eyebrows. "You heard him," he said. "We can't make him eat breakfast if he doesn't want to."

"But he's working so hard," Amy said as they walked Gypsy back to her stall.

"We can't really complain," Ty replied dryly. "Just think how he used to be."

Amy thought back to when Ben had first arrived at Heartland a month ago. He had been sent to work at the horse sanctuary by his aunt, Lisa Stillman, who owned a large Arabian stable. She had thought training at Heartland would be a great opportunity for Ben. At first, Ben had been skeptical of the alternative therapies and training methods used at Heartland. He didn't offer to help at all. However, since Ty and Amy had saved Red, Ben's beloved showjumper, from poisoning, he had started to make much more of an effort.

But he's doing almost too much, Amy thought. "It's like he's working so hard to make up for the way he was at first," she said out loud, opening Gypsy's door.

"At least it gets the work done," Ty said.

"Ty!" Amy exclaimed, but she wasn't totally surprised by his comment. When Ben hadn't been pulling his weight, Ty was the one who had to do the extra work. And even though things had improved a little since Ben had lost his attitude, Amy had a feeling it was going to be some time before Ty and Ben considered each other friends.

As Amy came out of the stall, Ty bolted the door, and the two of them headed down to the old clapboard farmhouse. They kicked off their boots and went into the warm kitchen. The smell of freshly brewed coffee and homemade muffins hung in the air.

Jack Bartlett, Amy and Lou's grandpa, was standing by the stove, stirring a pan of fluffy scrambled eggs. He looked up as they entered, his strong, weather-beaten face creasing into a smile. "Hungry?" he said.

"You bet!" Ty grinned.

"Can I do anything, Grandpa?" Amy offered.

"No, just sit down," Grandpa replied.

Lou was pouring out glasses of orange juice, her short golden-blond hair still mussed from sleep, her pale skin flushed pink from the heat of the kitchen. "Where's Ben?" she asked.

"Still out in the barn," Amy replied. "He wanted to keep working."

"We can't let him do that," Jack Bartlett said, a look of concern showing in his pale blue eyes. He took the pan off the heat. "Lou, go and call him."

"No, don't," Amy said hastily to her sister. "Besides, he said he wasn't hungry." She knew how stubborn Ben could be. Having made up his mind, nothing would change it. She had a feeling that if Lou tried to persuade him it would only cause a scene.

Lou looked at Grandpa uncertainly.

He ran a hand through his thinning gray hair. "OK," he said. "But next weekend, no excuses."

Amy picked up a plate of ham. "Is this ready to be put on the table?" she asked, changing the subject.

Grandpa nodded, spooning the pile of eggs into a

serving dish. "All right," he said. "Sit down, everyone. We're just about ready to eat."

Half an hour later, the dishes in the center of the table had been emptied and everyone's plates scraped clean. Amy put down her coffee mug and sighed contentedly. "That was great, Grandpa," she said.

"Yeah, Jack — one of the best," Ty agreed.

Grandpa smiled. "Glad you enjoyed it."

Just then, the phone rang. "I'll get it," Lou said, jumping to her feet and reaching for the handset. "Hello, Heartland, how may I help you?" Her voice suddenly became brisk and efficient.

There was a pause. Then Amy saw a look of concern cross her sister's face.

"I see," Lou said, her voice sounding serious. "Well, you are pretty far away. You don't know anyone else who could help, Mr. Phillips?"

Amy glanced at Ty. He raised his eyebrows. It sounded like whoever it was on the phone needed help with a horse.

"OK," Lou went on. "If you give me your number, I'll find out if we have room and get back to you as soon as possible."

"Who was that?" Amy asked as soon as Lou had replaced the phone.

"A guy named Ray Phillips," Lou said. "His wife died

recently, and he wants us to take on a mare that she kept at their farm over on Wilson's Peak. The mare's in foal, and he doesn't know much about horses."

"Wilson's Peak? It's fairly isolated over there," Jack commented.

Lou nodded. "That's why he wants to bring the mare over here. He doesn't think he can get her through the labor by himself."

"Of course, we'll take her," Amy said immediately. "Won't we, Ty?"

Ty nodded.

Grandpa frowned. "I thought all our stalls were full."

"Uh-uh. Charlie's being picked up by his owner this morning," Ty explained. "We were going to call the next name on the waiting list, but this mare sounds like she needs the stall more."

Amy turned to her sister again. "How pregnant is she?"

"Ten months," Lou replied.

"That means her foal is due in about four weeks," Ty calculated, looking concerned. "It's not a good idea for her to travel so late in her pregnancy."

"I guess Mr. Phillips doesn't have much choice," Lou said.

"Will you call him back, Lou?" Amy urged. "Tell him we'll take her right away."

"Sure," Lou said, picking up the phone.

"And ask him how tall she is and about her breeding. And find out her name," Amy added quickly as her sister punched in the number.

She waited impatiently while Lou spoke to Ray Phillips again.

"Well?" Amy demanded as soon as Lou hung up.

"Her name is Melody," Lou said, looking at the notes she had scribbled down. "She's seven years old, a fifteen-two liver-chestnut quarter horse. Mr. Phillips is going to bring her over this afternoon. He said he'll pay any veterinary fees and her feeding costs until we rehome her and the foal."

"I'm going to let Ben know," Amy said to Ty. She jumped to her feet, grabbed the two remaining muffins, and folded them into a napkin. "I'll take him these."

"Do you need a hand clearing the table, Jack?" Ty asked, looking around at the dirty plates.

Grandpa shook his head. "Thanks, but it's OK. You two can get back to the yard work."

"I can't wait for Melody to get here," Amy said as she and Ty pulled on their jackets and boots and hurried outside into the cold. "And for the foal to be born." Her mom had rescued several mares with young foals, but a foal had never actually been born at Heartland. "It's going to be so cool," she said. "Can you imagine how cute it will be?"

Ty glanced at her. "Just remember that it has to be re-homed as soon as it's old enough," he warned.

"I know," Amy said impatiently. It was one of the rules at Heartland — all horses were rehomed if they could be. It was only by sticking to this rule that new horses could be rescued or cured. But for now, she didn't want to think about that — she wanted to enjoy the thought of a foal cantering around the paddocks in the spring sunshine.

Ty saw her expression. "Oh, no, you're going to fall in love with it, aren't you?" he groaned.

Amy raised her eyebrows. "And you're not?"

"Me? Never!" Ty said.

Amy grinned. She knew Ty too well to believe him. He would adore a newborn foal as much as she would — if not more!

Just then, one of the stall doors opened in the front stable block and Ben came out. "I'm going to tell him the news," Amy told Ty.

She hurried over. "Hi!" she called, holding out the muffins. "I brought you these."

Ben unfolded the napkin. "Thanks," he said gratefully.

"We have some news." Amy eagerly told him about Melody. "She's coming after lunch. We can put her in Charlie's stall."

"Sure," Ben said, nodding. "It'll need to be cleaned and disinfected before Melody goes into it. We'll have to attach the water bucket to the wall so that she doesn't knock it over when she goes into labor. And after the foal comes we should remove the haynet — just to make sure the foal doesn't get caught in it." He stuffed the muffins in his pocket and set off up the yard.

"How do you know all this stuff?" Amy asked in surprise as she walked alongside him.

Ben shrugged his broad shoulders. "There were always foals being born at my aunt's place."

Amy thought about Lisa Stillman's stable with its modern barns and army of stable hands. Ben's mom had sent him to live there when he was twelve after she had gone through a difficult divorce with his father.

They reached the back barn. "I'll muck out the stall," Ben said.

Amy took Charlie's halter off the hook on his wall. "OK, I'll brush him so he's ready for his owner," she said, patting the palomino, who was looking out over the door. She knew she'd miss him when he returned home. He had been sent to Heartland to have his fear of trailers cured. Horses like Charlie and Gypsy, whose owners paid good money for them to be cured, made it possible for Heartland to rescue horses that needed help and had nowhere else to go.

Tying Charlie up in the aisle, Amy began to groom him. "Are you still planning to take Red to that show at the fairgrounds in two weeks?" Amy asked Ben as he began to fork the straw from Charlie's bed into the wheelbarrow.

"I'm hoping to," Ben replied.

He had been practicing hard for the show, as it would be Red's first attempt at the High Prelim class. Red was only six years old, but he was very talented, and Amy knew that Ben dreamed of him one day becoming a Grand Prix showjumper.

"Are you going to be able to come and watch?" Ben asked her. "The class is in the afternoon. You can come in the trailer with me if you want."

"I'd love to," Amy said eagerly. Then she thought about her best friend, Soraya Martin. "I bet Soraya would like to tag along, too, if there's room."

"Sure, that would be great." Ben nodded.

Amy smiled to herself. Soraya thought that Ben was totally cute, and she'd definitely welcome the invitation. "How about your mom?" Amy asked, knowing that Ben's mom had originally planned to attend the show but had then called to say she couldn't make it. "She's still not coming?"

Glancing into the stall, she saw Ben's face tighten. "We haven't spoken since she canceled," he said.

Amy frowned. "How come?"

"Why should I call her?" Ben replied, scowling. "It's just a waste of time. She doesn't care what's going on with me."

"Ben!" Amy exclaimed. "She's your mom. Of course she does."

"You're wrong. All my mom's concerned about is winning her next case," Ben said, his voice suddenly bitter. "She's always been the same. When I was living at Fairfield, she was always too busy working to visit me. She's a lawyer first, a mom second."

"What? She never went to see you?" Amy said, shocked.

"Oh, at first she did," Ben said. "But then she came less and less." He shook his head. "I told you — she's too busy to care."

Amy frowned. She couldn't believe it. Nothing Ben's aunt had told them about his past had ever suggested that his mom was more interested in her career than she was in him. "It can't be that bad," she protested.

Ben stared at her for a long time. "How would you know what it's like, Amy? You couldn't possibly understand." Swinging around, he began forking through the straw with short, sharp movements.

Amy stared at his tense back for a moment. Then she turned away and began to brush out Charlie's tail. *How dare he say I don't understand,* she thought angrily. *At least his mom's still around. And she hasn't abandoned him — not entirely. Not like Daddy did.* Just thinking about her father made Amy upset. An international showjumper, he had been in a terrible accident on his horse twelve years ago that had ended his competitive career. Unable to cope, he had left Amy's mom, who brought up Amy and Lou on her own. They hadn't seen or heard from him since. Amy had been just three years old when he had left.

But that was forgetting the letter from England that she and Lou had found after their mom had died. It had been from their father. He had sent it five years ago, begging for a reconciliation. Amy didn't know if her mom had replied, but nothing had ever come of the correspondence.

Just then, Ben came out of the stall. "Look," he said, awkwardly shifting from foot to foot. "I'm sorry. I had no right to go off on you like that. I wasn't thinking about what I was saying."

Amy felt her frustration subside as she saw the genuine apology in his eyes. "Don't worry about it," she said. "Hey, listen — do you want to go for a ride at lunch?" she asked, suddenly eager to make up. "Sundance could use the exercise. We can make sure we're back by two o'clock, when Melody's due to arrive."

"OK," Ben said gratefully. "Sounds good to me."

🕸

It was windy out on the trails, but neither Sundance nor Red seemed to mind. They cantered along the tracks that led across Teak's Hill, the wooded slope that rose steeply behind Heartland. Amy was relieved that Ben seemed to have forgotten about the heated exchange they'd had that morning. He talked easily about the show and about his plans for Red. When he was in a mood like this, he was a lot of fun to be around, Amy thought. She just wished she could get him to lighten up more often.

They got back to Heartland just before two o'clock. "Hey, Scott's here," Amy said, seeing the local equine vet's battered Jeep parked in the driveway.

There was no sign of Scott around the barns, so Amy put Sundance away and went down to the house. She found Scott in the kitchen, talking to Lou.

"Hey, Amy," he said. "Lou called me and told me about the mare that's coming. I thought it might be a good idea to check her over when she arrives." He grinned at Lou. "Anyway, it was a great excuse to stop by."

Lou blushed and moved quickly to the sink.

Seeing her practical sister become flustered by Scott's comment, Amy smiled to herself. Lou and Scott had recently started dating.

"I think Melody's here," Lou announced, looking out the kitchen window. "I'll go get Grandpa. He's upstairs."

Amy glanced out the window to see an old wooden trailer pulling up beside Scott's Jeep. She hurried outside.

A tall man in his sixties, almost bald with stooped shoulders, was getting out of the pickup.

Amy went over. "Hi," she said. "I'm Amy Fleming."

"Ray Phillips," the man said slowly. "I've brought the mare — Melody."

He looked around in a vague manner, his eyes showing an absent look as if part of him were elsewhere.

Just then Grandpa came out of the house with Lou and Scott.

"This is Mr. Phillips," Amy said to Grandpa.

Grandpa shook hands and quickly introduced the other two.

"Thank you for agreeing to take Melody," Ray Phillips said. "I don't know what I'd have done if you'd said no. Things have been a bit of a strain." He looked almost helplessly at Jack. "Are you married, Mr. Bartlett?"

Amy saw a muscle leap in Grandpa's jaw in response to the abrupt question. "My wife died of cancer more than twenty years ago," he replied.

Ray Phillips shook his head. "I'm sorry."

"It was a long time ago," Grandpa said quietly, "and it gets easier."

Ray Phillips looked at the ground, seemingly in thought.

After a moment, Lou cleared her throat. "I guess we should get Melody out," she said, breaking the silence.

"Sandy — my wife — loved her so much," Mr. Phillips said. He sighed and glanced up. "Somehow I feel I'm betraying her by bringing Melody here."

"You're doing the right thing and what your wife would have wanted," Lou said gently. "We'll take good care of her, Mr. Phillips."

They were interrupted by the sound of restless hooves against the side of the trailer.

Scott went toward the ramp. "Did she travel OK?" he asked.

"She kicked around a bit," Ray Phillips replied. "She's always been nervous, but more so since she's been in foal. Sandy and I lived on our own, and Melody's only ever been used to being at our farm."

"Sure," Scott said reassuringly. He started to undo the bolts on the ramp. "OK, let's get her out."

Ty and Ben headed over from the barn. "Here, I'll give you a hand," Ty offered, hurrying to help Scott.

"Do you want me to lead her out for you?" Amy asked Mr. Phillips.

He hesitated before replying. "I don't know. It might be best if I do. I'm not sure how she'll react to a stranger going in there with her." He stepped into the box through the side door. There was a startled snort and the sound of hooves shying to one side. "Steady now," Amy heard Mr. Phillips say in a nervous voice.

Amy went to the door and glanced in cautiously. She

could just make out a high chestnut head with wide, startled eyes and pricked ears.

"It's OK," she murmured instinctively, stepping closer.

The frightened horse didn't seem to hear her. She was trembling.

"OK, we're bringing the ramp down," Scott called. "Just bring her out nice and steady, Mr. Phillips."

Suddenly Melody plunged backward. Ray Phillips gave a startled cry, and the rope slipped out of his hands.

"Watch out!" Amy cried in alarm. "She's loose!"

Dropping the ramp, Scott and Ty leaped out of the way just in time to avoid being trampled as the horse came shooting backward out of the trailer. The surface of the ramp was old and worn, and suddenly one of Melody's hind hooves slipped. With a startled whinny, she swung around. Catching sight of the whites of her frightened eyes, Amy lunged at the dangling lead rope, but she wasn't quick enough. The mare swerved and cantered straight toward Ben, her pregnant stomach swinging.

"Grab her, Ben!" Scott shouted.

Ben made a dive for the rope, but the mare shied out of his reach and he fell to the ground, his fingers grasping thin air.

With a terrified snort, Melody spun away from him. Already Ty was running to block off the driveway, but the mare wasn't heading for the drive. She was cantering in a blind panic straight toward the nearby paddock fence.

Amy saw her stride lengthen and suddenly realized that Melody was going to try to jump the fence. "No!" she gasped in horror. The mare was too heavily pregnant — she wouldn't make it!

Amy tried to run to cut her off but was already too late. At that moment, Melody gathered herself and took off.

For a fleeting second, Amy thought Melody was going to clear the fence, but the weight of her pregnant body dragged her down. Failing to make the height, she slammed into the top bar. It broke with a loud crack.

With a horrifying thud, Melody crashed awkwardly to the ground.

Amy ran harder, and as she closed in on the mare, her fears were confirmed. All she could see was the jagged end of the broken fence rail piercing deep into the horse's side.

Chapter Two

Flinging herself down on the grass, Amy frantically checked the mare for signs of life. Relief washed over her as she realized Melody was breathing hoarsely. Her eyes were open.

"Quick!" Amy cried out, seeing the others approaching. She stroked Melody's warm, damp neck. "It's OK, girl," she murmured, her heart hammering at the sight of the broken piece of wood sticking out of her side. "You're going to be just fine." She wished with all her heart that she could believe her own words.

Melody lifted her head and began to move her legs. "Stay still, girl," Amy said, desperately worried that if the mare tried to get up she might do herself more damage. But Melody had been disturbed by the sound of running footsteps, and she struggled unsteadily to her feet, her ears flicking nervously. Amy quickly took hold of the lead rope just as the others reached them.

"Oh, my God!" Ray Phillips exclaimed. "What happened? Look at her side!" He moved toward Melody, but Ty grabbed his arm.

"Please, it's best if you stay back, sir," he said quickly.

"She might panic if there are too many people around her," Scott explained as he opened his veterinary bag and knelt down by the mare. "Hold her still, Amy," he said quietly. "I'm going to sedate her so we can see exactly what the damage is."

Amy nodded as Scott filled a syringe from a bottle and glanced over his shoulder. "I'll need some hot water."

"I'll get it," Ben offered immediately.

"How bad is it?" Lou asked, sounding close to tears.

"I don't know yet," Scott replied, beginning to administer the injection. He looked around. "Ty, can you give Amy a hand holding Melody? I'm sedating her, but she's still shaky and she might well go down again."

Ty quickly joined Amy at Melody's head. Their gazes met for a moment. "It'll be all right," he said to her in a quiet voice.

Amy bit her lower lip, trying to hold back her tears. She couldn't cry now. She had to be strong for Melody's sake. She stroked the mare's trembling neck and swallowed hard.

As the drug started to take effect, Melody's head hung down and her eyes began to look glazed, the lids drooping. Her legs trembled, and suddenly she sank to her knees and her hindquarters thudded onto the grass. Scott pushed her over onto her good side and then crouched to examine the wound. Rivulets of blood were running over the taut skin of her belly from where the wood had pierced her side.

Amy felt sick as she thought about the foal. Was it hurt? But she knew she couldn't ask. Right now, the foal would be the last thing on Scott's mind; he would be concentrating on saving Melody. Without her, the foal stood no chance at this premature stage.

As Scott's experienced hands explored the gash, Amy glanced around at the others. The anxiety she felt was reflected in their faces. Grandpa had his arm tightly around Lou's shoulder, and Ray Phillip's face was ashen with shock.

Scott continued to examine the wound, gently feeling around the sharp splintered wood before running his hand quickly over her legs. "She's been lucky," he said, looking up at last, relief in his eyes. "She doesn't seem to have broken any bones, and the rail just missed her abdominal cavity. If that had been pierced it's unlikely we could have saved her. But I think I'll be able to patch this up. As long as her blood loss is minimal, her chances are good."

"So, she'll be OK?" Amy said, her hopes suddenly leaping.

Scott shook his head. "I can't say at this point. It's too early to tell. There's a possibility she'll pull through, but then she may still go into shock or into labor, and if the foal's born now it would have only the slimmest chance of survival." Before Amy could ask anything else, he opened his bag again and began to fire out rapid instructions. "Ty, I want you to monitor her pulse. Amy, stay by her head. Let me know if she shows signs of getting up, and keep checking her gums. If they get pale, let me know immediately — it could mean that she's going into shock." He looked around and saw that Ben had come back with the hot water. "Ben, can you watch her hind-quarters, please? I need to know immediately if she goes into labor."

There was no time for questions. Everyone did as Scott had instructed. Amy crouched by Melody's head, her trembling hands gently smoothing and stroking the mare's face and cheeks. "Good girl," she murmured. "You're going to be just fine."

"OK," Scott said. "If everyone's ready, I'm going to start."

❧

It was a nerve-racking time, sitting by Melody's head while Scott used a local anesthetic in the mare's side. He gently eased the splintered wood out and then started cleaning the wound and removing the damaged tissue. Amy alternated between checking Melody's gums and massaging her ears. Her fingers worked in small circles as she concentrated on soothing the mare and keeping her still so that Scott could get on with his work unhindered. She tried not to look at the blood-soaked timber lying to one side. She tried not to think about Scott's earlier warning regarding blood loss. As Scott began to stitch up the injury, Amy glanced at Ty and Ben, dreading that at any moment one of them would say that something was wrong. Their faces were tense, but neither of them spoke.

At long last, Scott clipped the final suture and put down his scissors. "We're done," he announced. "I'll just give her a shot of antibiotics and a tetanus injection and then that's it. She can get back on her feet when she's ready. But it could take a while for the sedative to wear off."

Seeing him start to clear his things away, Lou, Grandpa, and Ray Phillips came over from the fence. Their faces were full of concern.

"Is Melody going to pull through?" Ray Phillips asked immediately.

Scott straightened up. "I hope so," he replied, wiping a hand across his forehead. "The wound's deep but shouldn't be life-threatening. She'll need very careful monitoring for the next week — antibiotic injections for at least two days and then powders in her food for another few days. Providing she doesn't go into shock, I think we can say she's had a lucky escape."

Amy asked the question that she couldn't hold back any longer. "What about the foal?"

"There's still a very real danger that Melody might go into labor at any time," Scott replied. "And like I said, if it does happen this early, the foal doesn't have a good chance of pulling through."

"But what about the fall? What if the foal was hurt?" Amy said anxiously.

Scott frowned. "It's impossible to know if the foal is OK, but it should have been well cushioned by the amniotic fluid and the walls of the uterus. We could scan Melody's belly to investigate, but I don't want to risk upsetting her. The calmer we can keep her, the better for both of them. Just keep a very careful eye on her. If she seems in discomfort or starts sweating or pacing around her stall, that might indicate the first stages of labor." Scott looked at the mare and shook his head. "The longer she can hang on to her foal, the better its chances of survival."

Just then, Melody lifted her head and neck. "OK, stand back, everyone," Scott said. "It looks like she's ready to get up."

"Should I unclip her lead rope?" Amy asked as Melody rolled shakily onto her stomach.

"No, you should stay with her," Scott replied as he and the others moved back. "Someone has to hold on to her in case she tries to get away. You've been talking to her for the last half hour — she's probably most comfortable with you."

Melody stretched out her front legs and, with a grunt of effort, struggled to her feet. She looked dazed and shaken. Seeing Amy, she snorted warily. Amy held out her hand. "Hey there, girl," she said.

Melody drew back, her ears flattening.

Remembering what her mom had taught her, Amy turned her shoulders sideways to the mare and made no attempt to approach her. Digging in her pocket she found a couple of mints. Careful not to alarm Melody by making direct eye contact, Amy offered one on the palm of her hand.

She waited. No one else made a sound.

With a cautious snort, Melody took a step toward Amy.

There was a pause, and then Amy felt the long whiskers on Melody's muzzle tickle her hand for an instant as the mare snatched the mint and backed off again. Amy still didn't move. Listening to the mare crunching the mint, Amy took the remaining one out of her pocket. She knew it was vitally important that Melody make the choice to approach her. If she walked up to the horse she would be seen as a predator, and the mare might try to escape.

Amy took a step away and held out the last mint. Holding her breath, she listened and waited and then heard the faint swish of Melody's hooves as she walked toward Amy and took it from her hand. This time she did not move away. In two crunches the mint was gone and Melody stepped closer to Amy, her soft muzzle exploring the pockets of Amy's jacket.

Slowly Amy turned and gently stroked the mare's forehead. Melody looked at her with wary dark eyes, but she accepted the caress and didn't move away. Amy heaved a sigh of relief. The first battle in gaining the mare's trust had been won.

Melody was soon settled in Charlie's old stall. Although she seemed to be just about prepared to accept Amy, she was still nervous of everyone else.

"I'm sure she'll come around in time," Scott said as he and the others looked over the stall door. "I have to go now — but make sure you call me if you have any concerns. I'll drop by tomorrow morning to check her over and give her some more antibiotics. Make sure her bed is well cushioned. And bank up the straw around the edges — it'll protect her from rolling into the walls."

"We will," Amy promised.

"I can't believe all this is happening," Mr. Phillips said suddenly. Amy turned to look at him and could see that he was overcome with guilt. "I should never have tried to bring her over here in her condition," he continued. "It's all my fault. I should have just kept her at home and managed as best I could."

"You can't blame yourself," Scott said. "You did the right thing. In another month there could be snow, and you might have found yourself with a foaling emergency and no way for a vet to get out to you. She'll have the very best care here."

"But what if the foal's injured — dead even?" Ray Phillips said, shaking his head. "Sandy would be so upset, seeing Melody like this. I've let her down."

"No, you haven't," Lou said quickly. "Scott's right, Mr. Phillips, you did what you thought was best for Melody. I'm sure your wife would understand. You couldn't have known that this would happen."

"We'll look after her really well," Amy said to him.

Ray Phillips looked at them. "You've all been very kind. Thank you." He glanced into the stall. "You will let me know how's she's doing, won't you?"

"Of course," Lou said. "We'll call you regularly with news of her progress."

"And maybe when the foal's born you could come and visit," Grandpa suggested, stepping forward.

Ray Phillips nodded and then swallowed. "If everything's OK, of course," he said in a low voice.

"It will be," Amy said, wanting desperately to believe it.

He took one last look at Melody. "'Bye, girl," he said, and then with the weight of guilt still etched into the lines of his face, he turned and walked slowly away. Grandpa and Lou followed.

"Poor guy," Scott said quietly.

Looking at the old man's bowed shoulders as he trudged toward his pickup, Amy nodded. What a horrible thing to have happened.

"I'll call tonight to see how she's doing," Scott said, glancing in at the mare. "But if you have any questions, call me right away."

"We will," Ty said. He walked down the yard with Scott, leaving Amy alone with Melody.

The mare stood at the back of her stall. Her chestnut coat was dull, and her frame looked thin compared to her bloated belly. She looked like she could use a good grooming and some supplements in her grain. She needed to be healthy to get through the last weeks of her pregnancy.

"And you need to learn to be less nervous," Amy said to her. "There's nothing to be scared of here."

Now that the others had left the doorway, Melody stepped cautiously forward. Her long forelock fell down over her broad, pretty face. She stretched her nose out toward Amy and blew softly down her nostrils.

Amy smiled and blew back, knowing that it was the mare's way of saying she wanted to be friends. Then, sliding the bolt on the door, she slipped quietly into the warm stall and waited for Melody to come right up to her. Amy stroked the mare's rough neck and smoothed her tangled forelock with her fingers. At first the mare was cautious, her muscles tense, but as Amy's fingers moved in small, light circles across her face and neck, she slowly began to relax.

Very gently, Amy moved so that she could place her hand on the taut, stretched skin of Melody's belly. She glanced at Melody's face, but the mare showed no sign of objecting so Amy let her hand rest there.

Somewhere, underneath her fingers, she knew, there was a foal. She shut her eyes and tried to imagine it. What would it be like? Was it OK? Or had it been injured by the accident? Was it still alive? She felt Melody's side rise and fall with every breath. *Be all right,* she urged, *please, please be all right.*

❧

Although Amy wanted to stay with Melody all afternoon, she knew that the other horses needed attention, too, and after spending another half hour with the mare, she went outside and began to help Ben and Ty with the chores, stopping every now and then to check on Melody.

"We should probably try to protect the wound. I know she's on antibiotics, but it would be good to apply a salve to the outside of the cut as well," Ty said, joining Amy at Melody's door before feed time. "We'll have to be careful about what herbs we use because of her pregnancy, but garlic and kelp should both be safe. What do you think?"

Amy nodded. She knew that putting kelp in her feed would help improve the mare's skin and coat and that a garlic ointment should also help combat any infection that might come from her wound. At Heartland, they often treated the horses with herbs and other natural remedies. "Good idea. We could also add some Rescue Remedy to her water."

"Yeah," Ty agreed. "That should help her settle down and cope with the stress of being in a new place." He looked thoughtfully at the mare. "It might be better if you handle her over the next few days, Amy. She seems to have accepted you. While she's still recovering from the accident it would be good if she didn't have to deal with too many new people."

"I agree," Amy replied. She looked at the chestnut mare, happy to take sole charge of Melody for as long as necessary.

❧

After all the other horses had been fed and bedded down for the night and Ty and Ben had left, Amy went back to Melody's stall and began to gently groom her with a soft body brush. After an hour, the mare's coat was smoother and her mane and tail finally untangled, but Amy was still reluctant to leave her. What if something happened in the night? She sat down on an upturned bucket and watched the mare pulling peacefully at the pile of hay on the floor.

At eight o'clock, Grandpa came up to the stall. "Are you going to come in, honey?" he said, his hands buried deep in the pockets of his winter jacket. "It's getting late."

Amy looked around. "But what if she goes into labor?"

Grandpa's eyes swept over the mare. "She's not showing any signs of it." He took in Amy's reluctant face. "You can't sleep here every night until she has her foal," he said gently. "Leave her now, Amy. You can always come and check on her before you go to bed."

Knowing he was right, Amy stood up and stretched her stiff muscles. "See you later, girl," she said softly. Fastening the stall door, she followed her grandpa down to the farmhouse.

"Soraya called," he said as they reached the back door. "I told her you'd call her back."

"Thanks," Amy said, pulling off her boots. She had left a message on her best friend's answering machine that morning, telling her that a new horse was arriving. "Did you tell her about Melody's accident?"

"Only briefly," Jack replied. "I said you'd fill her in on all the details."

Going into the kitchen, Amy picked up the phone and headed up the stairs to her bedroom. "Don't be long,"

Jack called after her. "Supper will be ready in ten minutes."

"OK," Amy called back, starting to dial the number. She knew Soraya would be curious to know all about Melody and what had happened.

She was right. Soraya was bursting with questions. "What happened?" she demanded, as soon as she realized it was Amy. "Is the mare OK? Your grandpa said Scott was there and that he stitched her up. What about the foal?"

Amy sat cross-legged on her bed and explained everything.

"Scott thinks she's going to pull through, but she might still go into labor early, and we don't know if the foal's injured or not."

"Can I come and see her?" Soraya asked.

"Sure," Amy said. "Why don't you come over in the morning?"

"Great!" Soraya said. There was a tiny pause. "Will, er, Ben be around?" she said, her voice suddenly sounding deceptively casual.

Amy grinned. "Why?" she teased. "Aren't you coming over if he's not?"

"Of course I am!" Soraya exclaimed defensively. "I want to see Melody. It's just . . . well . . ."

"Relax," Amy broke in, laughing. "He'll be here. He already had his day off this week, and besides, even on his days off he seems to be here all the time. He's working really hard." She remembered about the High Prelim class. "Oh yeah, Ben's still taking Red to that show in two weeks, and he said we could both go with him to watch. But only if you want to, of course," she added.

"Want to?" Soraya yelled incredulously. "Try and stop me!"

Just then, Grandpa called up the stairs. "Amy! Dinner's ready!"

"I've got to go," Amy said to Soraya.

"I'll be over around ten tomorrow," her friend promised.

"OK," Amy said. "See you then!"

Chapter Three

༄

Amy had trouble sleeping that night. She had checked on Melody before she went to bed and the mare had been quiet, but she still couldn't help worrying. Her dreams were full of images of the mare lying on the grass, the bar of wood sticking out of her side.

Amy woke early and glanced at her alarm clock. *Five-thirty.* It was still dark outside, but she felt wide awake. Immediately, the events of the day before flashed in her head. She anxiously threw back the covers.

Her jeans and sweater were lying on the floor where she had left them the night before. Pulling them on, she crept down the quiet stairs and went into the kitchen. She *had* to see how Melody was. Taking the flashlight from the pine dresser, she went outside.

The air was frosty, but she hardly noticed as she ran

up the dark yard. She pulled back the barn doors and went inside. Hearing the noise, several of the other horses came to their stall doors in surprise. Amy hurried past them, her heart beating fast when she reached Melody's stall.

She shone the light over the door. Melody was dozing on her feet. However, as the light flashed past her head, Melody's eyes shot open and she started backward in alarm. Amy hastily angled the flashlight beam down to the floor.

"Easy, girl," she whispered, relief rushing through her as she realized Melody was OK. "It's only me."

She switched off the flashlight. Plunged into sudden blackness, it was a moment before her eyes started to adjust. Sliding back the bolts on Melody's door, Amy entered the warm stall. She could just make out the mare's shadowy outline.

"There's no need to be frightened," she said softly. She waited a moment and then heard the straw rustle as Melody turned and stepped cautiously toward her. Amy held out her hand and felt the mare's warm breath on her palm. With a quiet snort, the horse lifted her muzzle and blew gently, her breath flickering like soft fingertips across Amy's face.

For a long moment they stood there together cocooned in the darkness, Amy gently stroking the mare and the mare breathing in Amy's scent. Then, with a small sigh, Melody dropped her muzzle onto Amy's shoulder and let it rest there. It was the gesture of trust that Amy had been hoping for. She gently massaged the mare's neck with small clockwise circles.

"Poor girl," she whispered, feeling the weight of the horse's muzzle become heavier as she relaxed. "Your life's changed a lot recently, hasn't it? I guess you can't understand where your owner's gone or why you've been brought to this new place. But I'll look after you, I promise, and one day we'll find someone to love you just like Mrs. Phillips used to."

She leaned her face against the mare's cheek. It would be so much easier if horses could understand human language. The only way that she could show Melody what she meant was to treat her with respect and kindness and never do anything to break the trust the mare had placed in her.

As the darkness outside slowly gave way to dawn, Amy stayed with Melody, massaging first her neck and shoulders and then her back, hindquarters, and legs. Gradually she felt the tension in the mare's muscles begin to seep away.

Engrossed in her work, the sound of the barn doors being pulled back at seven o'clock and the electric lights being switched on made her jump in surprise.

"Amy!" Ty said, seeing her look out over the stall door. "What are you doing?"

"I came to see Melody," Amy explained, yawning suddenly. "I didn't sleep too well last night."

Ty nodded understandingly and approached the stall. "How is she?"

"She seems fine," Amy said. "There's no sign of her going into labor. Her side's swollen and bruised, but I guess that's not surprising."

Ty rested his arms on top of the half-door. Melody, still not trusting anyone apart from Amy, shied to the back of the stall.

"It's all right, girl, Ty's not going to hurt you," Amy said, but the horse still looked wary.

Ty's eyes swept over her wound. "We could use some comfrey ointment. It should help reduce the bruising and speed up the healing process."

Amy nodded. "What do you think we should do about exercising her? We can't turn her out in the field. She might rip out her stitches if she rolls."

"We'll see what Scott says when he calls," Ty said.

They had just finished the feeding when Scott arrived. Amy held Melody while he examined her side. The mare flinched as the vet approached, but with Amy stroking and soothing her, she let Scott check her over. After the first few minutes, Amy felt her relax slightly.

"The wound's healing OK," Scott said as he finished

his examination, having given Melody a shot of antibiotics. "Just keep it clean, and make sure she doesn't rip
her stitches."

"So how should we exercise her?" Amy asked, stroking
Melody's dark muzzle.

"Walk her around on a lead rope," Scott replied, packing up his bag. "She needs to move her legs or they'll fill
up with fluid, but don't turn her out. You might also
want to get a foaling kit ready in a clean bucket with a
lid."

"What goes in it?" Amy asked.

"Iodine, wound powder, cotton wool, a tail bandage, a
towel, and a feeding bottle," Scott replied, going out of
the stall. "I'll bring you some milk replacer tomorrow as
well in case anything happens during the birth and the
foal needs to be hand-fed. And it's probably a good idea
to keep a bale of fresh straw and a pitchfork by her stall
so you've got them on hand if she goes into labor unexpectedly."

"I'll get all that together," Amy said tentatively, following him out.

Scott saw the worry on her face. "She's doing fine,
Amy," he said, gently. "It could have been a lot worse."

Amy looked into his reassuring eyes. "I just want her
and the foal to be all right," she said, swallowing.

Scott gave her a pat on her shoulder. "We all want
that," he said, looking at Melody still standing at the

back of her stall, "but right now, there's nothing more we can do."

❧

As Scott got into his Jeep to leave, Soraya's mom's car came up the drive and Amy ran to meet her friend.

"How's Melody?" Soraya asked, jumping out of the car.

"She's doing OK," Amy replied. "Getting better, Scott thinks." They both waved as the vet drove off.

"See you later, honey," Mrs. Martin, Soraya's mom, said, poking her head out of the car window. "I'll pick you up around four o'clock."

" 'Bye, Mom!" Soraya called. She and Amy walked up the yard. "So where is she? Which stall is she in?"

"She's in the back barn," Amy said. "She's a bit nervous around people, though."

Just then, Ben came out of Jake's stall in the front stable block. "Hi, Soraya," he called. "Amy says you might come to watch me and Red at the show."

"Yeah," Soraya said, nodding eagerly. "If you're sure you don't mind."

"It'll be good to have the support," Ben said.

Soraya beamed.

"How about we all go out for a ride later?" Amy suggested, eager to get Soraya and Ben together as much as possible.

"That would be great!" Soraya exclaimed.

Ben nodded, too.

"We should see if Ty wants to come as well," Amy said to Soraya.

Ty was mucking out a stall in the back barn. "I'll pass," he said when Amy suggested a trail ride. "I'll stay and work Dancer in the ring."

"Are you sure?" Amy said, not wanting him to think they were all deserting him.

Ty nodded. "Yeah. Anyway, one of us should stay and keep an eye on Melody."

"Is this Melody?" Soraya asked, looking over a stall door.

"Yes, that's her." Amy said as she joined her friend. The chestnut mare had backed off from Soraya, but she pricked her ears as Amy let herself into the stall.

"She's lovely," Soraya said.

Melody snuffled at Amy's pockets. "I don't have anything for you," Amy told her.

"Here," Soraya offered, holding out some apple slices she had brought.

Amy took two slices and fed them to the mare, who greedily gobbled them up. "See if she'll take one from you," Amy suggested to Soraya. "She's got to start getting used to other people."

Soraya held out an apple. Melody stretched her head

forward hesitantly. "It's OK," Soraya murmured. "I won't hurt you."

The mare stepped forward and quickly took the treat. Then she stepped back, crunching the fruit. Soraya offered her another. This time, Melody took a more confident step forward. She ate the slice and then nudged Soraya's hand for more.

"Come on, let's leave her alone now," Amy said, pleased that the mare was showing signs of accepting Soraya. "We'll come back later and take her for a walk together."

They moved quietly out of the stall.

"Scott said to get a foaling kit ready," Amy said. "Will you give me a hand getting stuff together?"

"Sure," Soraya replied. "What do we need?"

Amy explained as they went down to the tack room to collect the equipment that Scott had suggested.

"Let's keep it all together in a bucket with a lid," Amy said, "so everything stays clean."

Just then, the phone rang in the house.

"I'll get that," Amy said, knowing her grandpa had gone out shopping. She ran down the yard, but by the time she had reached the kitchen Lou had already picked up the receiver.

"It's Judy Stillman, Ben's mom," Lou said as Amy opened the kitchen door. "Can you get him for me?"

Amy went outside. "Ben!" she yelled. "Phone!"

Ben came down the yard. "Who is it?" he asked.

"Your mom," Amy replied.

Ben stopped dead. "Can you tell her I'm not here?"

Amy frowned in surprise. "But she wants to talk with you."

"Well, I don't want to talk with her," Ben said. He turned abruptly and headed back up the yard.

Amy ran after him. "Ben! Wait up! You shouldn't just ignore your mom like this."

"Watch me," Ben said, going into Red's stall and sliding the door shut in Amy's face.

Amy stopped. What could she do? She couldn't drag Ben to the phone and make him speak to his mom. She hesitated and then headed back to the house. Lou had left the receiver on the table and was busily typing away at her laptop. "Where's Ben?" she said, looking up.

Amy shook her head and picked up the phone.

"Um, hi, Mrs. Stillman," she said. "It's Amy here. Ben can't, er, come to the phone right now. He's busy."

"What you're trying to say is that he's avoiding me," Judy Stillman said astutely.

"No, it's not that. He's just, um, just —" Amy stuttered uncertainly.

"It's OK," Ben's mom said quietly. "You don't have to make excuses for him. I've been leaving messages on his answering machine all week and he hasn't called me back." She paused. "I don't suppose *you* know what's going on, do you, Amy?"

Amy felt awkward. She didn't want to interfere. "Well, I think he was kind of looking forward to seeing you at the show," she admitted.

"That horse show!" Judy Stillman sounded surprised. "I didn't realize it meant that much to him. He acts like I'd be in the way if I were there."

"Well, he's probably just nervous. It's a big show for him." Amy said. "It's Red's first time competing at High Prelim level."

"Well, thanks for letting me know," Mrs. Stillman said. "Look, would you please ask him to call me soon?"

"No problem," Amy said. She replaced the phone in its cradle.

"What was that about?" Lou asked. "Why didn't Ben take the call?"

Before Amy could answer, the back door opened and Grandpa walked in with a box of groceries. "Hi, there," he said. Putting the box down, he reached into his jacket. "There's some mail for you," he said to Lou, taking out a handful of envelopes from his pocket. "There's one from England."

"From England!" The words burst from Lou, distracting her from the topic of Ben.

Amy looked at her sister in surprise.

Grandpa also noticed Lou's reaction. "Were you expecting something in particular?" he asked.

"Yes." Lou's cheeks flushed as she saw their curious glances. "But . . . but it's nothing important," she added quickly.

Despite her words, when Grandpa held the letter out, she grabbed it quickly, her eyes scanning the writing on the front. Flipping it over, she read the sender's address on the back. "Oh," she said, her face falling suddenly.

"Not what you were expecting?" Jack inquired.

Lou shook her head. "It's from Joanna, a friend of mine from boarding school." Looking up, she seemed to make an effort to smile. "I haven't heard from her for ages. What a nice surprise."

Amy frowned. Try as she might to hide it, Lou was obviously disappointed. What *had* she been expecting?

She couldn't forget her sister's expression, and going back to the tack room she told Soraya about it. "As soon as she heard there was a letter from England, she acted kind of strange," she said. "Like she thought it was something important."

"Like what?" Soraya asked.

"I don't know," Amy said. Lou had lots of friends in England. After their father had left, their mom had decided to return to Virginia to live with Jack at her childhood home. She had taken Amy with her, but Lou, age eleven, had begged to be allowed to stay on at her English boarding school. "It didn't seem like it was just a letter she was expecting from a friend," Amy said. "It seemed like she was *really* waiting for something to arrive."

"Maybe she's applied for a job over in England," Soraya suggested.

"She couldn't have!" Amy said. "She's decided to stay here."

Before their mom's death, Lou had been working in Manhattan, and although for a while it had looked as if she was going to return to her city life, she had eventually changed her mind and announced that she would stay at Heartland.

Soraya nodded. "Yeah. After all, she'd have told you if she was thinking of leaving. And anyway, things seem to be going really well with her and Scott. It's probably something else."

Amy hoped Soraya was right. After spending most of her childhood apart from Lou, she hated the thought of her sister going to live abroad just as they were beginning to really get to know each other. She nodded. "But what could it be?"

Soraya shrugged. "Why don't you ask her?"

Amy looked doubtful. She recalled the way that Lou

had reacted when Grandpa had asked her about the letter. It was apparent that she had a secret and she wasn't about to tell anyone what it was.

Soraya saw the concern on Amy's face. "Look," she said, practically. "If it's really important you'll find out sooner or later. There's no point worrying about it now."

Amy sighed. She guessed Soraya was right, but she hated the thought of Lou keeping secrets. After everything that had happened over the past six months, she just wanted life to be uncomplicated for a while.

"Come on," her friend said, linking arms with her. "Let's go see Melody again and take her for that walk."

Chapter Four

On the way to Melody's stall, Amy saw Ben going into the feed room with a pile of empty haynets. She remembered the message from his mother.

"Ben! Your mom asked if you'd give her a call back," she told him.

Ben nodded curtly and walked on.

Amy hesitated for a second and then followed. After her conversation with Judy Stillman, she was convinced that Ben's mom really wasn't as bad as he made her out to be. "She sounded worried that you hadn't returned her calls," she said.

Ben swung around. "So?" he said. "What do I care?"

Amy tried to keep calm. "Look, why don't you just call her? Is it really that big a deal?"

"I'll do what I want! OK? She's my mom, and I'll deal

227

with her," Ben said furiously. He threw the haynets on the pile and brushed by her as he headed out the door.

Amy was just about to go after him when Soraya reached her. "What's going on?" she asked.

Amy sighed. "Ben won't talk to his mom." She quickly told Soraya what had happened.

To her surprise, Soraya frowned. "Actually, Amy," she said, "Ben's got a point. It is *his* problem, not yours."

Amy glared at her, but Soraya met her gaze calmly. "You think I'm interfering?" she said more quietly, feeling her temper begin to die down.

Soraya nodded.

"I just get so frustrated," Amy said emotionally. "You know, when I think about what happened to Mom and how I would do anything to have her here still . . ." Her voice trailed off.

Soraya squeezed her arm. "I know," she said. "But you can't tell him what to do. He has to figure it out himself."

Amy looked at her. "I guess," she said, her voice almost a whisper. "I guess you're right."

❧

Later that morning, Amy, Ben, and Soraya tacked up for their ride.

"Where should we go?" Soraya asked as they mounted.

She seemed determined to be extra cheerful to make up for the tension that was still lingering between Amy and Ben.

"How 'bout to Pine Ridge," Amy suggested. "There are some great open fields for cantering over there and logs to jump." She had decided to ride Gypsy, thinking that it would be a chance to take the mare out for a good long workout to see if she showed any hints of bucking again.

"Oh, good!" Soraya said enthusiastically. She patted Moochie, the big bay hunter she was riding. He had been found neglected in a tiny paddock several months earlier and had come to Heartland to be nursed back to health. He was sturdy and strong again and was ready to be rehomed.

They let the horses trot along the trail that led across to Pine Ridge, the trees shielding them from the worst of the wind. As they rode, Amy felt her frustration with Ben's situation drain away.

He seemed more relaxed, too. Seeing a couple of fallen logs at the side of the trail, he turned in his saddle. "Want to jump these?" he called.

"OK," Amy said. "I'll go first."

She clicked her tongue and cantered Gypsy toward the two logs. The mare jumped them without a problem and pulled up calmly on the other side. "Good girl," Amy praised, patting her and turning to watch the others.

Moochie cleared the logs easily. Soraya pulled up alongside Amy, and together they watched Ben. Seeing the other two horses jump had excited Red. He flung his head up and plunged forward. Red was taking short, agitated steps and pulling at the reins. Amy watched cautiously to see what Ben would do. At one time, she knew he would have seen the horse's behavior as a challenge, a battle that had to be won no matter how wound up the horse became. But now he trotted Red past the logs, patting the horse's neck as he veered away from the jumps.

"Aren't you going to jump them?" Soraya said as he trotted toward them.

"Yes," Ben said. "But not until he's calm."

He steered Red away from them in a large circle. The chestnut visibly started to relax, his head and neck lowering as he listened to Ben's directions. Gathering the reins up slightly, Ben turned him toward the logs. Calm now, Red kept an even stride and jumped both smoothly, his ears pricked.

"That was really good," Amy burst out as Ben cantered up to them. Amy was relieved that Ben was becoming a more patient rider. Red really seemed to be responding to Ben's new training methods — the same methods that Heartland endorsed, building a bond of trust and understanding between horse and rider.

"Red's a beautiful jumper," Soraya commented as they all continued along the trail.

"I know. He's getting better all the time," Ben said, stroking the chestnut's shoulder. "I'm lucky."

"You can't give him all the credit. He really responds well to you," Amy said.

Ben shrugged. "I tell you, it's all Red. He'd jump with a three-year-old on his back."

Amy knew it wasn't true. Although Red was very talented at jumping, he was also pretty sensitive and needed a rider as good as Ben to bring out the best in him. "I guarantee he wouldn't go as well for another rider," she persisted.

Ben flushed slightly and shortened his reins. "Come on," he said, looking like he wanted to change the subject. "Let's canter."

✇

They stayed out on the trails for almost two hours. Gypsy didn't show any signs of bucking, but when Soraya asked if she could go back to her owners soon, Amy shook her head.

"She still doesn't seem quite ready," she said. She glanced at the mare's arched neck. Maybe it was the way Gypsy's muscles tensed when she was excited, or the way she snaked her head down to free the reins whenever she felt her rider relax. Whatever the reason, Amy instinctively felt that she couldn't completely trust the black mare.

When Amy, Ben, and Soraya got back to Heartland, they turned the three horses out in the field and helped Ty finish off the remaining barn chores.

Soraya had to leave at four o'clock, but Ty and Ben stayed until all the horses had been fed and stabled and the yard swept.

"See you tomorrow!" Amy called as the guys finally got into their pickups to go home.

"Night!" Ty shouted back. "Don't stay up too late with Melody."

Amy grinned. Sometimes Ty seemed to know her too well!

She waved them off and then, collecting a grooming bucket from the tack room, went up to Melody's stall. The mare was looking over her door. She pricked her ears when she saw Amy and, for the first time since she had arrived at Heartland, whinnied a greeting.

"Hi, Melody," Amy said, delighted that the mare seemed so pleased to see her.

She stroked Melody's nose, then tied her up and began the grooming. As she brushed and curried, Amy let her mind go blank. She didn't think about Lou and the mystery letter she was waiting for, she didn't think about Ben and his problems, she just concentrated on rhythmically sweeping the brush across Melody's dull coat until a faint shine began to emerge.

At last she paused and wiped the back of one hand

across her hot, dusty forehead. "You're a good girl," she murmured. "I'll call Mr. Phillips tonight and tell him how you're doing."

She pulled the brush across the currycomb to clean its bristles of dirt and grease. But as she stepped toward Melody again, she froze. The mare's side seemed to jerk. Amy stared. There! It happened again! A definite movement!

Amy's heart somersaulted. Dropping the brush, she put her hand against Melody's side. This time she felt as well as saw it. A kicking movement! A kick so strong that the shape of a small hoof could almost be seen through Melody's coat. It was the foal! It must be alive!

"Oh, Melody," Amy whispered in delight.

Melody snorted softly. She seemed completely unconcerned about the kicking. Undoing her halter, Amy quickly kissed her nose and ran out of the stall. She had to tell Grandpa and Lou!

She raced down the yard, her heart banging. It was the first sign they'd had that the foal was alive. She couldn't wait to share the news.

Kicking off her boots, she ran into the house. A casserole was bubbling on the kitchen stove, but the kitchen was empty. Suddenly, Amy heard Lou and Grandpa talking in the hall. She hurried toward the connecting door, but as she reached it, her grandpa's words stopped her in her tracks.

"And you haven't told Amy?"

Amy paused, her hand hovering over the door handle. *Told me what?* she thought.

She heard her sister's voice. "Only Scott knows. I didn't want to say anything until I got a reply, Grandpa. I didn't want to get Amy's hopes up. It's been so awful waiting, knowing that each day there could be a letter."

A letter! Amy felt her spine tingle. They must be talking about the letter Lou was expecting from England. *But what's it got to do with me?* she wondered.

"Lou, you have to tell her," Grandpa said, and Amy noticed an intensity in his voice that she had never heard before. "You should have told her before you wrote in the first place."

"But what if he doesn't write back?" Lou said.

"Amy still has the right to know. You can't —"

It was too much. "I've got the right to know what?" Amy said, opening the door.

Grandpa and Lou swung around.

"Amy!" Lou exclaimed, shocked.

"How long have you been there?" Grandpa said quickly.

Amy didn't answer him. She was staring at Lou. "What should you have told me, Lou?" she demanded.

Lou looked desperately at Grandpa. "I — well —" she stammered.

"What is it?" Amy cried, feeling increasingly alarmed. "Lou? *Who* did you write to?"

Look took a breath. "Daddy," she said.

For a moment, Amy was too shocked to speak. *Daddy?* She stared at Lou. Somehow she knew that was the answer, but she was still caught off guard.

"I wrote to him after we found the letter in Mom's room." The words came out of Lou in a rush. "I sent it to the address on the back of the envelope in the hope that he still lives there. I told him about Mom and that — we wanted to see him."

"*See* him!" Amy exclaimed, finding her voice at last. She stepped backward. "Are you kidding?"

She felt as if her world were falling down around her. All her life, her father had been a distant, shadowy figure. Sure, she had sometimes felt curious about him, wondered what he looked like, whether she was like him, but she had never wanted to *meet* him. He had abandoned them, and although she could not remember him, she could remember the nights when her mom had cried as if she were never going to stop, when nothing and no one had been able to comfort her. Mom had recovered in the end, moved on, founded Heartland. But Amy had always known that the sadness from that time had never left her; it had just been pushed way under the surface.

She shook her head. "I don't want to see him! I won't!"

"But he's our father!" Lou exclaimed.

"So?" Amy cried. "He abandoned us!"

"He tried to make things right!" Lou protested. "You saw the letter, Amy. He wanted to get back together with Mom. He wanted to be with us again."

"I don't care!" Amy shouted.

"Amy, calm down," Jack Bartlett said, stepping toward her. "We don't even know if he got the letter. It's been five years since he wrote to your mom. That address is probably old."

Amy looked at him desperately. "But what if it isn't?" she exclaimed. "Grandpa, what if he writes back and wants to come here?" Her eyes frantically searched his face. Surely Grandpa didn't want Daddy to come to Heartland. "Think of what he did to Mom — to us!"

A shadow crossed Jack's eyes. "I . . ." His voice trailed off and in that moment, in the look she saw cross his face, Amy knew she was right.

Lou must also have seen the expression in their grandpa's eyes. "Grandpa!" she exclaimed, horrified.

"Lou —" Jack began, but then he broke off, shaking his head. "Look, let's not argue, we can discuss it more when — *if* — he writes back."

"He will!" Lou said defensively. "I know he will!"

"Honey, don't get your hopes up too high," Jack said wearily. "After all, he's always known the address here, and even if your mom hadn't wanted to see him, he could have gotten in touch with you at any time."

"But maybe he was worried about how Mom would react," Lou said. "Now he has my letter and he *knows* that we want to see him."

Amy felt indignant. "*You* want to," she said. "Don't go making promises for me, Lou. As far as I'm concerned, I don't have a father anymore."

Lou turned on her, her eyes flashing with exasperation. "Amy!"

"No more arguing!" Jack held up his hands and looked at them both. *"Please."*

Amy saw the tension around his mouth and eyes and bit back the angry words that were springing to her lips. It couldn't be easy for Grandpa. He had always tried to be neutral about their father when he came up in conversation, but now she realized how hard this must have been for him. He'd been the one who had helped their mom slowly piece her life back together after the breakup. Arguing with Lou would only upset him even more.

She stared mutinously at her sister but didn't say another word.

"Thank you," Jack said quietly. "Now, can we just agree to deal with this later?"

Amy and Lou stared at each other, the silence between them weighted with anger. But Lou seemed as reluctant as Amy to upset Grandpa further. She nodded. "OK," she said.

Amy nodded, too, and saw the relief on Grandpa's face. "I'm going to get changed," she muttered, heading for the staircase. Right now, she just wanted to be alone.

In her room, she sat down on the bed. Her thoughts were whirling, and it was only now that she remembered she had meant to tell Grandpa and Lou about Melody's foal kicking. Right this moment, even *that* didn't seem important. How *could* Lou have just written to their father without discussing it with her first?

But then, deep inside, Amy knew. Her mom had often told her about the special bond that Lou and Daddy had shared. She had said how similar they were — both practical, brave, determined. Amy had seen the photographs that her mom had kept of the two of them riding together. She couldn't imagine how Lou felt at eleven, when Daddy abandoned them.

Thinking about the photographs, Amy opened her bedside drawer and rooted around until she found a photo that she kept in there. It was one of all four of them — her, Lou, Mom, and Daddy — sitting on a beach beside an enormous sand castle. They were all smiling. She looked at herself, a skinny two-year-old with straight dark blond hair, standing by Mom. Daddy had his arm around Lou's shoulders.

Amy studied her father's features and then took the photograph over to the mirror. She looked more like him than her mom. They had the same thickly lashed gray eyes, the same high, wide cheekbones and determined mouths. And yet she didn't know him at all. They shared the same features, but they were strangers.

She looked at the photograph again. "I don't want to see you," she whispered.

Despite her words, Amy knew that deep down inside, in a hidden corner of her heart, she desperately longed to know what her father was like.

Chapter Five

When Amy opened her eyes the next morning, she lay in bed for a moment with the feeling that she had just woken from a horrible dream. Then everything came flooding back. It wasn't a dream; it was real. Lou had written to Daddy. He might write back. He might even want to come and visit.

Well, I won't be here, Amy thought, hurriedly pushing back the covers and getting out of bed. *I'll go stay with Soraya. I'm not seeing him. I don't care what Lou says.*

She got dressed quickly, wanting to get out of the house before either Lou or Grandpa got up. Dinner, the night before, had been strained. She and Lou had hardly spoken a word to each other, and Grandpa had been quiet, lost in his own thoughts.

As Amy got the morning feeds ready, she heard the

sound of a car driving up outside the house. She looked out of the feed room and saw Ben getting out of his sporty black pickup. "You're early," she called in surprise. She glanced at her watch. It was only six-thirty, an hour before Ben officially started work.

Ben shrugged. "It's always more of a rush to get things done the days you're at school. I knew it would help if I got started now."

He was right, but even so, Amy didn't want him to feel obliged to have such long days. "We can manage," she said, seeing shadows of tiredness under his eyes. "You don't have to put in all these extra hours."

"It's no problem," Ben said, coming into the feed room. "What should I do? The haynets?"

Amy gave a shrug and nodded. There was no point arguing. If he wanted to work so hard, she wasn't going to stop him.

Ben picked up the pile of empty nets and took them to the small hay storage bin that had been built on to the stone feed room. Every few days the hay bin was filled up with bales from the big barn behind the tack room. Grandpa had built it so that the full haynets didn't have to be lugged all the way from the barn twice a day. Amy heard the sound of Ben shaking out the compact flakes of hay. "How's Melody this morning?" he called.

With a start, Amy stopped mixing up the feeds. She had almost forgotten the news about the foal! She rushed around to the hay bin. "Her foal's definitely alive!" she said. She quickly told Ben all about seeing and feeling the kicking movement in Melody's side.

"That's great," Ben said, straightening up immediately. "They normally start kicking a couple of weeks before they're born. Jack and Lou must be relieved."

Amy hesitated. "They don't know yet," she admitted.

Ben looked at her in astonishment. "You haven't told them?"

Amy shook her head. "Things were weird last night. We had a bit of an argument," she said, realizing that she needed to give him some sort of explanation. "I just wasn't in the mood to deal with it." She didn't want to say any more and she turned hastily. "I'll go give the horses their feeds," she said, and grabbing a pile of feed buckets, she strode out into the yard.

❧

To Amy's relief, Ben didn't ask for any more details. They fed and watered the horses and then, leaving him to start on the stalls, Amy went inside to get ready for school.

Coming downstairs after taking a shower, she found Lou sitting at the kitchen table reading the paper over a cup of coffee. Hearing the sound of her footsteps, Lou looked up, but then seeing it was Amy, she immediately looked down again.

Ignoring her sister, Amy got a bowl and poured out

some cereal. She sat down at the far end of the table and ate it quickly.

Just as Amy was finishing, Grandpa came into the kitchen. "Morning," he said. The two girls looked up.

"Hi, Grandpa," Amy said, getting up and putting her empty bowl in the sink. "Do you want some coffee?"

Jack nodded. "Thanks."

Amy poured him a cup and was just about to tell him about Melody's foal when the back door burst open. Ty stood in the porch. "Ben just told me about Melody's foal!" he said, looking delighted. "It's great!"

Amy saw Grandpa and Lou look at Ty in confusion. "What?" Grandpa said blankly.

"About the foal kicking!" Ty said in surprise. He turned quickly to Amy, a frown crossing his face. "Ben said you saw it last night."

Amy felt herself start to go red. "Yeah, I did," she admitted.

"Well, that's wonderful!" Lou exclaimed, getting to her feet. "It must be a real survivor after that fall."

"Why didn't you tell us?" Grandpa said to Amy.

"I was just about to," Amy said. She grabbed her back-pack off the floor, not wanting to bring up the tension of the night before by explaining. "I'm going to school," she said, turning away from Lou's and Jack's astonished expressions.

"Amy —" Grandpa began, but Amy didn't stop.

"I'll be late. See you this afternoon," she said as she ran out of the house.

Ty followed her. "Hey, what's going on?" he asked, catching up with her.

Amy paused for a moment. "It's a long story," she said, her eyes begging him not to question her. "I'll — I'll tell you tonight." Shifting her backpack onto her shoulder, she set off down the drive.

"See you later," Ty called.

Amy nodded but didn't look back. She knew she'd have to explain things to him later, but right this minute she didn't feel like talking about it — not to Ty, not even to Soraya.

"You're quiet today," Soraya said, when the bus reached school. "Are you OK?"

"Yeah, fine," Amy said quickly.

Soraya didn't look convinced. "Are you sure?"

"Yes!" Amy insisted.

Soraya held her gaze for a moment but then, to Amy's relief, seemed to decide not to press the matter further.

❧

Amy couldn't concentrate at all that day. Every time a teacher started talking, she drifted off into her own thoughts. Had the mail arrived at home? Maybe even now Lou was opening a letter from their father.

Maybe, somewhere in England, he was reading Lou's letter, or at this moment he was sitting down and writing a reply.

Amy could tell that Soraya knew something was up. Being best friends since third grade, they knew each other inside out. On the way home in the bus that afternoon, Amy finally gave up trying to pretend nothing was wrong and told her everything.

Soraya's eyes widened. "Lou wrote to your dad!" She spoke in a low voice so that no one else could hear, but her face showed her shock. "When?"

"About six weeks ago," Amy said. "She's been waiting to hear back."

Soraya's eyes scanned Amy's face. "What are you going to do if he gets in touch with you?"

"I don't know," Amy said, pushing a hand through her hair. "Lou wants to see him, of course, but . . ." Her voice trailed off.

"You don't?" Soraya said, finishing the thought for her.

Amy saw the understanding in her friend's dark brown eyes. "No," she said, shaking her head. "I don't *ever* want to see him." She spoke the words as if trying to convince herself that what she was saying was true.

"What about your grandpa?" Soraya asked. "What'd he say?"

"That we should wait and see if he gets in touch," Amy

replied. She remembered the look that had crossed his face the night before. "No matter what he says, I *know* he doesn't want Daddy at Heartland." Her voice rose slightly. "I just don't get how Lou can be so selfish! She must know that Grandpa wouldn't want to see him. I mean, he was the one who had to look after Mom after my father left us. What was Lou thinking?" she demanded.

Soraya hesitated. "Well, I guess she misses your dad. She probably still loves him."

"How can she?" Amy exploded. Suddenly realizing that several kids nearby had turned to look at them both, she dropped her voice again. "I hate him," she hissed. The back of her eyes felt hot. "I'll never forgive him for what he did to Mom. *I can't!*" Her eyes blurred and she looked quickly down at her knees and angrily blinked back her tears.

Soraya reached out and squeezed her hand.

Amy continued to stare at her knees. *I mean it,* she thought. *I hate him, and I'll never forgive him!*

❧

When Amy got off the school bus she went straight to Melody's stall. She wanted to push all thoughts about her father to the back of her mind. "Hello, girl," she murmured as Melody gave a welcoming nicker. "Did you miss me?"

Melody nuzzled her shoulder in reply.

"She seems to be settling down a bit."

Amy turned when she heard the voice. It was Ty.

"I've been in with her a few times today," he said. "And I think she's beginning to get used to me." He came over to the door and offered his palm for Melody to sniff. The mare cautiously stretched her muzzle forward and blew in and out.

"That's a big improvement," Amy said. "A few days ago she wouldn't have come anywhere near you."

"We could take her out for a walk together," Ty suggested.

Amy smiled. "I'll just get changed."

She ran down to the house and quickly pulled on her old jeans and sweater.

"Let's walk down the drive," Amy said, joining Ty in Melody's stall.

At first, Melody's ears flickered backward uneasily, and she kept looking at Ty warily as he walked beside Amy down the drive, but after a few minutes, she began to relax.

"Have you called Mr. Phillips yet to tell him how she's doing?" Ty asked Amy as they stopped to let her graze for a few moments.

Amy shook her head, remembering that she had been going to. "I will. I was going to last night, but then" — she hesitated — "well . . . something happened."

She saw Ty's curious look and knew that she couldn't

keep it from him any longer. When she had finished relating the events of the previous evening, his reaction was much the same as Soraya's — concerned understanding.

"It must have been a real shock for you," he said.

"It was," Amy admitted. "But I'm not going to see him." She spoke the words more confidently than she had on the bus. The more she said them, the more she felt herself believing in them.

Ty nodded. "I can understand why."

"Lou doesn't," Amy said quietly.

Ty looked at her sympathetically. "It'll be OK," he said. "You'll see."

Amy wished she could believe him. Just the thought of Daddy coming back caused a wave of panic to well up inside her. She looked quickly at Melody and changed the subject. "Here, you hold her," she said, handing Ty the lead rope.

Ty took it and moved closer. Melody side-stepped away from him. "Easy, girl," he murmured.

Melody glanced at him suspiciously for a moment, but then she relaxed and began to crop at the short winter grass again. Ty reached out and gently stroked the mare's neck. She didn't flinch or move away.

"She's starting to like you," Amy said softly.

Ty nodded. "We'll get there in the end," he replied. "We just have to take things slowly for a while."

They had just put Melody back in her stall when Ben came into the barn. "Hi," he said, seeing Amy. "So, did Ty tell you about our mystery visitor?"

"Mystery visitor?" Amy echoed.

"Oh, it was just this guy who came up to the house," Ty said dismissively. "Your grandpa said he was looking for work."

"He kind of hung around after Jack talked with him, though," Ben said. "And before he left, he looked in all the stalls. I think he was a reporter."

"Yeah, right." Amy couldn't help smiling. "Why wouldn't he have said he was a reporter, then?"

"You never know," Ben said. "Maybe it's something undercover."

Ty grinned at Amy. "He's been going on about it all day. He was just some guy looking for work. Word is probably getting around that business has picked up for us." He shut Melody's door. "Ivy, Solo, and Sundance need riding. We could take them out on the trails."

Amy ran down to the house to get her hard hat. Grandpa and Lou were in the kitchen.

"Hi," Amy said, grabbing her hat from the easy chair by the TV.

Lou didn't say anything. She just went on looking

through the barn records, but Grandpa smiled and looked up from the catalog he was reading. "Hi, honey."

"I'm just going out for a ride with Ty and Ben," Amy said. As she reached the door, she remembered the conversation in the barn. "Oh, Ben and Ty were talking about the guy who came by today."

To her surprise, Grandpa started violently in his chair.

"A man?" Lou said, looking up curiously.

The shocked expression on Jack Bartlett's face quickly smoothed out. "It was just someone looking for casual work," he said, his voice light. "You were out, Lou. It was no big deal."

"Ben seems to think it was." Amy grinned. "He's convinced he was an undercover reporter. Maybe it was a spy sent by Greenbriar," Amy offered with a laugh. Greenbriar was a rival stable across town.

Lou shook her head and turned back to the records.

But when Amy glanced at Grandpa, his face looked taut with distress. "Are you OK, Grandpa?" she asked in concern.

"Me?" Jack said in surprise.

"Yeah, you don't look like yourself," Amy said.

Jack looked down at the catalog again. "I'm just a little tired. Old age catching up with me, that's all." He smiled at her but she noticed that his eyes looked distracted. "I'm fine, just fine."

Amy smiled back, but she couldn't help feeling

slightly concerned. Grandpa was very fit and healthy, and although he was sixty-eight years old now, he hardly ever showed any signs of old age. Hoping that he was telling the truth, Amy went back outside.

❧

Over the next few days, Amy continued to notice that Grandpa didn't seem to be his usual self. Quieter than normal, he seemed to be lost in thought. She was consumed with thought as well, wondering what the day's mail would bring. But by Friday, there was still no response to Lou's letter.

"Oh, Melody." Amy sighed as she groomed the mare on Friday night. "What's going to happen?"

Amy stroked the mare's smooth neck. With good food and daily grooming sessions, the mare's chestnut coat was at last beginning to shine and her skin had lost its dryness. The hollows in her flanks had begun to fill out, and most important of all to Amy, the wariness had left her eyes. "You're going to have the most beautiful foal," she said, watching Melody's side twitch with a sudden kick. "And it'll go out in the fields with you and graze on the grass and gallop at your side. Won't that be wonderful?"

There was a noise at the stall door and Amy swung around. Ty was standing there, car keys in hand. "One day I'm going to put a tape recorder in here," he said with a grin. "It would make very interesting listening."

"You talk to the horses, too," Amy protested.

"I don't have complete conversations with them," Ty teased. He shook his head. "Well, I'm off. I'll see you tomorrow. I was thinking of going to the cemetery to visit your mom's grave at lunchtime. Do you want to come?"

"I'd like that," Amy said. She tried to go to the cemetery as often as possible, but with the darker evenings and the winter chores it was getting more difficult to find time to visit.

"I'll get some flowers," Ty said.

Amy nodded. "See you tomorrow, then."

"Yeah, later," Ty said, and he left.

❧

The next day at lunchtime, Amy and Ty got into his battered pickup and set off for the cemetery.

"I'm glad you asked me. I haven't been over there for a few weeks," Amy said. "We've been so busy. I was going to go last weekend but then Melody arrived." She paused. "I wonder what Mom would have done with Melody." She often found herself wondering how her mom would have treated the new horses that came to them. She knew that she had to rely on her own intuition and knowledge, but it was hard not to wonder whether Mom would have done things differently.

Ty looked at her reassuringly. "Probably exactly what

we've done. Melody's wound's healing well; she's looking good. And she's a lot quieter. You've done a great job."

"I guess," Amy said, feeling a bit happier. "I just hope that the birth goes without a hitch. Now that we know the foal's alive, I hope it's healthy."

Ty nodded and they drove on in silence.

Finally, they reached the cemetery parking lot and got out. Tall trees loomed overhead, their bare branches outlined against the dull, gray sky. It was a cold, frosty day, and as they walked down the path toward Marion's grave, their breath froze like white smoke in the air.

"I wonder when we'll get the first snow," Ty said as their boots crunched on the stone path.

Amy nodded. When it snowed, the workload at Heartland increased, the water troughs froze, the yard became icy, and the ground in the schooling rings became hard, so there was less chance to exercise the horses. She dug her hands in her pockets and hoped that the snow would hold off for a while longer.

They rounded the corner that led to the quiet area of the cemetery where Marion was buried. Suddenly, Amy stopped. "Hey, is that man at Mom's grave?" she questioned.

A man was kneeling about thirty feet away, his head bowed. Hearing her voice, he looked around and rose swiftly to his feet. He was tall, with slightly graying hair.

He looked like he'd once been handsome, but now deep lines were etched across his face.

A swift rush of anger rose inside Amy. What was he doing? "Who are you?" Amy said under her breath. Then, as the curiosity swelled inside her, she repeated the question with more force. She began to stride down the path toward him. "What are you doing? This is my mom's grave."

The man stared at her as she approached, and for a moment, she thought he was going to speak. But then a strange, haunted look crossed his eyes, and he suddenly turned and cut across the grass to the far path.

Amy stopped and stared after the figure, noticing as he hurried away that he had a slight limp. She swung around to Ty. "What was that about?" she demanded indignantly.

Ty was frowning. He had an incredulous look on his face.

"What is it?" Amy said.

"I know this sounds odd, but that is the guy who came by Heartland the other day looking for work," Ty replied. "I'm sure of it."

Amy stared at him. "What was he doing here?"

"I don't know," Ty said, sounding mystified. "Maybe he *is* a reporter," he added, trying to break the tension.

Amy looked for the man, but he had vanished into the mist.

❧

"He was kneeling right next to Mom's grave!" Amy told Grandpa and Lou when she arrived back at Heartland, half an hour later. "I went over to talk to him, but he just ran away."

The two of them had been eating lunch, and now Lou put down her knife and fork. "And Ty said it was the same man who came by the other day?"

"He says he's sure of it," Amy said anxiously. Now that her initial shock had passed, she felt angry. She didn't like the idea of some strange guy hanging around her mom's grave. It was creepy and weird.

Lou frowned and turned to Grandpa. "Did this guy say anything about knowing Mom when he was here?"

For a moment, Jack looked like he was about to shake his head, but then he seemed to stop himself, and for the first time, Amy noticed that the muscles in his face were tense. A red tinge spread along his cheekbones.

"Grandpa, what is it?" Amy said, seeing his guarded expression.

But he didn't speak.

Amy's heart suddenly began to thump in her chest. There was something wrong — something dreadfully wrong.

"Grandpa?" Lou said, and from the high tone of her

voice Amy could tell that Grandpa's expression was unnerving her, too.

Jack cleared his throat. "There's . . . something you should know," he said. He looked at Amy. "The man you saw — the man who came around the other day — isn't a stranger. He's —" He took a deep breath. "He's your father."

Chapter Six

For a moment, the world stood still, and then the room and everything in it seemed to rush away from Amy at high speed. She clutched the back of the chair she was standing behind. "What?" she stammered in shock.

"That man is your father," Grandpa repeated.

"What do you mean?" Amy cried.

"No!" Lou gasped, almost at the same time.

Amy's gaze frantically scanned her grandpa's face, desperately looking for him to shake his head, to smile. But he didn't. His blue eyes were grave. "I should have told you right from the start," he said heavily. "I know it was wrong. When he came over, I told him that you didn't want to see him. I told him to leave."

"You did *what*?" Lou burst out, pushing her chair back violently.

257

Amy jumped. Through the shock of the announcement, she had almost forgotten about Lou. Now she saw that furious color was flooding her sister's cheeks.

"You told Daddy to go away?" Lou said, staring at Grandpa. "How *could* you?" she cried, her voice rising. "You know how much I want to see him!"

"Yes, I know," Jack said, sounding wretched. "But Lou, I had to." He stood up and stepped toward her. "I was the one who had to pick up the pieces after he left your mother. I saw how he almost destroyed her, Lou. I couldn't have him here."

He reached out for her, but Lou jerked her arm away. She stared at him. "You can't go on protecting her after she's gone. I wanted to see him. I need to see him. I'll never forgive you for this, Grandpa!" she spat, her eyes welling with tears. "Never!"

"Lou —" Amy said, going toward her.

"No! Leave me alone!" Lou cried. With a sob, she grabbed her car keys and ran out of the kitchen, slamming the back door.

"Lou!" Jack wailed. But by the time he and Amy had reached the doorway, Lou was already starting the engine of her car.

"What did I do?" Jack whispered as Lou drove off at high speed. He turned, his face pale.

Amy saw the despair in his eyes. "She'll be OK,

Grandpa," she said, desperately trying to ignore the frantic hammering of her heart. "She'll come back soon."

❧

But by six o'clock that evening, Lou still hadn't come back. Amy had briefly explained to Ty what had happened, and after the horses had been fed, he had come down to the house to wait with her and Grandpa.

"It's been three hours now," Grandpa said, getting up and pacing across the floor. "Where is she?"

"Maybe she went to Scott's?" Ty suggested.

Grandpa picked up the phone and began to dial the vet's number.

Ty pressed Amy's hand. "You OK?" he asked.

Amy nodded numbly. Since her grandpa has made the announcement, her mind had gone into shock. Every so often an image of the man — her father — standing by the grave flashed into her mind, but each time she pushed it away. To think that she had actually seen him, spoken to him, and not recognized him was just too much to think about. But thinking about Lou wasn't any easier. Where had she gone? Was she all right?

She looked at Ty and saw the concern in his dark eyes. "Lou will be fine," he murmured, squeezing her hand again. "She just needs some time to cool off."

Amy swallowed and looked down. She desperately

wanted to believe him, but she couldn't help thinking the worst. What if Lou had been involved in an accident? It was almost dark outside and it had begun to rain — the roads would be wet and slippery. She fought back the fear that rose inside her as memories flashed into her mind, memories of a day five months ago when she and Mom had been driving through the rain. In her mind, she saw the sodden road, the sleeting rain, the trailer skidding toward the fallen tree. . . .

"Scott, it's Jack here."

The sound of her grandpa's voice jerked Amy from her nightmare thoughts. Her eyes scanned his face as he asked if Scott had seen Lou. There was a pause, and then seeing the hope die from his eyes, Amy knew what the answer had been.

"She left here more than three hours ago," she heard Grandpa say. "We had an argument. It's too difficult to explain over the phone, but she's upset — very upset."

He replaced the handset. "Scott's going to come over."

Just then, the back door opened and Ben came in. "I'm going home now, if that's OK," he said, stamping his feet on the mat. He looked around at their worried faces. "Is everything all right?"

Amy nodded. She had simply told him that there had been a family disagreement. "Yeah, you call it a day," she said, forcing herself to smile. "We'll be fine."

"You're sure there isn't anything I can do?" Ben asked.

Amy shook her head. "See you tomorrow."

"'Bye, then," Ben said.

Scott arrived twenty minutes later. He came into the kitchen, shaking the raindrops off his jacket.

"So what happened exactly?" he said quickly.

As Jack explained, the concern on Scott's face deepened. "And she just took off without saying where she was going?"

Grandpa nodded. "I tried to stop her, but she wouldn't listen." He stood still by the sink and rubbed his face with his hands. "I should never have done what I did," he said to Scott with a sigh, "but when Tim just showed up, I couldn't stop myself. I know how he almost destroyed Marion, and I couldn't stand by and see him upset my granddaughters." He looked wretchedly at Amy. "Please try to understand, honey, I was just trying to protect you — to protect us all."

Amy hated seeing the guilt on his face. "I know, Grandpa," she said, going over and hugging him. "And I do understand. But I — I don't think Lou can." She swallowed, her eyes catching Ty's.

"You said you saw your father at the cemetery?" Scott asked her.

Amy nodded.

"Maybe Lou went there," he said abruptly. "She might have thought that he would go back." He took his car keys out of his pocket. "I'll go take a look."

"I'll come, too," Amy offered. At least then she would be doing something instead of just waiting around.

"OK," Scott said. He turned to Jack. "Call us if she comes back. I've got my phone. And we'll let you know if we find her."

🙢

Scott's Jeep bumped down the driveway. Rain spattered onto the windshield, and the wipers beat methodically as they swung back and forth. Amy huddled deeper into her coat. *Please, please let us find Lou,* she prayed.

She glanced at Scott's face. The skin around his mouth and chin were taut with worry. "What was Jack thinking?" he muttered savagely, as they turned on to the road.

"He was just trying to do what he thought was best," Amy said hotly, jumping immediately to her grandpa's defense. "He didn't want us to get hurt."

"But he *knows* how Lou feels about your father," Scott said.

Amy didn't answer. She could see why Scott was siding with Lou, but she also saw her grandpa's side of things. It must have been awful for him to have watched Mom suffering after Daddy had left.

Daddy. The word seemed to ring in Amy's ears. She had seen her father — even spoken to him. An image of his face sprang into her mind. The deeply etched lines, the distant look in his eyes. She shut her eyes, willing it to go away.

Neither she nor Scott spoke again until they reached the cemetery. There were no lights on, and the wrought iron gates that led into the memorial ground were shut and locked. The mist from earlier had grown thicker, and now it swirled about the deserted parking lot. Suddenly, Amy caught sight of a single, lonely car parked under the leafless canopy of an oak tree.

"That's Lou's Honda!" she gasped.

Scott put his foot on the gas, and his Jeep shot across the parking lot, stopping with a screech of brakes behind Lou's car. Even before the Jeep had completely stopped, Amy was leaping out. She ran to the driver's door, her heart pounding.

The windows were frosted over, but Amy could just make out a shadowy figure, sitting huddled in the front seat.

"Lou!" she cried out, banging on the window.

The next moment, Amy saw her sister's face looking around at her.

Amy tried the door, but it was locked. "Open the door, Lou!"

For a moment, Lou didn't move, but then, with fumbling fingers, she released the catch.

Amy flung the door open. "We were so worried!"

Lou stared at her, her face white. "He wasn't here. I

waited and waited and he didn't come back." Suddenly, her face crumpled and a strangled sob burst from her. "Oh, Amy, I'm never going to see him again!"

Amy flung her arms around her sister's neck. "You will," she gabbled. "He'll get back in touch, and if he doesn't, we'll find him, Lou. I'll help you."

"You will?" Lou sobbed.

"Yes!" Amy felt prepared to say anything to comfort her sister. She was so relieved Lou was safe.

They hugged tightly.

"Lou! Are you all right?" Scott's deep voice spoke from behind Amy.

"Scott," Lou said, pulling back from Amy in confusion and looking up at him. "What are you doing here?"

"Jack told me what happened," Scott said quickly. "Are you OK?"

Lou nodded.

Scott crouched down and spoke softly. "You had us so worried." He took her hands. "You're freezing." He tightened his grip on her fingers. "Come on, let's get you home. We'll pick up your car tomorrow."

Lou looked too worn out to argue. She got out of the car without a word and allowed Scott to put his jacket over her shoulders. Wrapping an arm around her waist, he helped her into the Jeep.

The backseat was crowded with boxes of medicines, plastic gloves, and map books. Amy pushed them to one side and climbed in. The first wild rush of relief she had felt when they found Lou was fading, and she was beginning to feel anxious about what would happen when they got back home.

❧

As soon as the Jeep drew up outside the house, the back door opened and Grandpa and Ty ran out. Amy had phoned them on Scott's cell phone to let them know that Lou was safe.

"Lou!" Grandpa exclaimed, hurrying over as Lou got out of the Jeep. "Thank heaven you're all right."

Lou ignored him and marched into the house without saying a word. With a look at her grandpa's hurt face, Amy ran after Lou.

"Lou!" she said, catching up with her sister in the kitchen. "Grandpa's been really worried about you."

Lou swung around, and Amy braced herself for a furious retort, but then Lou checked herself. When she spoke, her voice was quiet. "I'm not ready to talk to him right now, Amy," she said, the hurt showing in her eyes. "I just can't."

Scott, Grandpa, and Ty appeared in the doorway.

"I'm going to my room," Lou said bleakly.

"Lou," Grandpa said quickly, "we need to talk this through."

"There's nothing to discuss," Lou answered curtly.

She glanced at Scott. "Thanks for coming to find me," she said wearily. "I'll — I'll call you tomorrow."

Scott smiled. "Take care." He looked like he wanted to say more, but the presence of the others seemed to hold him back. "Get some rest," he said.

Lou nodded and then turned and walked out of the room.

There was a silence.

"I'd better go," Scott said at last. He glanced at Amy. " 'Bye."

Amy felt tears rise in her eyes as he left. Everything was going wrong.

Ty put a hand on her shoulder. "Maybe it's best if I go, too," he said, looking at her and Jack. "You've got family things to sort out." He hugged Amy briefly. "I'll see you tomorrow."

Grandpa made an effort to smile. "Thanks for staying, Ty."

"No problem," Ty said. "I'm just glad nothing happened to Lou." With a last look at Amy, he left.

Grandpa sat down at the table. "Oh, Amy," he groaned, putting his head in his hands. "What am I going to do?"

Amy sat down beside him, wishing she could say something to comfort him. "It'll be OK," she managed. "Lou will come around in the end."

Grandpa looked up at her. "What about you? How do *you* feel? Do you want to meet your father?"

A vivid image of the man she had seen that afternoon at her mom's grave flashed into Amy's mind. She swallowed. "I didn't recognize him, Grandpa," she whispered. "I didn't know who he was."

"How could you?" Jack replied. "You haven't seen him for twelve years. You were only a toddler when he left."

Amy looked down. Maybe Grandpa was right, but it didn't make her feel any better. How could she not have known him? How could she not have felt even the faintest glimmer of recognition?

Jack took her hand. "Amy, you can't blame yourself for not knowing him. It's his fault for not being around when you were growing up."

Amy lifted worried eyes to his. "But —"

"There are no buts," Grandpa said firmly. He put his arms around her and hugged her tightly. "Your father chose to leave and to not stay in touch. It was his decision."

Amy felt the rough wool of his pullover rub against her cheek. "He did write to Mom that time," she said.

"Yes," Grandpa said quietly. "He did."

Amy glanced up at him. "Did — she ever tell you about that, Grandpa?" Until she and Lou had found the letter, she didn't have any idea that her father had ever written. How had Mom felt?

"She showed it to me the day it arrived," Grandpa said, the wrinkles on his face seeming to deepen as he remembered the time. "I — I was so angry with him."

He must have seen Amy's shocked look, because he shook his head. "So many years had passed. Your mom had built a new life for herself, she was just starting to find happiness, and then he wrote and almost destroyed everything again. Just the sight of his handwriting was enough to make her consider giving up everything she had here. She seriously thought about leaving and going back to him. She loved him, Amy. Despite everything he had done, she loved him to the end."

"But why didn't she go back?" Amy said wonderingly.

"I think she realized that whatever she and your father had once shared had been irreversibly spoiled. She knew that going back could never be the same," Grandpa replied. "After she showed me the letter, we didn't really discuss it any further. We both knew it was a decision she had to make on her own." He kissed the top of her head. "She made the right decision, Amy. For herself — and for the family."

Amy rested her head silently against him and thought about her mom. It must have been a painfully hard decision to make, especially if she had still loved him. And poor Grandpa. How awful it must have been for him, seeing what his daughter had gone through. Amy couldn't blame him for hating their father or for turning him away.

But Amy wasn't sure Lou would ever understand that.

Chapter Seven

The next morning, when Amy got up and went downstairs to feed the horses, she found Grandpa already in the kitchen getting out the breakfast things. His eyes looked tired. "How did you sleep?" he asked.

Amy had slept restlessly, her dreams full of images of her father standing by her mother's grave. "Badly," she admitted, going over to the refrigerator.

"That makes two of us," Grandpa said.

Just then, the door opened and Lou came in. The air in the kitchen suddenly seemed to stiffen.

"Hi, Lou," Amy said, trying to act normal. "Do you want some orange juice?"

Lou shook her head. "No, thanks." She sat down at the table. She was dressed but looked tired and pale.

Grandpa put down the plates he had in his hand. "Did you sleep?" he asked her.

Lou shrugged. "On and off."

For a moment, Grandpa looked as if he was about to turn away, but then he changed his mind and sat down. "Look, Lou," he said. "I know what I did was wrong, but we can't let it come between us."

Amy watched her sister look at him with something resembling hope in her eyes.

"I've reached a decision," Grandpa continued. "Although I won't have your father here at Heartland, I can't — and I won't — stand in your way if you still want to find him."

Lou looked at him incredulously. "Did you really think you'd have been able to *stop* me?" she said, her voice rising.

"Lou —" Amy began, but her sister didn't even look at her. She had got to her feet and was staring at Grandpa.

"I'm not going to let you come between us again," she said angrily. "He's my father and I love him."

"I know you do, Lou," Jack Bartlett replied. "I'm just saying that I don't want him here at Heartland."

Lou shook her head and walked to the door. "I'm going to Scott's."

"You can't, Lou," Amy said, hurrying after her as she went outside. "Your car isn't here."

Lou paused for barely a second. "Then I'll walk," she said.

Grandpa joined Amy. "Don't be crazy, Lou. It's miles!"

For a fraction of a second, Amy thought that Lou was going to snap back, but she didn't; she just took a deep breath. "A walk will do me good," she said, her voice level. "I need some space."

Grandpa sighed. "Look, if you really want to go, Lou, I'll give you a lift. You can't walk all that way."

Lou hesitated, but just then both Ty's and Ben's cars came up the drive. A look of relief crossed her face. "It's OK," she said. "Ty will take me."

Lou hurried over to Ty's pickup and opened the passenger door, then the truck turned around and headed down the drive.

Grandpa turned and went into the house as Ben shut his car door and walked over. "What's going on?" he asked.

"Nothing," Amy snapped unhappily. She saw a hurt look cross Ben's face. Turning quickly, he marched up to the feed room. Amy kicked a nearby stone in frustration. Right now, she just didn't feel like coping with one of Ben's moods. Frowning, she followed him.

Ben was banging the buckets down onto the stone floor. Amy began to scoop grain into them. Neither of them spoke a word.

Eventually, Amy could stand the silence no longer. "I'll take these to the back barn," she said abruptly, picking up a pile of feed buckets. "You finish off here."

Ben didn't reply. Relieved to escape, Amy carried the feed buckets up the yard.

The horses in the barn were all looking over their doors. Seeing Amy, they whinnied excitedly.

"OK, OK, I'm here," Amy called, starting to empty the grain into the mangers. She reached Melody's stall last. The chestnut mare nickered softly as Amy came to her door.

"Hi, girl," Amy said, letting herself into the stall.

Melody nuzzled her shoulder as Amy tipped her feed into the manger. Amy let out a long sigh and watched the mare thrust her nose eagerly into the grain and begin to eat.

She put her arm around Melody's neck, taking comfort from the mare's warm, solid presence. Everything was so confusing. Grandpa and Lou had never argued like this before. She turned her face into the mare's rough mane.

She stood there for a moment and then felt warm breath on the back of her neck and looked around. As if sensing her unhappiness, Melody had turned her head to look at her. Lifting her nose, she gently nuzzled Amy's hair.

Amy swallowed. It was something her mom's horse, Pegasus, used to do before he'd died. Tears filled her eyes. "Oh, Melody," she whispered in despair. "I don't know which way to turn."

❧

Ty arrived back just after Amy and Ben had finished feeding and watering the horses. "So what's going on?" he said curiously to Amy. "Lou hardly said a word on the way to Scott's."

"She had an argument with Grandpa this morning," Amy replied, trying to sound composed. "And last night."

"About your dad?" Ty asked.

Amy nodded her head.

"How are you doing?" Ty asked, looking at her in concern.

Before Amy could answer, the phone rang. "I'll get it," she said, knowing that Grandpa would probably be getting dressed.

She ran down the yard and into the kitchen. "Heartland," she said. "Amy Fleming here."

"Hi, this is Judy Stillman. I was wondering if I could speak to Ben."

"Just a second, I'll get him," Amy said. Seeing a wheelbarrow by Red's stall, she went over. "Your mom's on the phone," she called.

"I don't want to talk to her," Ben replied tersely. "Tell her I'm busy."

"Go and tell her yourself," Amy retorted angrily.

Ben glared at her. "I said I don't want to talk to her!"

It was the last straw. Amy's temper finally snapped.

"Oh, come on, Ben!" she yelled in exasperation. "Stop being so stubborn. Just go and talk to her."

"No!" Ben said furiously.

"Well, I'm not going to!" Amy yelled. "You can't put me in the middle of it."

Ty came hurrying over. "What's going on?" he demanded.

"He won't talk to his mom," Amy said, turning to Ty for support. "She's on the phone."

"Ben, you can't make Amy deal with your mom," Ty said curtly. "You have to do it yourself."

For a moment it looked as if Ben was about to argue, but then he turned and stormed down the yard to the house.

Amy watched him, but Ty just shook his head and went back to the chores.

Amy waited at the top of the stable block for Ben to finish with the call. She felt like she had to apologize to him for overreacting. But when Ben came back, he just grabbed his pitchfork and headed toward Red's stall, obviously ignoring Amy.

"Ben!" Amy exclaimed, going after him.

He swung around furiously. "Look, I spoke to her, didn't I? Now just leave me alone. I've got to get back to the stalls."

Amy was exhausted by her conflicting emotions. "Ben, just take a break for a second. I want to talk. Mucking out isn't really important right now."

Ben stiffened. "Oh, sorry, I forgot," he spat. "Nothing I do here is important, is it?"

"What are you talking about?" Amy demanded. She had no clue what he was getting at.

"Nothing I do matters!" Ben shouted. "You and Ty treat the horses, I'm just a stable hand. It doesn't matter how hard I work — I'm still an outsider. Basically, there's all of you — and then there's me."

Amy was completely taken aback. "But that's crazy," she said in astonishment. "We don't think that way."

"No?" Ben said disbelievingly. "So how come you never tell me what's going on?" Turning on his heel, he marched back to Red's stall.

Amy was stunned. She'd had no idea Ben was feeling so left out. She paused for a moment and then went after him.

He was angrily forking damp straw into the wheelbarrow.

"Ben," Amy said, but he didn't look up or even acknowledge her presence. "Look, I'm sorry," she said quickly. "I wasn't leaving you out on purpose. I just wasn't ready to talk about what's going on. It's kind of complicated."

Ben seemed to hesitate for a moment, but he still didn't look up.

Amy swallowed. "It's my dad," she said to his back. "You know how he left us twelve years ago? Well, Lou's been in touch with him recently, and he tried to visit the other day. He was the man Grandpa said was looking for work."

Ben turned quickly. "That guy?"

Amy nodded and quickly explained everything else that had happened. "So now Lou's mad, and Grandpa's determined not to let him come here," she concluded. She looked at his astonished face. "I — I told you it was complicated."

Ben nodded. "Yeah, I guess." The fire had faded completely from his eyes and he looked awkward. "Thanks for telling me."

"I should have told you before," Amy said. "You're part of Heartland now."

Ben looked away. "Yeah, whatever," he muttered, not sounding as if he believed her.

"You *are*," Amy insisted.

Ben shrugged and turned back to the straw bed. After watching him for a few moments longer, Amy shook her head and walked away.

She found Ty in the back barn. "Still in one piece?" he said with a grin.

Amy was in no mood to be teased. She told him quickly about what Ben had said. "He doesn't feel like he's important here," she said.

"That doesn't make sense," Ty said.

"It's what he thinks," Amy replied. "I explained to him

what's going on with Lou and Grandpa, but it didn't seem to make much of a difference."

Ty frowned. "We should talk to him."

"I tried," Amy said, "but he's not in the mood to listen."

"We can try again later," Ty said. "You could say you need someone to ride Gypsy and go on the trails with him. It might be easier to get him to talk away from here."

Amy nodded. "OK, but what about you? Will you come?"

Ty shook his head. "I think it's better if I don't. He'll open up more if it's just the two of you."

✌

Two hours later, Amy and Ben rode away from Heartland on Moochie and Gypsy. The wind had picked up, and the horses jogged excitedly. Amy patted Moochie's bay neck. "Let's go on the field trail," she said. "It'll be more sheltered than up on the mountain."

Ben nodded, and they turned onto the trail that led down into the valley. They rode along the grassy path in silence. Amy tried to think of a way to begin the conversation she wanted to have, but whenever she glanced at Ben, the sight of his set profile made the words die on her tongue. What could she say? However she started, it was going to be a very awkward discussion.

Moochie pulled at his reins, and Amy decided to put off the conversation. "Want to trot?" she asked.

"OK," Ben said shortly.

Amy clicked her tongue, and Moochie leaped eagerly into a trot. The trees on either side of the trail were swaying in the wind, and Moochie's mane blew over Amy's hands. She looked across at Gypsy. The black mare was throwing up her head, looking as if she wanted to go faster, but Ben controlled her effortlessly.

"Gypsy's going well for you," Amy called.

They trotted around a bend in the path. Suddenly both Moochie and Gypsy shied violently. A pile of barrels covered with a plastic tarp had been left standing at the side of the trail. The tarp flapped wildly in the wind, making a thunderous noise.

Quickly recovering her balance, Amy brought Moochie under control and glanced over at Ben. He was soothing Gypsy, who was backing away from the barrels, trembling.

"It's OK, girl," Amy heard him saying. "They won't hurt you."

"I'll pass them first," Amy called, hoping that if Gypsy saw Moochie walk past the barrels, she would follow. She closed her legs on Moochie's sides. "Walk on," she said. But just as the big bay stepped forward, the tarp flapped furiously, and Moochie shied back again.

"Here, I'll try it," Ben said. Shortening his reins, he

urged Gypsy on. The black mare snorted, her eyes wide. But Ben insisted. Lifting her feet high, Gypsy approached the barrels, every muscle in her body tense.

Just then, a huge gust of wind blew under the tarp and tore it free from the weight of the barrel. It twirled upward. With a frightened whinny, Gypsy plunged sideways, but the wind whipped the tarp toward her, and the next moment it was caught between her back legs.

With a terrified snort, Gypsy began to buck viciously. "Ben!" Amy gasped in horror.

Gypsy's bucking had allowed the tarp to escape from her legs, and it was now twirling away across the field. But Gypsy seemed oblivious. With her head between her knees, she was still bucking wildly.

Amy's stomach somersaulted. There was no way Ben could stay on. She waited for him to come crashing to the ground. But he didn't. His body moved with the horse, his strong legs and seat anchoring him in the saddle. After three more bucks, he managed to pull Gypsy's head up. Amy saw his lips moving constantly as he sought to quiet the frightened mare. At long last, she came to a trembling halt.

"Are you OK, Ben?" Amy exclaimed, nudging Moochie and trotting forward.

Ben was leaning low over Gypsy's neck, his hands stroking and soothing as he calmed her down. He looked around.

"That was exciting," he said with a grin.

Amy stared at him in amazement. After what he had just been through, how could he smile like that? "How did you stay on?" she stammered.

"Guess it's just this special glue that I use," Ben joked.

"If you'd fallen off we'd have been back to square one," Amy said, suddenly realizing how lucky they'd been that Ben had stayed on and that all their work with Gypsy hadn't been ruined. "That was amazing!"

Ben suddenly looked embarrassed. "It's no big deal," he said awkwardly.

"Yes, it is!" Amy exclaimed.

But Ben didn't look convinced. "Anyone could have stayed on."

"That's not true," Amy said. "Ben! You're a great rider." She saw the doubt on his face, and all the words that she had been wanting to say tumbled out of her. "You don't realize how much work you saved us by staying on. I don't know why you feel like you're not a real part of Heartland. You really are, and if it took a wild mare almost throwing you off for me to convince you, then I guess it's a good thing."

Ben hesitated for a moment, trying to take in everything Amy had said. "Do you mean that?"

"Yes!" Amy cried. "We really need you. And we want you to feel like part of the team."

A flush of color crossed Ben's face. "Thanks," he said. "That really means a lot, Amy."

"It's the truth," she said simply. She grinned at him. "You're one of us now — whether you like it or not."

To her relief, Ben smiled back. "Sounds good to me," he said.

They exchanged smiles, and then Ben picked up his reins and asked Gypsy to walk on. "Looks like you were right about her," he said, changing the subject quickly. "She's not ready to go home yet."

"Definitely not," Amy agreed as she rode along the trail beside him. "So, are you looking forward to the show?" she asked, happy to go along with the change of subject now that the tension between them had subsided.

Ben nodded. "Yeah, I am. You and Soraya are still going to come, aren't you?"

"Of course," Amy said.

They rode on for a few more minutes in silence and then Ben spoke. "You — you know when my mom called this morning?" he said.

Amy nodded. How could she forget!

"Well, she said she can make it to the show after all," Ben said. "She's changed her meeting."

"That's great!" Amy exclaimed. She saw the frown on his face. "Isn't it?" she asked uncertainly.

Ben looked down at Gypsy's neck. "It's to the point that I don't care what she does," he said. "She doesn't care about me."

Amy stared at him. "But she's your mom."

"So?" Ben said. He shook his head bitterly. "I've never meant anything to her."

"I can't believe that's true," Amy said, thinking about the hurt in Mrs. Stillman's voice the day Ben had refused to speak to her on the phone.

Ben said, "Then why did she send me to live with my aunt? She just wanted me out of the way."

"I thought it was because you were getting into trouble," Amy said, remembering what she had been told about Ben's past. "You know, skipping school and stuff." She stared at his face. "If she didn't care, she wouldn't have done anything, Ben. It can't have been easy for her."

"Well, it wasn't easy for me, either!" Ben exclaimed with a sudden burst of anger. He shook his head. "It's not like I could make you understand. You can't know how hard it is. Your mom never abandoned you!" Almost before the words were out he seemed to regret them. He paled, but Amy hardly noticed. She was too angry.

"No! But my dad did!" she retorted with bitterness. "*My* mom's dead." Hot tears sprang to her eyes. "You don't know how lucky you are, Ben!" she yelled. "I can't believe you won't give her another chance."

Desperate to hide her tears, Amy dug her heels into Moochie's side. With a surprised snort, he leaped forward into a canter. Amy urged him on. She heard Ben yell at her to stop, but she ignored him. She wanted to get away from him — away from everything.

She pounded her legs against Moochie's sides, but no matter how fast he ran, images of her mother's and father's faces flashed before her eyes.

Moochie's canter became a gallop, his hooves pounding across the damp grass. The wind buffeted Amy's face, whipping tears from her eyes. She dug her heels in, trying to escape Ben, trying to escape everyone.

Through the mist of tears, Amy could see a sharp turn at the end of the path. She knew that they would never make it at such high speed, but for one wild moment she didn't care. Ben, Lou, Grandpa, Daddy — the only way to forget them was to keep going faster.

Suddenly, she heard the sound of hooves behind her. She glanced over her shoulder. Urged on by Ben, Gypsy was drawing near. Ben leaned low over the black mare's neck. "Amy, stop!" he yelled. "You can't make that turn!"

Ignoring him, Amy urged Moochie forward, the corner becoming impossibly close. In three powerful strides, Gypsy had caught up. Leaning over her neck, Ben grabbed at Moochie's reins.

Feeling the reins yank on his mouth, Moochie jerked his head up, his haunches skidding underneath him.

Amy was flung back in the saddle, and it was only by grasping a handful of Moochie's mane that she kept herself from falling off.

"What are you doing?" she screamed at Ben.

"Me?" he yelled back. "What about you?"

Amy was about to defend herself when suddenly she saw the corner, only a stride ahead of them, and realized how close she had come to hurting Moochie. At that speed, crashing off the path would have been devastating. Amy's emotions, stretched taut by the events of the last few days, snapped, and a sob burst from her. Scrambling down from Moochie's back, she collapsed on the ground and buried her head in her hands.

Within a few seconds, Ben had dismounted and was kneeling next to her. "It's OK," he said, putting an arm on her trembling shoulder. "Amy, I'm sorry. I just wasn't thinking. I've got a lot of things to work out. I'm sorry I brought you into it."

"It's not you," Amy said distraught. "It's everything — everything's gone wrong."

"Things will work out," Ben said. "You'll see."

"How can they?" Amy cried. "Grandpa and Lou are never going to agree about my dad. What if he comes back? What if Lou decides to leave Heartland and live with him?"

"That won't happen," Ben said. But Amy knew they were empty words. Who could tell what was going to happen in the future? And who knew what would happen if Daddy did come back? Her tears fell faster.

Powerless to say anything to comfort her, Ben kept his hand on her shoulder, gently rubbing until, at long last, her sobs started to subside. Amy took a deep breath and raised her head to look at him. "I'm sorry," she said, feeling horribly embarrassed. She rubbed her jacket sleeve across her face.

"Don't be," Ben said. "It's my fault. I'm too caught up in my problems. I forgot you've got your own things to deal with."

"It's OK," Amy said. She glanced at him and swallowed. There was something she had to say. "It's just hard sometimes. I can't help but think about how much I miss my mom whenever we talk about yours."

She saw Ben flinch and looked away. There was a long silence. Finally, Amy gathered up the reins and put her foot in the stirrup. "Come on," she said, not looking at him. "We should go."

She mounted. When she looked around, she saw that Ben was still standing beside Gypsy.

"Ben?" she said. "You ready?"

He didn't answer her question right away. "Yeah," he said quietly. "I guess I'm ready."

Not saying anything more, he mounted and clicked his tongue. The two horses moved forward.

They rode in silence. Ben seemed to be thinking about

something, but Amy hardly noticed. Her own thoughts had moved to the issue of Lou and Grandpa and the situation at home.

As they approached the barns, the two horses broke off, each heading to its stall. As they parted, Ben turned in his saddle. There was a decisive look on his face. "I'm going to go call my mom," he said.

Amy pulled herself out of her own thoughts and stared at him. "You are?"

"Yeah." Ben took a deep breath. "I was thinking that it doesn't matter what's happened, she's still my mom. And if she wants to come to the show, then it would be nice if she could be there."

Chapter Eight

Amy was untacking Moochie when Ty came to find her. "How did it go?" he asked her in a low voice.

After everything that had happened, Amy had almost forgotten that the reason for the ride had been to reassure Ben about the importance of his role at Heartland. "OK," she said. "I — I think we sorted things out."

"Good," Ty said, looking relieved.

"I'll tell you about it later," Amy said, letting herself out of the stall.

As Amy headed to the tack room, she heard Ben talking in Red's stall. She glanced in as she walked by and saw him on his cell phone. *All right,* Amy thought to herself, hoping the conversation with his mom was going well.

"So?" she demanded, stopping at the stall door when she heard him say good-bye. "How did it go?"

He shrugged. "Well, I told her she could come to the show."

"And she's going to?" Amy asked eagerly, shifting the weight of Moochie's saddle in her arms.

Ben nodded. "She's meeting me there." He ran a hand through his hair. "That's going to be fun," he said with sarcasm.

"It'll be fine," Amy said optimistically.

But Ben looked far from convinced.

Well, it may not have been a full-blown reconciliation, she thought as she walked away from Red's stall, *but at least Ben is speaking to his mom again — surely that's a step in the right direction.*

❧

For the rest of the day, Ben was like a different person around the yard. He laughed and joked and even came down to the house to have lunch with Amy and Ty.

"Well, whatever you said to him must have worked," Ty said to Amy that afternoon as they both filled water buckets at the faucet. "He's never been so relaxed."

Amy then told Ty about how Gypsy had shied when the tarp ripped free and about her conversation with Ben afterward, but she didn't say anything about the way she had taken off on Moochie. She felt ashamed of her reaction and wanted to forget what she had done.

"Best of all, he got in touch with his mom," Amy said. "She's going to meet us at the show next week."

"So you're still planning to go and watch?" Ty asked.

"Yes," Amy said. "Why don't you come?"

"I'd like to," Ty replied. "But I'm meeting some friends — it's my day off."

Amy looked at him in shock. Ty hardly ever went out unless it was to do something with horses. "Who are you meeting?" she asked.

"Pete and Greg. They're friends of mine from high school," Ty said. "We've been planning it for a while — a kind of reunion before they go off to college. I would have liked to have made it to the show, though. I hope Ben does well. He's been working so hard with Red — he really deserves it. I can't believe how much they've improved."

Just then, the farmhouse door opened and Grandpa looked out. "Amy!" he called. "Phone call! It's Mr. Phillips!"

Amy ran down to the kitchen and took the phone from her grandpa. "Hi," she said. "Amy speaking."

She heard the hesitancy in Mr. Phillips's voice. "I — I was just calling to find out how Melody is," he said. "I hope you don't mind."

"Not at all," Amy said. She hadn't spoken to him since just after Melody's accident. She had meant to call him, but the events of the last few days has pushed all other thoughts out of her mind. Now she was glad to be able to give him good news. "She's doing really well," she said. "Her wound's healing, and she's not showing any sign of going into labor." She remembered the best news of all. "And we've felt her foal kick, which means it's alive."

"Oh, how wonderful," Ray Phillips gasped. Amy heard him take a deep, trembling breath. "I've been so worried," he admitted.

"Well, like I said, she's doing fine," Amy said.

"My wife would have been pleased," Mr. Phillips said quietly.

Amy heard the note of sadness in his voice. "Will you come and see the foal when it's born?" she asked.

"I'd love to," Ray Phillips replied. He paused. When he spoke again it was with difficulty. "Maybe if I could just see for myself that Melody and her foal are OK, then I'd feel that I did the right thing after all."

"I'll call you and let you know as soon as the foal is born," Amy promised. "And, Mr. Phillips," she added quickly, "I'm sure everything will be just fine."

When she put the phone down, she was thinking hard. Mr. Phillips obviously still blamed himself for Melody's accident. She hoped that Melody's foal would be healthy, so Mr. Phillips could see for himself that everything had worked out. She hoped with all her heart that Melody and her foal were going to make it.

❧

Lou came back from Scott's that evening, but she hardly spoke to Grandpa. As the next few days passed, the silences between them grew longer. There were no more arguments, but the tension in the air was apparent. Lou was determined to find their father. She called all the hotels and lodges in the area to see if he'd been staying there, but apart from the time she was on the phone she avoided being in the house, spending her time in the yard with Ben and Ty, or going out with Scott.

For the first time in her life, Amy found herself almost looking forward to going to school each day; at least it meant she could escape from the atmosphere at Heartland. She longed to be able to do something about the growing rift between Grandpa and Lou but didn't know what she could do. Grandpa was adamant about not having their father at Heartland, and Lou was equally determined to track him down.

On Friday afternoon, Lou was waiting expectantly when Amy got home from school. "I think I've found where Daddy was staying," she said, her eyes sparkling. "There was a Tim Fleming staying at a place called the River House Inn. He checked out on Sunday."

Amy stared at her. With each day that had passed, she

had begun to think, with relief, that Lou wasn't going to be able to track their father down. "Was it definitely Daddy?" she stammered.

"I don't know," Lou said excitedly. "But I'm sure it must be. The name's right, and they said he was tall with dark hair and that he checked in there the day before Daddy visited here. They didn't know where he was going to next, but they have an address for him."

"Are — are you going to write to him again?" Amy asked.

"I already have," Lou replied. "I sent a letter off this afternoon. I told him that we were both desperate to see him." She must have seen the shock on Amy's face because she frowned. "Why are you looking like that? You told me that you wanted to find him. You told me that you'd *help* me."

Amy remembered her words the night that she and Scott had found Lou outside the cemetery. "I know," she said, trying to appease Lou. "And I do want you to find him, it's just —"

She broke off as Grandpa came into the room. The effect on Lou was immediate; a shutter seemed to fall across her face. "Well, I'll let you know if there's any news," she said abruptly to Amy, and then she turned and left the kitchen.

Amy looked at her grandpa. She didn't know what to say. The longer the argument went on, the less likely it looked that it would ever be resolved. She couldn't understand why they hadn't made up.

"Did — did Lou tell you she thinks she's found where Daddy was staying?" she asked.

"No," Jack said, looking shocked.

"She's got an address for him, and she's already written to him again," Amy said.

Jack shook his head. There was a moment's silence between them.

"Grandpa," Amy whispered suddenly, "I don't want to see him."

Jack looked at her and then held out his arms. "Come here," he said.

Amy stepped forward and felt his arms close around her, warm and comforting.

"You know, you have to make that decision for yourself, but whatever you decide," he said softly, "I'll always be here for you, no matter what."

‘’∞

Five minutes later, Amy was headed up the yard — she'd decided getting back to her chores was the best way to distract herself from what Lou had told her. It was cold outside, and she was glad of her warm jacket.

Seeing Ty come out of the tack room, she jogged up to meet him. "Have you checked on Melody today?" she asked.

"She's a bit restless," Ty replied, "but I've walked her around several times and that seems to have calmed her down a bit."

Amy nodded. Scott had told them that it was likely that Melody would get livelier as her wound healed and the infection went down. He'd also said that, all being well, they could start letting her out to graze for a few hours each day the following week.

"I'll go and see her," Amy said.

Just then, Ben appeared, leading Red down from the training ring.

"How was he?" Ty called.

"Great," Ben replied, stopping and patting Red's powerful neck. "We just worked on the flat so he can save his energy for tomorrow."

"I bet he'll be totally fabulous," Amy said confidently. "Are you going to bathe him?"

Ben glanced at the gray sky and shook his head. "I think it's too cold. I'll just wash his tail and give the rest of him a really good brushing. I'll braid him in the morning." He clicked his tongue and went on down the yard.

"The forecast says there could be snow in the next few days," Ty commented as he and Amy continued to Melody's stall.

"I hope it holds off until after the show," Amy said, shivering.

Ty nodded.

They reached the back barn. Melody was looking out over her door. "Have you been restless today?" Amy said, stroking the mare's warm neck and looking at her churned-up bed. "I could take her for another walk," she decided out loud.

"Sure," Ty replied. "I'll fix her bedding while she's out of the stall."

Amy slipped Melody's halter on and led the mare down the drive. Melody's pregnant belly seemed bigger than ever. It was hard to believe that she still had another two weeks to go before the foal was due. She walked slowly and heavily, and Amy noticed that her legs had filled up with fluid again.

"Poor girl," she said to the mare. "You'll be happier when you can go out and graze for a bit each day, won't you? That exercise will keep the swelling down."

She paused to let Melody nibble at the grass, but to her surprise, the mare didn't seem hungry. She tore at a few strands and then lost interest.

Amy decided to take her back to her stall. She bumped into Ben, who was carrying Red's tack. He frowned. "She looks close to foaling," he said.

Amy stopped Melody. "You think so?" she questioned anxiously. "She's still got two weeks to go."

"I'd say no more than a week, maximum," Ben said.

"Look at her hindquarters — all her muscles have slackened off. That normally only happens a few days before labor starts."

Feeling worried, Amy led Melody up to the barn and into her stall. What if Ben was right and Melody had her foal early? She would call Scott and give him a heads-up.

"He may be right," Scott replied when she got through to him and told him what Ben had said. "But don't worry. It's not really too early for her to have her foal. Mares rarely give birth on the day they're supposed to. Going into labor a couple of weeks either side of their due date is considered normal. The foal's health won't be at risk if it is born now."

"Will you come see her?" Amy asked, feeling slightly reassured. "Just to make sure?"

"I've got a really busy couple of days, I'm afraid," Scott said. "Why don't you see how it goes and give me a call if you get worried. Otherwise I'll try to come on Sunday."

℞

There was a thick frost on the ground when Amy got up early the next morning. As she strode up the yard, she glanced at the gray sky. The clouds looked like they were heavy with snow. She frowned, hoping that it would hold off at least until after the show.

Melody was walking restlessly around her stall. Amy went in and ran her hands over the mare's sides and hindquarters. Her muscles felt soft.

"How is she?"

Amy turned and saw Ben standing by the door. "You're here early," she said in surprise.

"I didn't sleep that well," he replied. "I couldn't stop thinking about the show — and about seeing my mom."

"Well, Melody seems about the same as yesterday," Amy said, patting the chestnut mare. "She still seems restless." She frowned. "Maybe I shouldn't go to the show, after all. Maybe I should stay here."

"But you've got to come," Ben said quickly. "I need your support. The showground's only an hour away," he added. "Can't you ask your grandpa to keep an eye on Melody? If anything happens he can call us on my cell phone and we'll come right back."

Amy felt torn, but she reluctantly agreed. "OK, if Grandpa doesn't mind."

Jack was preparing breakfast in the kitchen. He frowned as she came in. "You look worried, honey," he said. "Is everything OK?"

Amy explained about Melody. "I'm really not sure about leaving her, but Ben really wants me to go to the show."

"You go," Grandpa said immediately. "I can keep an eye on Melody. If there's any change, I'll call you right away." He seemed to see the uncertainty on Amy's face. "Don't worry about it. I might not have experienced many mares foaling, but I've seen plenty of calvings. If worst comes to worst, I'll be able to hold the fort until Scott gets here."

Amy still felt torn, but deep down she knew he was right. Grandpa had years of experience with farm animals. If anything happened, he would know what to do. "Thanks, Grandpa," she said. "I'll tell Ben I can go."

❧

Soraya arrived at eight-thirty. "Hey!" Amy called, coming out of Jake's stall.

"Hi," Soraya replied. She waved good-bye to her mom and ran up the yard to meet Amy. "So what can I do?" she asked, dumping her bag on the ground.

"Take your pick," Amy said. "There are the stalls in the other barn to finish and all the horses to water, and someone needs to walk Melody. We're going to have to work pretty hard, because Ben is busy getting Red groomed and braided. We're leaving for the show at noon."

Soraya immediately went to find a pitchfork and started helping Amy with Jake's stall. "Where's Ben now?" she asked.

"In the barn," Amy replied. She thought about the

way he had been hurrying through his chores that morning. "I think he's a bit nervous."

Just then, Ben came to Jake's stall. "The stalls in the barn are done," he said to Amy. "Is it OK if I braid Red now?"

"Sure," Amy said. "Soraya and I will finish off the stalls down here."

"Great," Ben said, and jogged off.

"He does look nervous," Soraya commented to Amy in a low voice.

Amy nodded as she watched Ben disappear into the tack room. She desperately hoped everything was going to go well for him that day — both in the ring *and* with his mom.

Chapter Nine

At noon, Amy, Soraya, and Ben loaded Red into the trailer and got into the pickup. Grandpa came out of the house to wave them off.

"Good luck!" he called out as Ben started the engine.

Amy took one last glance toward the back barn and Melody's stall. She hated leaving her but knew she could trust Grandpa.

They reached the showground an hour before the class was due to start. Ben carefully steered the trailer through the horses and ponies milling around and found a quiet corner to park. "I'll go and sign in," he said, jumping out of the pickup.

"Do you want us to get Red out for you?" Amy asked.

Ben nodded. "Yeah, thanks."

Soraya lowered the ramp while Amy went into the

trailer. As the ramp went down, Red let out a piercing whinny. The muscles on his neck were tense with excitement, and he danced out of the trailer beside Amy, his head held high.

While Amy held him, Soraya removed the protective wraps from his legs. He sidestepped excitedly.

"I think we'd better walk him around to calm him down," Amy said, seeing the damp patches of sweat darkening his neck.

"Do you think Ashley will be here?" Soraya asked as they put on Red's bridle.

"Probably," Amy said, making a face at the thought. Ashley Grant was in their class at school. Her parents owned a hunter barn — Greenbriar — and Ashley rode in shows nearly every weekend. The horses and ponies she rode were always expensive and very well trained. She and Amy had often competed against each other in the Large Pony Hunter classes, where, much to Ashley's disgust, Sundance had carried off the blue ribbon a good bit of the time.

However, as Amy and Soraya walked Red around the showground, they didn't see Ashley or her family.

They had just begun to tack Red up when Ben returned with his number.

"All right," he said, "the classes are running on time so I should start warming him up."

"He's kind of high-strung," Soraya commented.

"He always is when he comes to a show," Ben said, patting Red's gleaming neck. "He loves them." He glanced down at his jeans. "I need to get changed, too," he said. "Can you walk him around a little longer?"

Amy nodded. "At your command — we'll do whatever you need."

Soraya giggled as Ben disappeared into the living quarters of his trailer. "You said it!"

Amy chucked Red's bell boots at her. "Put these on!" she said with a grin. "And quit dreaming!"

Five minutes later, Ben came out of the trailer. Amy thought she was going to have to physically shut Soraya's mouth for her, it dropped open so far. Ben's jeans and barn jacket were gone, and in their place were spotless tan breeches, long leather boots, and a beautifully cut black show jacket. Even though Ben wasn't Amy's type, she had to admit that he looked very nice.

Seemingly oblivious to their reactions, Ben walked over to Red. "Thanks for tacking him up," he said, taking the reins.

"That's OK," Amy said, realizing that Soraya was incapable of speech.

Ben mounted. "I'll go and warm up," he said.

Amy and Soraya watched Ben ride off, Red prancing, his powerful muscles clearly defined under his glossy chestnut coat, Ben sitting effortlessly in the saddle. They looked perfect together.

"Wow! And I never thought I'd find a cute, nice guy who likes horses," Soraya breathed.

Amy gave her friend a knowing smile. "Come on, let's go and watch."

They found a space at the side of the schooling ring and watched Ben start to work Red. The ring was busy, with horses and ponies cantering around in all directions and several trainers standing in the middle, shouting out instructions. But Ben managed to find a reasonably quiet corner and began to get Red warmed up.

Suddenly, Soraya nudged Amy. "It's Ashley! Look!"

Amy glanced around. Ashley Grant was trotting into the ring on a beautiful bay hunter. Her long platinum-blond hair was tied back in a single braid, and her perfectly tailored navy show jacket accentuated her tall, slim figure. The only thing that marred the picture was the scowl on Ashley's face.

"Out of my way!" she snapped at a younger girl who was getting ready to jump one of the practice fences. Barging the bay hunter past the girl's gray pony, Ashley cantered toward the jump. The bay sailed over it, his dark coat gleaming. Ashley smiled smugly as if she was aware of exactly how good she looked.

"How come she always has such lovely horses?" Soraya said. "It's totally unfair."

Amy nodded. She wouldn't have swapped Sundance for anything, but Ashley did get to ride the most amazing horses. For a moment, Amy wished she had Sundance there so that she could at least attempt to wipe the self-satisfied smile off Ashley's face.

Just then, Ashley turned and saw them. "Oh, no!" Amy groaned under her breath as Ashley turned her horse and began to trot toward them. "How could she have spotted us?"

"It must be an evil sixth sense," Soraya whispered.

Ashley stopped along the fence rail. "What are you two doing here?" she said, as if they had no right to be at a show.

"What do you think?" Amy retorted.

"Well, you're obviously not competing," Ashley said, sweeping her green eyes disparagingly over their yard clothes. "Not even *you* would go in a ring looking like that, Amy."

Before Amy could reply, Ben came trotting over. "Can you take Red for me?" he said to Amy and Soraya. "I want to go and have a look at the course." Suddenly he seemed to notice Ashley. "Oh, sorry," he said quickly. "I didn't mean to interrupt."

"You haven't interrupted *anything*," Amy said pointedly.

"Of course we'll hold Red," Soraya said, jumping over the fence.

Ashley was looking at Ben. "Hi," she said, her lips curving into a smile. "I don't think we've met before. I'm Ashley Grant, and you're —"

"Ben Stillman," Ben said dismounting. "I work at Heartland." He held out his hand. "Nice to meet you, Ashley."

"And you," Ashley replied.

"Well, I'd better go walk the course," Ben said. "See you around."

"You can count on it," Ashley purred, giving him a little wave as he walked off.

Amy glanced at Soraya. She was biting her lip as she checked Red's girth.

"Ashley!" a voice bellowed. Ashley swung around. Her mother, Val Grant, was making her way through the crowd, a frown on her square-jawed face. "What are you doing?" she shouted. "Why aren't you working Dreamtime in?"

Ashley turned abruptly to Amy and Soraya. "See you, then," she said coldly, and cantered off.

"Can you believe Ashley?" Soraya exclaimed the second she was out of earshot. "Did you hear how she was cooing at Ben?"

Amy nodded. "He didn't seem that interested, though," she said quickly.

"I guess." Soraya sighed. "I just wish he was interested in *me*."

❧

After ten minutes, Ben came back from walking the course.

"What's it like?" Amy asked.

"Not too bad," Ben replied. He glanced at his watch.

"What time did your mom say she'd be here?" Amy asked, guessing what was on his mind.

"Three-thirty," Ben said shortly. "Fifteen minutes ago."

"I'm sure she'll make it," Soraya said reassuringly. "She probably just ran into traffic."

"Or she decided not to come," Ben said tersely. He swung himself back into the saddle. "I'd better keep Red moving. We're jumping fifth in the order." Without another word, he rode off.

Amy watched him trot around the schooling area, his eyes scanning the crowds. *Please let his mom get here on time*, she thought desperately.

The loudspeaker crackled and announced that the High Preliminary class was about to begin.

"Do we have a cloth to dust off Red before he goes in?" Soraya asked suddenly.

Amy shook her head.

"I'll run back to the trailer and get one," Soraya said. She ran off through the throngs of people and horses.

Amy looked around, hoping Ben's mom would appear. In the training ring, Ben turned Red toward a practice fence, but he didn't seem to be concentrating, and Red's forelegs clattered into the top rail. Glad for something to do, Amy slid between the fence boards, walked quickly into the ring, and put the fence up again.

"Thanks," Ben said, his face grim.

Dodging the cantering horses and shouting trainers, Amy went back to the fence. She saw Ben trying to canter Red in a figure eight, but the horse appeared to sense his owner's tension and threw his head up, fighting for the reins.

"And coming into the ring we have number 381," the loudspeaker announced.

"Ben!" Amy called. "You're in the hole."

Ben rode Red toward her. Despite the cold, the chestnut was sweating. He tossed his head in agitation.

Just then Soraya appeared. "Here, I have a cloth. I'll rub him down," she offered.

Ben's face relaxed for a second. "Thanks, Soraya," he said as she started to rub the sweat marks away from Red's side.

"That's OK," Soraya said, smiling up at him.

Ben looked at them both. "Thanks for coming today, you guys. It's good to have the support."

Amy heard a hard edge to his voice and realized he was thinking about his mom.

The loudspeaker crackled into life. "That was four faults for number 381, and now we have number 382 in the ring."

"You'd better get to the ring," Amy said quickly. "You're two away."

Ben nodded and took up his reins.

As Red stepped forward, a voice called out. "Ben!"

Ben swung around abruptly. "Mom!" he exclaimed.

A woman was hurrying through the crowd toward them. The thick blond hair that fell around her shoulders was exactly the same shade as Ben's, and her blue eyes were the mirror image of his.

"I got held up on the way here," she gasped. "I thought I wasn't going to make it."

"Well, it wouldn't be the first time," Ben said, his voice suddenly cool. "Something came up at work?"

"No," Judy Stillman said, looking at him in surprise. "I told you, I canceled my meeting today. It was the snow. It's really falling north of here."

"It's snowing!" Soraya said.

As Judy Stillman nodded, the loudspeaker made an announcement. "Will number 384 come to the collecting ring, please. Number 384."

"Ben! That's you!" Amy exclaimed.

Ben seemed to hesitate for a moment.

"Go on," his mom said. "We can talk later. I want to see you jump."

Amy saw some of the tension leave Ben's face.

"Number 384!" the loudspeaker said.

Ben loosened his reins and Red plunged forward.

"Good luck!" Soraya called excitedly.

Ben turned in his saddle. "Thanks!" he shouted, and then he jogged Red toward the collecting ring.

"I'm Amy Fleming," Amy said to Mrs. Stillman, realizing that they hadn't been introduced. "And this is my friend Soraya Martin."

"Judy Stillman," Ben's mom said. "It's nice to meet you both. I really thought I wasn't going to get here."

"We'd better go into the arena," Soraya said quickly, "or we'll miss Ben's round."

They hurried to the viewing gallery of the indoor arena, found three empty seats, and sat down.

"Our first clear round," the announcer said as the rider before Ben rode out of the arena to a round of applause. "And now we have number 384, Ben Stillman, riding What Luck."

"Here he is!" Amy exclaimed, grabbing Soraya's arm.

Ben came trotting into the arena on Red. He looked calm and utterly focused, his lips moving inaudibly as he spoke quietly to the horse. Red seemed to mirror his rider's confidence. Amy crossed her fingers. They just *had* to do well.

The starting bell rang out, and Ben turned Red toward the first fence, a solid green-and-white oxer. Amy leaned forward in her seat as the chestnut approached it smoothly. She was so nervous it felt as if she were riding the course herself, as if she could feel every stride Red was taking. Ben met the jump perfectly and Red soared over it, his forelegs snapping up neatly.

Then he was cantering toward the gate. He sailed over that and then over the upright, the wall, the red-and-blue double, another oxer, and finally turned toward the treble. As he approached the line of three jumps, Amy held her breath. "Go on!" She breathed, knowing that if he could just clear this last combination, he would be in the jump-off. "Go on!"

Red took off over the first. He cleared it. He seemed to hesitate, but Ben sat down in the saddle and drove him on, and in one stride he was over the second. Again he seemed to falter as he approached the third, but Ben urged him on and Red responded. Taking two neat strides, he cleared the final fence.

"Yes!" Amy and Soraya exclaimed in delight as the audience broke into a round of applause.

"And that's a clear round for Ben Stillman on What Luck," the announcer said over the clapping.

Amy was totally delighted. "He's in the jump-off!" she cried, turning to Ben's mom.

Judy Stillman's eyes were shining with pride. "He was wonderful!"

Soraya jumped to her feet. "Let's go and find him!"

Quickly, they made their way outside. Ben had

jumped off Red and was patting the chestnut as if he were never going to stop.

Amy raced up to him. "Nice round!" she gasped, patting Red, too.

"Wasn't he amazing?" Ben said to her, his eyes filled with happiness. "He didn't touch a single rail."

Soraya reached them. "Way to go, Ben!" she cried.

Caught up in the moment, Ben gave her a hug. "We're in the jump-off, Soraya!" he exclaimed.

Amy saw the look of shock on her friend's face as Ben hugged her. However, it was quickly replaced by a smile of utter elation. "You were amazing!" Soraya said. "Oh, Ben."

Hearing his mom's voice, Ben pulled away from Soraya and turned. Judy Stillman was standing behind him, her eyes shining with delighted tears. "You looked great. I'm so proud of you," she said.

"Really?" Ben said, frowning suddenly.

Judy Stillman looked at him in surprise. "Of course! You rode a wonderful round." She looked at him for a moment and then shook her head. "Why wouldn't I be proud?"

"I've just never heard you say anything like that before," Ben said.

"That's not true, Ben," Judy protested.

"Are you sure?" Ben said, his voice suddenly cold. "I can't remember the last time you watched me ride."

"Ben," Judy began, "I know the last eight years have been hard for you, but you have to believe me, I've only ever done what I thought was best for you."

Ben laughed bitterly. "Including leaving me at Lisa's?"

"Leaving you?" Judy echoed. "But I came to see you every weekend."

"Yeah — that didn't last long," Ben said.

Judy stepped toward him. "Did you think I didn't want to come?" she said intensely. "Ben, the reason I stopped coming all the time was because it seemed to upset you so much. You hardly ever spoke to me. It seemed like you didn't want me around. I talked it over with Lisa, and we figured that it might be best if I gave you some space to settle in."

Amy saw the confusion in Ben's eyes. "But you always said it was your work." His voice, still angry, was now edged with uncertainty.

"That was just an excuse," Judy said. "I couldn't just stop coming without an explanation. It made it easier for me, that way."

Ben looked confused. "I've always believed it was your work. I thought it meant more to you than I did."

Judy stared at him. "Ben, nothing has *ever* meant more to me than you," she exclaimed. "I worked because I had nothing else in my life." Her voice suddenly shook.

"Having you was the best thing that ever happened to me. You're my son, and I love you."

There was a moment's silence. Slowly the confusion and hurt left Ben's face. "I didn't know, Mom," he said quietly. "Really, I didn't."

Mrs. Stillman reached out with both hands to Ben. He hesitated for a brief second, and then he stepped forward to hug her.

Amy and Soraya exchanged delighted grins.

Mother and son held each other for a long while. The moment was eventually broken by the sound of Red stamping his front hoof impatiently into the ground.

"I think Red's had enough of this sentimental moment," Judy said, pulling back from Ben with a smile.

Ben nodded. "Getting jealous, boy?" he said, patting the big chestnut.

Red tossed his head.

"Come on, let's get you back to the trailer." Ben smiled. "You get a break before the next round."

❧

There were ten horses in the jump-off. "So the fastest one wins?" Judy asked as Ben waited to go in the ring.

"The quickest round with the fewest penalty points," Ben explained. "But I'm not going to hurry Red. He's still young, and I'd prefer he jumped a clear round than rush it and knock down a load of fences. We've been working on keeping a steady pace at home. I don't want him to get overexcited and forget what he's learned. There'll be plenty of time for him to build up speed when he's more experienced. I'm just happy he made it in the jump-off."

Amy had to agree with Ben. She hated it when people raced young horses before they were ready. She thought Ben was smart to take it one step at a time. It would make Red a better jumper in the end.

The horse before Ben came trotting out of the ring. "Good luck!" Amy and Soraya called before going back to the stands with Judy.

Red tossed his head and snorted as he came into the ring and saw the jumps. He was obviously excited, but Ben kept to his word, steadying him at the start before guiding him through a fast but careful, clear round. When Red cantered out of the arena, his ears were pricked and his eyes confident.

"It was perfect — just the round I wanted," Ben said happily to the others as they hurried to congratulate him afterward.

"You were fantastic!" Amy exclaimed, feeding Red a mint from her pocket.

And it was enough to earn Red a yellow ribbon for third place. Only two other horses jumped clear, the rest completing fast rounds but gaining penalty points after knocking fences down. Amy, Soraya, and Judy watched proudly as Ben rode Red into the ring to collect his ribbon.

Amy turned happily to Soraya. "This has been a great day!" she said.

❧

As they untacked Red and got him ready for the journey home, Amy realized with a start how much colder it had become. Her breath froze in the air, and as she fastened the wraps on Red's legs, a few flakes of snow drifted down from the sky and landed on the nylon straps.

"You'd better get going," Judy said, helping Ben put his tack away. "It's coming in from the north, and the forecast said it would pick up toward nightfall."

"What are you going to do, Mom?" Ben asked.

"I was planning to head home," Judy said. "But looking at this weather, it might be best to find somewhere to stay around here for the night."

"You can stay at my place," Ben said quickly. "It's nothing special, but I have a fold-out bed."

Judy smiled at him. "That sounds perfect. I'll follow you back."

It didn't take long to get Red loaded up.

Amy, Ben, and Soraya climbed into the pickup. It was starting to get dark now. "I hope we get back before too much snow falls," Amy said, looking up at the ominously thick clouds as Ben started the engine and the wipers swept across the windshield.

"We don't have too far to go," Ben said.

"And it's not snowing that hard yet," Soraya pointed out. She smiled at Ben.

As Ben and Soraya talked happily about Red's performance in the jump-off, Amy watched the snowflakes falling through the dusk and thought about Melody. There had been no phone call from her grandpa, which must mean that she was OK. Amy was relieved. The last thing they wanted was for Melody to go into labor if there was a heavy snowfall that night. The farm's winding drive could become impassable in deep snow.

As they drove north toward Heartland, Judy following, the snow started to fall more quickly, and the drifts on the sides of the roads became noticeably deeper. Amy couldn't remember the last time it had snowed so much so early in the autumn.

❧

Eventually, they turned up the drive to the farm, the truck's wheels crunching into the frozen snow.

"Looks like we got here just in time," Ben said.

The farmhouse door opened as they drove into the yard, and Grandpa came out. He looked relieved to see them. "I was just about to call you," he said. "I was worried about you getting back in this weather."

"It didn't start really falling until we were almost here," Amy said.

"Well, at least you're here now," Grandpa replied. "I've fed the horses and put their blankets on. There's feed waiting for Red in his stall."

"Thanks, Grandpa," Amy said gratefully. "How's Melody?"

"Just fine." Grandpa turned to Soraya. "Your mom's been on the phone," he said. "I think you'd better call her and let her know that you're back safely."

"Sure," Soraya said.

"I'll give you a lift home," Ben called as Soraya headed for the house. "It'll save your mom coming out."

Soraya smiled at him. "Oh, that would be great!"

Judy parked her car and got out. "This is Ben's mom," Amy explained to Grandpa. "She's staying with him tonight."

"Pleased to meet you." Judy smiled at Grandpa.

"Why don't you come and wait inside while Ben gets things put away?" Grandpa offered.

Amy helped Ben unload Red and settle him into his stall. "I'll unbraid him for you," Amy offered. "You should head out before the snow gets any worse."

"Are you sure?" Ben said.

"Of course, no problem," she replied.

Ben went up to Red. "'Bye, big fella," he said softly. "You were the best today." The chestnut snorted and nuzzled his head against his owner's chest. Ben rubbed his forehead and then turned and smiled at Amy. "Thanks for all your help today."

"My pleasure," Amy said. "See you tomorrow."

She waved good-bye as Soraya, Ben, and his mom got into the pickup, and then she went back to Red's stall. She had just taken out the first braid when Grandpa appeared with a mug of chicken soup. "Here," he said. "You must be starving."

"Thanks, Grandpa." Amy took it gratefully. She wrapped her fingers around the hot mug, savoring the warmth. It was impossible to take out braids with gloves on, and her hands were freezing.

"So how was the show?" Grandpa asked.

Amy told him about Red's success and also about how Ben had made peace with his mom. "They finally seem to have put the past behind them." She grinned.

"That's good," Grandpa said quietly. "There's nothing worse than a family at odds." Amy heard the sadness in his voice and knew what he was thinking.

"How — how's Lou been today?" she asked tentatively.

"She's been in her room most of the evening," Grandpa

said. "Though she did come out and help me feed the horses when it started to snow."

"Oh, that's good," Amy said, feeling encouraged.

"Except she didn't speak to me." Grandpa sighed. "She hasn't said a word to me all day." He suddenly looked old and tired. "I'm going to start dinner. Don't be out here too long."

Amy watched him go, wishing more than ever that there was something she could do to sort things out between him and Lou.

✒

After unbraiding Red, Amy brushed out the horse's mane and then left him to a well-earned rest. She checked on all the other horses and then went down to the house. Lou only made a brief appearance at dinner and didn't even talk much to Amy, disappearing to her room again as soon as the plates were cleared. Amy sat with Grandpa in the warmth of the kitchen, watching TV while the snow continued to fall outside.

At ten o'clock, Amy reluctantly got up from her chair. "I'm going to check on Melody again," she said to Grandpa.

"I'm sure she'll be fine," Jack replied.

But Amy knew she wouldn't be happy unless she made sure. She pulled on her boots, thick coat, and gloves and stepped outside. Snow swirled around her and a freezing wind bit into her cheeks. Shivering with cold, she fought her way through the drifts and up to the back barn.

Snow had piled up outside the doors, and she had to get a shovel to clear it. With a great effort, she heaved the door open and staggered into the quiet warmth of the barn. Sighing with relief, she shut the door behind her and felt for the light switch. As the lights lit up the darkness, she heard a few surprised snorts and rustles from the stalls.

She hurried down the aisle. "How are you, girl?" she said as she looked over Melody's door.

The words died on her lips. Melody was standing in her stall, her head down, her tail swishing. Damp patches of sweat stood out on her sides. Just then, a groan erupted from her and she sank to her knees. Amy caught sight of the beginnings of an opaque sac protruding from under Melody's tail and gasped.

Forgetting about the cold, Amy turned and raced back up the aisle and out of the barn. Stumbling and tripping she ran, half-blinded, through the snow.

"Grandpa!" she shouted, bursting into the kitchen. "Come quick! Melody's having her foal!"

Chapter Ten

Grandpa was on his feet almost before the words had left Amy's mouth. "What? Now?" he exclaimed.

"Yes!" Amy gasped. "I could see the sac coming out of her."

Grandpa strode into the hall. "Lou!" he shouted. "It's an emergency." He began to pull on his coat and hat. "Where's the foaling kit, Amy?"

"In the tack room," Amy said. "Should I call Scott?"

Before Grandpa could answer, Lou came running into the kitchen. "What is it?" she asked, her eyes flying from Amy to Grandpa. "What happened?"

"Melody's having her foal early," Grandpa said, going to the door. "Can you get in touch with Scott? I'm going up to the stall with Amy."

Lou grabbed the phone, her argument with Grandpa

seemingly forgotten in her desire to help. As she punched in the number, she asked, "Do you need anything else?"

"Boil some water and bring it up to the stall," Grandpa said.

"Sure." Lou nodded as Grandpa strode outside.

Amy ran after him, and together they fought their way through the blizzard, stopping only in the tack room to collect the foaling kit.

"I hope this is going to be a regular foaling," Grandpa shouted as they stepped out into the wind and snow again. "Scott's going to find it hard to get through to us in this!"

Amy's heart was pounding so fast that she thought it was going to burst. "Come on, Grandpa! We have to hurry!" she said.

They reached the barn, its electric lights shining out like a beacon into the darkness. Amy ran down the aisle, hugging the foaling kit against her ribs. She could hear Grandpa behind her.

"She's still down!" She gasped as Grandpa caught up with her at Melody's door.

The chestnut mare was lying in the straw, groaning as her sides heaved with a fresh contraction. Amy reached for the door bolt, but Grandpa stopped her.

"We'd better stay out here," he said in a low voice. "Animals don't like being disturbed when they're giving birth. If we go in, it might upset her. As long as there aren't any complications, she's better off on her own."

Amy looked at Melody's hindquarters. More of the opaque bag — the amniotic membrane that covered the foal — could be seen pushing through, under Melody's tail.

"The front hooves are out," Grandpa said, nodding toward the bag. "That's a good sign. The foal must be facing the right way."

Amy looked more closely and could see what he meant. She could make out two tiny hooves through the protective covering of the bag.

Melody's sides heaved again, and the hooves and front legs slid out a little more.

"Will we see the muzzle soon?" Amy asked.

Grandpa nodded. "It should come right after the front legs."

They watched as Melody continued to strain, but nothing happened. No muzzle appeared. Melody continued to groan.

"What's happening? Why's the head not coming?" Amy asked Grandpa anxiously.

Jack shook his head. "I don't know." Wrinkles of concern creased his forehead. "I hope it's not a malpresentation."

"What's that?" Amy asked quickly.

"It's when the foal isn't lying correctly," Jack explained. "The head is bent back either along the back or through the front legs. If that happens, the foal gets stuck and can't be born. If it *is* a malpresentation, Melody's going to need help."

Just then, the barn door opened, and Lou walked in with a covered bucket of water.

"Did you get through to Scott?" Grandpa said.

"Yes," Lou replied, quickly heading toward them, "but he says all the roads around here are blocked. He's already had another call that he couldn't get to."

Amy's eyes flew to her grandpa's face. "What are we going to do?" she asked.

"I'm going to have to find out what's holding up the foal," Grandpa said quickly. He shrugged off his coat and began to empty the equipment out of the foaling bucket. "Can you find me the antiseptic soap, Amy?"

"What's wrong?" Lou asked as Grandpa tipped some of the hot water into the bucket that had held the foaling kit. He began to soap his hands and arms.

"Grandpa thinks the foal's stuck," Amy said, so worried that she was hardly able to get the words out.

"But that's serious, isn't it?" Lou said.

Grandpa nodded and went into the stall. "It's OK, girl," he murmured to the mare. Hearing his footsteps, Melody looked around, her eyes wide and alarmed. As he approached, she began to try to struggle to her feet.

Jack quickly backed off. "I think she's going to panic if I get too close," he said.

"I'll hold her," Amy said.

"She might not let you," Jack said. "She'll be in so much pain, she won't be thinking straight."

"Let me try," Amy said.

She saw Grandpa nod and went quietly into the stall. Hearing the rustle of the straw, Melody's head shot into the air. "It's OK, girl, it's only me," Amy whispered.

Melody's head stayed high, but she didn't try to stand up. Her ears flickered as Amy slowly approached. "Steady now," Amy murmured. She knelt down beside the mare's shoulder and began to move her fingers in quick, light circles over Melody's damp skin. Although she desperately wanted Grandpa to be able to find out what was wrong as soon as possible, she forced herself to control her movements.

"You've got to let us help you," she said softly as her hands worked. Gradually, she felt the mare start to relax. She slowly worked her fingers up Melody's neck toward her head and ears. As she worked, she moved around until she was kneeling in front of the mare. With a sigh, Melody dropped her muzzle into her lap.

"I think she'll be OK now," Amy said softly, glancing over her shoulder to where Lou and Grandpa stood by the door. They both looked pale and worried.

After scrubbing up again, Grandpa came quietly into

the stall. Melody's eyes flickered uneasily, but she didn't move. Trying to keep her own breathing regular because she knew it would help to calm the mare, Amy started to work in small circles on her ears, her fingers stroking and soothing.

Grandpa approached quietly, and then, crouching down in the straw, he inserted his arm inside the mare. He felt around for a few minutes and let out a frustrated sigh.

"What's the matter, Grandpa?" Lou asked quickly.

"The foal's head is bent back along its sides," Grandpa said. "I was afraid of this." He straightened up and went back out of the stall to wash his arm. "It's stuck fast in the birth canal."

"So, what do we do?" Lou asked.

Grandpa's face was serious. "We need to turn the head. The problem is, it's so far back I don't think I can reach it." Amy saw the lines of worry etched along his face. "I'm going to have to call Scott and see what he thinks."

He hurried out of the barn. Amy looked at her sister. "Oh, Lou, is she going to be okay?" she said.

"I don't know," Lou replied. She looked around. "Would it be a good idea if I put this straw down?" she asked. "I guess we should have the bed as clean as possible."

Amy nodded. "Do you want me to help?"

Lou's eyes flickered to Melody. "No, you stay there."
She worked quietly. Melody groaned again.

Feeling close to tears, Amy kissed the mare's face. "It's going to be OK," she whispered. "It is!"

They heard the barn door open, and Grandpa appeared in the doorway. "What did Scott say?" Lou asked quickly.

Jack's face was serious. "We have to turn the foal around," he said.

"But I thought you said you couldn't reach it," Lou said.

"There isn't a choice," Jack said grimly. "If I can't reach the muzzle and turn it, we'll lose both Melody and the foal."

Amy felt the blood rush from her face. "They'll die?" she whispered.

Jack nodded. "Scott says there's no chance he can get through." He stripped off his coat and shirt again. "We have to do this ourselves."

Amy heard him plunge his arm into the bucket again.

Melody's sides contracted, and Amy caught back a sob. *Please, please don't die,* she prayed, seeing the pain and distress in the mare's eyes.

Grandpa came into the stall and inserted his arm inside Melody again.

Forcing herself to focus, Amy worked on the mare's ears to help settle her. However, by now Melody seemed to be past caring about Grandpa. Her breathing was hoarse, and her neck was soaked in sweat.

For what seemed like ages, Jack struggled to get a hold on the foal's head. "I can't get hold of it," he gasped. "If I could just hook my little finger in the corner of its mouth, then maybe I could turn its head around, but I just can't reach."

"Keep trying, Grandpa," Lou said, her eyes scared.

Amy looked anxiously at Melody. The mare was starting to tire. What if they were too late?

"It's no use!" Grandpa said, after five more minutes.

"You can't give up!" Amy said.

"I don't think there's anything more I can do," Jack said desperately.

The next minute, Lou entered the stall. "You can do it, Grandpa," she urged, kneeling down beside him. "I know you can."

Jack took a deep breath and reached deep inside Melody again. His face contorted as he struggled to get hold of the foal's muzzle.

"Come on," Lou whispered.

Amy saw their grandpa's face crease as he stretched his arm with one last enormous effort. "Got it!" he gasped suddenly. "I've reached its mouth."

Amy caught her breath, hope flooding through her as Grandpa began to ease the foal's head around, inch by difficult inch.

She bent her head to Melody's. *Please, please, please*, she prayed frantically. *Please be OK.*

"That's it!" Grandpa exclaimed suddenly, collapsing back onto the straw.

"I can see its nose!" Lou gasped. The mare's sides heaved with new force. "And here's its whole head!"

"She's tiring — she's going to need a hand," Grandpa said, struggling to his feet. "Lou, help me. We need to take hold of the front legs just above the fetlock joints, and pull as she pushes."

Lou did as he asked. Melody's sides shook in another contraction. "Pull now!" Grandpa cried.

Amy saw their faces grimace with effort as they both pulled. She had been holding her breath for so long now that she felt as if she was going to pass out.

Melody groaned.

"Here it comes!" Grandpa gasped. "Pull, Lou!"

Suddenly the foal's damp body slid out onto the straw.

Amy's heart almost stopped. "Is it OK?" she whispered, not knowing now whether to be relieved it was out or terrified by the foal's stillness.

Being careful not to break the umbilical cord that attached the foal to Melody, Grandpa bent over to examine it. As he did so, Amy saw the foal's tiny ears flicker and its head move.

"It's alive!" she cried, relief sweeping over her like a wave.

"Oh, Grandpa!" Lou exclaimed, flinging her arms around Jack.

He grinned happily. "Exhausted but alive," he said.

The tension in the stall dissolved. Grandpa stood with his arms around Lou while Amy stroked Melody's face, and they watched the foal start to move in the straw. It was perfect. A tiny, chestnut replica of Melody with a white blaze on its forehead. First, its eyes blinked open, and then it struggled onto its chest, its legs breaking through the membrane that still coated its body. As it struggled and kicked, the umbilical cord broke, and the foal took its first breath of real air.

Grandpa grabbed the iodine, cotton wool, and antibiotic powder from the foaling kit and quickly dressed the umbilical stump while the foal was still lying down.

"It's a filly," he said with a smile. "A little girl."

Suddenly, Amy felt Melody's nose move in her lap. Lifting her head, the exhausted mare looked around. Her ears pricked as she saw the foal. Amy hesitated for a moment and then edged away and joined Grandpa and Lou at the stall door.

Grandpa put his arm around her, and together they watched mother and foal meet each other for the first time.

Melody struggled to her feet. Blowing down her nose, she sniffed all over the filly with loud snorts. The foal snorted back, her tiny nostrils opening wide, her bedraggled ears pricking clumsily. Melody nuzzled the foal's damp face and then began to lick its coat.

"They're bonding," Grandpa said softly.

Happy tears filled Amy's eyes. "I can't believe they both survived," she said. She turned to Grandpa. "And it's all thanks to you."

"Thanks to *all* of us," Jack said, looking at her and Lou.

"But it was your determination, Grandpa," Lou said. "You were the one who wouldn't give up."

Amy saw an expression almost like regret cross Grandpa's face as he nodded. "I've always been stubborn," he said.

There was a pause. "Then I guess that makes two of us," Lou said softly, looking at her grandpa's worn features. "I knew you didn't mean to hurt me, Grandpa. I'm sorry I've been holding it against you."

"It's OK, Lou," Grandpa said. He looked at them both. "You two mean more to me than anything," he said. "Hurting you is the last thing I'd want to do. Please forgive me."

"Of course, Grandpa. If you'll forgive *me*," Lou said as he wrapped his arm around her shoulder.

"Thank goodness!" Amy said with a deep sigh of relief. It looked like the argument had finally been resolved.

"Oh, Amy," Jack said, looking at her. "Sorry you've been caught in the middle of all this."

"I'm just glad you finally worked it out," Amy said truthfully. She joined in the embrace. "You guys are the most stubborn people in the world."

Grandpa and Lou looked at each other.

"Well, apart from you," Lou said.

They all laughed. "Come on," Grandpa said as they separated. "Let's go inside. Melody and the foal will be just fine now."

"I think I'll stay for a little bit longer," Amy said, glancing at the foal. "Just until she gets up."

"OK," Grandpa said, nodding with understanding. "But don't try to help — it's important that she learns to stand on her own."

"We'll see you later," Lou said.

Amy leaned over the entrance to the stall and listened to the barn door banging shut behind them. Feeling totally drained, she sank down in the straw and looked at the chestnut filly lying there, her long limbs so tiny but perfect, the white blaze streaking down her forehead. There was only one more problem to be solved. "What shall we call you?" Amy whispered.

The little filly looked at her, her dark eyes bright.

Melody snorted softly, and suddenly the foal began to make her first attempt to stand. Stretching out her long, spindly legs, she got halfway to her feet and then collapsed into the straw with a soft thud. Amy longed to help her, but she knew Grandpa was right, it was a lesson the foal had to learn on her own.

With a toss of her head, the filly tried again. Her legs stretched and braced, and then with a heave she was on her feet. She wobbled for a second and fell over.

"Come on," Amy urged under her breath. "You can do it!"

The filly rested in the straw for a few minutes, and then Melody nudged her side. Out came the foal's legs again. She paused, a look of determination on her face, and then she struggled to stand. Her legs braced, she swayed a little, but this time she stayed on her feet. For a few moments, she just stood there, wobbling slightly. Then with a quick wag of her fluffy tail, she took an uncertain step forward and thrust her muzzle under Melody's belly.

Melody nuzzled her flank, and the filly began to feed.

Amy smiled and leaned her head back against the wall, shutting her eyes. It had been a long day, but at last, everything was OK.

🙣

Several hours later, she awoke with a start. She looked around and everything came flooding back. Melody and the foal were safe. They were lying in the straw, the foal's head resting against Melody's side.

Glancing at her watch, Amy saw that it was six o'clock. She'd been in the stall all night.

Feeling stiff, she got slowly to her feet. The foal's eyes blinked open and she raised her head, her tiny ears twitching.

Amy stood still. "It's all right," she murmured. "Stay there."

The foal looked at her for a long moment, and then with a sigh, she dropped her muzzle and shut her eyes again.

Amy crept out of the stall and shut the door as quietly as she could. There would be plenty of time to get to know the foal later in the day, but right now, she knew that Melody and her baby needed to rest. Stretching her cramped muscles, she walked to the barn door. Then, taking hold of the handle, she braced herself for the blizzard outside. As she pushed it open, she heard nothing but the silence of the morning.

As she stepped out, her boots crunched into the deep snow. The blizzard had stopped. The air was still, and in the night sky above, a tapestry of stars glittered. Amy shut the door and took a deep breath of the clear, cold air. Silence surrounded her — intense, deep, and peaceful.

Amy looked around at the buildings and fields of Heartland spread out before her. Everything was covered in a blanket of thick snow. As she looked toward the east, she saw the first pale gray glimmers of daybreak creeping across the dark sky, and suddenly she knew what Melody's filly should be called.

"Daybreak," she whispered. For a new beginning and the start of a new life.

Heartland

❧

One Day You'll Know

To Mary Ritchie — a wonderful friend who listens with
her heart, not just her ears — just like Amy

Chapter One

❧

"Easy now," Amy Fleming murmured to Melody as the mare pulled against the lead line and whinnied restlessly to her foal. Unaware of Melody's concern, Daybreak, the four-day-old filly, trotted inquisitively around the field, her arched neck and intelligent head held high, her tiny hooves flicking lightly over the snow-covered grass. The pale November sun shone down on her bright chestnut coat. *It was a perfect Thanksgiving day. . . .*

Amy held back her thoughts. No, she didn't want to think about it being Thanksgiving. That's why she was out here with Melody and Daybreak instead of in the farmhouse with Grandpa and her older sister, Lou. That's why she'd been working nonstop in the barn all day. She didn't want to think about it being her first Thanksgiving without Mom.

339

Melody whinnied again.

"It's OK, girl," Amy said, her fingers moving in light circles on Melody's neck. "Your baby's safe. She's just taking a look around."

Registering the familiar, comforting touch of Amy's hands, Melody turned her head. Amy rubbed the mare's forehead and felt her relax slightly and nuzzle Amy's arm. *If you're here,* Melody seemed to be saying, *then everything must be OK.*

A warm glow spread through Amy as she saw the trust in the mare's eyes. Only a month ago it had all been so different. When Melody had first arrived at Heartland, the horse sanctuary founded by Amy's mother, she had been exceptionally wary. But gradually Melody had overcome her nervousness and had grown to trust Amy. And since Amy assisted at Daybreak's birth, the bond between them had seemed to deepen further.

An icy breeze blew Amy's long light-brown hair across her face. She pushed it back, her gray eyes moving toward the little foal. Every step the filly took looked so full of energy; it was hard to believe that just a few days ago they had feared for her life. Her birth had been difficult, and for a while it had looked as if both the mare and foal might die. However, Amy, Lou, and Jack, their grandpa, had refused to give up, and at long last, as the stressful night gave way to morning, Daybreak had been born.

The filly stopped, her nostrils quivering, her beautiful proud head held high. As the rays of sun caught her coat, each chestnut hair seemed to flame brightly, but then the moment broke. With a toss of her head, Daybreak swung around. Cantering across the grass, she butted her head hungrily underneath her mother's belly and began to drink.

Amy watched her short, fluffy tail flicking from side to side and smiled. Ever since Daybreak's birth, she had felt an intense connection with the little foal. She wondered if it was just because she had been there at the filly's birth or whether it was something more than that. Her mom's voice came back to her: *Every so often a special horse will come along — a horse that will touch your life forever.* Looking at Daybreak, Amy was sure she knew what her mom had meant.

"Here, Daybreak," Amy murmured as the foal finished feeding. Daybreak took a step forward and sniffed Amy's outstretched hand, her intelligent eyes bright. "Good girl," Amy said softly, reaching to pat her neck.

With a squeal, Daybreak wheeled around. Amy jumped back just in time, gasping as the spirited filly kicked her back hooves feistily into the air and cantered off.

A voice hailed Amy. "Looks like she's going to be a handful."

Amy swung around. Scott Trewin, the local equine vet, was standing at the gate with Lou.

"Scott!" she exclaimed. "What are you doing here?"

"Oh, that's nice," Scott teased. "It's good to see you too, Amy."

"I didn't mean it like that," Amy grinned, going over. "I just thought you'd be at home, with it being" — she struggled with the word, "Thanksgiving and all."

"He just stopped by to wish us a happy holiday," Lou said, turning to smile at Scott.

He took her hand and smiled back down at her. "Well, I couldn't *not* see you, could I?"

For a moment Amy thought they were going to kiss. "OK — enough already," she said hurriedly. Scott and Lou had recently started dating, and although she was thrilled about it, there was a limit to how much she could stand!

Scott and Lou pulled apart, Scott grinning, Lou inspecting the tassels on her scarf. "So . . . how's Daybreak today?" Lou asked Amy, her embarrassment accentuating her English accent.

"Crazy," Amy replied, thinking, not for the first time, about how different she and her sister sounded. While Lou had lived nearly all her life in England, Amy had moved to Virginia when she was three. "But then she always is."

Lou smiled. "Well, Grandpa said to tell you everything will be ready in half an hour, Amy."

Amy felt her stomach contract at the thought of

Thanksgiving without Mom. "But there's these two to bring in and the back stalls to be mucked out," she appealed, "and the feeds to do. There's no way I can be ready in half an hour. Maybe you and Grandpa should go ahead and eat without me."

"Amy." Lou's voice interrupted her. Her cornflower-blue stare was sympathetic but firm. "You know Grandpa's put a lot of effort into this dinner. We all have to eat it together — that's the point. We'll give you a hand with the horses, won't we, Scott?"

"Sure." Scott nodded.

Amy's throat felt dry, but she knew that Lou was right. "OK," she said, fighting to keep her voice steady. "If you open the gate, I'll lead Melody in. Daybreak should follow."

However, when Amy led Melody out of the field, Daybreak stayed stubbornly where she was. Having tasted freedom for the first time, she seemed reluctant to give it up. Melody whinnied anxiously to her. Daybreak's eyes flickered from the field to her mother.

Scott stepped into the field, headed toward the foal. "Go on," he said encouragingly.

With a pert toss of her head, the filly put her ears back and cantered after Melody. Reaching the mare, she nipped her flank sharply as if to scold her mother for leaving her.

"Hey!" Amy protested. Flattening her ears, Daybreak

gave Amy a threatening glare, but Amy simply laughed and pushed her away. "You're going to have to learn some manners, baby," she told the foal. Daybreak looked at her haughtily, and Amy was reminded of Scott's earlier words. Daybreak was going to be a handful — no doubt about that.

❧

After Melody and Daybreak had been settled in their stall in the back barn and the final stalls had been cleaned, Scott left for his family's Thanksgiving. Amy watched from the stone-flagged feed room as Lou walked across the yard with him. Stopping by his car, they kissed. Lou watched until the vehicle disappeared out of sight and then came back toward the barn, a dreamy smile playing at the corners of her mouth.

"What do you want me to do?" Lou asked as she entered the feed room.

"Can you add some cod liver oil to those buckets and then mix them?" Amy said, pointing to a pile of feeds she had made up earlier.

Her sister nodded absentmindedly. "OK." She looked out the door again and then turned back to Amy, frowning. "What did you just say?"

"Lou!" Amy exclaimed. At twenty-three, Lou might be eight years older than Amy, but at that moment it felt like the other way around. Amy picked up the dusty cod liver oil can and put it into her sister's hands. "Cod liver oil — in buckets — then mix." She grinned as she propelled her normally sensible sister toward her task.

Lou started to pour dollops of the oil into the horses' food. "Scott's invited me to a Christmas reunion dinner in three weeks," she said breathlessly. "It's for all the vets in his year at college. It's black tie, so I'll have to find something formal to wear. Will you come shopping with me next week?"

"Sure," Amy said, starting to stir the feeds. She never had time to do much clothes shopping for herself, but helping Lou buy a gorgeous dress might be fun.

"I was thinking, you and Matt should get together," Lou said. "Then we could all go out on a date."

"Well, it's not going to happen," Amy said, thinking of Scott's younger brother, Matt. He was one of her best friends, and he'd been trying to get her to go out with him for ages.

"Why not?" Lou said. "Scott says Matt really likes you."

"Yeah, and I like him," Amy said. "But not like *that*."

"So who do you like?" Lou said.

Amy shrugged and started to pile the feeds up. "No one." It was the truth. There wasn't anyone at school that she wanted to date. *And probably just as well,* she thought. With winter setting in, there was always so much to do in the yard. Up at six o'clock every morning, she rarely stopped before midnight. The only boys she ever saw outside school hours were Heartland's two stable hands, Ty and Ben. For a moment an image of quiet, dark-haired Ty rose in her mind. She blushed as she remembered a day way back in the summer when he had touched her cheek and a shock like fire had run through her veins.

Lou obviously saw the blush. "Amy?" she said in delight. "There *is* someone, isn't there? Who is it?"

"There isn't anyone," Amy said quickly, pushing Ty out of her mind. She was being dumb. Ty was like a brother and best friend to her, not a boyfriend. "There really isn't." She grabbed the pile of feeds. "I'll go and hand these out," she said, hastily leaving the feed room before Lou could question her more.

❧

The two sisters were rinsing the buckets by the water tap when the back door of the farmhouse opened and the tall figure of Jack Bartlett, their grandpa, appeared.

"Almost finished?" he yelled, his deep voice trailing across the yard. Suddenly, his upright shoulders jerked forward and he coughed heavily.

Amy frowned. "Are you OK, Grandpa?"

Jack cleared his throat as he walked toward them. "It's just a bad cold," he said, nodding. "I guess I picked

it up the other night when we were foaling Daybreak."
He changed the subject. "Now, are you coming in? Dinner's ready."

"We're coming," Lou replied.

As Grandpa turned back into the house, Lou gently took the water bucket from Amy. "Come on, Amy," she said. "It's time to eat."

Amy took a deep breath and followed Lou down to the back door. *It's going to be all right,* she told herself. She looked at Lou. Her sister appeared so composed; it was almost as though she didn't care that this was their first Thanksgiving since Mom had died. But Amy knew her sister better than that. Lou cared as deeply as she did. It was just that she had a different way of coping. Lou channeled all of her energy into being practical and sensible.

Reaching the porch, Amy pulled off her boots as Lou opened the door into the warm, brightly lit, cluttered kitchen. Grandpa was lifting a perfectly golden roasted turkey out of the oven.

"It all smells delicious, Grandpa," Lou said, going over to the sink to wash her hands. "Can I do anything to help?"

Amy stopped in the doorway, her heart pounding. Everything looked so familiar — the white candles on the table, the huge pumpkin pie cooling on the counter, the dishes of homemade cranberry sauce, sweet potatoes, and chestnut stuffing. As her eyes fell on the place settings, she tried to hold back the tears. At the far end of the table, where Mom had always sat, the tablecloth was bare.

Lou and Grandpa turned around at the sound of her crying.

Grandpa, his face creased in concern, put down the turkey and hurried over.

As his arms folded around her, Amy felt the grief that she'd been controlling so well during the last few months overwhelm her. She remembered so clearly the day when she had persuaded her mom to take the trailer out to lonely Clairdale Ridge to rescue Spartan, a half-starved stallion. She also remembered the storm and the tree falling, then waking up in the hospital and Lou telling her the news. Mom was dead.

She didn't know how long she cried, but at last she became aware of the room again and of the rough wool of her grandpa's sweater prickling her face.

"I'm sorry," she muttered, pulling back and trying to regain some control over her feelings.

"It's OK, honey — it's natural," her grandpa said. "Times like these are never easy when we've lost someone we love."

Amy looked into his blue eyes and saw the understanding there. "I miss her, Grandpa. So much . . ." she whispered, her heart clenching with loss. "And it's not just today, it's every day."

Grandpa kissed her hair. "We all miss your mom. We always will. But we've got each other, and today of all days we need to give thanks for that. It's what your mom would have wanted. You know how much she believed in looking forward to the future, not back at the past."

Lou rubbed Amy's arm. "Grandpa's right, Amy."

Amy swallowed and nodded.

"Come on," Grandpa said, hugging her one more time. "Let's eat."

The atmosphere around the table was subdued as they sat down. "I wonder what Daddy's doing right now?" Lou said, breaking the silence as they began to pass around the hot vegetable dishes.

Amy glanced quickly at Grandpa. His face had tightened. "Probably nothing special," she said quickly. "They don't have Thanksgiving in England, do they?"

"No," Lou admitted. "But he might be thinking of us."

"I'm sure he is, sweetheart," Grandpa said, only his taut mouth betraying his feelings. Amy knew Grandpa had never forgiven Tim, their father, for abandoning them and their mom after a riding accident had ended his international show-jumping career twelve years ago.

"I hope he got my last letter," Lou said, referring to the one she had put in the mail the previous week. "I asked him to call us today."

"Well, maybe he will," Grandpa said.

Sensing the awkwardness, Amy hurriedly looked at her grandpa. "We haven't said thank you for the horses yet," she said, blurting out the first thing she could think of to change the subject. "Mom always used to. We should, too."

Grandpa nodded. "You're right." He stood up and took down a thick, dusty photograph album from its place on the top shelf of the chest. He offered it to Amy. "Would you like to?"

Amy hesitated for a moment. She hadn't really thought beyond the need to divert the conversation from Daddy. "Oh," she said slowly. She took the heavy leather book and opened it, swallowing a lump in her throat. Page after page was filled with photographs of horses they had treated at Heartland. Amy looked inside the front cover and saw her mom's familiar writing: *By healing, we heal ourselves.*

"If you don't want to . . ." Grandpa began, looking at her face in concern.

"No," Amy said. "I want to." And suddenly she meant it. "Mom often told me how privileged she was, being able to work with the horses, and, well, I feel the same," Amy said, thinking of all the horses *she* had helped in the five months since her mom had died — Sugarfoot, Spartan, Promise, Melody. Glancing up at Lou and

Grandpa, she continued, "Every Thanksgiving, Mom said that by healing, we heal ourselves, and it's true. The horses I've helped have given me so much, and so I'd like to give thanks to them, just like Mom would have done."

Grandpa lifted his glass. "To the horses," he said. "To those in the past, the present, and those still to come."

"To the horses," Amy and Lou echoed quietly.

They put their glasses down and picked up their knives and forks. They had been eating in silence for a few minutes when Amy glanced across at her sister. Lou was looking at the photograph album, her eyes shadowed. "I wish I could have been here to hear Mom say those words," she said sadly.

Grandpa looked at her sympathetically. "You were never able to get off work, Lou."

"No," Lou said slowly. "I suppose I wasn't."

✒

When they had finally finished eating the pumpkin pie, Amy and Lou cleared away the dishes and plates and then they all settled down in front of the TV for the evening. Around ten o'clock, Amy glanced at her watch. "I'd better go and check on the horses," she said, standing up.

As Grandpa stood up, he started to cough. "Do you want a hand?"

Before Amy could reply, Lou jumped to her feet. "You don't sound very good, Grandpa. You should stay in here where it's warm. I'll help."

After pulling on their jackets and boots, the girls went outside into the frosty night air. Lou seemed unusually subdued as they went around the stalls, collecting the empty hay nets and checking the water buckets and blankets. Amy looked at her sister and wondered what was on her mind.

When they'd finished, Lou went over to Sugarfoot's stall, and leaning against the stall door, sighed. "I wish I'd been here for at least one Thanksgiving with Mom."

Amy felt awkward. "You were always too busy. It was hard for you to come to Heartland, Lou."

"I could have come," Lou said. "I didn't really have to work every holiday."

"Mom understood how you felt," Amy told her. "She knew that the horses reminded you too much of Daddy and that it was easier for you to stay away."

"That doesn't seem like a good enough excuse any-more. I should have come." Lou stretched out her hand to stroke the little Shetland. "I should have made the effort. I didn't, and now —" She paused and looked down. "Now, it's too late."

Amy squeezed her arm.

Lou turned. "I missed out on really getting to know

one parent. I'm not going to make the same mistake again."

Unease stirred through Amy. "What do you mean?"

"Daddy," Lou said. "I can't stop thinking about him. I'm going to find him, Amy. I don't care what I have to do."

Chapter Two

That night, Amy thought about what Lou had said as she tried to fall asleep. Amy had been just three years old when Daddy had left and she had no real memories of him, except for the photos her mom had kept of him riding his horse, Pegasus. After the accident, she and her mom had left England to live with Grandpa in Virginia, while Lou, convinced that Daddy would one day return, had begged to continue going to her English boarding school. It was a hard decision, but their mom, reluctant to upset Lou any more, had agreed to let her stay. On Lou's rare visits to Heartland, she made no secret of the fact that she thought Mom and Amy had been wrong to leave England.

Shortly after their mom's death, Amy and Lou had

discovered a letter sent by their father to their mom five years before, begging for a reconciliation. Marion had never replied, but, determined to find their father, Lou had written to the address on the letterhead asking if they could arrange a meeting.

Amy hugged her knees to her chest and tried to imagine what it would be like to meet her father. Three weeks ago she had caught a fleeting glimpse of him at her mom's grave, but she hadn't realized who he was. It was only later that Grandpa had admitted that their father had visited Heartland earlier that day and Grandpa had refused to let him see his daughters. For a while Amy had thought that Lou would never forgive Grandpa, but eventually, on the night of Daybreak's birth, the two had made their peace.

Amy sighed. What would happen if Daddy *did* come back into their lives? After her mom's death, everything had been turned upside down — Lou had come back from her big job in Manhattan, and Ty and Amy had learned how to treat the horses on their own. It had been a time of upheaval and change, but at last life had begun to settle down again. If Daddy did contact them, then surely there would be many more changes to cope with.

Amy shut her eyes. It felt as if a distant storm cloud was looming ominously on the horizon. With a shiver, she tried to blank the thought out of her mind.

❧

Amy woke up early the next morning. The air was still and frosty when she took her pony, Sundance, for an early morning ride.

When she returned forty minutes later, Amy heard the familiar noisy rattle of Ty's pickup coming up the drive. She put Sundance away in his stall and strode down the yard to greet him.

"Hi," she called. "How was your Thanksgiving?"

"Pretty good," Ty called back, slamming the truck's door shut and running his hand through his dark hair. Slim but muscular, he stood only a few inches taller than Amy. "How about you? I guess it was probably kind of hard."

Amy shrugged. Having worked at Heartland for the last two and a half years, Ty knew her so well that it was pointless trying to pretend otherwise. "It wasn't easy," she admitted, "but we made it through." Not wanting to think about it anymore, she changed the subject. "I turned Daybreak and Melody out in the afternoon."

"How were they?"

As they walked up to the tack room, Amy filled him in. "Daybreak isn't having any trouble finding her independence," she said. "I think the sooner we teach her to lead the better."

Ty nodded. "We can start today."

"How about this morning?" Amy said. "I'm meeting Matt at the mall this afternoon."

Ty raised his eyebrows. "Oh, I see, you and Matt have a date, huh?"

"Come on!" Amy exclaimed. "For your information, Soraya's going to be there, too. We're *all* going Christmas shopping together." She shook her head. "Honestly! What's wrong with everyone here? Matt's just a friend — that's all!"

❧

After the horses had been fed and the stalls cleaned out, Amy and Ty went to Melody and Daybreak's stall. Their goal was to teach Daybreak to walk to the field on a lead rope instead of letting her just run loose and follow her mother as she had the day before.

Amy knew that it was very important that Daybreak learn to be led. Her mom had always said that learning to accept the restraint of a halter and lead rope was the most important lesson you could teach a young horse. But her mother had been totally against training techniques that involved any kind of physical domination. She believed a horse should learn to submit willingly to the handler. *Force destroys trust,* she had always said, *and without trust, there can never be a true partnership.*

Amy remembered those words as she walked to Daybreak and Melody's stall. She had been handling the little filly regularly to try to gain her trust. Although at first Daybreak had resisted, Amy had been calm and persistent with her, and now she would stand while Amy ran her hands over her head, legs, and body. Admittedly, Daybreak didn't seem to enjoy it, but she accepted it and that was the main thing.

"How about I take Melody, and you follow with Daybreak on the lead?" Ty said. Amy nodded as they headed to the stall. She knew she had to be careful, that she shouldn't use the lead rope to pull or force Daybreak but simply to guide her in the right direction. If the foal stopped, then Amy would have to place her arm around the foal's hindquarters and try to encourage her to move forward with a gentle nudge. Amy had seen her mom do it many times, and she was confident that they wouldn't run into any problems.

As Ty opened the stall door, Melody whinnied a greeting. "Hi, girl," Amy said. Daybreak was standing behind her mother. Amy clicked her tongue, but the little foal gave her an arrogant look and didn't move.

"We'd better just thread the lead rope through the back of Daybreak's halter rather than hooking it to the metal ring," Ty said, starting to put on Melody's halter. "Then if something happens and she *does* get loose, the end of the rope will just slide through the leather. We don't want to risk her running around the yard with the rope attached to her halter."

Amy nodded. What Ty said made sense. As she approached Daybreak, the filly turned her hindquarters to Amy and lifted one back leg warningly. "Come here," Amy said, neatly sidestepping the filly's back end and closing in on her head. Almost before Daybreak knew what was happening, Amy had slipped the halter over her nose and was slipping the end of the rope through the back.

Daybreak tossed her head but Amy kept hold of her. "Don't be silly," she said. "It's going to be OK."

Ty led Melody out of the stall. At first, all went well. Daybreak, realizing that she was going to the field, followed her mother eagerly. Amy simply held the lead rope loosely and walked alongside her. Then, halfway up the path, Daybreak suddenly stopped.

"Walk on," Amy encouraged, clicking with her tongue. Daybreak did not move. The foal watched Ty lead her mom farther away, but she stubbornly stood still. "Walk on," Amy repeated, now putting her right hand around the filly's hindquarters and pressing lightly. Whenever she had seen her mom apply the same method, the foal had always walked forward, but not Daybreak. Throwing her head high, she dug her heels in. Amy increased the pressure. "Come on, Daybreak, walk on," she said more firmly.

But instead, Daybreak shot backward with a speed that took Amy completely by surprise. The lead rope slid through her hands, and she instinctively grasped it. As the rope tightened and halted her with a jerk, Daybreak gave an enraged squeal and rose on her back legs, her head fighting against the restraint, her front legs striking the air.

"Let go of the rope!" Ty shouted, looking around and seeing the foal rearing, pulling full force against the lead. "Let go, Amy, or she'll go over!"

But Amy had realized the danger the foal was in and had already loosened the rope. The end of it slithered through the halter, and Daybreak was free. As her front hooves landed on the path with a thud, she plunged sideways and came to a trembling halt.

"Easy, Melody, easy," Ty said, trying to calm the mare, who was struggling to get to her foal. "What happened?" he demanded.

"I don't know. I put my arm behind her and she just went crazy," Amy exclaimed, staring at the foal. Her heart was pounding as she thought about how close Daybreak had come to toppling over backward and really hurting herself. Amy stepped toward the foal to try to catch her again, but she shied away.

"Leave her," Ty said quickly. "She needs to calm down. Let's just put them out in the field."

"But if we do that, she'll think that by fighting the lead she can get her own way," Amy protested.

"I know, but look at her," Ty replied. "She's too tense

to learn anything now. She'll fight us no matter what we do."

Amy hesitated. It was a hard decision. If they gave in to Daybreak now, she would have learned a damaging lesson, but Ty was right. They didn't want to have to use force to teach her a lesson. And Daybreak was not in the mood to give in. Nodding her head, she reluctantly agreed, going ahead of Ty to open the field gate.

Ty led Melody into the field and unhooked her lead. Keeping a wary eye on Amy, Daybreak shot through the gate and up to her mother. Stopping dead, the filly shoved her head against Melody's belly and began to feed. She didn't seem at all fazed by what had just happened. In fact there was an almost mischievous wag to her tail as she suckled.

Amy felt awful. It was Daybreak's first lesson in leading, and it had ended disastrously. "What did I do wrong?" she said. "I never saw a foal act that way with Mom. Did I scare her or something?"

"Scare her?" Ty echoed in astonishment. "I don't think so. You saw her. She wasn't scared of that lead, she was fighting it."

"But why?" Amy said.

"She's just headstrong," Ty said. "You can see it in her eyes. You know, most horses are willing to give in. In the wild, the herd follows the lead stallion or mare. When we train them, most horses follow us in the same way.

But sometimes you'll get one who isn't willing to give in — a horse who would have been a lead stallion or mare in the wild. Some horses will fight anything." He looked at Daybreak. "They used to be called rogue horses."

"But Mom always said that there's no such thing!" Amy burst out. "Horses aren't born bad, it's people who make them turn bad."

"I know," Ty said quickly. "And I agree with her. But there are exceptions. Some horses are born with a strong instinct to fight control. I think Daybreak's one of them. It doesn't mean she's bad, but she won't be easy to train."

"She'll learn," Amy protested. "She's only a baby."

Ty didn't say anything for a moment. "Yeah," he said at last. "You're probably right. She's young, and if we're patient, she'll learn." He fastened the gate. "But I don't think we should try leading her in the open again for a while."

Amy nodded. He was right. Until Daybreak was willing to listen to her cues and walk on a lead, they shouldn't work with her in areas where she could get loose. She looked at the fiery little filly in the field and acknowledged that training her to be led was going to be far more difficult than she'd imagined.

❧

Lou dropped Amy off at the mall just after two o'clock. Lights glittered on every tree and storefront and canned seasonal songs boomed out through the loud-speakers as she made her way through the crowds. Just about everyone seemed to be out shopping. At last she caught sight of Matt and Soraya, waiting by their old meeting place, Huckleberries Ice Cream Parlor.

"Hi!" she gasped as she reached them. "Sorry I'm late. I got busy with Daybreak and turning out and —"

Matt grinned. "Yeah, yeah — why change the habit of a lifetime?"

"I'm not *always* late," Amy protested.

"Only ninety-nine point nine percent of the time," Soraya teased. "So what shopping do you still have to do?"

"Everything," Amy said as they started to make their way through the crowds. "All my Christmas gifts — *and* it's Ty's birthday soon. I've got to get something for that."

"Hang on, I need to find a belt for Scott," Matt said, dashing into a leather store they were just passing.

Soraya looked at the display of belts, wallets, and coats in the window. "Maybe I should get something for Ben," she said. "What do you think?"

"I don't know," Amy said. It was a tough question to answer. She knew Soraya liked Ben, but he hadn't shown any sign of asking her out even though they seemed to get along very well. "I mean, you don't want to get him a gift if he doesn't give you anything."

"I know," Soraya said. "But what if he does get me something and I don't have anything for him?"

They frowned at each other, appreciating the difficult dilemma. "I know. I'll try to find out if he's going to get something for you," Amy said.

Just then, Matt came back out of the store with a shopping bag in his hand. "That's one gift down," he said with some satisfaction. He dug a list out of the pocket of his jeans.

"You're so organized," Amy said as they set off through the crowd again. "How do you know what to get everyone?" Her own shopping was much more haphazard. She tended to buy things on impulse, not having any clear plans but just waiting until she saw something she liked.

"I just asked everyone before I came here. It makes my life a lot easier." Matt grinned as Amy began to think that she should have been a bit more practical.

"But you didn't ask me what *I* wanted," she teased.

"Me, neither," joined in Soraya.

"Er . . . well, it's a surprise," Matt started. "Now, I could go to that store that sells aromatherapy stuff," he said, consulting his piece of paper. "I want to get something for my mom. You know about aromatherapy, Amy. Can you give me some help?"

"I thought you made a list!" Soraya exclaimed.

"I did, but — er — Scott was the only one around when I filled it out," Matt admitted. "I'm guessing at the rest."

"So much for making your life easier," Amy laughed. "Come on, let's go." She began to think what *she* might buy at the aromatherapy shop — some oils for Lou, maybe something for Ty. Suddenly, her eyes fell on a group of three girls approaching from the opposite direction. "Oh, great!" Amy groaned to Soraya. "Look who it is."

Ashley Grant and her two friends, Jade Saunders and Brittany Phillips, were sauntering through the crowd, perfectly put together in their designer clothes. Ashley Grant was Amy's least favorite person in the world. Her family owned a highly successful hunter-jumper stable called Green Briar. It was close to Heartland, but the methods they used couldn't be more different. Val Grant, Ashley's mom and the head trainer at Green Briar, believed in using force and firm discipline.

"Maybe we should go to the music store first," Soraya said, grabbing Amy's arm. She wanted to avoid Ashley's crew as much as Amy did.

"Is Dan still dating Brittany?" Amy asked Matt as they followed Soraya. Dan Evans was one of Matt's friends from the soccer team.

"Yeah," Matt replied. "They've been seeing each other a lot. We all went to a movie on Wednesday night — Ashley came, too."

Amy raised her eyebrows sarcastically. "That must have been fun."

Matt smiled. "You know, she's not that bad when you get to know her."

Amy stared at him in disbelief. "This *is* Ashley Grant we're talking about, isn't it?"

"She's sent me an invitation to her Christmas party," Matt said.

This piece of information was enough to stop Soraya and Amy in their tracks. "What? *You're* going to the Grants' Christmas party?" Soraya exclaimed.

"Hey, not just me," Matt said hastily, seeing the expression on their faces. "There's a lot of guys from the soccer team going."

Amy could hardly believe it. Every year the Grant family held a huge Christmas party at their very large house. Ashley talked about it for weeks in advance and afterward; it was considered *the* party to be invited to by the people at high school who cared about that sort of thing. However, the invitations were very exclusive, and even Matt, who was very popular, had never been invited before. "And you're going to go?" Amy said incredulously.

"Sure." Matt shrugged. "Why not?"

"Amy! Wait up!"

Amy swung around. It was Ashley. She was pushing her way across the crowded mall, waving.

Amy's muscles tensed. The only time Ashley ever spoke to her was to make sarcastic comments, usually about Heartland. However, Amy knew there was no way of getting out of talking with her. Lifting her chin, she held her ground. "Hello, Ashley," she said coolly as Ashley reached her. She waited for the cutting remark, but to her surprise Ashley's lips, perfectly defined by rose-red lipstick, curved into a smile.

"Hi," she said. "How are you?"

Amy stared at her in astonishment. Ashley Grant had just asked her how she was and, even weirder, sounded like she *meant* it. She looked at Soraya and saw that her friend's brown eyes were wide with disbelief.

Hardly noticing that Amy hadn't replied, Ashley carried on. "Did you have a good Thanksgiving?" She paused for a fraction of a second. "It must have been busy with all the horses you have at the moment. Were Ty and Ben around to help?"

Having expected a standoff, Amy could hardly get her head around this new-style Ashley. Feeling like she was in some sort of crazy dream, she shook her head. "They both had the day off."

"Are they going to be away for the whole weekend?" Ashley asked.

"No, Ty's back today and Ben's back tomorrow," Amy said.

"Oh, that's good," Ashley said. She looked up at Matt with her catlike green eyes. "Did you get my invitation for the party, Matt?"

"Yeah," Matt replied. "Thanks."

Ashley turned back to Amy. "You must come as well, Amy," she gushed.

"You're inviting *me* to your party?" Amy said in absolute astonishment.

"Of course." Ashley said it as though it was the most natural thing in the world for her to invite Amy. Suddenly, she seemed to remember Soraya. "You, too, Soraya," she added. "I'll drop your invitation off with Amy's tomorrow."

Amy frowned. The last thing she wanted was to go to the Grant's party. "It's OK," she began, about to tell Ashley not to bother, but Ashley interrupted her.

"Sorry, Amy," she said, smiling widely. "I'd really love to stay and talk but I have to go. I'll see you tomorrow!" And with that she turned and flounced away to where Jade and Brittany were waiting.

For a moment, Amy and Soraya stared after her in stunned silence.

"Did I just dream that?" Soraya said in a strangled voice. "Or did Ashley really just come over here and invite us to her party?"

"It *has* to be a dream," Amy said.

"Or else there's something totally weird going on," Soraya said. "Like aliens have come and taken over Ashley's body."

"Come on, you guys," Matt protested. "I told you — Ashley's not that bad. It's Thanksgiving. She must have remembered about your mom, Amy. Maybe she was just trying to be friendly."

Amy and Soraya looked at each other. At the same moment they shook their heads. "No — aliens," they said together.

Soraya grinned at Amy. "So, are we going to go?"

"Are you kidding?" Amy asked. She caught a look of disappointment cross Soraya's face and she frowned in surprise. "Why? You don't want to, do you?"

Soraya hesitated. "Well, it could be kind of fun, but there's no way I'm going without you," she added hastily.

"Yeah, come!" Matt urged. "I'll have a way better time if you guys are there."

Amy frowned. She didn't really want to go, but Matt and Soraya both looked so eager. "Let's see if Ashley actually delivers the invitations first," she said skeptically.

❧

Much to Amy's surprise, Ashley turned up at Heartland the next morning. It wasn't ideal timing. Having decided to work with Daybreak once more before trying to use the lead rope again, Ty was holding the foal in the field while Amy was running her hands over the filly's body, legs, and head.

Daybreak had managed to stay reasonably still for five minutes. However, at exactly the moment that Val Grant's silver Mercedes pulled into the driveway, Amy decided to try to persuade Daybreak to move forward a step. The second the little filly felt Amy's left arm pressing around her hindquarters, she shot violently backward in protest. Amy jumped back just in time to avoid being trampled, and Ty barely managed to hang onto Daybreak.

"Looks like you've got a difficult one there!"

"Oh, no," Amy groaned to Ty as she looked around and saw the figure of Val Grant striding toward the gate.

Ashley followed her mom. Ashley had on expensive black breeches, and her pale blond hair fell to her shoulders in a gleaming sheet. She looked like a glamorous model from a magazine advertising riding clothes — the models whom Amy suspected had never even touched a currycomb. Still, Amy suddenly felt very aware of the straw in her own hair and the stains all over her worn jeans.

"Causing you some problems, is she?" Val Grant said, nodding at Daybreak.

Amy gritted her teeth. "Nothing we can't manage," she said. "We just need some time."

Val Grant ignored her words. "I wouldn't let a little thing like that mess with me," she said, her eyes narrowing as they swept over the defiant filly. "I'd tie one of her legs up and force her to the ground. Keep her there until she gives up fighting. You need to show her who's the boss right from the start."

A string of angry words leaped into Amy's mouth, but before she could say anything Ty stepped forward. "That's not how we go about things here," he said levelly, only the darkening of his eyes revealing how angry *he* was, too. "But thanks for your advice, Mrs. Grant."

Val Grant's face hardened, and for a moment tension crackled in the air. It was broken by Ashley producing a bundle of envelopes from her pocket. "Here are the invitations to our party," she said, handing them to Amy. She'd been so busy looking around at the yard that she had hardly seemed to notice the exchange between her mom, Amy, and Ty. "I brought one for you as well, Ty, and one for Ben. Do you think he might like to come, Amy?"

Amy was still fuming from Val Grant's comments. "Why don't you ask him yourself?" she said hastily. "He's over there."

Ashley spun around. Ben was walking across the yard with a water bucket in his hand. "Ben!" Ashley called out, waving.

Ben looked around. He had only met Ashley once before, and for a moment a frown creased his handsome face as he tried to place her. But then Amy saw a look of recognition dawn in his eyes. "Hi," he said, coming over. "It's Ashley, isn't it? You're one of Amy's friends."

Ashley flicked her long hair back and smiled up at him. "That's right," she said. "I met you at the show last weekend. This is my mom, Val. Mom, I want you to meet Ben Stillman."

"Pleased to meet you," Ben said, holding out his dirt-caked hand to Val Grant.

Val looked at Ben with interest. "You're Lisa Stillman's nephew, aren't you? From the Fairfield Arabian Stables?"

"Yeah," Ben said. "My aunt sent me to Heartland to learn about treating problem horses."

Val Grant snorted derisively. "Well, I'm not sure what she thinks you'll be learning."

Ben looked confused.

"We just stopped by to drop off some invitations for a family party we're having in two weeks," Ashley stepped in quickly. "There's one for you. I thought with you being new in the neighborhood you might like the chance to meet some people." She fluttered her long eyelashes at him. "Oh — you *will* come, won't you?"

"Sure," Ben said, looking pleased. "Thanks for asking me."

Ashley held his gaze. "It's my pleasure."

Instantly, it was like a light had come on in Amy's head. *That was it!* That was why Ashley was being so friendly — she liked Ben, but she couldn't invite him to the party without asking everyone else, too. Suddenly, it all made sense.

But what about Soraya? Amy glanced anxiously at Ben for a sign he was attracted to Ashley, but to her relief he was simply smiling in his usual easy way.

"Well, I guess I'd better get back to work," he said. He turned to Val Grant. "Nice to meet you, Mrs. Grant."

"You, too, Ben," Val replied.

"See you," Ben said to Ashley, and then with a quick smile at Amy and Ty, he headed back to the water tap.

Ashley watched him go and then turned around. "Come on, Mom, let's go. See you at school, Amy," she added almost curtly as the Grants walked back to their car.

"OK," Ty said slowly, looking down at the invitation in his hand as Ashley and Val got into the car. "Do you have any idea what *that* was all about?"

"Yep," Amy said, and explained her theory to him.

"So, Ashley likes Ben!" Ty repeated in astonishment.

"I'd bet on it," Amy replied. "That's the only reason she'd invite us to the party. Did you see the way she was looking at him?" She dropped her voice in an imitation of Ashley's husky purr. "Oh, Ben, you really *must* come."

Ty grinned. "Poor Ben — do you think he has any idea what he's in for?"

"I don't know, but I guess it's only fair to warn him,"

Amy said. She headed down to the faucet where Ben was just rinsing his hands. "Looks like you've got a fan," Amy said. Her voice was teasing, but inside, her heart was thumping. She hoped — for so many reasons — that he wasn't going to say he liked Ashley.

A look of surprise crossed Ben's face. "What do you mean?"

"Ashley Grant," Amy said. "Ben!" she exclaimed seeing his blank look. "You can't tell me you missed the way she was flirting with you."

"Ashley?" Ben said incredulously. "That girl who was here just now?"

"Yeah, blond, skinny, looks like a model," Amy said.

Ben shrugged. "She's not my type. I met a lot of girls like that when I was living at my aunt's — rich, beautiful, and almost always boring."

Amy felt a rush of relief. "So, you're not interested?" she asked casually.

Ben shook his head. "I'm not ready to get involved with anyone yet. There's enough going on in my life, with Red, and learning about things here, and trying to spend time with my mom again." He picked up the bucket. "But this party sounds like fun. Are you, me, and Ty going to all go together?"

Amy shook her head. She knew Soraya and Matt wanted her to go, but she really didn't want to. "I don't think I'm going."

"Why not?" Ben said, surprised.

Amy shrugged. "It's not really my crowd. I don't think Ty will go, either."

Ben looked disappointed. "You've got to be kidding. I only accepted the invitation because I thought you guys would go. I don't want to go by myself."

Amy felt bad. It was mean to make Ben go alone. He would hardly know anyone there. And what would Soraya say if Ben decided not to go because of Amy and Ty?

"Come on, Amy," Ben pleaded. "Don't do this to me. You've got to come."

Amy thought for a second. "All right," she said. "I'll come." As much as she hated to admit it, there was a little part of her that was curious about the Grants' house and what their famous party might be like. And who knew when she'd be invited again.

"You will?" Ben looked very relieved. "Thanks. I owe you one."

Amy returned to Ty, who was handling Daybreak's legs again. "Well, I guess I'm going to the Grants' party after all," she sighed.

"Why?" Ty said in surprise.

"Ben told Ashley he'd go, and I'd feel bad if he went alone. We're the only people he knows around here," Amy explained. She looked at him. "You should come with us, Ty."

Ty shrugged. "I don't know Amy. It's not really my

kind of thing . . ." he hesitated. "But if you and Ben are going, then it might be fun." He stroked Daybreak. "She's pretty calm now. Should we try again?"

Amy nodded and positioned herself at the side of the foal. "You're sure you don't want to try Val Grant's suggestion?" she teased.

Ty's eyes met hers. "Quite sure," he said, and they both smiled.

❧

The training session with Daybreak didn't go well. Time after time, when they applied gentle pressure to her hindquarters to encourage her to move forward, the little filly either ran backward or simply refused to move. Amy and Ty grew warmer and warmer from the workout and soon took off their heavy winter jackets.

"We can't give in," Amy said through gritted teeth after fifteen minutes. "She *is* going to move forward."

Even Ty, whose patience was normally endless, was beginning to look exhausted. "Come on, girl," he encouraged, taking a deep breath and taking hold of the halter again.

Suddenly, Daybreak took a tiny step forward.

"Good girl!" Amy cried, immediately releasing the pressure she had been applying under the foal's tail.

"It's about time," Ty exclaimed.

Amy rewarded Daybreak by rubbing her head. Most

horses love being stroked, but the little foal looked at Amy mutinously — not pulling away from the caress but not looking as if she was enjoying it, either. Amy sighed. It would be nice if, just once, Daybreak showed some affection.

"Let's call it quits for the day," Ty said, wiping his arm across his forehead.

As they released the foal, Daybreak shook her head, wheeled around, and plunged away, every muscle in her body declaring independence now that she was free. Amy watched as she cantered around the field. She loved the fire that burned so strongly within Daybreak. The challenge would be to harness that fire and channel it so that Daybreak wanted to work with, rather than against, them. Picking up her jacket, Amy left Ty to shut the gate and walked toward the front paddock deep in thought.

"Amy!"

Amy looked up. Lou was getting out of her car, a bundle of mail from the mailbox at the end of the driveway in her hand. Her eyes were bright as she waved a pale-blue envelope at Amy.

"Amy! Hurry up! It's a letter from Daddy! Come and see what it says!"

Chapter Three

Amy stopped dead in her tracks, her eyes locked on Lou. Having put the other mail on the roof of the car, Lou was tearing open the airmail letter, her face flushed with excitement. Amy felt her stomach suddenly tighten. *A letter from their father.* She walked slowly toward her sister.

Lou's eager blue eyes were scanning the page. "He says he's really sorry he didn't get to see us. And he wants to come and visit."

Amy peered at the unfamiliar handwriting. It was slightly slanted, the letters neat and precise.

"Oh," Lou said suddenly. "He says he wants to meet in February. He'll be over here on business then."

For one brief second, Amy found her mind catching

on the word "business." *Business — what sort of business? What does he do?* And then she registered the flatness in Lou's voice. "February?" she echoed. "That's three months away."

Lou nodded, and Amy saw that the excited glow in her sister's eyes had been replaced by a faded look of disappointment. "I guess he must be busy until then." She looked at the letter again. "There isn't even a telephone number, so I can't call him to see if he can come sooner. There's just an address." She handed the letter to Amy.

Tim Fleming, Amy read on the back, *Oak Farm, Willoughby, Gloucestershire, England.* She turned the letter over and skimmed the contents.

My dear Lou,

Thank you so much for your letter. I so wanted to meet you and Amy when I came over, but your grandfather told me to stay away. I can't blame him for that — I know he was only trying to protect you. I just wish you could know how much I've wanted to see you, how often I've thought about you — my two girls. What are you like now? Who do you take after? I would dearly love to meet up with you both. Unfortunately, I can't return to the States at the moment, but perhaps in February? I'll be in New York on business then so I could fly down and visit. I'm sorry it can't be sooner but things are a bit difficult right now —

*I'll explain when I see you. Till then, take care, give my love
to Amy, and remember that I think about you both every
day.*
       All my love,
              Daddy

Amy had to struggle to compose her thoughts. *Give my
love to Amy.* She reread the words three times. It was as if
an invisible thread were stretching across the world,
linking her with the father she had never really known.
But she didn't want his love. What right did he have to
suggest that she did? He wrote as if he had just been
away on vacation, not missing from her life for twelve
long years. And there wasn't even a single mention of
their mom.

She handed the letter back to Lou. "What are you going to do?"

"I don't know," Lou replied slowly.

"It's not that long till February," Amy said.

Lou stared down at the letter and didn't reply.

For the rest of the day, Amy tried not to think about
the letter. She didn't want to think about meeting
Daddy. She wanted to block the whole thing from her
mind. That evening, she called Soraya and told her all

about Ashley's visit. "You should have seen the way she was flirting with Ben!"

"Oh, great," Soraya groaned. "Like I stand a chance if Ashley's after him."

"But he's not interested in her," Amy told her. "I asked him." She wondered whether to tell Soraya Ben's comment about not wanting to get involved with anyone at the moment, but she held back. There was no point in depressing Soraya, and besides, she reasoned, he might not have really meant it. She tried to remember what he'd said about Ashley. "Ben said he'd met tons of girls like her before, and that they were all boring."

"Oh, come on!" Soraya exclaimed. "If Ashley's boring, then what am I?"

"Interesting," Amy said.

"Interesting!" Soraya exclaimed. "That makes me sound like a total freak."

Amy grinned. "Stop worrying. You are *not* a freak! So, are you going to come over here to get ready for the party? Ben said he'd give me and Ty a lift. I'm sure he can squeeze all of us in."

"Then definitely," Soraya said. "There's no way I'm showing up at Ashley's on my own."

"Soraya! It's only a Christmas party," Amy said.

"Correction: the Grants' Christmas party," Soraya

said dramatically. She changed the subject. "So what else did you do today besides hanging out with Ashley?"

"Well, Lou got a letter from our dad," Amy said. "He wants to come and see us in February."

"February!" Soraya replied. Amy could hear the surprise in her friend's voice. "But that's months away."

"I don't care," Amy said, her voice getting harder.

"Really?" Soraya said.

"Yes, really," Amy replied. "He can do what he wants as far as I'm concerned. It's Lou who wants to see him, not me."

❧

Later that evening, Amy thought about what she'd said. It was true. She didn't care what her father did. But at the back of her mind, there was a haunting suspicion — was it that she didn't care or that she didn't *want* to care? There was a huge amount of difference.

❧

Heartland's stalls were all full, so the next two weeks raced by as Amy juggled her time between the horses, school, and seeing her friends. But as usual, every spare minute she had was spent working with Ty and Ben in the barns. She was also trying to avoid being alone with Lou in case the conversation turned to Daddy. However, to her relief, Lou made no attempt to bring up the subject when they were alone, and when they were with Jack neither of them spoke about it, in case it would upset him. Grandpa wasn't looking well — the cold he had picked up the night of Daybreak's birth seemed to be lingering and the cough was getting worse. Amy and Lou tried to persuade him to see a doctor, but he kept putting it off.

With everything that was happening, Amy managed to push the letter to the back of her mind. Whenever thoughts of it crept back to disturb her, she forced herself to think about Daybreak instead. Despite Amy and Ty being patient and gentle, the little filly was still resisting their attempts to train her. Some days she would move forward when Amy gave her the cue, but mostly she would simply refuse to acknowledge her and would fight them every step of the way. Amy was starting to get worried. With each day that passed, Daybreak was getting physically stronger and harder to manage.

"I just don't understand why she's being like this," she said to Ty on a Friday afternoon as they looked over Daybreak and Melody's stall door after yet another unsatisfactory training session with the foal. "We've done everything we should."

"I was looking at one of your mom's books this morning," Ty said. "Maybe we should have handled her more in the first twenty-four hours after she was born."

Amy thought back to Daybreak's first day. "But we

were letting her bond with her mother," she said, remembering how they had decided to leave handling the little foal until the following day for that reason.

"I know," Ty said. "But this book said that if you handle a foal first thing, it will bond with you as much as with its mother. They call it 'imprinting.' But you have to do it that first day. After that it's too late."

"But I spent that first night in Melody's stall." Amy frowned. "And Mom never had a problem with the foals she handled, and they weren't even born here, they were close to two or three months old when she started working with them."

"But I bet none of them was as headstrong as Daybreak," Ty said. "I'm not saying we can't train her. I just think we'd have better luck if we'd been more hands-on from the start."

Amy looked at the little filly. She was lying down in the straw, her muzzle resting on one of her slender front legs, her hind legs curled up beneath her. Her dark eyes were focused on them — fearless, intelligent, and confident. Amy turned to Ty. "So what do we do?"

"I guess we've just got to be patient," Ty replied. "But we should try using some oils to calm her, so she'll listen better. Vetiver oil's relaxing. It's good for bold, headstrong horses."

Amy nodded. At Heartland they often used aromatherapy, herbs, and Bach Flower Remedies to help deal with horse's behavioral or emotional problems. "I'll get some vetiver from the tack room," she said.

"OK," Ty said. "I'm going to groom Jasmine and Dancer."

Amy walked across the frosty yard to the tack room where the essential oils were kept in the medicine cabinet. Taking out the vetiver and jojoba oils and an empty bottle, she put thirty milliliters of the jojoba into the empty bottle and then added twelve drops of the vetiver. It was very important to dilute potent oils like vetiver into a base oil to prevent them from irritating the horse's skin. She was closing the cabinet when Ben came into the tack room with a grooming kit.

"Hey, what are you doing?" he asked, looking at the solution in the bottle with interest.

Amy was eager to get back to Daybreak and quickly replied, "Just working on something for Daybreak."

She was about to leave the tack room when she caught sight of Ben's disappointed face. Amy felt a pang of guilt — Ben was working at Heartland so he could learn about the alternative therapies they used. She and Ty were so used to working together that they often forgot to explain the treatments to him.

"She's being real stubborn. Do you want to come and see what I'm going to do?" she asked him.

"Sure," Ben said. He dumped the grooming bucket in the trunk and joined her.

As they walked by the old stable, Amy saw a ladder leaning against the eaves. Grandpa was standing near the top, replacing some missing shingles on the roof. All of a sudden, his upper body folded over in an intense coughing spasm.

Amy stopped at the foot of the ladder. "Are you OK, Grandpa?" she asked when his breathing returned to normal.

Wiping his mouth with his sleeve, Jack looked down and attempted a smile. "I'm just fine," he said, his blue eyes watering. But suddenly, he started to cough again, his hand grasping at his chest as if he were in pain.

Amy felt concerned. "You don't sound fine at all," she said forcefully. "You have to see the doctor. At least you should get off the roof until you're feeling better. If you're not careful, you could fall off."

"I've got to finish this before the weather gets really bad," Jack said, determinedly picking up another shingle. "Then I'll go in and call the doctor."

"All right, but you have to promise me you will," Amy sighed. Knowing how obstinate Grandpa was about these kinds of things, Amy reluctantly gave up.

"He's been up there all afternoon," Ben told her as they walked out of Jack's earshot.

They reached the warmth of the barn. Amy unbolted the stall door. Daybreak was still lying down. She lifted her head and stared at Amy with wary eyes. "First we've got to see her reaction to the prepared oil," Amy explained to Ben. "If she likes it, I'll massage a little into her muzzle."

"If she likes it?" Ben echoed. "What do you mean?"

"Watch," Amy said. As she headed toward the little foal, Daybreak scrambled to her feet. "Steady," Amy soothed, quickly grabbing the little foal's mane before she could swing her haunches around. Grabbing the filly's nose with her free hand so that she had some control of the foal, she unscrewed the top of the oil bottle and offered it to Daybreak to smell. At first she threw her head back in defiance at being held, but then the fragrant scent of the oil reached her nostrils. Blowing out in surprise, she seemed to forget about fighting Amy and lowered her muzzle close to the bottle. Amy held the bottle tightly in case Daybreak suddenly decided to nibble it out of curiosity. The filly sniffed the oil with each nostril and then, lifting her head, she rolled her top lip back and showed her teeth.

"She likes it," Amy said, pleased.

"How do you know?" Ben asked.

"If she didn't, she'd just have sniffed it once or she'd have turned away and put her ears back," Amy said.

"You can't treat a horse with something they instinctively don't like. Somehow they seem to know which oils will help them and which won't. You have to listen to the horse and trust her to guide you."

"So what do you do now?" Ben asked curiously as Daybreak lowered her head to sniff the oil again.

Amy poured a little of the diluted oil into the palm of one hand and then handed Ben the bottle to hold. "Now I massage her with it," she said, catching hold of Daybreak's nose again and beginning to work the oil into the skin just between the filly's ears. "It might not work immediately, but hopefully there should be a gradual change in her over the next few days. If nothing happens after a week or two, then we'll have to try something else." Turning her attention to Daybreak, she focused on massaging in the oil. For once, the foal stood calmly, her delicate nostrils trembling as she breathed in and out. Enjoying this unfamiliar moment of peace between them, Amy began to feel a flicker of hope — maybe the oil would be the solution to Daybreak's problems.

"There," Amy said at last, when the oil was completely massaged in. "I'll do that twice a day for a week. If she isn't any easier to work with after that, then we'll try something different."

As they left the stall, Ben looked puzzled. "But how does it actually work?" he said.

"Well, no one knows for sure," Amy said. "But it's thought that as the chemicals in the oil are inhaled and absorbed through the skin into the bloodstream, they reach the emotional center of the brain where they affect the horse's mood and attitude." She saw the slightly skeptical look in Ben's eyes. "Mom always said as long as it works, it doesn't matter how it happens." She bolted the stall door and took the bottle from Ben. "Come on, let's start on the hay nets."

❧

Amy woke early the next morning. As soon as she got dressed she went to see Melody and her foal. Melody whinnied when she saw her and came over to nuzzle at Amy's hands. Amy rubbed her head and looked at Daybreak. The foal was standing in the back of the stall. Amy held out a hand. "Hi, girl."

With a squeal, Daybreak swung around and gave a discreet buck, her tiny ears flat against her head. Amy sighed. It didn't look like the vetiver oil was working just yet.

After she had fed the horses, she went back down to the house to grab some coffee. To her surprise, the table was set and Lou was bustling around the kitchen, cooking breakfast. "I've made some waffles," she said brightly as Amy came in. "Sit down. There's maple syrup and bacon on the table and some fresh coffee in the pot."

Amy stopped and stared. "You made *waffles*?" she said. Normally, the only person in the house who cooked breakfast was Grandpa. If Lou was in charge of breakfast, it was never anything more than a bowl of cereal and a slice of toast.

"Yes, I thought I'd cook for us all," Lou said. "I told Grandpa to sleep in for a while. I heard him coughing really badly last night."

"Again?" Amy looked worried. "I told him he had to get an appointment at the doctor's."

"Yeah, and he has," Lou said. "But the doctor can't see him for three days." She busied herself around the kitchen. "Now, sit down. Are waffles OK? Or do you want some scrambled eggs? I can whisk some up in no time."

"OK," Amy said, realizing there was something on Lou's mind other than breakfast. "What's going on, Lou?"

"What do you mean?" Lou said. "I just thought it might be nice if I organized breakfast for a change."

Amy raised her eyebrows. "But all *this*?" She pointed at the table piled with waffles, bacon, orange juice, and steaming coffee.

Lou hesitated and then suddenly her shoulders sagged. "Well — you're right," she admitted, sinking down onto a chair. "There *is* a reason." She looked at the tablecloth. "I've — I've got something to tell you."

From the tone of her sister's voice, Amy could tell that she wasn't going to like what she had to say. "What is it, Lou?"

Taking a deep breath, Lou lifted her eyes. "I've made a decision, Amy," she said resolutely. "I'm going to England. I have to find Daddy."

Chapter Four

Amy stared at her sister, her heart thudding. "What do you mean?"

"I've booked a flight to London on Wednesday." Lou's eyes begged her to understand. "I know Daddy said he's coming over in February, but I can't wait till then. Thanksgiving made me realize that life's too short for family rifts. I need to see him now."

"But it's only two weeks till Christmas," Amy stammered, hardly able to take in what Lou was saying. "How long will you be gone?"

"I'll be back before then," Lou said. "I've got his address, so it won't take me long to find him."

"But can't you just call him?" Amy said desperately. "There has to be some way you can find his phone number and talk to him that way. Why do you have to go to see him?"

"I tried to get the number, but the operator said it wasn't listed," Lou replied. "Anyway, I don't just want to talk to him. I want to *see* him and get this all sorted out." She grasped the back of a chair. "I've been waiting twelve years for this, Amy. Please say you understand."

For a moment Amy battled with a desperate urge to beg Lou not to go. Part of her was terrified that she would never come back. *Don't go, please don't go,* she thought.

"Amy?" Lou said.

As much as Amy wanted her to stay, she knew she couldn't convince her. This was something Lou had to do. She took a deep breath. "I understand," she whispered, the words hurting her as she uttered them.

But she was rewarded by the look of intense relief that crossed Lou's face. She hugged Amy. "Thank you. It means a lot to me. I know it's hard at the moment with Grandpa not being very well and —"

"I'm fine. What do you mean I'm not well?"

Amy and Lou turned around. Jack was standing in the kitchen doorway, pale and tired.

"Grandpa," Lou stammered. "How long have you been there?"

"I just came down." A frown deepened on Jack's face as he looked from one granddaughter to the other. "What's going on?"

Lou glanced nervously at Amy. "I think you'd better sit down, Grandpa."

Lou told him what she'd just told Amy. "I have to go, Grandpa," she said.

Amy looked anxiously at their grandpa's face. She knew how he felt about their father. How would he take the news?

For a moment, Jack didn't say anything, but then he squared his shoulders. "Lou," he said quietly, "I've always said that you should follow your heart, and if that's what it's telling you to do, then that's what you should do." He looked at Amy. "We'll get along fine, won't we, Amy?"

"I'm not going to leave you completely on your own," Lou said quickly. "I've called my friend Marnie — you remember her, Grandpa? She came to visit that time you were away at Glen and Silvia's. Well, she's got some time off and said she'd love to come and stay again. I'll leave instructions so she can take over my work while I'm gone. She'd already talked about coming to visit over the holidays — her parents are away in Fiji for Christmas and New Year's, so it works out perfectly. When I asked her if she'd come a little early, she was really excited."

Amy was surprised but pleased. She liked Lou's friend Marnie a lot.

"What about Scott?" Grandpa asked. "Have you told him?"

"No, not yet. I just made up my mind yesterday that I was going to go, and I wanted to tell you two first," Lou replied. "He's stopping by this morning. I'll tell him then."

Amy remembered something. "But you'll miss his reunion dinner."

"He'll understand," Lou said confidently. She smiled, looking as if a weight had lifted from her shoulders now that she had told them. "I just can't wait to see Daddy again. Imagine his face when I just show up at his door."

"Lou, you've got to remember you don't know anything about your father's life now," Grandpa said warningly. "Maybe you should write to him and let him know you're coming."

"There's no point," Lou said. "I'm flying out on Wednesday, so I'll probably arrive before a letter could get to him anyway." She saw the concern on Grandpa's face. "Daddy wants to see me — his last letter made that clear."

"Yes, I know, but —" Grandpa broke off as Lou's face narrowed. "Look, just be careful, honey," he sighed, "that's all I'm saying."

Lou smiled. "I will." She hugged him. "You worry too much, Grandpa. Everything will be fine, you'll see."

❧

After breakfast, Amy went out to the barns. Going up to Daybreak and Melody's stall, she leaned over the door, thinking about Lou's trip.

"Hey, you." Amy turned around to see Ty coming down the aisle toward her. He frowned as he saw her face. "What's up?"

"It's Lou," Amy sighed. "She's going away." Miserably, Amy told Ty about Lou's plans. "What if she doesn't come back?" she said.

"She'll be back," Ty said reassuringly. "Her life's here now. You know she decided that when she gave up her job in New York."

"But what about Daddy? What if he wants her to stay with him?" Amy voiced her worst fears.

"Hey." Ty squeezed her shoulder. "Take it easy, Amy. A lot has changed since she last saw him. Lou has changed."

Amy took a deep breath and forced herself to stay calm.

"Come on," he said practically. "You can't stand around worrying about it. Let's get started on the stalls."

❧

At eleven o'clock, Scott drove up and parked outside the house. "Hi!" he called, jumping out as Amy came down the path with a wheelbarrow. "Is Lou around?"

"She's in the house," Amy replied, for once hoping that he wouldn't come and talk to her.

He took a white envelope out of his pocket. "The tickets for the dinner arrived. Do you know if Lou has gotten her dress yet?"

Just then, the front door opened and Lou came out. "Hi, Scott," she said quietly.

Scott bounded over to her. "Hi," he said, seeming not to notice her subdued manner. He kissed her enthusiastically. "Our tickets are here."

Lou glanced in Amy's direction.

Amy immediately took the hint. "I better go and turn Jasmine and Sundance out," she said, hastily dumping the wheelbarrow.

As she headed back to the barn, she heard Lou say, "Scott — we need to talk."

Out of earshot, Amy stopped and took a deep breath. She couldn't help wondering how Scott would take the news about Lou going away.

Ten minutes later, she heard his engine start up. She headed cautiously toward her sister.

Lou was watching Scott drive away. Her face looked worried.

"How did it go?" Amy asked her tentatively.

Lou sighed and turned round. "It was all right — although he was disappointed about the dinner," she said. "I don't think he understands why I have to go to England right now." Lou paused for a moment. When she next spoke, her voice had a note of doubt in it for the first time. "I — I am doing the right thing, aren't I, Amy?"

Amy struggled hard against her feelings. She knew Lou needed her support. "Of course you are," she said as convincingly as she could. "You heard what Grandpa said this morning. You've got to follow your heart, Lou."

Lou looked slightly happier. "Yes," she said. "You're right. That's what I'm going to do."

❧

Soraya came around that afternoon, and as soon as the horses were fed, she and Amy went inside to get ready for the Grants' party. Amy had been saved the trouble of worrying about what to wear by the simple fact that she only had one dress that was suitable. It was a pale, shimmery, silver color with tiny straps and sequins and beads sewn along the hem of the floaty skirt that ended just above her knees. Lou had bought it for her at Bloomingdale's a year ago, when Amy and Grandpa had gone to visit her in Manhattan. Amy had worn it that night in the city, but since then it had stayed in the back of her closet.

"I love that dress," Soraya said as Amy took it out of its garment bag. "You should wear it more often."

Amy grinned. "Yeah, it would be perfect for mucking out the stalls." She shook out the dress. "What are you going to wear?"

Soraya took down two outfits from the back of Amy's door — a long black dress with a low back and a short lilac shift dress with tiny butterflies embroidered on the bodice. "I couldn't decide. Which do you think?"

Amy looked from one to the other. "The lilac," she said decisively.

"But you haven't even thought about it," Soraya complained.

"I just like it best," Amy said. She couldn't see the point of agonizing about clothes for hours.

"But which do you think *Ben* would like?" Soraya asked.

"Both of them," Amy grinned, going over to her desk and putting a CD on. "Now, stop worrying and take a shower."

〰️

An hour later they were just about ready. Amy sprayed on some perfume borrowed from Lou while Soraya finished fixing the clips in her hair. Amy's party dress swished elegantly as she walked, and her strappy silver shoes emphasized her slender ankles and calves. Usually when Amy went out she just wore a dash of mascara, but tonight Soraya had persuaded her to be more adventurous. She had used silver eye shadow and eyeliner to emphasize her gray eyes, and she had even blow-dried her long silky hair.

"You look great!" Soraya said as Amy looked critically at her reflection in the mirror.

"I just feel weird," Amy complained. "It doesn't look like me."

"You could always put your riding boots on underneath your dress," Soraya said teasingly.

"Don't tempt me!" Amy smiled.

Soraya put the final clip in place.

"I love your hair like that," Amy told her.

Soraya anxiously worked a few curls down around her face.

Amy glanced at her bedside clock and saw that it was nearly seven o'clock. "Come on, we'd better go downstairs!"

Grandpa and Lou were sitting in the kitchen watching a game show. Grandpa was drinking a steaming hot mug of honey and lemon tea. They looked up as Amy and Soraya entered.

"Wow! You should take a shower more often!" Lou teased.

Feeling very self-conscious despite her sister's sarcasm, Amy hurried across the kitchen and grabbed her jacket.

"That's a gorgeous dress, Soraya," Lou said.

"Thanks," Soraya smiled.

"You both look perfectly beautiful," Jack said warmly, getting to his feet. As he did so, his chest rumbled with a single deep cough.

Amy looked at him in concern. "You sound awful, Grandpa."

"I'm all right," Grandpa said. "And if it doesn't get any better, I've got that doctor's appointment."

"All right, Grandpa," Lou said. "But promise you'll stay inside tomorrow."

"I'll see," Jack replied.

Just then there was the sound of a truck drawing up outside the house. Grandpa looked out the window as a horn blew. "It looks like your ride is here. You girls enjoy yourselves."

"Yeah, have fun!" Lou said.

"We will," Amy replied. "See you later."

Ben and Ty were standing by the pickup. Ben gave an appreciative whistle as he saw them. "Hey, look at the two of you!"

"You like?" Soraya said, giving a twirl.

"I do," Ben grinned.

Amy found her eyes drawn to Ty to see his reaction.

"You look really nice," Ty said to her.

Amy felt the blood rush to her cheeks. She hurried to the door of the pickup, glad that the darkness hid her blush. "It's freezing out here," she said quickly to disguise her embarrassment.

Ben held out his hand to Soraya with a fake English accent. "May I escort you to your carriage, ma'am?"

Soraya giggled. "You may," she said, pretending to curtsy. Taking his hand, she let him help her into the pickup. Amy and Ty followed her in.

It was a squeeze with all of them squished in the bench seat. Sitting between Ty and Soraya, Amy was acutely aware of Ty's legs pressed against hers. Trying to reposition herself, she leaned back and then flinched slightly as their shoulders touched.

"Here," he said, moving over to make more room for her.

"Thanks," Amy muttered, not wanting to look him in the eye. The air was cold but her cheeks were burning. She looked down at her lap. She couldn't imagine why she felt the way she did.

❦

The Grants lived in a sprawling mansion on the edge of town. A wide gravel driveway led to the grand front entrance, which was decorated with an oversize holly wreath. On either side of the door were tall Christmas trees, covered with thousands of twinkling fairy lights.

Candles flickered in every window. "Whoa!" Soraya said. "It looks like a palace out of some fairy tale."

"It looks like an electrical fire hazard to me," Amy muttered, but even as she spoke she had to admit that she was impressed. The place looked beautiful.

As they entered the house, the smell of balsam and pine seemed unusually strong. There were Christmas trees in every room, and the mantels were weighed down with swathes of dark green foliage and shiny red berries. Waiters bustled around with trays of drinks and beautifully prepared morsels of food — miniature quiches, smoked salmon canapés, delicate asparagus spears, tiny pizzas, and Thai prawns. For the first time, Amy began to see why everyone made such a big deal about the Grants' Christmas party. She looked around at the masses of people. "I wonder if Matt's here yet?"

"Over there!" said Soraya, nodding to a group standing by one of the Christmas trees. Matt was talking with Dan and Ashley, Jade and Brittany.

"Matt!" Amy called out as she waved.

Matt looked around. His handsome face broke into a smile. "Hey, Amy," he said, coming over. "You look great."

"As do you," she replied.

"Well, hi there!"

Amy glanced over Matt's shoulder. Ashley had left her little group and was heading through the crowd toward them. She was wearing a stunning silvery-green long dress that shimmered in the lights. Noticing how her blond hair cascaded over her shoulders in a riot of artfully styled curls and her green eyes were emphasized by glittery mascara, Amy couldn't help but think that Ashley looked like a mermaid.

"Hi, Ashley," Amy said. Reminding herself that this was the Grants' party, she was determined to be polite. "You look lovely."

"Thank you." Ashley's eyes swept over Amy's outfit. "That's a nice dress — I remember it from the sales rack at the end of last season, but some styles don't really date, do they?" She smiled sweetly and turned to Ben and Ty. "Let me get you a drink."

Amy looked at Soraya and rolled her eyes. She knew Ashley had been trying to insult her, but it didn't faze Amy; she didn't care whether her dress was the latest look or not.

Ashley waved a waiter over and then looked up at Ben through her long lashes. "I'm so happy *you* could come," she said.

"Thanks," Ben replied, smiling easily.

"You *must* come and meet my friends," Ashley said, putting a hand through his arm. "They're *dying* to meet you."

Shooting a rather helpless look at Amy, Ty, and Soraya, Ben allowed himself to be led away.

Ty grinned at Amy. "Well, I guess we won't be seeing much of Ben this evening."

Amy glanced at Soraya. The sparkle in her eyes had immediately gone flat. "Don't worry. We'll rescue him in a bit," Amy said quickly. "We won't let her monopolize him all night."

Just then, the live band started playing in the far room. "Come on," Amy said, desperate to get Soraya to cheer up. "Let's go dance!"

🙠

At first Amy danced with Ty, Soraya, and Matt as a group, but gradually Matt started to draw her away from the other two. "You really do look amazing tonight," he said.

Amy grinned at him. "Thanks."

For a few minutes they danced without saying anything else, but Amy became conscious of Matt's eyes never leaving her face. She found herself purposely avoiding his eyes. As the song ended, the music changed tempo and slowed down.

Amy glanced around. "Well, I guess we should find Ty and Soraya," she said quickly. But before she could move, Matt had grabbed her hands.

"Don't go, I love this song," he said, the tone of his voice becoming serious.

Amy swallowed. This wasn't what she wanted at all. "But it's a slow song," she said.

"I know," Matt said, smiling at her. He slipped his left hand around her back and tried to draw her closer. "Come on, Amy. You know that I like you."

Amy pulled back. Her heart was pounding now, but she didn't want to make a scene. "Matt, I like you, too," she stammered, desperately wishing she was some-where — *anywhere* — else. "But I don't think I'm ready for anything more. If we started dating it would change everything."

"Yeah — it would be great," Matt said. He gripped her hand. "We'd be good together, Amy."

Amy saw the hope on his face. She didn't want to hurt him, but she didn't want him to go on thinking there could be something between them. It wouldn't be fair. She just didn't like him that way. "Look, Matt, I really like you as a friend. . . ."

Matt's face stiffened, and before she had a chance to go on to explain, he dropped her hand.

Amy saw the hurt in his eyes. "Matt —" she began.

Ignoring her, he turned around and started to walk away.

At that moment Soraya came bounding across the dance floor. "Ty and I are going to get something to eat," she said brightly, stopping in front of Matt. "Are you two coming?"

For a fraction of a second, Amy thought Matt was going to brush past her, but then he shrugged. "Sure."

Breathing out a trembling sigh of relief, Amy watched him walk over to join Ty at the edge of the dance floor.

"You OK?" Soraya asked her in a low voice. "That looked kind of uncomfortable."

"It was," Amy said, with feeling. "Thanks."

They followed Ty and Matt to the side of the dance floor where a long table had been set up with drinks and finger food. As they reached it, Ty looked at Amy. She was sure he must have noticed what was going on, too, but he didn't say anything. Matt's face was hidden as he leaned over the food table and filled a plate.

"Where's Ben?" Amy said.

"Where do you think?" Soraya sighed, nodding toward Ashley's group of friends.

Amy looked over. Ben was standing near Ashley's crowd. She was trying to persuade him to dance.

"Come on, you haven't danced all night," Amy heard her say.

Ben looked awkward. "Maybe later."

"Can't Ashley take no for an answer?" Amy said to Soraya.

Ashley flicked back her hair. "But this is a great song. Come dance with me." She took Ben's hand.

Ben gently freed himself. "No, thanks."

"Why not?" Ashley pouted. "Don't you like me?"

An embarrassed look crossed Ben's face. "Ashley, you've picked the wrong guy," he said. "I'm not looking for a relationship right now."

Ashley stared at him and then drew back as if she'd been slapped. "What makes you think I want a relationship!" she exclaimed, her face flushing hotly. "I only asked you to dance!"

Ben stood there helplessly as Ashley stormed off, her friends close behind her.

"Well, Ben told her," Amy said to Soraya with a giggle.

"Oh, yeah — that's real funny, Amy!" Amy swung around. Matt was standing a few paces behind her, glaring at her. "You know, Ashley might actually be upset. What if she really likes Ben?" He didn't give her time to let her answer. "You never thought of that, did you?"

Amy felt awful. She hadn't thought anyone had been close enough to hear. "Matt —" she began, not knowing what to say. She realized how insensitive her comment must have seemed to him, so soon after what he had said on the dance floor.

"Forget it, Amy," Matt said coldly as he walked off. "Just forget it."

Chapter Five

Amy looked at Soraya and Ty's stunned faces. "I'll go after him," she said quickly.

She set off across the dance floor. She felt awful. She had to figure out how to apologize to Matt. But she stopped when she turned around the corner. Matt was walking up to Ashley. At first Ashley didn't look at Matt but continued talking with Jade and Brittany. When Ashley finally turned to him, her face was hard. But then he held out his hand, and to Amy's astonishment, a look of gratitude crossed Ashley's face. With a faint smile, she took Matt's hand and allowed him to lead her onto the dance floor.

Soraya came up behind her. "What's going on?" she asked, looking bewildered. Her eyes widened as she saw

Matt and Ashley together on the dance floor. "What's Matt doing?" she gasped.

"Dancing," Amy snapped, a sharp pang of betrayal shooting through her as Matt's arms encircled Ashley's slender waist. He was supposed to be *her* friend.

"But he's dancing with *Ashley*!" Soraya said as they watched Ashley's arms curve around Matt's neck. She turned to Amy. "What happened?" she demanded. "Why did he get so mad at you?"

"I don't know," Amy lied. She saw the disbelief in Soraya's eyes. "OK, I guess he might have been a little upset because I didn't want to slow dance with him," she admitted reluctantly.

"So he asked Ashley?" Soraya said, as if she still couldn't believe it. "But he doesn't even *like* Ashley."

"Well, he certainly doesn't seem to be giving that impression at the moment," Amy said sarcastically as she saw Matt draw Ashley closer.

As she spoke, the song came to an end and the music became faster again. Amy watched Matt and Ashley, expecting to see them go their separate ways. But they didn't. Matt said something to Ashley. She smiled, and then they separated slightly. Still holding hands, they started to dance again.

Amy was still watching Matt and Ashley when she realized that Ty was standing beside her. Soraya was nowhere to be seen.

"Do you want to dance?" he asked.

Amy looked at him in surprise. "With you?"

Ty grinned. "No — with the giant nutcracker in the corner."

Amy saw the teasing glint in his eyes and smiled. "OK," she said.

They found a space on the dance floor. Trying to forget about Matt dancing with Ashley, Amy let the music swell through her mind. As her body swayed in time with the beat, she glanced at Ty. His gaze was fixed on her face. As she looked into his familiar eyes, Amy's heart somersaulted, and she suddenly seemed to lose the ability to breathe. For a moment they just stared at each other, and then without saying a word, Ty stepped closer and took her hand.

The rest of the world seemed to swirl and fade away. Amy could think about nothing except the heat of Ty's fingers clasped around hers. They moved together in time with the music, their eyes fixed on each other's face.

Amy didn't know how long they'd been dancing when Ben came up to them.

"We've got some drinks and a table to sit at!" Ben shouted over the music. "Soraya's guarding it!"

Ty dropped Amy's hand.

"What?" Amy stammered to Ben. She suddenly became aware of the crowd of people around them, the sound of talking and laughing, of Ty standing there and looking at her with an unreadable expression in his eyes.

Ben bellowed out his message again.

Amy glanced at Ty and saw his face smooth into its usual friendly expression. "Great," he said easily. "You coming, Amy?"

Amy forced herself to nod. "Sure." Her voice came out high and breathless, but Ben and Ty didn't seem to notice. Taking a deep breath to calm her pounding heart, Amy followed Ben and Ty over to the table.

❧

It was two o'clock in the morning when they finally got back to Heartland. Ty jumped out of the pickup to let Amy out.

"Thanks for the ride, Ben," Amy said.

"No problem," Ben replied. "See you later."

Amy looked at Soraya. She was scooting over in the seat, taking advantage of the extra room now that Ty and Amy were out. But Amy thought Soraya had looked pretty happy when she was squished in next to Ben.

"Call me," Amy said, giving her a meaningful look. As far as she knew, nothing had happened between Ben and Soraya, but they had been together all evening and Amy wanted to know the details. Besides, Amy also wanted to know what Soraya thought about Matt and Ashley, who hadn't left each other's sides all night.

A grin twitched at Soraya's lips. "I will," she promised.

Amy got out. The frosty air stung her bare legs, and her breath froze like smoke as it left her lips. "Night," she said to Ty, who was standing by the pickup door. Since the moment on the dance floor they hadn't been alone together, but now she found herself looking into his eyes and felt a blush creep up her neck.

"Good night, Amy," Ty said softly.

Amy hesitated. She felt as if they were both waiting for something, but she didn't know what.

"See you later," she said breathlessly as she hurried indoors.

❧

As she got into bed and turned off the light, Amy's thoughts raced back to the moment when she'd been dancing with Ty. Shutting her eyes, she could see his face as clearly as if he were there, could feel his fingers touching hers, could feel her heart pounding. She'd never felt like that before.

But this is Ty you're thinking about, she quickly reminded herself.

She curled her knees up to her chest. It was just so confusing. How could she feel like that about Ty, of all people? *I see him every day,* she thought. *He's one of my best friends.* But still, the memory of him holding her hand came back to her. She tried to push it away. After all, she didn't even know how Ty felt. It wasn't like he'd tried to kiss her or anything.

But what if he had? she thought.

She stopped herself before she went any further. Nothing was going to happen between her and Ty — nothing!

❧

Four and a half hours later, Amy woke up to the blare of her alarm clock. She groaned and staggered out of bed. She was in the middle of mixing the feeds when Ty arrived.

"You look as good as I feel," he said, coming into the feed room.

Amy jumped at the sound of his voice. "Morning," she said, hastily trying to cover her confusion. After the events of the night before, she sort of felt that he should look different, but he looked exactly the same as he always did every morning. "I can't believe I've only had four hours' sleep," she said.

"Me, neither," Ty said. "But," his voice softened suddenly as his eyes met hers, "it was worth it."

Feeling suddenly flustered, Amy grabbed a pile of the feeds. "I'll go get started on the back barn," she said.

For the rest of that morning, she avoided being alone with Ty. Trying not to think about the night before, she threw herself into the regular routine of cleaning the stalls and taking the horses out to the paddocks. Just before lunch, she was on her way to bring Moochie and Jake in when she heard the telephone ringing. A few seconds later, Lou opened the back door. "Amy! It's Soraya on the phone!"

Amy hurried to the kitchen. Kicking her boots off, she took the phone from Lou. "Hey," she said, carrying the phone up the stairs to her bedroom and shutting the door. "How are you?"

"Fine," Soraya said, and Amy could hear the grin in her voice. "Oh, Amy, I've got a lot to tell you."

"About you and Ben?" Amy said eagerly.

"Yes!" Soraya said. "Do you remember when you and Ty were dancing?"

Did she remember? Amy didn't think she'd ever forget. "Yes," she said.

"Well, did you notice how long Ben and I were gone when we disappeared to get drinks? " Soraya asked.

Not wanting to admit that she hadn't noticed at all, Amy quickly lied. "Yes, of course. So what happened?"

"Well —" Soraya stopped.

"Go on," Amy urged.

"Well, there was a long line for drinks, so we went outside onto the veranda for a while," Soraya sighed dreamily. "It was, like, really romantic. There were loads of stars in the sky and just me and Ben standing there."

"And?" Amy said in an agony of impatience. "What happened?"

"Well, nothing happened exactly," Soraya admitted. "We just stayed there and talked. He told me all about what it was like growing up on his aunt's farm instead of with his parents and about how he feels about getting to know his mom all over again. I felt like he was being very honest. He said he could really talk to me."

"Soraya, that's great," said Amy, even though she detected some hesitation in her friend's voice. She was eager to get to the important point.

"Yeah," Soraya admitted. "I wish he would have kissed me. It would have been so perfect, but he said that he's got so much stuff going on with his mom and everything else that he just doesn't want to date anyone yet. But I don't care. I'll wait. I'll just be his friend for now, if that's what he wants." Amy could hear the happiness in Soraya's voice. "When he dropped me off at home he said he'd really enjoyed the evening and that maybe we could go out sometime."

"On a date?" Amy exclaimed.

"Well, not a date exactly," Soraya said. "But you never know — it could lead to that."

"That's wonderful!" Amy said. "Just think how mad Ashley will be if you start dating him!"

"Speaking of Ashley, what do you think's going on with her and Matt?" Soraya said eagerly.

"I think they both just wanted someone to hang out with last night, but I don't think it's going anywhere," Amy said. "He can't possibly *like* her."

Soraya suddenly sounded more serious. "But what if they do start going out? Do you think we'll have to hang out with her?"

"They won't start dating," Amy said. "Matt's got better taste than that."

Soraya didn't say anything.

"He does!" Amy insisted, trying to suppress a vision of what it would be like if Matt and Ashley were going out and always hanging on each other at school.

"Well, I guess we'll see tomorrow," Soraya said.

After Soraya hung up, Amy sat in her room, thinking about what Soraya had said. There was no way Matt and Ashley would start dating — was there?

She looked at the phone and then punched in Matt's number.

"Hello, Mrs. Trewin," Amy said when Matt's mom answered. "It's Amy. Is Matt there?"

"I think you're in luck," Mrs. Trewin said. "I just heard him get up. Let me call him for you." Amy heard Mrs. Trewin shouting for Matt and then she came back on the phone. "It must have been some party last night," she said with a laugh. "He hasn't been out of his room all morning."

"It was," Amy said.

Just then, Matt took the phone from his mom.

"Hi," Amy said brightly.

"Hello." Matt's voice sounded guarded.

Amy suddenly felt awkward. "Last night was a lot of fun, wasn't it?" she said.

"I had a good time," Matt replied briefly.

There was a pause. Amy wanted to ask about Ashley, but Matt sounded so cool and reserved that she didn't dare. For the first time since they had become friends she found herself searching for something to say to him. "So — what are you doing today?" she said at last.

"Just stuff," Matt said noncommittally. He didn't expand, and there was another uncomfortable pause.

"OK, then, I better get going," Amy said. "I — I just thought I'd call to say hi."

"Yeah," Matt said. "See you tomorrow at school."

As Amy put the phone down she realized that her face was flushed. Matt had sounded like he didn't want to talk to her at all. She remembered how hurt he had looked when she had been laughing with Soraya after Ben refused to dance with Ashley. More than anything she wished that she could take that moment back. Matt was her friend, and although she didn't want to go out with him, she had never meant to upset him. He acted as if she and Soraya had been laughing at him.

It'll be OK tomorrow, she told herself, trying to be positive. *He'll have forgotten about it by then.*

❧

But the next day she couldn't help feeling nervous when they reached Matt's stop. Matt's tall figure got onto the bus, and to Amy's relief he made his way to the seat in front of her and Soraya, just like he usually did.

"Hi," he said. He sounded normal, but Amy noticed how his eyes slipped quickly away from hers as he greeted them.

"Hey," Soraya grinned, unaware of the slight tension in the air. Amy had been too embarrassed to tell Soraya about the phone conversation she'd had with Matt. "So, what was going on with you and Ashley on Saturday night?" Soraya teased.

Matt looked uncomfortable. "We were just dancing."

"Are you going to start dating?" Soraya said. "Go on — tell us."

Amy saw how awkward Matt was looking. "Of course Matt's not going to start dating Ashley," she said quickly, wanting to stop Soraya's teasing.

But it was the wrong thing to say. Matt turned to her. "What do you mean I'm not?" he demanded.

"Well, I mean, it's *Ashley*," Amy said, taken aback by the anger in his eyes.

Matt glared at her, obviously misinterpreting her words. "It may be hard for you to believe, Amy, but there are some people who would go out with me."

Amy stared at him. "I didn't mean it that way, I just — "

Matt got to his feet. "You know, sometimes you can be so selfish. You only see what you want to see," he said, and with that he marched off to sit farther down the bus.

Amy and Soraya looked at each other in stunned silence for a moment and then Amy jumped to her feet. "Matt," she said, following him, "I didn't mean that she wouldn't want to go out with you. I meant it the other way around."

Suddenly, Matt looked very weary. "Look, just forget it," he said. "I don't want to talk about it." Opening his bag, he took out a paperback and began to read.

Glancing around, Amy was suddenly aware of the curious looks they were getting from the other students. She hesitated, hoping Matt would look up, but his head stayed resolutely bent over his book. With her cheeks burning, she made her way back up the bus aisle.

✌

At school that day, Matt hardly said a word to Amy. He hung around with Ashley and her friends. Every so often Ashley would link her arm through his and look triumphantly over in Amy's direction.

"I don't know why she's looking at me that way," Amy muttered to Soraya at lunchtime. "Everyone's going to think that I had wanted to go out with Matt and she stole him from me."

"Sure you're not jealous?" Soraya said.

"*Jealous!*" Amy exclaimed. "Of course I'm not jealous. Matt can do whatever he wants!"

But despite her words, she had to admit that she would miss being with Matt. Not in a romantic way, like Soraya meant, but they'd been friends since sixth grade and it felt strange to see him hanging around with other people — especially Ashley and her friends.

❧

By the time Amy got home that afternoon, she was in a very bad mood. She dumped her backpack in the empty kitchen and went upstairs to get changed. Lou was in her bedroom, packing for her trip. "Had a good day?" she asked as Amy went past.

"No," Amy replied abruptly.

"Oh," Lou said. She came to her door. "Do you want to talk about it?" she said.

"No," Amy said again, and going into her bedroom, she pointedly shut the door.

She went to the window. The cold gray sky seemed to press down on the muddy fields. Sundance and Jasmine were grazing in the field by the back barn. Amy suddenly frowned. Grandpa was working on the paddock gate. As he bent to pick up some nails, she saw him start to cough. He leaned weakly against the fence, his shoulders shaking.

"Oh, Grandpa," Amy muttered, exasperated.

She pulled off the sweater she'd worn to school and grabbed a sweatshirt, determined to go straight out and tell him to come inside. But just then she saw Grandpa stagger. He grasped at the fence, and then suddenly his knees seemed to sag. He sank to the ground with his hands clutching his chest.

"Lou!" Amy screamed, throwing her sweatshirt down and running to the door. "Lou! Come quick!"

Chapter Six

"Dial 911!" Lou shouted as she ran down the stairs and out of the house. "Call an ambulance!"

Her heart pounding, Amy grabbed the portable phone in the kitchen. It only took a few seconds to get through to the emergency medical services. "I need an ambulance!" Amy gasped when an operator answered. All the time, she never took her eyes from Grandpa's bent-over body.

By now Lou had reached him. Amy saw Lou's arms go around his shoulders, saw her turn and yell for Ty and Ben.

"Name, please," a voice spoke in Amy's ear.

"Fleming — Amy Fleming," she burst out.

"Address?"

Amy rattled off the address.

"And what seems to be the problem, Amy?" the woman on the other end of the phone asked calmly.

"It's my grandpa," Amy said, barely able to get the words out. "He's collapsed."

She was asked more questions — what exactly had happened, whether Grandpa was conscious, how old she was, who was with her. She answered them almost without thinking as she watched Lou, Ty, and Ben help Grandpa to his feet. Half carrying him, they brought him back to the house.

"An ambulance is on its way," the woman said. "I need to know as much as you can tell me about your grandpa's condition so I can help you to help him while you wait for the ambulance to arrive. Does he have a fever?"

"I don't know," Amy replied anxiously. "Hang on —"

Lou came through the door, opening it wide so Ty and Ben could help Grandpa inside. "Lou! They want to know about Grandpa's condition. Does he have a fever?" Amy gasped.

"Here, I'll talk to them." Lou grabbed the phone from her. "Lou Fleming here," she said.

Amy looked at Grandpa. He was conscious but his lips were blue and he was breathing in quick, shallow gasps. Beads of sweat stood out on his forehead.

As Amy watched Ty and Ben lower Grandpa onto the sofa, she heard Lou answering the woman's questions. Despite her obvious concern, Lou's voice was brisk and in control. "I see," she said, scribbling notes on the pad. "Keep him warm, change his clothes if they're damp, give him fluids if he'll take them. And how long did you say the ambulance would be?"

Amy crouched beside Grandpa's side. "It's going to be OK. The ambulance will be here soon."

"No ambulance. I'll be all right," Grandpa said, wheezing between each sentence. His normally sharp blue eyes looked dazed and confused. "Got to fix the gate."

"The gate!" Amy exclaimed. "The gate doesn't matter, Grandpa!"

A spasm of coughs burst from Jack, his face screwing up in pain.

Amy couldn't bear it. "What's the matter with him?" she cried, looking at Ty and Ben.

"Pneumonia." There was a click from behind them as Lou replaced the hand set. They all turned to look at her. "That's what the woman thinks from his symptoms." She hurried to Grandpa's side. "Come on, we've got to keep you warm and dry until the ambulance arrives."

㋢

The next few hours passed in a blur for Amy. The ambulance seemed to take forever to get there. However, when it did, the paramedics immediately assessed the situation. Grandpa was lifted into the ambulance and given an oxygen mask. Then the doors shut and the ambulance set off for the hospital. Leaving Ben and Ty to take care of the horses, Amy and Lou followed in Lou's car. Neither of them spoke much on the way. Staring out the window, Amy just kept seeing Grandpa collapsing on the ground, his face contorting in pain.

At the hospital, Grandpa was taken away immediately, and she and Lou had nothing to do but wait. At last a young female doctor came to find them to confirm that Jack did indeed have pneumonia.

"So what exactly does that mean?" Lou demanded.

"Well, as you may know, pneumonia is a serious inflammation of the lungs," Dr. Jane Marshall explained. "The air sacs in the lungs fill with liquid, and this keeps the correct amount of oxygen from reaching the blood." She paused, watching them to see if they were following. "Your grandfather has a bacterial form of pneumonia. It can affect people of all ages. It's most likely to take hold in someone whose immune system has been weakened in some way by an illness. When a person's resistance is lowered, the bacteria that normally live in the throat can work their way into the lungs. That bacteria causes the air sacs to become inflamed."

Amy thought about the cold that Grandpa had picked up when helping Melody to foal. "Grandpa has had a bad cold for several weeks," she interrupted. "He hasn't rested and it's just gotten worse and worse."

"That would certainly weaken his immune system," Dr. Marshall replied, nodding.

"How long will it take him to get better?" Lou said quickly.

"It all depends on how he responds to treatment," Dr. Marshall said. "The inflammation is very severe, which is why he has such a high temperature and is in such pain. We're giving him antibiotics to combat the infection and painkillers to help ease the pain in his chest from coughing. He's also on a respirator, which will help get his oxygen levels back to normal. Providing he responds to the treatment and there are no complications, we're probably looking at a hospital stay of about a week."

"Can we see him?" Lou asked.

"Yes, but just briefly," Dr. Marshall said. "We're still trying to stabilize his condition."

Amy and Lou followed her down a succession of long white corridors. At last the doctor stopped outside a door. "He's in here," she said.

Amy took a quick look through the glass in the door. Grandpa was lying in bed on his back, his eyes closed. Long thin tubes traveled from machines into his arm and nose.

Dr. Marshall opened the door. "You can go in," she said quietly.

They walked into the room. Lou sat down by the bed and took Grandpa's hand. "Hello, Grandpa," she murmured.

Amy followed her. Standing beside Lou's chair, she saw Grandpa's eyelids blink. "Lou?" he whispered hoarsely, turning to look at her.

Lou squeezed his hand. "Yes, Grandpa, I'm here. So's Amy."

Grandpa's clouded blue eyes found Amy. She felt a lump of tears form in her throat as she saw the confusion in his face. "Hello, Grandpa," she said, longing to hug him but not quite daring to because she didn't want to interfere with the tubes.

"Where am I?" Grandpa asked.

"In the hospital," Lou replied. "You've got pneumonia, and you need to stay here a while — until you get better."

Amy half expected Grandpa to object, but his illness seemed to have drained all the fight from him. He nodded wordlessly.

Lou squeezed his hand. "We're going home now. You need to rest." She leaned forward and kissed his cheek. "But we'll come back tomorrow. You take care now."

She stood up and let Amy take her place. "Bye, Grandpa," Amy whispered. "We love you."

A faint smile caught at the corners of Grandpa's mouth. "I love you both, too."

✖

Amy and Lou got back to Heartland at ten o'clock that night. They found the lights on and Ben and Ty waiting for them.

"How's Jack?" Ty asked as soon as they got out of the car.

"They're still trying to stabilize him, but they think he's going to be OK," Lou said. She explained about the pneumonia, her voice as brisk as the doctor's. "We can go back first thing in the morning."

"Well, don't worry about the horses," Ben said. "We'll take care of them, won't we, Ty?"

Ty nodded.

"Thanks," Lou said gratefully. "That would be a real help."

"Do you want us to do anything now?" Ty asked, looking from her to Amy.

"No, we'll be fine," Lou said. "You two go home."

Ben said good night and went over to his pickup, but Ty paused by Amy. "How are you doing?"

She shrugged. She had a feeling that if she spoke she would start to cry.

Ty squeezed her shoulder. "Look, I'll see you tomorrow," he said, and walked to his truck.

As she watched his taillights disappear down the drive, Amy felt tears spill down her cheeks.

"Hey, Amy," Lou said, noticing and hugging her. "Don't cry. You heard what the doctor said. Grandpa's going to be OK."

Amy wiped her sleeve across her eyes. "But it was just seeing him like that, Lou — with all those tubes, barely able to breathe."

"I know," Lou said. "But he'll be out in a week or two." She took Amy's hands. "Come on, we need to be strong — for Grandpa."

🙦

Amy stayed home from school the next day. She and Lou went to the hospital in the morning. They found Grandpa looking a bit brighter. He was still pale, but his skin had lost the horrible blue-white tone of the day before. An IV was still attached to his arm, but the tube had been taken out of his nose.

Lou sat down next to him and Amy sat on the edge of the bed. "How are you feeling?" Lou asked him.

"Better," Grandpa said weakly.

"That's good," Lou told him. "Now, you're going to do exactly what the doctor says, aren't you? You're going to rest and get better."

Jack nodded. "I've learned my lesson." He looked at Amy. "How's everything with the horses?"

"Fine," she reassured him. "Ty and Ben said they'd cover for you."

"You don't need to worry about a thing," Lou said quickly. "I'm going to cancel my trip to England. We'll easily manage till you come back."

Jack stared at her. "No, Lou — you can't cancel it, not for me."

"Don't be silly, Grandpa," Lou said. "I'm not going away while you're in the hospital."

"But I don't want you to stay because of me." Grandpa pulled himself up so he was leaning against his pillows. "No, I mean it, Lou," he insisted as Lou opened her mouth to argue. "I want you to go." The exertion of sitting up made him start to cough. He bent over, his face turning white as he grasped at his chest.

Amy looked at Lou in alarm. Lou quickly picked up a glass of water from beside the bed. "Here, Grandpa, drink this."

Grandpa swallowed a few sips. "Please," he said weakly as he caught his breath and his coughs died away. "Go to England like you'd decided."

Lou shook her head. "I couldn't. Now let's stop arguing about this."

"Go," Grandpa said, starting to look agitated again. "I won't be happy till I know you're going, Lou."

Lou hesitated. She looked at Amy, who shrugged.

"OK, Grandpa — I'll go, as long as the doctor says you're getting better," Lou said slowly.

Amy stared at her sister.

"Good," Grandpa whispered, a look of relief crossing his face as he sank back against the pillows. His chest moved up and down in short, shallow breaths.

"You're worn out," Lou said, looking worried. "We'd better leave."

But Jack shook his head. "No. I want to tell you something first."

"We'll come back later, Grandpa," Amy said, standing up. "You can tell us then."

"I want to tell you now," Grandpa insisted. "It's about your parents."

Amy sat back down on the bed slowly, wondering what he was going to tell them.

Jack took a wheezing breath. "It's something your mother never told you. I realized this morning that if anything ever happened to me you might never know. Or if you found out, you might be upset that you heard it from someone else."

"What are you talking about, Grandpa?" Lou asked.

Grandpa paused for a moment. "There's no easy way to say this," he said, looking from one sister to the other, "but your parents got a divorce three years ago."

Amy stared at him. "A divorce! What do you mean?"

She saw the shock on Lou's face. "Mom would have told us!"

"She didn't tell anyone apart from me," Jack said. "Your father initiated the divorce. Your mom didn't want to agree — despite everything, she still loved him — but as you know, she'd already turned down his attempts to reconcile and try to get back together. I think she probably felt she had no choice."

Amy struggled to take it all in. She'd always thought her mom and dad had stayed married. *Well, does it really matter?* she thought. *It's not like they were ever going to get back together.* But it mattered to her, and she couldn't pretend it didn't. Being divorced seemed so much more final than just being separated. "Why didn't you tell us before, Grandpa?" she asked, trying to understand.

Jack sighed. "I wanted to respect your mother's wishes," he said. "She didn't tell you when she was alive, so I didn't see how I could after she died. I don't know why she decided not to tell you, and I feel like I've betrayed her. But I couldn't keep it from you — you have the right to know."

There was silence for a moment and then Lou spoke. "Thank you for telling us," she said, squeezing Grandpa's hand. "You did the right thing."

Jack looked at her anxiously. "I hope it won't stop you going to England."

Lou shook her head. "Divorced or not, he's still my daddy." She smiled. "The only thing that will stop me going is if you don't start getting better."

Looking as if a weight had been taken off his shoulders, Jack leaned back against the pillows. "Oh, I'll get better," he said, smiling weakly back at her. "I'll be out of here in no time — just you wait and see."

Chapter Seven

"So, how is he?" Ty said. He and Ben were waiting for Amy and Lou when they pulled into Heartland's driveway.

"It looks like Grandpa will be in the hospital for at least a week," Lou explained, stepping out of her car. "But then, providing there are no complications, he can come home and recuperate here."

"That's great news," Ben said, looking relieved.

Lou smiled. "Yes, it is."

Not a single muscle in Lou's face betrayed the impact of Grandpa's recent announcement. Amy wasn't so able to hide her feelings. "I'm going to get changed," she said, just wanting to be on her own.

In her bedroom, she sank down on her unmade bed. Mom and Dad were divorced. She thought about the letter her father had written to her mother, begging for a reconciliation. *I'll never stop loving you,* he had written in that letter. She picked up the photograph of her mom and Pegasus that she kept beside her bed.

As always when she saw that photograph she'd have given anything to have her mom back for half an hour — to talk to her again, to tell her how much she loved her. But this time she would ask her mom questions. Why did she keep Daddy's letter secret? And why hadn't she told them about the divorce?

❧

When Amy finally went back downstairs, she found Lou, Ty, and Ben in the kitchen having coffee.

"Do you want some?" Lou asked, gesturing toward the coffeepot.

Amy shook her head. She didn't feel like talking. "I'll go get started on the grooming."

Ty jumped to his feet. "I'll go with you," he said, dumping his coffee mug in the sink and following her outside.

"Are you all right?" he asked as they walked up the path.

Amy nodded. She didn't want to talk to anyone, not even Ty.

Ty looked up at the sky where dark rain clouds were gathering on the horizon. "We should hold off on the grooming," he suggested, "and take Daybreak for a walk before that rain sets in."

"OK," Amy agreed, feeling relieved. She knew that if she was with Daybreak she wouldn't have a chance to think about anything else. And right now, that was just what she wanted.

They headed toward the back barn. As always, before trying to lead Daybreak out, Amy spent at least five minutes running her hands over the filly's body and legs, trying to get her used to being handled.

Daybreak seemed quieter than normal. "She's being good," Amy said to Ty, who was holding the filly's head. "Maybe the vetiver oil's working."

"Or maybe she's not feeling very well," Ty said, pointing to Daybreak's muzzle. "She might have a cold."

Amy joined Ty and saw that Daybreak had a runny nose. She felt worried. She knew that any illness in a young foal had to be watched carefully. Foals less than eight weeks old are especially vulnerable because they don't have an older horse's ability to fight off disease. "I'll check her temperature," she said.

Amy went to get the thermometer. "One hundred degrees," she said, checking the reading twice to make sure. "So it's normal."

"Well, I guess we don't need to call Scott then," Ty said. "But we should keep an eye on her for the next few days."

❧

Later that morning, Amy saw Scott's Jeep coming up the driveway. "Amy!" he said, looking worried as he got out of the car. "Ty called me this morning and told me about Jack. I came as soon as I could. How is he?"

"He's a bit better," Amy said. "The hospital said that he'd probably be out in a week." She was about to ask him to take a look at Daybreak when the back door opened and Lou came out.

"Scott, what are you doing here?" she said, surprised.

"Ty told me the news," Scott said, going over to her. "I came as soon as I could." He held out his arms. Lou stepped forward and Scott's arms folded around her. Bending his head, he kissed her hair. "I'm really sorry."

It was such an intimate moment that Amy felt awkward witnessing it. She started to back away.

Scott noticed Amy's expression and broke away from Lou. "It must have been terrible for both of you," he said, including Amy in his glance. "So what exactly did the hospital say?"

Lou explained. "I don't know how we're going to make him take it easy when he comes out." She looked at Amy. "You can't let him do anything outside while I'm away — no fixing the roof or gates."

"I won't," Amy said. She saw Scott frown.

"What do you mean — when you're away?"

Lou's cheeks flushed pink. "I'm — I'm flying to London tomorrow."

Scott stared at her in astonishment. "What? When Jack's in the hospital?"

"Grandpa wants me to go," Lou said quickly. "He knows how important this is to me. I feel like there's something missing from my life. I get this empty feeling whenever I think of Daddy."

Amy saw Scott's jaw tighten. "I see," he said flatly. "I didn't realize how hard it's been on you."

"I want to stay — really, I do," Lou went on, "but Grandpa won't hear of it — he's made me promise to go."

"*Made* you?" Scott snapped angrily. "Jack would never make you do anything, Lou. You know that. This is your choice. Don't try to pretend it's not."

Lou looked astonished at his outburst. "Scott —"

"No, Lou," Scott interrupted icily. "If you want to go chasing halfway around the world after the father who deserted you when your grandpa is right here sick in the hospital, then that's fine — it's your decision. Just don't try to justify it to me." Scott's face was thunderous as he strode down to his Jeep and, slamming the door shut, drove away.

Amy looked quickly at Lou. She was staring at Scott's car with a shocked expression on her face and then, tears suddenly filling her eyes, she rushed into the house.

Amy followed her.

"Lou?" she said tentatively, going over to her sister, who was standing by the kitchen table.

"I can't believe Scott said those things!" Lou exclaimed. She sank down in a chair. "Of course, I don't want to leave Grandpa while he's sick, but he understands. You heard him today — he wants me to go."

Well, maybe he wouldn't if he thought that you really wanted to stay, Amy thought to herself, but looking at the confusion on Lou's face she bit back her words.

"If I could be in two places at once, I would be," Lou said, shaking her head. "But I have to go to England. You know that."

Amy didn't know what to say. It would be really tough to deal with everything on her own, but she knew it would be selfish to ask Lou to stay.

Lou stared at her. "You agree with Scott, don't you?" she said. "You think I should stay."

"I don't," Amy lied quickly, not wanting to upset Lou even more. "You *should* go to England, Lou. Grandpa will get better soon, and it'll only make him feel guilty if you stay." Her words sounded false even to her own ears, but Lou didn't seem to notice. She nodded, looking slightly comforted.

"You're right. I mean, it's not like I'm going to be gone long." She managed a smile. "Thanks, Amy. It's good to know I've got your support."

Amy smiled, trying to ignore the voice in her head that said, *Just tell her that you think she should stay.*

Lou sighed. "I wish Scott could be so understanding." A frown crossed her face. "I can't believe he blew up at me like that."

"He was probably just hurt," Amy said. She saw her sister's surprised expression. "I mean, you did say that you have an empty feeling. That can't have made him feel too great."

Lou looked at her in astonishment. "But I didn't mean that my life was bad, just that it sort of feels incomplete without Daddy."

"But that's not what it sounded like," Amy said.

"Scott *knows* how important he is to me," Lou said. "He won't take it that way." She shook her head and stood up. "You'll see. He'll think it over and change his mind."

Amy got up at six o'clock the next morning to see Lou off. "Now, you've got Marnie's phone number," Lou checked as she put her bags in the car.

Amy nodded. "What time do you think she'll arrive?"

"Around five o'clock," Lou said.

"What about you?" Amy said. "Where can I contact you?"

"I'll call from London when I get in," Lou said. "I'll be

staying one night in a hotel near the airport, then I'll head to Gloucestershire, where Daddy lives." She gave Amy a slightly nervous look. "I'm not sure where I'll be staying after that."

Amy hugged her. "Good luck."

"Thanks," Lou said, hugging her back. "Now remember to go back to school tomorrow."

"I will," Amy sighed. They'd agreed that she would stay home from school until Marnie arrived. "But I don't see the point of going back at all. Term ends soon anyhow, and I don't have any more tests."

Lou smiled at her. "You should still go back until then."

They embraced for a long moment and then Lou got in the car and drove off. Amy waved until her sister's car disappeared from sight, then she looked around. It was still dark, and suddenly everywhere seemed very quiet. She went into the house, trying to get used to the strange sensation of being on her own.

Back in the kitchen the silence pressed down on her. She switched the radio on and sat down at the table, wondering what to do. Picking up the latest issue of the local paper, she tried to read, but the words just wouldn't sink in. So much had happened in the last few days — the Grants' party, Grandpa going into the hospital, and now Lou leaving. She shook her head. The Grants' party seemed like weeks ago.

At last she gave up trying to read, and pulling on her jacket and boots, she went outside to get started on the horses.

When Ben arrived, he volunteered to finish off the jobs that Grandpa had been working on. Amy agreed, thinking that at least then Grandpa wouldn't be tempted to go outside when he came home from the hospital. But it meant that she and Ty had to do all the stalls and exercising on their own. The phone — which Lou normally answered — seemed to ring constantly with inquiries from prospective clients and people looking for horses to rehome. As Amy answered the sixth call that morning, she silently thanked Lou for getting the portable phone. How had they managed before?

Walking into the feed room after the last call, Amy remembered that she needed to call the feed merchants because they were running low. That was when she began to realize, for the first time, just how much Heartland's day-to-day business depended on her sister.

❧

At lunchtime, Ty drove Amy to the hospital.

"Did Lou get off all right?" Grandpa asked them as they sat down.

"Yes, she left at six this morning," Amy answered.

Grandpa nodded. "And how's everything going?"

"We're getting along just fine," Amy told him. "Ben's

been fixing the fences this morning and just about all the horses are done," she lied, trying not to think about the five stalls that still needed to be mucked out, the unswept yard, and the fact that it looked like none of the horses were going to get worked that day.

Grandpa looked relieved. "Good," he said.

Amy looked at him with concern. He was paler than the day before, and when he coughed, she saw his knuckles clench the bedsheets. "How are you feeling?" she asked.

It seemed to take an effort, but Grandpa managed to smile. "I'm on the mend," he said. "Don't you worry about me. You've got enough to think about with the horses and all."

But Amy wasn't convinced he was improving, and as they left she told Ty that she wanted to find a doctor. They asked at the reception desk and were told to wait. They had been sitting on hard plastic chairs in the lobby for fifteen minutes when, to Amy's relief, Dr. Marshall came to find them.

"I'm afraid your suspicions are correct. Your grandfather's not responding as well as we had hoped to the medication," she admitted to Amy. She saw Amy's face became pale. "But please be assured, we're monitoring his progress carefully."

Amy's throat felt dry. "Will — will he still be able to

come home soon?" she asked, trying to sound calm. "Before Christmas?"

Dr. Marshall looked at her sympathetically. "I'm afraid I can't say at the moment. We'll just have to see how he feels over the next few days."

Amy nodded, unable to speak.

"Do you have any other questions?" the doctor asked.

Ty looked at Amy, who shook her head. "Thank you," he said to the doctor.

Amy followed him out of the hospital, her stomach churning with worry.

"He'll be all right, Amy," Ty said, looking at her white face as they went outside.

Desperately wanting to believe him, Amy nodded.

"If it was anything more serious the doctor would have told you," Ty reassured her.

Amy took comfort from his words. "Yeah," she whispered, trying to be positive. But she couldn't help thinking that Grandpa was sicker than she'd even imagined.

Chapter Eight

Just as they were finishing feeding the horses that evening, a yellow sports car came up the drive. "Marnie!" Amy exclaimed as it stopped in front of the house and a tall, slim woman in her twenties got out. Dumping the hay nets she was carrying on the ground, Amy raced toward the driveway.

"Hi, Amy!" Marnie said, hugging her. Marnie's blond hair bounced on her shoulders as she looked around. "Wow!" she said. "It's so good to be back."

Amy grinned, feeling really happy for the first time in days. She knew Marnie loved Heartland — that was one of the reasons why she liked her so much. "I love your car," she said, looking at the shiny new sports car.

"Well, there have to be some perks to working in the city," Marnie said. She took a deep breath of the frosty air. "Though I have to admit that being here again really makes me wonder."

"Do you want some help with your stuff?" Amy offered.

Marnie glanced at the hay nets lying on the ground. "No, you go ahead and finish what you were doing. I can manage — am I in the same room as last time?"

Amy nodded. It was her mom's old room. "Just make yourself at home," she said.

Marnie smiled at her. "That'll be easy. This place feels like home already."

❧

After unpacking and walking through the barns, saying hi to all the horses and to Ben and Ty, Marnie declared she would make supper. "I'll go shopping tomorrow," she said, peering into the almost empty fridge. "But for tonight, I could make us some pasta with —" She looked in the cupboards. "Tuna, tomato, and olive sauce. How does that sound?"

"Great," Amy said.

"Do Ty and Ben want to stay for supper?" Marnie asked. "I can easily make enough to feed all of us."

Amy went to ask. "They both said they'd love to," she said, returning to find that Marnie was already preparing enough for four hungry people. "They're just finishing up in the feed room," she smiled.

Marnie handed her a jar of olives. "Then let's get this food moving. You start chopping those tomatoes, and I'll put the pasta on."

Amy sat down at the table and got to work. A few minutes later, Ben and Ty came in. They shrugged off their jackets, washed their hands, and began to help. The kitchen, which only that morning had seemed so silent and empty, was now suddenly bustling with life.

In the middle of the supper preparations, the phone rang. It was Lou.

"Lou!" Amy exclaimed. "Hi! Where are you?" Hearing her exclamation, Marnie, Ty, and Ben immediately quieted down.

"I'm in London," Lou replied. "At the hotel."

"How was the flight?" Amy asked.

"We were a bit late getting in, but it was OK," Lou said. "How's Grandpa?"

Amy hesitated. She didn't want to worry Lou now that she was so far away. "Fine," she said.

"That's good." Lou sounded very relieved. "I haven't been able to stop thinking about him, wondering if I made the right choice."

"Marnie's here," Amy said quickly, wanting to get off the subject of Grandpa. "Do you want to say hello?"

"Yeah!" Lou replied.

Amy held the phone out to Marnie, who handed Ben the cheese to grate while she spoke to her best friend.

"How are you doing?" she said, taking the phone from Amy.

Lou and Marnie spoke for a few minutes and then Marnie handed the receiver back to Amy.

"I'd better go," Lou said. "This call's going to cost me the earth. Give Grandpa a big hug for me."

"I will," Amy promised.

"And wish me luck for tomorrow," Lou said, sounding nervous. "I've rented a car, and I'm going to drive over to Gloucestershire to Daddy's house in the morning."

Amy's heart flipped. With everything that had been happening, she had pushed the thought that Lou might be seeing their father the next day to the back of her mind. "Good luck," she said.

"I'll call tomorrow night and tell you all about it," Lou said. "Bye for now."

"Yeah, bye," Amy said, and with a click Lou was gone.

"Lou sounds good," Marnie said to her as she replaced the handset on the charger.

Amy nodded slowly. "Yeah." She chewed on a fingernail. "She's going to try to find our father tomorrow."

Marnie looked at her quizzically. Amy thought she was going to say something, but she didn't. Instead she swung back into action. "OK, supper's almost ready," she said, taking the cheese grater from Ben. "Someone get the drinks together. Then we can all sit down and eat."

❧

After supper, Marnie and Amy went to the hospital. Grandpa was lying in bed, looking pale and tired. Talking seemed to hurt him and he didn't say much, but he was evidently pleased to see Marnie.

"I didn't realize he was quite so ill," Marnie said as they walked back to the car. "Lou seemed to think he was getting better when she called me last night."

"He was," Amy said. "But now I'm not so sure. Ty and I spoke to a doctor this morning, and she said he's not responding to his medication."

"You didn't mention it to Lou when she rang this evening?" Marnie said.

"No," Amy admitted, wondering whether Marnie would think she'd done the right thing. "I didn't want to worry her."

"That was probably smart," Marnie said reassuringly. "After all, she can't do anything about it while she's in England." She frowned. "Still, if he gets much worse, you should probably tell her."

Hoping that it wouldn't come to that, Amy nodded. "Yeah, I will."

❧

Amy didn't sleep well that night. One minute she was thinking about Grandpa in the hospital and the next she was thinking about Lou. In just a few hours' time Lou was going to drive up to their father's house and knock on his door. What would happen?

By the morning, Amy's stomach was knotted with tension. "Maybe I won't go to school today," she said to Marnie as they got breakfast together. "If I don't go, I could visit Grandpa this morning."

"Why don't you call the hospital and see how he is?" Marnie suggested. "He might be feeling better."

Amy agreed. But when she got through to the ward, they told her that they couldn't put her through. "I'm sorry, but he's asleep," the nurse told her. "He's had a difficult night and he needs to rest."

"Can I come see him?" Amy asked quickly.

"It might be best if you wait till later," the nurse replied. "He really needs to be kept quiet. Why don't you come later this afternoon?"

"What did they say?" Marnie asked, her eyes scanning Amy's face.

Amy told her. "I'm definitely *not* going to school," she said.

"But it'll keep your mind off worrying," Marnie said. She must have seen the uncertainty on Amy's face. "Look, if there's any news, I'll phone the school right away," she promised. "If I don't hear anything, then I'll come to pick you up after school and we can go straight to the hospital."

Amy reluctantly gave in. In a sense, she knew that Marnie was right. She would only think about Grandpa and Lou all day if she were at home.

Marnie gave Amy a ride to school. "I promise I'll call if the hospital calls," she said as Amy got out of the car. "Try not to worry."

Amy walked slowly into the school. She was so wrapped up in her own thoughts that she hardly noticed Ashley and Jade standing nearby.

"Hi, Amy," Ashley said, following her. "How's that foal coming along?" She probed. "Have you gotten her to lead yet?" Since she had lost interest in Ben, Ashley had dropped all pretense of being nice to Amy. "Or is she still standing in the middle of the field?"

Amy stopped. For a moment the insult made her temper rise, but as she looked into Ashley's taunting face, she suddenly didn't care. "Yeah, whatever, Ashley," she said flatly as she walked on. But not before she had caught the look of triumph in Ashley's eyes. She ignored it. Right now, she didn't have the energy for a fight. Walking around the corner, she almost bumped into Matt.

"Amy!" he exclaimed. "How are you? Scott told me about your grandpa being in the hospital. I'm really sorry."

"Thanks," Amy said briefly, walking on.

"Look," Matt said following her. "I'm sorry about what I said on Monday. I shouldn't have taken it all out on you."

"It doesn't really matter," Amy said flatly. "Just forget it."

Matt looked hurt. "I'm trying to apologize, Amy. I don't see why our friendship should suffer just because I'm dating Ashley."

Amy stopped and stared at him. "You're *dating* her?"

"Yeah," Matt admitted awkwardly. "Look, I know how you feel about Ashley," he said quickly, "but if you just spent some time with her —"

"Spend time with Ashley!" Amy exclaimed, feeling nothing but frustration. How could he think spending time with Ashley was even a possibility? "Get real, Matt! That's the last thing I'd want to do."

"Amy —" Matt said, stepping forward.

Amy shook her head. "Look, if you want to go out with Ashley, that's fine. Go ahead. Just don't expect me to be friends with her as well." And with that she swung her backpack onto her shoulder and marched away.

❦

For the rest of the day, Matt avoided Amy. The sight of Ashley's hand resting possessively on Matt's arm at lunch made Amy so annoyed that it reinforced her initial disgust. She felt completely betrayed. Matt *knew* she couldn't stand Ashley. How could he even think about dating her?

As soon as school finished, she grabbed her books and set off at a run. Marnie was already parked on the road outside the school, ready to take her to the hospital.

"Relax," she said as Amy pulled open the car door. "I called the hospital before I left. They said it's OK to visit. Your grandpa's not any worse."

Amy felt a wave of relief rush over her. "Thanks, Marnie," she said. "Has Lou called?"

Marnie shook her head. "No."

Wondering whether that was good or bad, Amy sat back as Marnie drove through the traffic to the hospital. When they got there, Marnie suggested she wait in the reception area for Amy in case having two visitors tired Jack out.

Amy went nervously to Grandpa's room on her own. It quickly became clear that his condition might not be any worse, but it wasn't any better, either. His breathing was short and shallow, and every so often he reached for the mask at the side of the bed to get a boost of oxygen to his lungs.

"You don't sound too good, Grandpa," Amy said from the doorway as he coughed painfully.

"The doctor says it's just a small setback," Grandpa

wheezed. "Nothing to worry about. Is there any news from Lou?"

Amy shook her head. "Not yet."

"I guess she'll phone tonight," Grandpa said. He took a deep breath. "Well, tell me about you. How was school?"

Amy sat down next to him and told him a little about her classes and then started talking about the horses, hoping that if she kept talking, Grandpa wouldn't try to say anything. He listened and nodded. "And Marnie's settling in?" he said as Amy paused for breath.

"Yeah, she's great," Amy said. "She's been helping Ty and Ben today while I've been at school."

"Good," Grandpa said, looking relieved. "So you're all managing?"

"Yes," Amy told him firmly. She squeezed his hand. "You shouldn't worry about us, Grandpa. You just think about getting better."

❧

When Amy and Marnie returned to Heartland, they found Scott there. "I just dropped by with a birthday present for Ty for tomorrow," he said as Amy jumped out of the car and walked over to him. "How's your grandpa?"

"He's not doing all that well," Amy admitted, realizing

that she'd totally forgotten it was Ty's birthday the next day. It was a good thing she'd ordered him a gift that day at the mall, and it had been delivered to Heartland already wrapped.

"Well, send Jack my best wishes," Scott said. "I'll stop by and visit him when he's feeling up to it."

Just then, Marnie came over. "Hi, Scott," she said warmly. "It's nice to see you again."

"You, too, Marnie," Scott smiled. He opened the car door to get in but stopped. "So, have you heard from Lou?" he asked casually.

"She called last night," Amy replied. "Didn't she call you, too?" As soon as the question left her lips, she couldn't believe she said it.

Scott's mouth tightened slightly. "No," he said.

"She sounded really tired," Amy stammered quickly. "She'll probably be in touch tonight or tomorrow."

"Yeah, maybe," Scott said, but he sounded as if he didn't quite believe her.

Amy suddenly remembered that his alumni dinner was scheduled for the next evening. "Are you still going to the reunion at your old vet school?" she asked.

Scott nodded.

"Oh, your reunion is tomorrow?" Marnie asked.

Scott explained about the dinner. "It's black tie. All very formal."

"It sounds kind of fun," Marnie said.

"You think?" Scott said.

"Sure," Marnie said. "I love things like that."

Scott frowned. "What would you think about coming with me?"

Marnie's eyes widened in surprise. "Really?"

"Yeah, I've still got Lou's ticket, and if you want to use it you're more than welcome," Scott replied. "It would be a lot more fun than going on my own."

"Well, if you're sure," Marnie said, beaming. She turned to Amy. "You'll be all right on your own tomorrow evening, won't you?"

"Of course I will," Amy said. "You go."

Scott smiled at Marnie. "Then in that case, I'd be honored if you'll be my date. I'll pick you up at seven." Getting into his Jeep, he drove away.

Marnie looked stunned. "Wow!" she said to Amy. "I wasn't expecting that." She glanced at her watch. "If I'm quick I'll just have time to get into town to find something to wear." She headed back to her car. "I'll be back in time to make dinner."

"See you," Amy called after her.

As Marnie turned the car around and drove off, Ty came across the yard.

"What's going on?" he asked, surprised. "Where's Marnie going?"

"Scott's invited her to his vet reunion dinner tomorrow," Amy told him. "So she's buying something to wear."

"How is Jack doing?" Ty asked.

Amy quickly filled him in. "He says it's just a setback, but he didn't look good. It seemed to hurt him to talk — even to breathe." She looked into Ty's familiar, understanding face and suddenly felt the urge to confide the fears she had been having since leaving the hospital, fears that she hadn't even admitted to Marnie. "You know what he's like, Ty, he'll never admit that there's anything wrong. I just hope he's not keeping something from me."

"You didn't see a doctor?" Ty said.

Amy shook her head. "They were all busy."

"Well, make sure you talk to one tomorrow," Ty said.

"I will," Amy sighed. Just then the phone rang. "That might be Lou!" she exclaimed.

She ran to the kitchen. "Heartland, Amy Fleming speaking."

"Hi, Amy, it's me."

"Lou!" Amy sat down with the phone, her heart starting to pound. "How are you? What's happened? Have you seen Daddy?"

"No," Lou said, sounding very disappointed. "I went to the address but it's not Daddy's house, it belongs to some friends of his. A neighbor I spoke to said that the family who lives there, the Carters, are away until Saturday. She also told me that Daddy had been staying with the Carters for a while but she didn't know where he is now."

"I don't get it," Amy said, confused. "Why did Daddy leave that address at the hotel then?"

Lou sighed. "I don't know."

"There must be some way of finding out where he is," Amy said, hating to hear Lou sounding so miserable. "Maybe these people — the Carters — will be able to tell you where he lives when they get home. I mean, he could have just been staying with them while his house was being remodeled or something."

"I guess," Lou said.

"You'd only have to wait two more days," Amy told her, trying to cheer her up.

"Yeah, you're right," Lou replied. "I'll find somewhere around here to stay and go to see the Carters on Saturday. How's Grandpa?" she asked anxiously.

"He's doing just fine," Amy lied, hoping it was the right thing to say. Lou sounded so down she couldn't tell her about Grandpa's setback.

"That's good," Lou said. "Is Marnie there? Can I talk to her?"

"Actually, she's out," Amy said.

"Out?" Lou echoed.

Amy hesitated, suddenly wondering how Lou would

take the news. "Yes. She's, um, gone out shopping for an outfit. Scott's invited her to that dinner tomorrow."

There was a silence on the other end of the line.

"It's just as friends," Amy said quickly, in case Lou was getting the wrong idea. "I mean, you know Marnie and Scott would never —"

"I know," Lou broke in. There was a pause. When she spoke again, her voice was flat. "Well, I'd better go. Tell Marnie that I hope she has a good time tomorrow. I'm glad Scott will have someone fun to go with."

"I'll tell her," Amy promised.

When Amy walked out of the house, she found Ty waiting for her. "Was it Lou?" he asked.

"Yep," Amy said.

"So?" Ty prompted, when she didn't say anything more. "Did she see your father?"

Amy told him what had happened. "She sounded so disappointed," she said to Ty. "I wish I could do something."

"Well, you can't. You're doing all you can," Ty said gently. His eyes searched hers. "Look, you shouldn't be on your own tomorrow night," he said suddenly. "How about I come over and we can cook dinner?"

"But it's your birthday!" Amy said. "Don't you want to go out?"

"I can go out anytime. And my family isn't celebrating until Sunday."

"But — " Amy began.

"No buts," Ty interrupted. "It's decided. I'll stay and keep you company tomorrow night until Marnie gets back."

He looked so determined that Amy gave in. "OK," she smiled gratefully. "Thanks."

Chapter Nine

When Amy woke up the next morning, the air had a strange, silent feel to it. Jumping out of bed, she went to the window. It had snowed heavily in the night, and the yard and the fields were covered in a thick white blanket. Everywhere looked very bleak.

"I'm not going to school today," Amy told Marnie when she went downstairs. "Now that it's snowed there's going to be loads to do in the yard, and I don't want to wait until this afternoon to see Grandpa."

Marnie took one look at her steadfast face and seemed to realize that there was no point in trying to argue. "OK," she said. "I'm not going to force you. But you will go back on Monday, won't you?"

Amy nodded and pulled on her boots. Right now

school just seemed so unimportant, but she guessed she couldn't stay away forever.

She went outside to give the horses their breakfast. As she fed Melody, she heard a muffled cough come from the back of the stall. She looked carefully at the foal and could see that Daybreak's nose was still running and her eyes looked dull. She checked the foal's temperature. It was normal, but Amy made a mental note to call Scott if the filly didn't seem any better by the following day.

Ty and Ben arrived and they all got to work. The snow meant that there were a lot of extra chores to do — ice in the water troughs to be broken, extra straw to put down on the horses' beds, the paths to be shoveled. Amy hurried around, trying not to think about Grandpa and Lou, just hoping to keep things going.

When Amy visited Grandpa later she forced herself to be as cheerful as possible so that he wouldn't worry. "How are things?" he wheezed.

"Everything's just fine," Amy told him.

Grandpa studied her with concern. "You're looking tired, honey."

"Me? No, I'm all right," Amy said, smiling and trying to look wide awake. "Lou called last night," she said, changing the subject quickly. "She sent her love."

Jack took a sip of water from the glass by his bedside. "Has she been able to talk with your father yet?"

"No, she went to the address, but it isn't Daddy's house," Amy replied. "It just belongs to some friends of his, and they're away until Saturday. She's hoping to see them then to find out where he's living."

For a moment Grandpa didn't speak. "I hope she's doing the right thing. I don't want to see her hurt," he said at last.

Amy decided not to tell him how unhappy Lou had sounded on the phone. "I'm sure she's fine," she said, wishing she could believe it.

🙥

When Amy got back to Heartland she immediately went back to work. There was something soothing about working. It meant she didn't have to think.

At half past six, Amy and Ty turned off the stable lights and went into the house. They had just gotten out some cookbooks and were arguing about what to eat for supper when Marnie came downstairs. "Well, what do you think?" she demanded, appearing in the doorway.

"You look amazing!" Amy exclaimed.

It was true. Marnie was wearing a long black evening dress. It had a low back, and the neckline and straps were intricately beaded with delicate crystals. Her wild blond hair was wrapped up in a tight bun, and she was wearing high-heeled, strappy shoes.

"Well," Ty said. "You're certainly not dressed to hang out with us."

Marnie grinned. "Well, I wanted to look my best. Just think of all the young vets who'll be there. If I find a good one, we can double-date with Scott and Lou."

Just then Scott beeped his horn outside. "See you later," Marnie said, going to the door.

"Bye!" Ty and Amy called together.

As the door shut behind her, Ty grinned. "I hope they have a good time. Now," he said, turning back to a cookbook on the kitchen table, "what do you mean, you don't like eggplant?"

"I just don't," Amy said. "Can't we have" — she pulled the book away from him — "farmhouse chicken casserole?"

"Too boring," Ty said. He stood up. "No, it looks like I'm just going to have to cook you my specialty."

"I'm afraid to ask what it is," Amy said dubiously.

"You'll have to wait and see," Ty said. "You should go upstairs and get changed, and I'll start cooking."

"I'm glad it's not your birthday every day — it makes you very bossy," Amy teased. But as she went upstairs she couldn't help feeling glad that he had insisted on staying.

When she came downstairs, Ty was busy frying some bacon.

"What can I do to help?" Amy asked.

"You can peel those potatoes," Ty said, nodding to a bag he'd put on the table. "Then they need slicing." Amy grabbed a peeler and a bowl of water and set to work.

As they worked, they chatted about the horses.

"Daybreak's been coughing a little today," Ty said after a bit. "And her nose is still running."

"Yeah, I noticed that, too," Amy said. "I thought I might call Scott tomorrow and get him to take a look at her."

Just then the phone rang. Amy picked up the receiver.

It was Lou. "How's Grandpa?" she asked.

"He's doing just fine," Amy lied. "How are you?"

Lou sighed. "OK, I suppose." She paused. "It's — it's just strange. England seems so different." She forced a laugh. "I've always thought of it as my home, but suddenly it doesn't seem like that anymore. Maybe it's because it's almost Christmas, but I can't stop thinking about all of you. I'm really missing everyone. I just keep wondering whether coming over here was a big mistake."

Amy heard the unhappiness in her sister's voice. "Of course it wasn't," she said firmly. "You'll meet the Carters tomorrow, they'll tell you where Daddy is, and then you'll be able to go and see him. It's all going to be worth it in the end."

"I suppose so," Lou said. She sighed. "Still, right now, I wish I was there with you."

As Amy put the phone down, Ty looked at her. "What's the matter?" he asked, looking at her face.

"It's just more of the same," Amy said, sitting down. "Lou's feeling down." She shook her head. "I wish there was something I could do to help."

Ty looked at her sympathetically. "She'll be back soon."

Amy nodded. "Yeah."

"Come on, cheer up," Ty said softly. He crouched beside her, taking her hands. "You've got to stop taking on everyone's worries. You're being too hard on yourself."

Amy looked down into his familiar green eyes, and for a moment it was as though she was seeing his face for the first time. Her gaze followed the sweep of his cheekbones down to his serious, sensitive mouth. Meeting his eyes again, she saw a warmth just like there had been the night of the Grants' party. Feeling herself blush, Amy jumped to her feet.

"I haven't given you your birthday present yet," she stammered. "I'll get it."

She ran up the stairs, her heart pounding and her palms damp. What was the matter with her?

Reaching her bedroom, she picked up the gift from her dressing table. Forcing herself to stop, she took a few deep breaths. *It was just the stress of everything,* she told herself. She was overreacting. All Ty had done was hold her hands and try to reassure her. But as she shut her eyes, the image of his face forced itself into her mind. It was the way his eyes had looked at her — so deep and so searching.

Looking in the mirror, she saw that her cheeks were still flushed. She took another few deep breaths to calm down and then went back downstairs with the gift.

Ty was setting the table. "Here," Amy said, holding out the box and the card she had gotten him. "There's a card and present from Lou and Grandpa as well," she said.

Ty opened the cards first and then Lou and Grandpa's gift — a new riding hat and a pair of gloves.

"Wow," Ty said, "these are great!"

"Now open mine," Amy said, eager to see what he would think of the present she had bought for him.

Ty picked up the package and began to open it. Amy watched his face as he took out her gift, a leather-bound book on herbal remedies for horses signed by the author, George Verrall. She knew Ty had been wanting it for ages, and she had requested the mall bookstore to special order it.

"Look inside," she said eagerly as Ty took the book out of the gift wrap. Below George Verrall's signature Amy had written her mom's words: *By healing, we heal ourselves.*

"Do you like it?" she asked anxiously as Ty read the words.

"This is something I've always wanted," Ty said softly, touching the quotation with his forefinger and looking at her. "Thank you."

Amy was so relieved he liked the gift, she couldn't stop smiling. For a moment the two of them just stared at each other. Almost before Amy knew what was happening, Ty stepped forward and his arms seemed to fold around her.

Suddenly, the phone rang.

Amy and Ty broke apart. Amy darted across the kitchen and grabbed the hand set. "Heartland," she stammered. "Amy Fleming speaking."

An efficient voice spoke on the other end. "Hello, Amy, this is Dr. Marshall at Meadowville Park Hospital. I'm glad I reached you."

Amy's heart skipped a beat. "Dr. Marshall," she echoed. "Is it Grandpa? Is he all right?"

There was a slight pause. "I'm afraid I've got some troubling news," Dr. Marshall said gently.

Amy felt her insides turn to ice. "What is it?"

"Your grandfather's condition has deteriorated in the last few hours," Dr. Marshall replied. "One of his lungs has collapsed. He's now in Intensive Care. I think you had better come to the hospital right away."

Chapter Ten

Ty was beside Amy even before she had put the phone down. "Was that the hospital?" he demanded. "What's wrong?"

Amy started to shake. "It's Grandpa," she whispered, so distraught that she could barely get the words out. "He's been moved to Intensive Care. I've got to go. I have to be with him."

Not stopping to ask any more questions, Ty grabbed their coats from the back of the door. "Come on," he said, handing Amy her jacket. "I'll drive you."

Moving automatically, Amy pulled her jacket on. "What about Marnie?" she said suddenly. "She'll wonder where we are."

"I'll leave her a note to tell her we're at the hospital," Ty said. He tore a piece of paper from the notebook by the phone and scribbled a message. He left it in an obvious place on the table and turned off the oven. "Let's go."

Too scared to think straight, Amy followed him out of the house. A light snow was falling, but she hardly even noticed as the flakes caught in her hair. She got into the pickup and huddled against the cold seat. Ty turned the key and the engine rumbled into life.

"So what did the hospital say?" Ty asked, swinging the truck around and setting off down the driveway.

"One of Grandpa's lungs has collapsed." Amy's teeth began to chatter.

Ty looked at her with concern. "Here," he said, pulling a travel blanket out from beneath the seat and tossing it to her. "You're in shock."

Amy wrapped the blanket around herself, but neither it nor the roaring heater could stop her from shivering. At the first set of traffic signals, Ty stopped, rummaged in the glove compartment, and pulled out a small brown bottle with a dropper in the top. "Bach Flower Rescue Remedy," he said softly, handing it to her. "It's not just for horses. Put four drops under your tongue."

Amy did what he said. All she could think about was Grandpa. A collapsed lung sounded so critical. What if he didn't get better?

Oh, please, she prayed desperately as the wheels of the

truck cut through the slush on the roads and the lights of the late-night stores flashed past. *I'll do anything. Please just let Grandpa get better.*

❦

The half-hour journey to the hospital seemed to take forever, but at last Ty pulled up in the empty visitors' parking lot outside the sprawling complex of low white buildings. Once in the hospital, they were shown into a small room, and a few minutes later Dr. Marshall joined them.

"How's my grandpa?" Amy asked, jumping to her feet.

"His condition's very serious," Dr. Marshall said gravely.

"Will he be OK?" Amy whispered.

"Collapsed lungs aren't usually life-threatening, providing treatment is administered quickly," Dr. Marshall replied. "However, in your grandfather's case, there have been complications."

"Complications?" Amy echoed.

"He has what is known as a tension pneumothorax, which means that the air can't escape properly from his good lung," the doctor explained. "It's potentially fatal. Now that doesn't mean he's going to die," she added quickly, seeing Amy's face. "We've stabilized his condition. But I have to tell you the next few hours will be critical."

"Can I see him?" Amy asked, hardly able to get the words out.

Dr. Marshall nodded. "He's sedated at the moment, but yes, you can see him."

Amy and Ty followed the doctor down the corridors. When they reached the Intensive Care Unit, Dr. Marshall opened the door.

Grandpa was lying immobile on the hospital bed, his eyes shut. Tubes led into his nose, chest, and wrist, and beside the bed several machines blinked and whirred. A nurse was bustling around. Seeing Amy, she looked at her sympathetically. "Are you Mr. Bartlett's granddaughter?"

Amy nodded, her eyes on the still figure. She felt Ty's hand squeeze her shoulder, and as the nurse moved out of the way, she went over to the bed. Grandpa's skin was very pale and he hardly looked like himself.

Swallowing hard, Amy sat down on the chair beside the bed and put her hand over one of Grandpa's. It was cold and clammy and motionless.

"We'll leave you for a few moments," Dr. Marshall said. "If there's any problem, just press the red button on the wall."

The door shut behind the doctor and nurse.

"Do you want me to stay, or do you want to be on your own?" Ty asked softly.

Amy looked up at him. "Stay — please." She turned to Grandpa again. "I just can't bear to see him like this."

Ty put his arm around her shoulders. "It'll be OK, Amy."

"First Mom and then Pegasus and now —" She bit her lip, struggling not to give way to the familiar anguish that was threatening to overwhelm her again. She bent her head, her long hair falling across her face. "I love him so much."

"And he loves you," Ty said, crouching beside her, his eyes intense. "Come on, you know what your grandpa's like. He won't give up. He's a fighter."

Amy swallowed, knowing Ty was right. "Grandpa, can you hear me?" she whispered, clutching her grandfather's limp hand. "You've got to fight — please, do it for me. Please fight."

❧

The long hours of the night slowly passed. Amy hardly moved from Grandpa's bedside. Just after two o'clock in the morning, Scott and Marnie appeared at the door of the Intensive Care Unit.

"Amy," Marnie whispered. "We came as soon as we saw the note."

Pulling away from Grandpa, she went to the doorway and hugged them both.

"Does Lou know?" Scott asked.

Amy shook her head bleakly. "I don't know where she is."

Scott cursed under his breath.

Amy glanced at the door. She didn't want to be away from Grandpa for even a second. "I'm going back in."

Leaving Ty to explain exactly what had happened, she returned to Grandpa's side.

After ten minutes, Ty returned. "Marnie's offered to stay here with you," he said. "I'm going to go back to Heartland so that I can feed the horses in the morning. Ben should probably know, too. Is it OK if I tell him?"

Amy nodded. She didn't want Ty to go, but she knew that it made sense. Marnie didn't know enough about the horses to handle the morning feeds, and Ty was right, Ben needed to know what was going on.

"It'll mean someone will be there if Lou calls, too," Ty said. "You'll be all right with Marnie, won't you?"

"Yeah," Amy said. She forced her lips into a smile and stood up. "Thanks, Ty."

"No problem," Ty said. "I'll see you soon." He hugged her for a moment, then left.

❧

Marnie sat with Amy through the remainder of that long night. They talked a little but mainly sat in silence as the hours ticked by. Amy was glad for the quiet. Her mind felt as if it had shut down, as if all normal actions like speaking and smiling were beyond her. All she wanted was for Grandpa to open his eyes and speak to her, to show her that he was going to get better.

She remembered the hours she had spent with him when she had been too little to help her mom in the stables — helping him clean the house, weed the vegetable garden, do the grocery shopping. All the games he'd played with her. She remembered how he had always been there for her when Mom was too busy. Grandpa had been the one who listened when she wanted to talk, who helped her with her school projects.

As she looked at his lined face lying against the pillow, she realized that he had grown older without her noticing. He always had such energy that she had never really thought of him as old, but now her gaze traced the deep grooves on his forehead, the wrinkles around his eyes. She and Lou should have insisted that he take things easier.

As the gray light of dawn streaked across the dark sky, she scooted her chair forward and put a hand to his face, trying to imagine what life would be like without him. "Grandpa," she whispered. "I love you."

Her hand froze. She was sure his eyelids had moved. Had she imagined it?

"Grandpa?" she said.

This time she knew there was no mistake. He blinked.

His lips moved but his voice barely made a sound. "Amy?"

"Yes, Grandpa!" Amy gasped. "It's me!"

Behind her, she heard Marnie jump to her feet. "I'll get a doctor."

Amy barely registered the sound of the door opening and shutting. Grandpa's eyes blinked open again. "Throat's dry . . . water . . ." he croaked.

"The doctor will be here in a minute," Amy told him, clutching his hand, silently praying that Grandpa was now going to be OK.

🙞

Over the next half hour, a succession of doctors and nurses hurried in and out of Jack's room, until at last Amy was left alone with him again. He was still attached to all the tubes, and his face was still pale, but at least he was awake.

Amy kissed him gently on the cheek. "I was so worried about you, Grandpa," she said.

Jack spoke slowly, every breath an effort. "It'll take more than a bit of pneumonia to get rid of me," he whispered. He covered her hand with his. "You look tired, honey. What time is it?"

"It's early in the morning. I've been here all night, but I'm OK."

"Lou —" Jack began.

"As soon as she calls I'll tell her what's happened," Amy said quickly. "She'll be back in no time, Grandpa."

"No," Grandpa wheezed. "Don't worry her. I don't want her to come back just for me. Make her stay until she's seen your father."

"But, Grandpa," Amy began, "she'll want to be here. She'll —"

"No, Amy," Jack said weakly. His words were slow, but his tone was insistent. "I stopped her from seeing your father before. I'm not going to be the one to stop her again. Please, promise me you'll make her stay."

Amy stared at him. How *could* she promise that? But then she couldn't bear to see the distress in Grandpa's eyes. "I'll try," she agreed reluctantly.

"Thank you," Grandpa said, the words no more than a whisper as he sank back against the pillows.

"I'd better go," Amy said, "but I'll be back later. You get some rest now, Grandpa."

He nodded and closed his eyes. Amy heard him sigh with relief as he drifted off to sleep.

❧

Amy followed Marnie out of the hospital and into the parking lot. It had stopped snowing now, but the heavy morning clouds seemed to promise that there was more to come. The freezing air hit Amy's face like a splash of icy water, but instead of making her feel more awake it seemed to have the opposite effect. The adrenaline that had been surging through her body over the last fourteen hours suddenly drained out of her and all her muscles turned to lead. Getting into Marnie's car, she leaned her head heavily against the window.

"I think it's bed for us when we get back," Marnie said, starting the engine.

As Marnie drove home, Amy blinked hard to stop her eyes from shutting. She looked at Marnie. Her blond curls had long since escaped from the bun, and her evening dress was creased and rumpled. "Thanks for staying with me, Marnie," Amy said gratefully.

Marnie turned her tired eyes to her and smiled. "That's what friends are for. I couldn't have left you there on your own." She yawned. "I'm just glad Jack's getting better."

When they reached Heartland, Ty and Ben came hurrying to meet them.

"How's Jack?" Ty asked.

"Still improving," Marnie said.

Amy noticed the dark shadows beneath Ty's eyes. He looked as if he'd hardly slept. "Has Lou called?" she asked.

Ty shook his head.

"Come on," Ben said, leading the way to the house.

"We've got some coffee on, and you both look like you could use some breakfast."

They followed him into the house. Once in the kitchen, Amy collapsed onto a chair at the table and let her head rest on her arms.

Her mind was just starting to swim toward sleep when she felt Marnie's hand on her shoulder. "Go to bed," Marnie said gently. "You can eat later. Right now you need rest."

❧

Amy fell into bed and slept for six straight hours. When she woke up, daylight was streaming in through her window. She looked around in confusion. What was she doing in bed? Gradually the events of the last twenty-four hours came rolling back. Grandpa. The hospital . . .

Jumping out of bed, she went downstairs. The kitchen was deserted. Picking up the phone, she dialed the hospital. Dr. Marshall had gone off duty, but one of her colleagues came to the phone to speak to Amy.

"Your grandfather's doing well," he said reassuringly. "His lung has stabilized, and providing all goes well the damage should now start to heal. We'll need to monitor his condition very carefully over the next week. In this sort of case, there's always the danger that the lung could collapse again. If that happens, then we'll be looking at major surgery. However, such relapses are rare, and we're hopeful that your grandfather will make a rapid and full recovery."

Feeling comforted by the doctor's words, Amy replaced the receiver. As she did so, her gaze fell on Ty's birthday presents. They had been piled up on the dresser, forgotten in the drama of the night before. The sight of them brought a vivid memory flashing into Amy's mind — Ty's arms wrapping around her, his eyes looking into her own.

The back door opened. Amy jumped and swung around. It was Ty.

"Ty," Amy stammered, acutely aware of what she'd just been thinking.

Ty didn't seem to notice her confusion. "I was just coming in to leave you a note," he said, rubbing a weary hand across his eyes. "Ben offered to finish the work, so I thought I'd head home and get some sleep. If that's OK."

"Of course," Amy said. "You've got to be exhausted."

Ty forced a smile. "I'm a little tired. Have you talked to the hospital?"

"Yeah." Amy told him what the doctor had said. "He sounded pleased with Grandpa's progress," she finished.

"Good," Ty said, looking relieved. "Well, I'll see you tomorrow then."

"Don't forget your birthday presents," Amy said quickly as he turned to go.

Ty glanced at the dresser and then he looked at her. From the suddenly guarded look on his face, Amy was sure that he, too, was thinking about the night before. She caught her breath, thinking that he was about to say something, but then in a split second he seemed to change his mind and the tension left his face.

"Thanks for reminding me," he said, going to the dresser and picking up his gifts. When he turned to Amy again, his eyes showed nothing more than genuine concern. "Look, if you need me for anything, just give me a call."

Not trusting herself to speak, Amy nodded.

As the door closed behind him she sank down on a chair, feeling confused and mixed up. Her thoughts whirled. There was so much to think about. Grandpa, Lou, Ty . . . She put her head in her hands. It was all getting to be too much.

Hearing footsteps on the stairs, she looked up as Marnie came into the kitchen. "I thought I heard you down here," Marnie said, yawning. "Is there any news from the hospital?"

Quickly pulling herself together, Amy filled Marnie in on her conversation with the doctor. Just as she was finishing, the phone rang.

"Hi, Amy." It was Lou. Her voice sounded shaky.

"Lou!" Amy exclaimed, glancing at Marnie in relief.

"I'm so glad you've called. It's —" But before she could finish, Lou broke in.

"Oh, Amy," she said, bursting into tears.

For a second, Amy was almost too shocked to speak. Lou never cried. "Lou!" she said in alarm. "What happened?"

"It's Daddy," Lou sobbed.

Horrible thoughts raced through Amy's mind. Daddy! Was he injured? Dead? "What's the matter?" she said quickly. "He's not —"

"No," Lou said, seeming to read her thoughts. "He's OK. It's just — just — he's not even here. He's in Australia."

"Australia!" Amy echoed, astounded. "What's he doing there?"

"He lives there," Lou said.

Amy began to feel that she was losing her grip on the conversation. "What do you mean?"

"I went to see the Carters today," Lou explained, sounding like she was struggling to control herself. "Michael Carter is not just friends with Daddy, he's his business partner as well. They have a company that specializes in importing and exporting horses between England and Australia. He told me that when Daddy's over here he stays with them but that he actually lives in Australia."

"But Daddy never said anything about Australia in his letter," Amy said, trying to get her head around what Lou was saying.

"I can't believe I've come all this way for nothing," Lou said.

Amy didn't know what to say. She understood the disappointment Lou must be feeling — to have psyched herself up for meeting their father only to find he was thousands of miles away.

"You'll get to see him soon," Amy said, trying to comfort her.

"But I've been so stupid," Lou sniffed. "I should never have left Heartland. Especially with Grandpa being ill and everything. How is he today?"

Amy paused. The last thing she wanted was to make Lou feel worse, but she knew she had to tell her the truth. "Um . . . he's not good, Lou," she said. She took a deep breath. "One of his lungs collapsed last night."

Lou gasped. Amy quickly explained what had happened.

"What am I going to do?" Lou said in an anguished voice. "I need to see him. I'm coming home," Lou said with determination. "I'm going to change my flight tomorrow, get the first seat out I can." She swallowed hard. "Tell Grandpa I love him, Amy."

When Amy replaced the receiver, she stood by the phone feeling stunned.

"What's the news?" Marnie asked anxiously.

Amy told her.

"Poor Lou," Marnie said, aghast.

"I wish she was here, Marnie," Amy said.

Marnie put an arm around her shoulders. "Don't worry," she said, hugging her. "She'll be back soon."

🙊

After supper Amy and Marnie returned to the hospital. Grandpa was awake when they arrived. He was still connected to the various tubes and machines, but Amy was relieved to see that some color had returned to his face. She decided to keep the truth about Lou and Daddy for when he had recovered some more.

When Amy and Marnie got back to Heartland, Marnie announced that she was going to go to bed. "You look like you could use some sleep, too," she said to Amy.

But Amy's mind was buzzing with thoughts of Grandpa, Lou, and Daddy. "I think I'll stay up for a bit," she said, sitting down in an armchair and picking up the remote control. "I'll watch TV."

"Do you want some company?" Marnie asked her.

Amy shook her head. "No, I'll be fine. You should go to bed."

"Night, then," Marnie said, and she went upstairs.

Amy flicked through the channels and eventually

settled on a sitcom. By ten-thirty she was almost asleep in the chair. Yawning widely, she got to her feet and turned the TV off. She went to the kitchen window. Apart from the lights on the front stable block, everywhere was dark. She was about to go upstairs to bed when she hesitated. For some reason, she felt that something wasn't right. She glanced outside again. Everything seemed quiet enough, but still she felt a nagging urge to go and check.

With a sigh, she pulled on her jacket and boots. She knew she wouldn't be able to relax until she had looked around the yard and checked that everything really was OK.

She went out into the darkness. As she walked toward the barns she thought about Lou. She hoped her sister could get an early flight. It would be wonderful to have her home again.

The top doors of the stalls in the stable block were all shut. Amy opened each one and checked inside, but all the horses appeared to be happy and content.

She turned and trudged through the snow to the back barn. Pulling back the door, she slipped inside and pressed the light switch. There were a few startled snorts from the stalls as the lights flickered on but nothing out of the ordinary. Still, Amy walked down the aisle, checking over each stall door. Dancer, Sundance, Jasmine . . .

She reached Daybreak and Melody's stall. The mare was pulling at her hay net, and the little filly was standing beside her. Amy was about to move on to the next stall when she paused. Daybreak was standing unusually still, her sides visibly moving in and out.

Feeling a sudden prickle of worry run down her spine, Amy pushed back the bolt on the door. Melody looked around but Daybreak didn't. Lowering her head, the foal coughed. Amy went over. For once, Daybreak didn't try to move away. She stood submissively as Amy gently felt her glands. They were swollen. With mounting concern, Amy noticed that the filly had a thick yellow discharge running from her nose and that her eyes were dull. There was no doubt about it, Daybreak was ill — possibly very ill.

Chapter Eleven

❧

"Equine herpes virus," Scott said an hour later as he stepped back from examining Daybreak. "I'm sure of it." He patted the foal. "But I'll still need to run a few tests to confirm it."

"What does that mean?" Marnie asked from where she stood in the doorway, with a coat on over her pajamas.

"It's a virus that causes respiratory infections," Scott replied. While Amy held Daybreak he took a blood sample and a sample of mucus from the foal's windpipe. "It particularly affects young horses," he went on. "At first the symptoms are mild — a clear nasal discharge, occasional cough, and possibly a rise in temperature. It doesn't look too serious at that point, but if left untreated a more serious secondary bacterial infection can develop. That's what's happened to Daybreak."

"But how would she have gotten it?" Amy asked.

"I imagine one of the other horses must have brought it to the yard," Scott said. "It generally doesn't affect adult horses to this degree so you probably haven't noticed it. Daybreak's been affected more severely because, at her age, she still has a relatively immature immune system." He looked at Amy. "Did you notice her nose running in the last week or so?"

"Yes," Amy said, feeling horribly guilty. "I was going to call you yesterday, but then with Grandpa at the hospital, I just forgot."

Scott nodded sympathetically. "That's understandable. You've had a lot going on. Well, don't worry. I think we've caught it early enough. Daybreak will need a course of antibiotics to control the secondary infection and some drugs to help break up the mucus in her lungs. Nursing is also very important if she's to recover quickly. She needs that liquid. She needs warmth and rest — keep her to just short lead walks each day. Here's the hard part. She needs to avoid dust. Do you think you could move her and Melody to one of the front stables so she can get more fresh air?"

"Yeah, we'll go work that out," Amy said.

"Keep the bedding deep and clean," Scott continued, "and try to see if she keeps feeding. I'll stop by tomorrow and vaccinate the other horses to stop the virus from spreading any further."

"OK. And should I use any herbs on her?" Amy asked.

Scott nodded. "Anything that will help her expel the mucus is ideal. You might want to try eucalyptus or tea tree oil."

He rummaged in his bag and took out a syringe and a bottle of antibiotics. After shaking the bottle, he filled the syringe and injected the antibiotics into Daybreak's hindquarters. "OK," he said. "I'll come back tomorrow morning and see how she's doing."

❦

It was past midnight when Scott left and Amy went into the tack room. Near the medicine cabinet was a shelf of books that had once belonged to her mom. She picked one on herbal remedies and began to leaf through the pages.

"You're not going to do anything more tonight, are you?" Marnie said, coming into the tack room.

Amy looked up. "I want to see if I can find anything to help her."

"But Amy, you're exhausted," Marnie said.

"I'm OK," Amy replied. She did feel incredibly tired, but she also felt incredibly guilty. How could she have forgotten about calling Scott? If she'd asked him to come a few days earlier maybe Daybreak wouldn't be so ill now. She saw Marnie's worried face. "I won't stay out long. I promise," she said. "But I'm not coming in just yet."

Her voice was so determined that Marnie had no choice but to give in. "All right," she said reluctantly. "But I'll make you some hot chocolate to keep you going."

Alone in the tack room, Amy ran her eyes over the pages on respiratory infections and herbal expectorants. Although garlic was highly recommended, the book suggested that it could upset the digestive system of young foals, so she decided to use echinacea roots instead. Echinacea, she read, had excellent antiviral and antibacterial qualities. It would stimulate the body to produce more white blood cells to fight the infection, and it could safely be used with antibiotics. She checked the dosage — ten grams of the cut root a day — and took some out of the cabinet. She also took out a bottle of eucalyptus oil and some cotton before returning to Daybreak's stall.

The little filly was still standing dejectedly beside Melody. Her head was hanging and her nose streamed. Her ears barely flickered as Amy looked over the door.

"It's all right," Amy told her softly. "You'll soon get better."

Marnie appeared with the hot drink for Amy and helped her bring a pitchfork and some fresh straw to make the bed clean and deep, like Scott had suggested.

Once the stall had been cleared and the new straw added, Amy crouched down beside Daybreak's head and encouraged her to eat the cut-up pieces of echinacea root. At first the filly simply mouthed it with her lips, but as soon as she tasted the plant she began to nibble on the pieces with more interest. It was almost as if she sensed they would help her.

When all the root was gone, Amy wiped Daybreak's nostrils with clean cotton and then poured a few drops of eucalyptus oil onto a fresh piece of cotton. Keeping the pad a few inches away from Daybreak's nostrils in case the concentrated oil irritated the foal's skin, Amy let Daybreak inhale the strong scent. She knew eucalyptus oil was supposed to be good for clearing blocked airways and loosening any infected mucus.

After a few minutes she decided that Daybreak had inhaled enough and she took the cotton away. As she took it over to the door, Daybreak lay down heavily in the straw. Amy went over and knelt beside the filly. "You're going to be OK," she murmured, stroking Daybreak's neck.

At her touch, the filly lifted her head slightly, a hint of her old spirit in her eyes, but she was too sick to really object. With a cough, she let her muzzle sink back heavily onto the straw. Amy looked at her for a long moment and then crept out of the stall.

🙲

As soon as Amy got up the next morning, she pulled on her clothes and went straight to the barn, her head feeling dizzy from lack of sleep. Dawn had hardly broken and the freezing wind whipped her face. Winter was really closing in. The turnout paddocks looked bleak and cold, the thick layer of snow seeming to suffocate the ground.

"How are you, girl?" Amy said, her gloved fingers fumbling with the bolt on the stall door.

The little foal was standing beside her mother. Her breathing was just as fast and shallow as it had been the night before and her eyes were dull. She didn't look any better. Amy's heart sank. "We'd better get you cleaned up," she said, looking at the foal's streaming nose.

The other horses in the barn had seen Amy and had started to kick their doors and call expectantly for their breakfast. But for once Amy ignored them. Using cotton and warm water, she bathed Daybreak's nostrils and dried them thoroughly before offering the foal some eucalyptus oil to sniff again. Daybreak inhaled listlessly, her ears drooping. All the spirit seemed to have drained out of her.

🙲

When Ty and Ben arrived, she told them about Daybreak. A pained look crossed Ty's face. "I can't believe I didn't notice," he said. "I knew she wasn't well. I should have kept a closer eye on her."

"I should have noticed, too," Ben said. "I knew you were both distracted."

Even though Amy still felt guilty herself, she was too tired to waste energy on placing blame. "Look," she said wearily, "none of us noticed. Let's just leave it at that. Now we just need to try to get her better." She told them what Scott had said.

"She can have Red's stall," Ben offered immediately, heading for the door. "It's the biggest. I'll go get started on cleaning out his bed."

"Thanks, Ben," Amy said gratefully.

Ty was still angry with himself. "I can't believe I didn't notice," he said under his breath as Ben left. "I just forgot about her."

Amy sighed. "Ty, don't be so hard on yourself."

Ty looked at her. "But I should be making things easier for you."

Amy looked at him, too tired to smile. "You are," she said.

❧

Amy and Ty took turns monitoring the little filly until Scott arrived. He gave her another shot of antibiotics.

"Her temperature's still too high," he told them. "Is she feeding?"

Amy nodded. Daybreak wasn't feeding very hard or for very long, but she was still suckling.

Scott looked relieved. "Good. Let me know immediately if she stops. It's vital that she keeps it up. If she doesn't, she'll become dehydrated very quickly."

"We'll keep an eye on her," Ty promised.

Amy told Scott about the remedies she had been using. "Keep going," Scott said. "We need to do whatever we can to help her to fight this infection off as quickly as possible." He picked up his bag. "OK, let's go and vaccinate the other horses."

❧

Amy spent the rest of the day with the filly, only leaving her to visit Grandpa in the hospital. The tube to his nose had been removed, although a drip still ran into his arm and the chest tubes were still in place. He seemed a little more alert, but he told her that the doctors didn't think he would be able to leave hospital for another two weeks.

"But that means you won't be home for Christmas," Amy said, aghast.

"I'm afraid so, honey," Grandpa replied. "But you'll have Lou and Marnie for company and you can come visit." He squeezed her hand. "It won't be that bad."

496 HEARTLAND

It will! Amy wanted to cry, but seeing the worry on Grandpa's face she smiled as cheerfully as she could. "Of course we'll manage," she said, "but we'll miss you."

In the car on the way back to Heartland, Amy felt a tide of emotion threaten to overwhelm her. Her first Christmas without Mom, and now she wouldn't have Grandpa, either. *Oh, Lou,* she thought desperately, looking out the car window with tears stinging the back of her eyes, *please hurry home.*

❧

When Lou called that evening, she had more bad news. "I went to the airport but I couldn't get a flight," she told Amy. "The air traffic controllers over here are on strike, and it doesn't look like I'll be able to get back for a couple more days."

"But you have to!" Amy burst out, feeling a hard lump pressing in her throat. "Lou! I —" she caught the words "need you" just before they left her lips. Lou was upset enough already; she didn't need to be made to feel any worse. "Well, I guess it's only a few more days," Amy said, forcing herself to sound calm.

"But I don't want to wait," Lou said. "I want to come home."

"You'll be here soon," Amy said as brightly as she could.

The second she put the phone down though, the

brightness faded from her face and a wave of bleak misery engulfed her. She couldn't bear it.

A floorboard on the landing above creaked. Guessing that Marnie was coming down, Amy grabbed her jacket and ran outside. She simply couldn't pretend to be strong and cheerful for one second longer.

She ran to the front stable block, her breath coming in short bursts. Unbolting the door of Melody and Daybreak's new stall, she went in and, collapsing on the straw in the corner, she burst into tears.

She looked toward Daybreak lying beside Melody, her head resting on the straw, her breathing noisy. Amy remembered the night the filly had been born. Life had seemed so full of hope then.

"Amy?"

Amy looked up. Marnie was standing in the doorway of the stall, a horrified look in her eyes as she took in Amy's distraught face. "Amy, what's wrong?" She came over and knelt beside her. "What's happened?"

Amy knew that there was no way she could hide the truth from Marnie. "It's Lou," she cried. "And Grandpa and Daybreak and everything! I just can't deal with it anymore."

Marnie put her arms around her. "It's all right," she said soothingly. "I'm here. You don't have to deal with it alone. Now, tell me what's wrong. What's happened with Lou?"

"She can't get home," Amy said, and she told Marnie all about Lou's phone call. "She's so unhappy and there's nothing I can do to help her. I'm useless."

Marnie hugged her fiercely. "Amy, you've been wonderful," she said. "I've seen how cheerful you've been with your grandpa and how you've been trying so hard not to worry Lou. You've kept things going, and it's taken real courage." She shook her head. "I tell you, there's been such a big change in you since I was last here."

Amy looked up at her. "Really?" she asked, surprised at the statement.

"Really," Marnie said softly, her blue eyes searching Amy's face. "Your mom would have been proud of you, Amy. I know she would."

For a moment neither of them spoke.

"Look," Marnie said softly. "Don't worry about Christmas. We'll spend it with your Grandpa in the hospital, and if Lou's still in England, we'll call her every hour if it makes you happier. You shouldn't worry about Daybreak, either. She's going to get better. It'll just take a little while for the medicine and herbs to work, like it did with your grandpa." She squeezed Amy's arm. "Things will turn out OK, you'll see."

Amy nodded slowly.

Marnie hugged her again. "Come on, let's go back inside."

Amy hesitated. "I will," she said. "In a moment."

Marnie studied her face and then stood up. "OK," she said, seeming to sense Amy's need to be on her own. "But don't stay out here too long."

As Marnie's footsteps faded away, Amy leaned back against the stall wall. *Would Mom have been proud of me?* she wondered wearily. *I just don't know.*

She looked at Daybreak lying in the straw. The filly's sides heaved painfully in and out, and getting to her feet, Amy went over to her. Crouching down, she laid her hand on Daybreak's neck. Some of her old fire flared in the filly's eyes and she threw her head up, but the sudden movement made her cough painfully. With a heavy sigh, she let her muzzle sink back on the straw.

Amy began to massage the foal's neck with slow circular movements. When she felt Daybreak's muscles start to relax, she let her hands work up over the foal's neck and then, with a lighter pressure, over her delicate ears, face, and nose. Closing her own eyes, she focused completely on the instinctive movement of her fingers. As she breathed in the warm scent of horse and straw, the stress and tension of the last few days seemed to fade away. The world seemed to shrink until it contained nothing but her fingers and Daybreak's skin.

She wasn't sure how long she worked on the little filly, but when she finally opened her eyes she found that a feeling of peace had crept over her. She glanced at the foal's sides. Daybreak's breathing had slowed; the tension around her muzzle had relaxed. Her eyes were half shut.

Amy gently eased backward and stood up, her heart turning over as she looked at the little foal lying so still in the straw. With one last glance at Daybreak, she crept quietly out of the stall.

Chapter Twelve

Amy slept better that night. Although the things she had been worried about the evening before hadn't changed, the time in the stall with Daybreak had somehow calmed her, and she awoke with a new sense of strength. *I can cope,* she thought. *Christmas might not be perfect, but Grandpa and Daybreak will get better and Lou will be home sometime soon — I know she will.*

Downstairs, she found Marnie in the kitchen putting on some fresh coffee. "How are you feeling?" she asked.

"Good," Amy replied, and instead of it being just something she said automatically, she found that she really meant it. She smiled. "Yeah, I'm feeling good."

The first thing Amy did when she went out to the stables was to go to Daybreak and Melody's stall.

The little foal was still lying in the straw, but even from the door Amy could see that her breathing looked calmer. She went into the stall and crouched beside the filly. "Hi, little one," she said, reaching out to gently scratch Daybreak's neck.

At the touch of her hand, the foal lifted her head, but for once her eyes didn't fill with hostility. She stared at Amy for a moment, and then, turning her head, she sniffed the back of Amy's hand. Amy felt a flicker of surprise. "Good girl," she said, tickling Daybreak's muzzle.

As she did so, she noticed that the filly's eyes were brighter. Maybe she was finally beginning to get better.

Feeling much happier, Amy left the stall and went to start the feeds.

🙈

She had just finished the feeding when Scott's Jeep came bumping up the drive. As he parked, Amy saw that he wasn't alone — Matt was with him.

"Hi," Scott said to Amy and Marnie as he and Matt jumped out of the Jeep. "How's the patient today?"

"A bit better, I think," Amy said.

"Good," Scott said. "That's what I want to hear."

As Scott got his bag from the backseat, Amy looked uncertainly at Matt. "Hi, Matt."

He smiled awkwardly. "Hi," he said. "Scott's giving me a ride to school. How are you?"

"OK, thanks," Amy replied.

There was a silence. The angry words they had exchanged the last time they'd met trembled in the air between them.

Scott walked over to them. "Should we go and see Daybreak?" he said. Not waiting for an answer, he headed to the stables. Marnie shot a curious look at Amy and Matt and then joined him.

Amy was about to follow when Matt caught hold of her arm. "Amy —" he said.

Amy stopped and looked at him.

"I really am sorry," Matt said. "About your grandpa and Daybreak and — and about the argument we had."

Amy nodded.

"Can't we make up?" Matt continued. "I don't want us to argue about who I'm dating. We've been friends for too long, and I don't want that to change."

"But why *Ashley*?" The words burst out of Amy. "I mean, of all the people in the world, Matt, why her?"

"I like her," Matt said simply. "Since Jade's been going out with Dan, I've really gotten to know her better."

Amy raised her eyebrows sarcastically. "And that's a good thing?"

Matt sighed. "Look, this isn't getting us anywhere." He looked at her. "I might be dating Ashley, but you're still one of my best friends, Amy. Don't ask me to choose between you — please."

Amy wavered. She hated the thought of Matt dating Ashley, but she couldn't bear the thought of losing him as a friend. "OK," she said at last. "I guess it really isn't my business who you go out with."

"So we're friends again?" Matt smiled.

Amy nodded. "Yeah, we're friends." She managed a teasing smile. "Even if you do have awful taste in girl-friends."

"Well, I did ask *you* out, didn't I?" Matt grinned.

Amy punched his arm and they walked toward the barn.

Reaching Daybreak and Melody's stall, they found the foal standing up, suckling vigorously. Scott and Marnie were watching.

"Hey, girl," said Amy, going into the stall.

"She's feeding. That's a good sign," Scott said.

Amy held the filly still while Scott checked her over.

"Yes, she's definitely on the mend," he said at last as he folded up his stethoscope. "Her breathing's improved, her temperature's almost back to normal, and her glands aren't as swollen. I think we can safely say she's over the worst."

Amy breathed out deeply in relief.

"Now, keep up the treatments and the nursing," Scott said. He glanced out the door. "She needs as much fresh air as possible. The wind's died down, so you can take her and Melody out for a gentle walk on the lead, but don't turn them out in the field until the weather improves. She's OK to go out in the snow for a while if it's sunny, but keep her out of wind and rain for now. She needs to stay warm and dry."

"Sure," Amy nodded.

Scott smiled at her. "You're doing a great job, Amy. Daybreak's very lucky to have you around."

Amy felt embarrassed by his words of praise. As they all walked back across the yard together, she changed the subject. "Has Lou called you yet?" she asked Scott as they reached the Jeep.

Scott nodded. "She called last night. She was pretty upset about your dad and everything."

"I know," Amy agreed. "I just hope she gets home soon."

Scott was silent for a moment. "Me, too," he said at last, and climbed into the driver's seat.

"See you, Amy," Matt said, opening the passenger door and getting in. "That is, if you ever decide to come back to school."

"Yeah," Amy said with a smile. "Say hi to Soraya, and tell her I'll call her tonight."

She felt hopeful as she watched them drive off. Things were somewhat back to normal with Matt, and Lou must have apologized when she'd called Scott. Amy couldn't really ask Scott. She knew her sister, and Lou was very strong — and also *very* stubborn. But Amy was certain she was missing Scott, or she wouldn't have phoned him. *Perhaps they've made up after all,* she thought.

Ty came down the yard. "So what did Scott say about Daybreak?"

"He's really pleased with her progress," Amy said. "He said we should walk her and Melody out in the yard this afternoon."

Ty raised his eyebrows. "That'll be fun. A loose foal is just what we need right now."

"Come on, she was getting better at leading before she got sick," Amy said hopefully. "She might not be that bad."

Ty didn't look convinced.

🙿

"So how are all the horses?" Grandpa asked when Amy and Marnie visited him at lunchtime.

"OK," Amy said, glad to be able to tell the truth for once.

"What about Lou?" Grandpa asked. "Has she seen your father yet?"

Amy hesitated. All the tubes and drips had been re-moved from Grandpa's body and he was starting to look much better. She decided it was best to tell him the truth. "No," she said. "It turns out that he's living in Australia."

"In Australia?" Grandpa echoed.

Amy nodded and told him everything.

"Oh, poor Lou," Grandpa said when she finished. "She must be so disappointed."

"She is," Amy said quietly. "It sounds like she feels the whole trip was a mistake."

"So when's she coming home?" Grandpa asked.

"As soon as possible," Amy replied. "There's a strike at the airport, but she's going to get the first flight out that she can."

Grandpa looked worried. "I hope she's back in time for Christmas."

"I know," Amy said. "I do, too."

🕊

That afternoon Amy fetched Melody's and Daybreak's halters. "Now be good," she told Daybreak.

She haltered Melody and then approached Daybreak. To her surprise, the little filly stood quietly.

"Good girl," Amy praised Daybreak as she buckled up the halter and slipped the lead rope through the leather band. She rubbed the little foal's head. Daybreak looked at her and then lowered her nose.

"Are you ready?" Ty said, coming into the stall.

Amy nodded. Ty led Melody out, and clicking her tongue, Amy followed with Daybreak.

Daybreak's ears pricked as soon as Ty opened the door to the outside and the daylight streamed in. She surged slightly ahead of Amy. "Easy now," Amy said, checking her. As she did so, Amy tensed, half expecting Daybreak to explode with indignation. But to her surprise, the filly slowed down obediently. "Good girl," Amy praised, astonished.

They continued to walk around the yard without incident. It turned out to be a pleasant jaunt.

"She was great," Ty said when they put Daybreak and Melody back in their stall ten minutes later.

"I know," Amy said. "She didn't barge or push me or try to rear."

"She's probably still feeling too weak to put up a fight," Ty said.

Amy stared at the filly for a moment. She wasn't sure. She might have been imagining it, but out in the yard it had seemed to her that Daybreak hadn't *wanted* to fight anymore. She wondered whether to say anything to Ty and then decided not to. He was probably right. Daybreak was still recovering from a serious illness. No wonder she was being quiet.

🕮

However, over the next few days, as Daybreak regained her strength, she also continued to behave. It was too windy for her and Melody to go out in the pasture, so twice a day Ty and Amy led the mare and her little foal around the yard. Not once did Daybreak show any sign of fighting the lead rope. And not only did she not fight it, she seemed willing to follow Amy on a loose rope wherever Amy wanted to go.

And it wasn't just the leading in the yard. Even in the stall, Amy noticed a change in Daybreak. Although the filly never whinnied to Amy like Melody did, she did whatever Amy asked without trying to resist.

By Friday, two days before Christmas, Amy was convinced that she wasn't imagining the change in the foal. "I'm sure she's getting better," she said to Ty as they brought Melody and Daybreak back to their stall after one of their yard walks. "Look." She stopped the foal with the lead rope and, by pressing on her sides, got her to move forward, sideways, and backward. Daybreak's eyes didn't even flicker. She moved where Amy wanted, responding to the lightest pressure from Amy's hands, her intelligent eyes calm. "She wouldn't have done that before she was sick," Amy said, patting her.

"You're right," Ty admitted. "There has been a change in her."

"Why do you think it's happened?" Amy asked.

"I don't know," Ty said. "Maybe it had something to do with the virus. Maybe she learned that she could trust you when you took care of her and helped her feel better."

An image came into Amy's mind of the night she had worked T-touch on Daybreak. She remembered how upset she had been and how massaging Daybreak had put her at ease. And she remembered, too, how the resentment in the foal's eyes had gradually faded as her fingers had worked on and on. Maybe the change in Daybreak had happened then. Maybe that feeling of peace had enveloped them both. Who could tell? She stroked the little foal. All that mattered was that Daybreak had come to respect and trust them and now she was willing to work with them.

She and Ty put the mare and foal back into their stall. As they came out of the barn Ty said, "Have you had any news from Lou?"

"She called last night," Amy replied. "The strike's still on." She swallowed. "It's beginning to look like Marnie and I might be having Christmas on our own."

Ty looked at her sympathetically. "Look, why don't I come over — spend the day here with you."

Amy smiled but shook her head. "Thanks, Ty, but your family will want to see you. You're here enough as it is."

"I don't mind," Ty said softly.

Amy's mind suddenly filled with the memory of his birthday. "Marnie and I will be fine," she managed, feeling a blush flooding into her cheeks.

Just then there was the sound of the phone ringing. "I'll get it," Amy said, relieved.

She ran to the kitchen and grabbed the receiver. "Hello, Heartland," she said.

"Hi, Amy, it's me."

"Grandpa!" Amy said with surprise. She felt suddenly worried. "Are you OK? There's nothing wrong, is there?"

"No," Grandpa said. "There's nothing wrong. In fact," Amy heard the smile in his voice, "there's something very right."

"What?" Amy asked.

"The hospital has told me I can come home, Amy. I'll be back for Christmas after all."

Chapter Thirteen

Amy could hardly believe it. "But that's fabulous!" she gasped.

"I know." Grandpa sounded equally amazed. "I've had to promise to take it very easy, of course, and I need to come back for a checkup on the twenty-sixth, but at least I'll be with you for the holiday."

"So when can we come and get you?" Amy said.

"Anytime," Grandpa said.

"I can't wait to tell Marnie!" Amy exclaimed. Just then she saw Marnie's car pulling up outside. "Look, I'd better go," she said, wanting to tell her the good news about Grandpa. "We'll be over to get you in about an hour."

Putting the phone down, she ran outside. Marnie

grinned excitedly as she told her about her Grandpa's call. "That's wonderful news," she cried, hugging Amy.

"What is?" Ben said, turning off the water tap and heading over. "Did Lou get a flight?"

Amy shook her head. "Not yet. But Grandpa's coming home!"

"Oh, wow!" Ben exclaimed. "So you're not going to be on your own for Christmas after all?"

"No," Amy said, her eyes sparkling with happiness.

Ben smiled. "I was going to offer to stay."

Amy grinned. "Not you, too?"

Ben looked confused. "What?"

"It doesn't matter," Amy said. She hugged him. "But you and Ty are really the nicest guys!"

♨

Amy set off with Marnie to the hospital. They went in Grandpa's car so there would be more room. When they got there, they found him already waiting, his bag packed.

"Now you take it easy, Mr. Bartlett," Dr. Marshall warned, coming to see him off. "And remember your antibiotics."

"I will," Grandpa smiled. "Thank you for everything, Doctor."

"No problem," she said with a smile. "And we'll see you right after the holiday for one final check."

"I can't believe you're really coming home, Grandpa," Amy said happily as they went to the car.

"No, I can't either," Grandpa said, smiling. "And it's Christmas Eve tomorrow!"

"I'm afraid we're not really in the Christmas spirit," Marnie said.

"The decoration boxes are still stacked in the hallway where you left them," Amy explained.

"Well, we'll soon see to that," Grandpa said.

"Grandpa! Were you even listening to the doctor? You've got to take it easy!" Amy protested.

"Oh, I'm planning to take it easy," Grandpa said, coughing slightly. "But that doesn't mean I can't organize *you* two."

On the way home, he made them stop and buy the biggest Christmas tree they could find.

"I'm glad we brought your car," Marnie said, easing into the driver's seat after she and Amy had securely strapped the tree to the roof.

"We can't have Christmas without a tree," Grandpa said.

When they got back, they found that they hadn't been the only ones thinking about Christmas. Ty and Ben had found the battered boxes of old decorations in the hall and had set to work making the yard and the house look as festive as possible. Fairy lights flickered along the roof of the front stable, and the kitchen, porch, and tack room had been decorated with Christmas garlands.

"Oh, cool!" Amy said, jumping out of the car.

Ty and Ben came down the yard.

"Welcome home, Jack," Ty said, helping Grandpa out of the car. "It's great to have you back."

Grandpa looked around, a contented smile on his face. "It's good to *be* back," he said.

🙠

With Grandpa back at Heartland, the whole house came alive again. He spent the evening supervising Amy and Marnie as they decorated the Christmas tree and put up all the cards that had arrived. Amy tried to call her sister to tell her that Grandpa was home, but when she spoke to the hotel, they said that Ms. Fleming had checked out several hours earlier. Knowing that Lou had been planning to stay with friends if she didn't get a flight home that day, Amy wasn't too worried. She just wanted to tell her the good news.

Later that evening, the phone rang. Amy raced to answer it but it wasn't Lou. It was Soraya. "Have you had any news from Lou?" she asked.

"No," Amy replied, "but Grandpa's home from the hospital. They discharged him early."

"That's great!" Soraya said.

"I know. I just wish Lou was going to be here, too. We'll just have to celebrate again when she gets home," Amy said. She sighed and then changed the subject. "So, are you coming over tomorrow?"

Every Christmas Eve Soraya came over to help with the horses and they went out for a long trail ride in the afternoon after the chores were done.

"Of course," Soraya said. "I'll come just after nine."

"Great," Amy said, pleased. "I'll see you then."

❧

When Amy woke up the next morning she became aware of a change in the air. She went to the window. There had been another fall of snow overnight. A heavy white blanket covered the fields and trees and everything was quiet and still. The chill wind that had been blowing for the last week or so had finally died down.

Amy pulled on her clothes and went downstairs. Both Grandpa and Marnie were still in bed. Taking a few cookies from the tin on the shelf, she went outside and stood for a moment in the quiet world. *It's Christmas Eve,* she thought, a pleasant tingle of anticipation running down her spine.

Ty and Ben arrived an hour later at seven o'clock, and they all set to work on the horses. They were mucking out when Marnie came outside with coffee for everyone.

"I'm going to cook a huge brunch," she announced, handing Ty and Ben insulated mugs. She grinned at Amy. "It's the only way I can stop your grandpa from doing it."

"Thanks," Amy said gratefully, blowing on her steaming coffee.

"No problem," Marnie replied. "It'll be ready about ten."

🙊

Amy forked the last few pieces of dirty straw from Jake's stall into the wheelbarrow. She was so glad that Grandpa was home for Christmas. *If only Lou were here, too,* she thought, *then everything really would be perfect.*

She had just emptied the wheelbarrow when she heard the sound of a car engine. Thinking it would be Soraya, she ran outside. To her surprise, she saw Scott driving up.

"Hey," Scott said as he got out of his Jeep. "I - wasn't doing anything this morning so I thought I'd drop by and see if you could use some help with the horses."

"That's really nice of you," Amy said, touched at the gesture.

"How's your grandpa?" Scott asked.

"He's better. In fact, he's here," Amy said, realizing that Scott wouldn't have heard the news. "We brought him home last night."

"That's wonderful!" Scott exclaimed. "Is he well enough for me to go in and say hello?"

"I guess so." Amy thought about the way Grandpa had been bossing her and Marnie around the night before and smiled. "He'd love to see you."

Scott went down to the house.

Amy had just started on Sundance's stall when Soraya arrived. She jumped out of her mom's car almost before it had stopped. "Hi!" she said, hugging Amy. "How are you?"

"Great," Amy said, and she really meant it.

✍

With Scott and Soraya helping, the mucking out took no time at all. As Amy was finishing Moochie's stall she realized that the clouds overhead had parted and blue sky was showing through.

She went into the next stall where Ty was grooming Jake. "Do you think the wind's calm enough to turn out Melody and Daybreak for a while?"

"Yeah, definitely," Ty said, glancing out of the stall. "Do you want a hand?"

"Thanks," Amy said gratefully.

They got the mare and foal and led them out through the snow to the paddock beside the house. Daybreak looked around excitedly, her nostrils flaring as she breathed in the crisp, clear air. Despite her eagerness to be out in the field, she walked obediently beside Amy.

"She's so much better," Ty said, looking at her.

"Yeah." Amy grinned happily. "She's a little lady now."

They reached the field gate and unclipped the lead ropes. With a loud snort, Daybreak trotted out across the snowy grass.

In the center of the field she stopped, her beautiful head held high, the tips of her tiny ears almost meeting. For a moment she stood poised and statuelike, every muscle tense. Then, with a sudden toss of her head, she squealed mischievously and plunged forward in a blur of glowing chestnut, her back legs kicking up a clump of snowflakes.

Amy's heart swelled with happiness. The little filly might submit willingly to a halter and lead rope now, but her spirit was far from broken. She was still fiery, proud, and free.

Wheeling around, Daybreak cantered toward the gate. Amy expected to see her go over to Melody. Instead, she trotted slowly past her mother, stopped, and looked at Amy.

Very slowly, wondering what she wanted, Amy stepped into the field and held out her hand. "Here, girl," she said softly.

Daybreak hesitated and then, with the faintest of whickers, she walked forward. Stretching her head forward, she nuzzled Amy's upturned palm. Then, lifting her tiny muzzle to Amy's face, she breathed out warmly, love and trust glowing in her dark eyes.

Amy was filled with triumph and delight. Daybreak's fight was over. Suddenly, all the frustration and sleepless nights that the foal had caused her were forgotten. Breathing in the sweet scent of Daybreak's breath, she kissed the little filly's nose.

"Daybreak," she whispered softly. "My Daybreak."

The moment was shattered by the sound of the back door opening and Marnie calling out, "Brunch is ready, everyone!"

With a swift toss of her head, Daybreak plunged away.

Amy turned and met Ty's eyes.

"I can hardly believe it, Amy," he said softly. "You've won her trust."

Amy's face glowed as she went over to the gate. "We did it together," she said, knowing that she could never have done it without him.

He smiled at her and they headed to the house.

❧

The kitchen table was piled high with food. There were dishes of crispy bacon, grilled sausages, and golden scrambled eggs, two huge bowls of fresh fruit salad, a platter of steaming blueberry pancakes, two pitchers of maple syrup, and a mountain of freshly baked muffins and cinnamon rolls.

"Sit down, everyone," Marnie said as they all kicked off their boots.

"Wow!" Ben said, looking around. "This is some spread."

Grandpa was sitting at the head of the table. "Who wants coffee?"

"I'll do that, Jack," said Scott, taking the coffeepot from him. "You just sit there and enjoy."

Talking and laughing, everybody pulled chairs up to the table.

"This is incredible, Marnie," Amy said, carrying a pile of warmed plates to the table.

"Thanks," she replied. "Jack instructed me from the armchair!"

Amy put the plates down on the table. "Now, everyone help themselves," she said, handing them out.

She had just sat down between Ty and Soraya when the back door opened.

Amy jumped to her feet and turned around. "Lou!" she exclaimed.

A silence fell on the room. Lou stood in the doorway. Her hair was disheveled and her face was tired. She was looking around in astonishment at the crowded kitchen.

"What's — what's going on?" Suddenly, her eyes fell on Grandpa. "Grandpa!" she gasped. "You're home!"

Dropping her bag, she rushed over to him. He rose to meet her. "Oh, Lou, it's so good to see you! We weren't expecting you for ages."

"I got a flight!" Lou said. "The strike was suddenly called off. I couldn't call. There was no time. As soon as I found out I could get a seat I had to get on that plane and come home," she said, pulling back from him with a relieved smile. "I still can't believe it. And to get here and find you home, Grandpa! I thought you'd still be in the hospital."

"They released me yesterday," Grandpa said.

"On strict instructions that he take it easy," smiled Amy, butting in.

"I've been so worried about you!" Lou exclaimed. "Leaving here while you were so ill was the stupidest thing I could have done. I don't know what I was thinking."

"But I made you go, Lou," Grandpa said, reaching for her hand. "I thought it was something you needed to do."

"You knew how important it was to me," Lou said sadly. "I *thought* I needed to go, too, but being away from here and away from all of you helped me figure things out." She sighed deeply. "I was just too focused on finding Daddy. I was blind to everything else. Please forgive me."

Jack smiled. "There's nothing to forgive," he said.

"But there is," Lou insisted. "I was really selfish." She turned to her sister. "I should have been here to help while Grandpa was sick instead of running off to London. It must have been really hard on you. I'm so sorry, Amy."

"It doesn't matter anymore," Amy said, hugging her in delight. "I'm just glad you're back."

"You're don't know how glad I am to *be* back. Being away made me realize a lot of things." Lou paused. "I can't go on searching for my father anymore. I know that's a mistake — we'll meet up soon enough. I don't need to put my life on hold waiting for him. There are more important things for me here." Lou smiled and looked across the room at Scott.

She walked over to him. "Scott, I need to apologize to you, too. I'm sorry I missed your dinner, and I'm sorry I couldn't see your side of things. I didn't mean to —"

Before Lou could finish apologizing, Scott wrapped his arms around her. "It doesn't matter, Lou. I know you didn't mean it. I missed you so much."

"I've missed you, too," Lou said, half laughing, half crying. "I'll make it up to everyone, I promise."

Amy sank down in her chair, her legs feeling suddenly shaky. Lou was back. Now *everyone* was home for Christmas.

Just then the phone rang. Marnie picked it up. "Hello, Heartland."

She looked at Lou, frowning. "Lou," she said. Amy couldn't help noticing a strange tone in her voice. "It's for you."

"Can you tell them I'll call back?" Lou said, turning happily in Scott's arms.

"Well — it's a long distance call," Marnie said. "It's — from Australia."

Lou's face suddenly paled. "Australia?" she whispered.

Marnie nodded. "It's your father."

"You don't have to talk to him, Lou," Amy said quickly. "You —"

But Lou had already pulled away from Scott and taken the phone. "Hello," she said, her voice catching in her throat. "Daddy?"

Turning, she walked out of the room and into the hall. She shut the door behind her.

No one spoke. Amy looked at Grandpa. His face was tense.

After about five minutes, the door opened and Lou came back in. Amy's eyes flew to her sister's face. She was even paler and her blue eyes looked shocked. She handed the receiver to Amy. "He — he wants to speak to you," she said, her voice now low and shaky.

Amy shook her head frantically, but Lou shoved the

receiver in her hand and walked away to the sink. For a moment Amy didn't know what to do, but then very slowly, she lifted the phone to her ear. "Hello?" she whispered, turning away from everyone in the room.

"Hello, Amy." The strange English voice on the other end of the line seemed unfamiliar at first, but deep in the corners of Amy's mind a long-forgotten memory stirred. She wanted to speak but just couldn't.

"I guess you don't remember me that well."

"No," Amy said, her heart beating fast.

"Well, I remember you," her father said, his voice warm. "In fact, I've got a photo of you in my wallet. You and Lou at the seaside. I carry it with me all the time."

Amy didn't know what to say. For twelve years her father had been absent from her life, and now suddenly, here he was, talking to her on the telephone.

Her father seemed to feel the awkwardness of the situation, too. "Look, I'm sorry for calling out of the blue like this," he said. "I wanted to meet you face-to-face after all this time, but when I heard from the Carters that Lou had been to England to find me, I knew that I had to call and explain."

Amy was silent.

"I live on a large farm here," her father went on. "I raise horses. Lou said in her letter that you're really into horses. You'd like it here."

Amy didn't say anything. Suddenly, she heard the sound of crying in the background. "Is that a baby?" she asked.

"Yes," her father said. There was a pause. "My wife gave birth to our little girl last week."

For a moment the world seemed to stop. The words ran through Amy's head. *Wife. Baby.* She looked at Lou's back and suddenly she understood the shocked look she had just seen in her sister's eyes.

"I just explained to Lou that's why I can't meet you until February," their father continued. "I need to be here at the moment. It's also why I didn't tell you that I'm living in Australia. I thought the news that I'd re-married and that you had a half sister might be better if I told you in person."

"I understand," Amy whispered.

There was a silence.

"Look, I think I'd better give you a little time to let all this news sink in," her father said. "There's much more that we need to talk about, but that can wait. I'll call again after the holidays, if that's OK. For now, let me just wish you a merry Christmas, Amy, and I look forward to seeing you in the new year."

"O — OK," Amy stammered. "Bye, Daddy."

As Amy put the phone down, Lou turned and met her eyes. Her face was wet with tears.

"What did he say?" Grandpa asked, looking anxious.

Amy looked around, her head spinning. "That he's married and they've just had a baby girl."

She saw the shock register on everyone's face.

"A baby!" Grandpa echoed. He stood up, his face suddenly dour. "Lou —"

"I'm all right," Lou interrupted. She lifted her head and brushed the tears away from her eyes. "I'm — I'm *glad* that Daddy's found some happiness at last."

"Do you mean that?" Grandpa said.

"Yes," Lou replied, going to Scott's side and taking his hand. "Daddy's got his life now, and I've got mine. And it's here at Heartland with all of you." Tears still glistened in her eyes, but she smiled and took a deep breath. "I don't know about everyone else, but I'm starving," she said. "Are any of those eggs for me?"

🙠

It didn't take long to reheat the food. Soon everyone was sitting down, passing the dishes around, and eating heartily. As the noise level rose Amy thought about everything that had happened in the last six months. There had been so much grief, so much pain, and so many tears.

But not everything that had happened had been bad, she thought, looking at Ben and Marnie laughing with

Soraya. New friends had been made, old friendships strengthened. *And not just friendships*, she thought, her eyes looking to Lou. For so much of her life, her sister had been almost a stranger to her, but over the last six months a new bond had been forged between them. Now they didn't just love each other, they understood and needed each other, too.

As she finished the last piece of muffin on her plate, Ty nudged her with his elbow. "We should probably bring Melody and Daybreak in. We don't want Daybreak to be out too long."

Amy nodded and they stood up.

"You're not going back out already, are you?" Lou said to them. "I was just going to make some fresh coffee."

"We'll be back soon," Amy replied, smiling at her big sister. "We're just going to bring Melody and Daybreak in from the field."

She and Ty pulled on their boots and left the warmth of the house. After the laughter and noise of the kitchen, the stables held a soothing silence for them both. Only the occasional snort of one of the horses in the stalls broke the calm.

"Look," Ty said, pointing to the field.

Amy smiled. Melody and Daybreak were standing by the water trough. The foal was suckling, her fluffy tail switching from side to side as Melody gently nuzzled her hindquarters. The rays of the winter sun shone down on their backs.

Amy and Ty stopped by the gate.

"Everything seems so peaceful," Ty said.

Amy nodded and leaned against the gate. "It's so quiet," she said softly. "It makes it easy to forget all the craziness we've been through."

Ty's eyes met hers. "It's been a tough six months, Amy."

"Yeah — but it's been good, too," Amy said. "Lou's come back to live here, Grandpa's on the mend, Heartland's doing well, and I know how lucky I am to have my friends and family." She looked up at Ty, knowing he'd understand. "I still miss Mom and Pegasus — I always will — but it's time to move on." She paused for a moment and watched the mare and filly in the field. When she spoke again, her voice was quiet. "You remember how Mom used to say, 'One day you'll know when the good times are here'?"

Ty nodded.

"Well, I had some wonderful times *with* Mom," Amy said slowly. "But now I know I've got to find my own good times, too. It's what Mom would have wanted."

"You're right," Ty said softly. "It is."

Amy met his gaze. She didn't know what she'd have

done without him over the last six months. "Thank you," she said suddenly.

"For what?" Ty asked, looking surprised.

"For being here," Amy said. "For helping me." She saw him about to speak, to shrug it off, but she shook her head, wanting to tell him just how much he meant to her. "If it hadn't been for you, Ty, Heartland wouldn't even exist anymore. You're very important to Heartland — and to me."

"And you're important to me," Ty said warmly. He stepped closer.

Amy felt her stomach somersault as she looked up at him. "Ty?" she said as his hands touched her shoulders.

But Ty didn't speak. His eyes looked deep into hers and then his lips met her own.

Amy didn't know how long the kiss lasted. But when it stopped, her heart was pounding so hard she thought it was going to burst. "Ty?" she stammered.

Ty looked down at her and smiled. "Merry Christmas, Amy," he said. "I hope the good times come soon."

Amy glanced at Melody and Daybreak, then around at the house. Through the kitchen windows, with their festive decorations, she could see everyone she loved most in the world gathered together. "I think they're here already," she said, looking back at Ty. "They really are."

As she opened the field gate Daybreak whinnied, and with a smile, Amy walked across the snow toward the little foal.

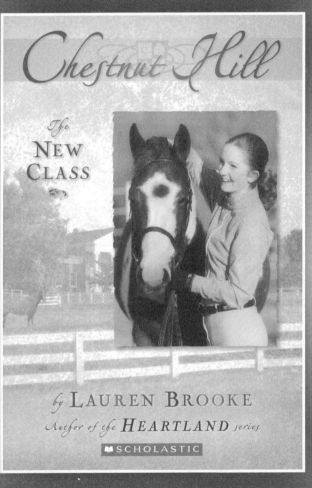

It takes more than talent to win

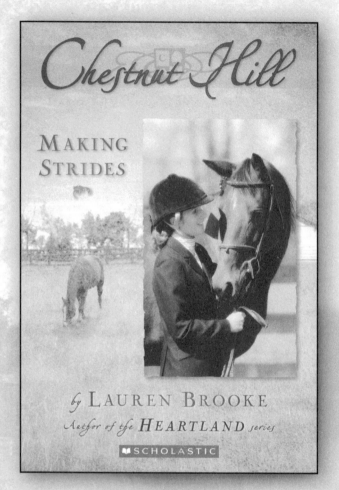

Heartland comes to Chestnut Hill when Malory, one of the school's premier young riders, contacts Amy Fleming to treat a talented, young and defensive horse with a mysterious history. Malory isn't sure how to help this horse, but she's willing to bet her future at Chestnut Hill that he can win.

Discover the place where neglected horses learn to trust again.

Visit
Heartland

on the Web
scholastic.com/heartland

- Join Amy and share her adventures
- Read sample chapters from the Heartland books
- Collect the new Heartland trading cards
- Find out about Heartland writing contests and much more

Come home to Heartland one last time...

In this moving conclusion to the beloved series, Amy is graduating from high school. She knows she should feel excited for college, but she dreads leaving home. And now she must decide what her future holds, and whether it will take place at—or away—from Heartland.

www.scholastic.com/titles/heartland

HFBTA